BOUND
BY
BLOOD

BOUND
BY
BLOOD

TIMECASTER CHRONICLES
—— BOOK THREE ——

R.L. PEREZ

WILLOW
HAVEN
PRESS

BOUND BY BLOOD

Cover Art by Blue Raven Book Covers

ISBN: 978-1-735049-22-9

www.rlperez.com

For Colin, my curious little learner, and all the ways you inspire me to think outside the box.

CHAPTER 1

Wind whipped at my face so hard it burned. I crammed my eyes shut, and my fingers gripped Oliver's hand so tightly I knew it hurt him. But I couldn't let go. I couldn't lose him.

Kismet screamed. *Kismet.* My mentor. My Familiar. Though she was younger now than when I first knew her, she was still my friend. I couldn't lose her either. I tried calling out for her, but my voice was lost in the tornado.

Colonel Greenwood—or rather, El Diablo—roared, his voice a deep bellow. Was he angry? Triumphant?

Please let the spell fail. Wherever he's trying to go, please don't take him there. Please, please, please.

I'd never been very religious, but in that moment,

amidst the spinning cyclone of the time travel spell, I prayed to every god I knew of to thwart El Diablo's plan.

My stomach churned. I felt no sense of gravity. The ground vanished from under me, and I was floating and spinning. I pressed my lips together to keep from puking. I knew something heavy would smash into me at any second and knock me out.

Then I slammed into something hard and cold. A bright light shone against my closed eyelids. I rolled and groaned, my stomach spinning from the movement. My shoulder throbbed from the impact as if I'd fallen several feet to the floor instead of getting swept away in a Wizard-of-Oz-worthy tornado.

I slowly shifted and turned back over. Prickles of pain shot through me from my head, stomach, and face. I couldn't remember each injury, but the fight from moments ago flashed through my mind. The voodoo doll of the dark warlock, Isko, who had tried to sacrifice me in a blood ritual; El Diablo drinking my blood; scrapes on my arms from repeatedly falling on the ground.

Oliver.

My eyes snapped open, and I winced against the bright fluorescent lights.

Fluorescent?

My heart rate accelerated. I scrambled backward on all fours until I hit a wall. Eyes wide, I scanned the room.

I was in a . . . *bathroom.*

A toilet stood in the corner, opposite from a clean, white sink and a mirror. In front of me was a small set of shelves with paper towels and hand sanitizer. Above the shelves, a sign on the wall politely requested that all employees wash their hands before returning to work.

A quick glance around the bathroom told me I was alone.

No, no, no.

"Oliver?" I cried, staggering to my feet.

I tore open the door and found a startled woman with red hair and deep purple lipstick. She clutched her designer bag close to her chest. I pushed past her, knowing I was disheveled and covered in injuries. I didn't care.

"Oliver?" I asked again, louder this time.

The smell of leather and fresh paper tickled my nose. I searched frantically around the room. I was in a bookstore, surrounded by towering bookshelves. A narrow flight of stairs rested against one wall and led to even more bookcases high above me.

Several customers stared at me as I raced up and down aisles of books. My tight, messy curls bounced against my face. After checking the entire store—even upstairs—I approached the counter where a bored-looking cashier sat thumbing through a magazine.

I cleared my throat. "Excuse me, have you seen a man in a . . . blue uniform? He's got short blond hair. Really tall." *Have you seen a soldier from the year 1899 wandering around?*

The man sighed and looked up at me. His eyes widened as they roved over my bedraggled appearance and my nineteenth century tunic and trousers. "Uh, no. Sorry. Haven't seen him."

"Please," I begged, placing my palms against the counter. "It's urgent. Are you sure?"

Alarm flickered in the man's eyes. He leaned away from me, and his gaze flicked to the phone on the desk as if he was considering calling security. "Look, I already answered your question. If you need help finding a book, I'd be happy to help. If not, there are other customers waiting."

He gestured behind me to where another man waited, his arms full of books.

I swallowed, trying to squash the mounting panic inside me. "Okay. Sorry."

I turned away and pressed a hand to my forehead. A glass window faced the street and sidewalk outside. I dropped my hand, my mouth falling open as I stared at the people passing by the bookstore. Dozens of men and women walked by, dressed in expensive suits. Some wore sunglasses, and others clutched bags or briefcases.

My head spun and ached as I tried to drink in my surroundings. *What year is it? Where am I?* My eyes rested on a woman's cell phone pressed against her cheek, then another man's headphones as he listened to music, and lastly the cars that passed by.

Cell phones. I had to be in the twentieth century . . . unless I'd traveled to the future? Further than the year I'd originally left? The idea made me feel sick.

Oliver. Where was Oliver? I'd been holding his hand right up until I landed in that bathroom. Surely he couldn't be far.

But a gnawing, sinking sensation settled in my stomach as I remembered something I'd heard when I'd first arrived in Santiago. Sofia—the Santería priestess whose mother had also cast the time travel spell—had mentioned something about Timecasters being linked to their own time. She'd said my connection to the future would steer the spell in the right direction toward the time I was from. If my year of origin pulled me back to the year 2000, then where would Oliver go? Would he have been dropped back in 1899 even though we'd held on to each other?

That couldn't be right. Oliver had cast the same spell

when El Diablo stabbed me in Santiago, and we'd still traveled together.

But this was different. Somehow, I *knew* it was. El Diablo had killed several powerful Kulam warlocks to fuel the spell. That act had to provide more power than when Oliver had cast the spell.

"Focus, Desi," I muttered to myself. "Find Oliver."

I pushed open the door and stepped outside. An array of noises surrounded me, suffocating me: cars whooshing, horns blaring, people chattering, shoes clacking. A throng of people immediately pressed in on me. Startled, I backed against the glass display of the bookstore to avoid being trampled. I glanced up and down the sidewalk, and my head reared back in shock.

Buildings and skyscrapers loomed over me, taller than any I'd ever seen in my life. Crowds of people bustled down the sidewalk and crosswalk. Dozens of yellow taxis passed me on the road.

I'm in a big city. Definitely not North Grove. North Grove, Wisconsin was a small town, and my parents had been too busy hunting demons to ever take me on a vacation. I'd never traveled outside Wisconsin before. At least not in my time. Surely never to this place. New York maybe? Or Chicago? I couldn't tell.

Focus, I told myself again. *You can do this. You're a witch and a Huntress. Use your abilities.*

I closed my eyes and sniffed the air deeply. But there were so many people that my nose was overwhelmed by all the scents: perspiration, cigarette smoke, minty gum, hot dogs, perfume. Too many smells to sift through.

Instead I focused inward, seeking out our blood oath —the mental and physical connection Oliver and I had forged when I saved him from being enslaved by El Diablo. Would it still work if we were in different times?

Oliver, I pleaded, *where are you? Show me the way. How do I find you?*

I waited, feeling ridiculous with my back pressed against the glass as people rushed past me. I knew I looked like an idiot.

Oliver, please.

I felt nothing but the frantic beating of my heart and the imminent panic and devastation that threatened to swallow me whole.

I'd lost everything. Everyone.

Stop it, I ordered myself. My eyes felt hot, and my throat swelled up. *Don't give up. Not yet.*

Then I felt it: alarm, confusion, fear.

Desi?

Shock rippled through me. Though I'd heard his voice in the past, we'd never actually talked mentally before.

Desi!

7

I exhaled, and my breath came out as a half sob. Tears of relief stung my eyes.

Oliver's warmth and gratitude spread through me. Unsure if he could hear me, I thought to him, *Stay where you are! I'll find you.*

I opened my eyes and pressed a hand to my chest, unable to wipe the grateful smile from my face. Tears streamed down my cheeks. My breaths came in sharp wheezes. I straightened and walked toward the emotions I felt coursing freely through our blood oath: disbelief, awe, panic.

Stay there, Oliver. I'm coming.

I pushed against the thick crowd, weaving through bodies and bumping against shoulders. I ignored the outbursts and dirty looks of the passersby. The emotions in my chest intensified, growing louder and stronger until they were bound to rip right through me. I stopped as the strength of our blood oath thrummed through me like electricity.

I turned and found myself in front of a sandwich shop. I opened the door, breathing heavily. My fingers clenched and unclenched into fists.

A long line of people waited at the counter to order food. Judging by the height of the sun and the crowds in the street, it must have been right around lunch time.

A quick glance at the line of people told me Oliver

wasn't there. Frowning, I gazed around the booths and tables. Still no Oliver.

Where was he? Unless—

My eyes fell on the sign for the restrooms. "No way," I whispered, almost laughing in disbelief. Had the time travel spell really spit us both out in bathrooms? *Why?*

I hurried to the restrooms and lingered uncertainly outside. Was he in the men's room or women's room? Would the time travel spell even know which bathroom to put him in?

The energy of our blood oath churned in my chest like boiling water. Tentatively, I said, "Oliver?"

Nothing.

A little louder: "Oliver?"

A few people in a nearby booth glanced at me with a "she's crazy" look, but I ignored them.

Something bumped against the men's room door, and my heart jolted in my chest. Then, very slowly, the door opened.

The first thing I saw was the dark blue uniform covered in dust, soot, and drops of blood.

Then I lost it. Tears streamed down my face as I leapt toward him. My trembling fingers weaved through his short, honey-colored hair. His arms hovered over my waist. I sensed his uncertainty and fear.

I drew away from him and wiped tears and snot off

my face. "Lilith, Oliver," I said in a broken voice. "I thought I'd lost you."

His face was ashen and completely drained of color. His eyes were wide as saucers as they gazed frightfully around the room. "Desi," he said weakly. "Where are we?" His back was stiff and straight, and he moved forward with slow, careful steps. His head darted left and right as he took in our surroundings.

I took his hand in mine and squeezed. "We're in the future. I think. I'm not sure exactly what year, but it's close to when I left."

His dazed eyes met mine for a brief moment before darting to the glass door that people shuffled past.

"Was anyone else with you?" I asked, looking over his shoulder toward the men's room.

"What?" He met my gaze again. He looked as lost and forlorn as a child. It broke my heart.

I stepped closer to him and touched his cheek. "Oliver. Was anyone else with you?"

He swallowed and shook his head. "No. It was only me."

I dropped my hand, my mind racing with possibilities. *Who traveled with us? Where did they all go? El Diablo, Kismet, Bay?* I swallowed down the knot in my throat as I thought of Bay, the dark warlock who had betrayed me to his coven—and then fought alongside me, saving my life. El Diablo stabbed him just before casting the spell. Had Bay survived?

A few customers nearby cleared their throats and gave Oliver and me strange looks.

"Come on," I said quietly, urging Oliver toward the door. The last thing we needed was to cause a scene and draw El Diablo here. Assuming he was even in this time.

We stepped outside. Oliver gasped, straightening as he tilted his head back to gaze up at the skyscrapers. "Mother of Lilith," he whispered, teetering backward.

I gripped his shoulder with both hands. "Easy now. I know it's a lot to take in. You need to trust me, okay? Oliver, look at me."

He tore his gaze away from the buildings and looked at me.

I leaned closer to him. "Trust me. I know this time period. Stick with me, and you'll be fine. We can drink in the sights later. But right now, we need answers. We need to know what year it is. Can you handle this?"

I felt his heavy breaths brush against my forehead. Slowly, he nodded. "Yes. I'll be fine."

"Good." I looked up and down the sidewalk, squinting. Then I saw it. A newspaper stand. "There." I pointed, and we both set off.

At first, Oliver fell behind, bumping into people and muttering apologies. After a moment, he seemed to realize this was slowing him down, and he pushed onward until he was right behind me. I took his hand in mine and squeezed his fingers reassuringly.

When we reached the newspaper stand, I crouched down to peer inside. The glass was smudged and stained, but I just barely made out the year.

"It's 2001," I told Oliver. I leaned closer but couldn't make out the month because of a smear of bird poop on the glass. I pushed against the glass, but it was locked. "Damn." I certainly didn't have any pocket change on me.

I stood and met Oliver's panicked gaze. "Over one hundred years, Desi," he said hoarsely. "A *hundred years.*"

"I know." I glanced up at the buildings, squinting against the afternoon sun. My eyes widened when I recognized a building a couple blocks away. Its towering spire stretched high in the sky and pierced right through the clouds.

I nudged Oliver. "Look! That's the Empire State Building. We're in New York." I sniffed the air and scrutinized the passersby. Some wore light jackets and scarves, but there were no thick coats or gloves.

"It might be fall," I muttered to myself. "Or late spring? I can't tell. I've never been to New York before."

"I have," Oliver said, his voice strengthening as if being useful made him feel more certain. He sniffed too.

"It's late summer. Early fall. There's no pollen in the air."

I frowned, doing the math in my head. "So I've been gone . . . more than a full year. Maybe a year and a half." Everyone I knew probably thought I was dead. And even if they didn't, I didn't know anyone in New York City who could help us.

"Clocktower," Oliver said suddenly, his eyes wide as he looked at me. "We need to find a clocktower."

I pointed at him and nodded enthusiastically. "Yes. Good thinking."

We started back toward the skyscrapers, but a light *pop* stopped me in my tracks. I grabbed Oliver's arm as three figures approached us from the shadows of a nearby shop. Each person smelled strongly of magic. The man in front had long, disheveled, brown hair and a short goatee. Two women in pantsuits stood behind him. I caught Oliver frowning curiously at them and their attire.

"Thank Lilith," I said, sighing with relief. "We need your help."

The man jerked his head toward us, and the two women surged forward. A burst of magic tickled my nose, and suddenly my hands were bound behind my back.

"Ah—what?" I sputtered.

"You two are under arrest for unsanctioned time travel," the man said in a monotone like he was reciting a script. "You will be tried according to the magical law of the Council of America. If found guilty, you will serve a prison sentence of eighteen years, provided you have passed the necessary safety measures."

Oliver struggled next to me, and I knew he was bound by their magic as well.

"You don't understand," I said through gritted teeth. "A Third Tier demon lord traveled with us. He's extremely dangerous. We have to find him!"

The man raised an eyebrow. "Our intelligence only picked up two travelers within a fifty-mile radius. You're the only ones around who aren't from this time."

I stilled, my heart frozen with shock.

We're the only ones?

So where did the others go?

CHAPTER 2

My body stiffened, frozen by a magical vise. I couldn't move, but somehow my legs pushed forward. One of our captors must have used their powers on me. I struggled, but it was like an imaginary puppet master controlled my limbs and moved me forward one step at a time despite my efforts to stop. A quick glance at Oliver's panicked expression told me the same thing had happened to him.

Our captors casually led us down the sidewalk to the tallest and most intimidating buildings. Our hands remained bound behind our backs. Oliver and I were each flanked by someone to mask the fact that we were prisoners. To any passerby, we would appear to be an ordinary group of nobodies strolling down the sidewalk like everyone else.

Well, except for our hundred-year-old attire. And the dirt and blood on our clothes.

We followed the tall goatee man to a towering building that was so narrow it reminded me of pictures I'd seen of the Washington monument, only this one was more rectangular. My mouth fell open in awe, my eyes widening as I tried to absorb it all. The sun shone off the glass of the building next to it, almost blinding me. Something in the back of my mind prickled with recognition. I felt like these were important government buildings, but I couldn't remember.

A chill pressed in on me once we entered the glass doors. Behind us, a pattern of rectangular windows covered the wall and bathed the area in sunlight. The smooth, tiled floor stretched on and on, adjacent to several counters that were longer than an all-you-can-eat buffet line. The spotless lobby was filled with people in business suits. A woman with a headset sat at the counter closest to us. She raised a thin eyebrow at us and nodded as we passed.

"Please," I muttered, trying again to explain the situation. "We didn't cast any time travel spell. It was the Third Tier demon. He must've traveled to a different time, but I swear, he's the one behind this."

Goatee man and the two women ignored my pleas. As I figured they would.

Panic blossomed in my chest. I suppressed a shiver as goosebumps tickled my arms. The air conditioning in this building was so *cold*. I'd grown accustomed to the heat of Santiago without the luxury of indoor cooling systems.

I glanced at Oliver next to me and tried to offer a reassuring smile, but it came off as more of a grimace. His face was colorless and terrified. His wide eyes flitted from me to our grand surroundings.

Soon, we approached a set of elevators. Though a few elevator doors opened for us, Goatee man waited for one that was completely empty before leading us inside.

As soon as the elevator doors slid shut, the man waved his hand, and a button appeared at the very bottom of the panel. Instead of a floor number, there was just a symbol: a white circle overlapping a black circle, creating a sort of Venn diagram with a slice of gray in the middle—similar to the yin and yang symbol but slightly different.

The man pushed the button, and the floor beneath us shifted. Oliver gasped and jerked backward in alarm, no doubt feeling that exhilarating sense of weightlessness I remembered as a kid.

"It's okay," I whispered to him.

The elevator floated higher and higher. I looked up

to see the floor numbers, but the screen was completely blank. My shoulders ached from the position of my arms, and my head throbbed. My stomach growled. How long had it been since I'd eaten?

At long last, the elevator doors slid open, but I hesitated. "Where are we?"

No one answered.

We stepped off the elevator and into a long hallway with glass doors. Our captors led us past several reception desks. I quickly read the labels on the doors we passed: *Criminal & Legal Assistance, Courtrooms, Investigators & Detectives,* and finally, *Criminal Holding Cells.* Fear crawled up my throat as we entered the last door.

Oh, Lilith, I thought, fidgeting against my magical restraints. *We're going straight to a prison cell. We'll be sitting ducks for El Diablo.*

Goatee man approached the woman at the desk and muttered, "Unsanctioned time travel."

The woman's eyes widened, which probably meant this crime didn't happen often—or at least, the criminals weren't caught often. She picked up her phone and pressed a few buttons. "I have a Code 43 . . . Yes . . . Yes." She hung up the phone and jerked her head to the hallway behind her.

My heart raced, my breaths turning shallow as we passed several ominous, gray doors. Goatee man pushed open one and pointed to Oliver, who cast me a frightened look before stepping inside. I tried stepping forward to follow him, but the invisible vise held me in place.

"I—but—" I sputtered, looking from the women to Oliver. "Please! I can't leave him."

"It's all right, Desi," Oliver said softly. I turned to look at him, and though his face was still pale and his eyes were wide, there was a calmness in his expression that I envied. His jaw tightened and he nodded.

I swallowed. *I can't leave him.*

Oliver nodded again. I tried to shake my head—to shout and fight my way back to him—but the women were already guiding me down the hall. My traitorous feet followed them obediently. Oliver's door shut with a loud slam, reverberating in my ears and heart.

You'll be fine, I told myself, though my breaths were so sharp and intense I felt a panic attack coming on. *You'll get this sorted out, and you'll get back to him. You* will *get back to him.*

But horror settled in my stomach. Had I just parted with my only friend here? The only person who knew me and could help me in this time period?

And worse—Oliver. At least I had a chance of knowing someone in this time, if only because my parents had been well-known Demonhunters. But

Oliver had left everyone and everything he knew. He wouldn't be treated kindly here. No one was here to vouch for him.

Yet *he* was the one reassuring *me* that it was all right.

Get a grip, Desi.

My captors led me to an identical gray door and opened it to a dark room with a lone table and chair. Goatee man stretched his hand forward to the cold metal chair, and I sighed before walking over and sinking into it. This room reminded me of those interrogation rooms in crime shows. I pictured being locked in here for hours while someone grilled me until I finally cracked and admitted to some horrendous crime.

The women said nothing as they placed something heavy and metal around my wrists. I wriggled slightly and concluded the metal object must be like a dampener on steroids—too thick for me to slide off on my own.

Goatee man turned to leave, and I yelled, "Wait! What's going to happen to me? To Oliver?"

The man hesitated. His cold, indifferent eyes swept over me, and for a moment I thought he might ignore me like he had before. But he inhaled and said quietly, "You'll be questioned shortly."

He and the women left, and the door slammed shut.

The vise on my body immediately lifted, and I slumped forward. My body ached from being stiff for so long. *I guess one of my captors had some special ability to keep me from running away.* That would explain why they handcuffed me before leaving.

I shivered, leaning forward and pressing my forehead against the cool surface of the table. The chill soothed the throbbing of my head for only a moment before my panicked thoughts took over.

El Diablo. Oliver. Time Travel. A prison sentence.

A small *pop* made me jolt upright, my head still spinning.

A plump, older man stood in front of me with thin, gray hair and glasses. In his hands, he gripped a small notepad and a pen. If I'd been anywhere else, I would've assumed he was some nerdy accountant. But the magic emanating from him made me shrink back in my chair.

He lifted his chin at me, his dark eyes boring into mine. "What's your name?" His voice was much deeper than I'd anticipated.

"Desiree Campbell."

The man arched an eyebrow and jotted something down on his notepad. "And where did you travel from? Or I suppose I should ask *when* did you travel from?" He smirked at his own joke.

"February of 1899 in Manila, Philippines."

The man nodded and wrote something else down. "And what brings you here?"

"I don't know."

The man looked at me with doubt in his eyes. "What?"

"I don't know. I didn't cast the spell."

"Ah." He adjusted his glasses on the bridge of his nose. "Who cast the spell?"

"A man named Colonel Greenwood. He's a Third Tier demon known as El Diablo."

The man's expression didn't change even though I'd just given him groundbreaking news. A freaking *Third Tier* demon had traveled to the future for some unknown purpose. Shouldn't he have been more worried?

"Is that so," the man said in a monotone. It wasn't a question.

I shifted in my seat, my body itching to stretch or dance—my usual coping mechanism for my anxiety. "You don't believe me?"

"I'm afraid not. You see, we have the strongest security measures in place, and our equipment only detected two magical beings who Teleported to this time. And that was you and the man you were with."

"I—I can't explain it. This time travel spell has a mind of its own. If it's cast with multiple people, some end up in different places—"

"So you've cast the spell before?" The man scribbled furiously in his notepad.

Frack. "I, uh, no, that's not what I meant, I just mean—"

"When and where did you travel from last time?"

I swallowed. Well, he was going to find out sooner or later that I was from this time. "I traveled in March of 2000 from North Grove, Wisconsin."

The man's pen froze above the notepad. His eyes were fixed on the floor. His brows pinched almost imperceptibly. "And where did you travel to?" he asked, his voice much quieter.

"July of 1898. Santiago, Cuba."

The man frowned, still not looking at me. "Why?" The question almost seemed rhetorical like he was muttering it to himself.

"I—I don't know. Like I said, the time travel spell does what it wants." Alba and Sofia had hunches, but I wasn't about to share them here. Not with this man who clearly didn't trust my story.

"The man we found with you—is he from North Grove as well?"

"No. He's from Cuba. I met him in 1898."

The man's head shot up, his eyes drilling into me. "*What?* You brought back someone from the past?"

My head reared back from his reaction. "It—it was an accident! Like I said, I didn't cast the spell—"

"You keep saying that," the man said with a touch of impatience. "But you don't have any proof to back up your claim."

"I didn't even know what was happening!" I cried as hysteria bubbled up within me. "We might not even be the only ones who traveled. There were two others, I think. One of them might be—might be dead." I almost choked on the words. *Bay isn't dead. He's not dead.*

The man slid his pen into his breast pocket and rubbed his forehead. "Miss Campbell, I regret to inform you that your situation doesn't look good. Time travel alone is a serious offense, but bringing someone who isn't from this time? One of our Teleporters will have to send him back where he can be tried by his own Council. And you'll almost certainly face charges as well."

My blood chilled. "Send him back? No—*no*! You can't do that! Please, I'm begging you." My throat closed, and I shook my head. *Send Oliver back . . . and keep me here? Lilith, please no!*

"I'm sorry, Miss Campbell, but the laws of our timeline are quite clear. We aren't supposed to alter any fixed point in time."

"But—but what if it *isn't* fixed?" I asked quickly, grasping at straws. "What if we were supposed to travel here? Look, I don't know all the answers, but something pulled me to Santiago, and something else pulled us here. Ask Oliver. Neither of us are very powerful—we practice light magic, so we haven't Ascended or anything. How could we possibly travel that far unless this was *meant* to happen?"

The man squinted at me thoughtfully. His lips turned downward in a contemplative frown.

That's it, I mentally urged him. *Believe me. Be on my side.*

He blinked and shook his head. "I'm sorry. But the law is clear. I'll forward your statement to my superiors, and your case will move forward from there."

Tears pricked my eyes. My throat dry, I whispered, "No. Please."

"You'll receive legal assistance to plead your case, but your fate is in the hands of the Council."

He slipped his notepad in his breast pocket and offered a sad, sympathetic smile. "Good luck, Miss Campbell."

I wanted to scream, to grab him by the collar and force him to believe me. But I just sat there numbly as he strode to the door.

Just before he left, the door burst open, and a woman stood there, panting. Her blond hair was tied in a ponytail, but loose strands rested against her cheeks. Her wide, blue eyes met mine. Her face was so familiar but so foreign. Wrinkles lined her eyes and mouth. Though she was much older than when I last saw her, I knew her like my own mother.

Kismet.

CHAPTER 3

"Kismet," I breathed, my eyes wide and my body frozen with disbelief.

My interrogator adjusted his glasses. His brow furrowed as he stared at Kismet. "Miss Harrington, this is very unorthodox—"

"I have explicit permission from Councilman Burke to intervene," Kismet said breathlessly, pulling a folded piece of paper from the pocket of her black dress pants.

I gazed at her pantsuit and purse and tried not to laugh. When she'd been my Familiar, she had one hour every day to be human, and she usually wore jeans and a grubby T-shirt. I'd never before seen her dressed like this. Even in 1899, she wore the fashions of the era.

Seeing her here in this time—*not* cursed to be a raven

for twenty-three hours of the day—made my head spin even more.

The man cleared his throat and took the slip of paper. He squinted at it, his mouth moving incoherently as he read. When he finished, he raised an eyebrow at Kismet. "Even so, it's highly unconventional to turn a criminal over to an investigator. You haven't received any official training in law enforcement."

Kismet offered a cold smile, and her eyes blazed. "I served as Miss Campbell's Familiar for almost eighteen years. She went missing for the last year of my sentence, but I still taught her everything she knows. I don't think she'll pose a threat to me."

I bristled at that but didn't want to argue. I certainly didn't want this man thinking I was capable of overpowering Kismet. And I probably wasn't.

When the man still looked doubtful, Kismet added, "She's a minor, John."

The man called John blanched and whirled to face me, his brows up to his hairline. "What?"

I squirmed in my chair. "Well, I—"

"Don't say anything, Desi," Kismet snapped. "Look, this is unprecedented. No minor has ever been charged with unsanctioned time travel in our entire magical history. And *yes*, legally she's a minor. For the last year and a half, she hasn't been here. She wasn't present for her eighteenth birthday, and I can attest to that. When my enchantment was broken, she was *not* here. Now, as far as we know, she could've time traveled and then come right back to this year. Which would still make her underage."

I held very still. I'd been in the nineteenth century for over six months. We both knew full well that I was a bona fide adult. But I knew what game she was playing.

John frowned, his gaze directed toward the floor.

"At least release her and her companion on house arrest," Kismet said. "They can stay with me, and the wards surrounding my apartment are more than sufficient."

John looked at her. "You live alone?"

Kismet stiffened. "No. My fiancé is a trained dark warlock who also works for the Council."

I froze, my mouth falling open. *Kismet has a fiancé? And he's a dark warlock?* Questions bubbled in my mouth, ready to burst, but I clamped my lips shut and waited.

John's eyes widened. "Really? Who is he?"

For some reason, Kismet's gaze flicked to me briefly before returning to John. "He's one of the trainers in the Blue Division. Badge number 537."

John's face slackened, his eyes brightening. "Ah. Why didn't you say so in the first place? Yes, this will work out nicely. Just bring the charged persons in for their trial next week, and it'll all be sorted out." He smoothed the slip of paper and frowned at it again. "And, I'll discuss this with Councilman Burke right away. Thank you for intervening, Miss Harrington."

Kismet's eyes darkened, but she offered a stiff nod and stretched her hand toward me. "Let's go, Desi."

I rose from my chair and glanced from Kismet to John. John wore an apathetic smile like the kind you give to that one classmate you can't stand but have to pretend to like. Kismet wouldn't look at him. Or me.

"Her cuffs?" Kismet asked.

"Oh, yes," John said as if he'd forgotten—though I was pretty sure he hadn't. He pressed his fingers against my wrists. The metal surrounding them grew so hot I winced in pain. Then they fell into John's palms.

A sharp ache ran from my shoulders to my elbows. I stretched my arms and rubbed my wrists. Kismet still wouldn't look at me. She strode purposefully to the door, and I followed behind her. She was taller than I remembered. Had she always been this tall, or had she somehow grown after her years of serving as a Familiar?

Once we were in the hall, I hissed, "Kismet, what—"

"Not now," she muttered. "Where's Oliver?"

I swallowed and pointed to the door where Goatee man had deposited Oliver. Kismet raised a hand, indicating I should wait in the hall. She knocked on the door and slid inside. My heart raced, and I rubbed my arms. Nervous energy flowed through me. I paced several steps, listening hard to the muffled voices on the other side of the door. But I couldn't make out anything.

Please let him go, I thought. *Please.*

At long last, the door opened again, and Kismet stepped out with Oliver right behind her.

I gasped and ran into his arms, clutching him in a tight embrace. "Thank Lilith," I whispered. "Are you all right?"

"Later," Kismet said sharply. "We have to leave *now.*"

I drew away from Oliver, my eyes wide, and looked at Kismet. The urgency in her voice scared me. Her eyes darted up and down the hallway like she was afraid of encountering other people on our way out.

She was in trouble. *We* were in trouble.

Oliver stared at her, his brows pinched and his eyes curious. He looked at me questioningly, but I shook my head. We followed Kismet down the hall, past the reception desk, and back to the elevators. Kismet pressed the button for the ground floor, and the elevator shifted. I was acutely aware of Oliver's body heat next to me. I wanted to take his hand, but I resisted the urge.

"Do you have an undershirt on?" Kismet asked Oliver.

My head jerked back in surprise.

Oliver's mouth opened and closed. "I . . . uh—yes."

"Take off your shirt, and put it in my bag. *Now.*"

Never one to refuse an order, Oliver unbuttoned the top of his uniform, revealing a loose, white undershirt. Kismet quickly shoved his uniform shirt into her large purse just as the elevator doors opened.

His uniform draws too much attention, I realized. *People will be watching us.* I glanced at my own outfit, which was covered in dirt. But at least I was wearing trousers, which was acceptable in this time. I rolled the collar of my shirt to hide a small bloodstain.

"Walk quickly," Kismet hissed. "Stay with me. Don't make eye contact with anyone."

I nodded and glanced at Oliver. His gaze was fixed determinedly forward, his jaw set and his eyes fierce. Right now, he was a soldier. Regardless of how confused or shocked he was, he followed orders.

I, however, was completely out of my element. Sneaking out of the Council headquarters after my raven Familiar mysteriously bailed me out? I couldn't wrap my head around it, and I was never good at acting.

Once again, I marveled that Oliver was more at ease than I was, even though he'd traveled one hundred years in the future. We were in my time, and I was a mess while he was cool, calm, and collected. How did *that* work?

I straightened my shoulders and relaxed my hands as we filed into the lobby. Dozens of people bustled by us, but I kept my gaze straight ahead. I felt several pairs of eyes on me, and I tried not to fidget. *Keep walking. Keep walking.* My erratic heartbeat was sure to give us away. My shoulders shook with each shallow breath. I focused on Oliver's gold hair just in front of me and Kismet's lighter blond hair ahead of him.

We passed through the glass doors, and I exhaled with relief. But Kismet's pace never slowed. Following her lead, I kept up with her and Oliver, struggling to keep my expression neutral.

Suddenly, Kismet stopped short. I peered around her, and my blood chilled.

A tall, black creature stood in front of us on the sidewalk. The only way I could describe him was *gargoyle.* His skin was wrinkly and charcoal-colored, and he had a large snout on his face with sharp fangs. Giant, black wings stretched out behind him, and long, knife-like claws extended from his fingers.

I looked nervously around at the passersby, but no one glanced twice at the demon. He must've been cloaked.

His black eyes glittered when they rested on us.

Kismet's fingers curled into fists. "Damien."

Damien's mouth stretched into a wide, sinister smile.

He cocked his head at us and ran a long tongue across his teeth.

Fear crippled me, seizing my limbs and locking me in place. I focused on my breaths. *I'm a Huntress. I've faced monsters before.* I wiggled my fingers, triggering my magic as if summoning it from its hibernating slumber.

The fear melted away into nothingness. Adrenaline pulsed through me as I glared at the creature.

"Let us pass," Kismet said, her voice hard.

A low growl rumbled from Damien's throat. His lips pulled forward, and he spoke in a smooth, deep voice. "You know I can't do that, Kismet. He wants to keep a close eye on them." His beetle-black eyes shifted to me and Oliver.

I stiffened. *What?* Was he working for El Diablo? My eyes darted to Oliver, but his steely gaze was fixed on the demon. Oliver's jawline was tense, and his teeth clenched. His lips moved as he whispered a spell. His voice was so faint, I might not have noticed if I hadn't been watching him.

"Magic above, in the wind and skies,
Hide our magic from mortal eyes."

A sharp, lime scent tickled my nose. I watched the gargoyle, whose eyes narrowed. He smelled it too.

Without waiting for him to strike, I thrust my arms forward. My magic Pushed him to the ground. He slid backward several feet, and the surrounding mortals mysteriously sidestepped him.

"Run!" Kismet shouted.

We turned away from Damien and bolted down the sidewalk. Then, an invisible vise wrapped around my throat. I choked and clawed at my neck. A sticky, rubbery substance was glued to my skin. I couldn't peel it away.

"Desi!" Oliver shouted.

The vise tugged me backward.

No. My neck will snap!

I flexed my hands behind me, blindly Pulling whatever was attached to me. My fingers twisted and yanked as I tried to magically grab the creature without looking at him.

Oliver shot a ball of flame past me. Damien howled in pain, and the pressure on my throat vanished. Coughing, I rubbed my neck. Black spots danced in my vision. I yanked the sticky, web-like rope away from my body.

Another ball of fire flew forward and blasted against the gargoyle. I cleared my throat and whirled to face the demon again. His wrinkly skin was scorched and smoking, but his enraged eyes told me he wasn't too injured to keep fighting.

Oliver and Kismet sent more flames into Damien's chest. I stretched my arms forward and Pushed him, freezing him in place. My fingers shook as he thrashed against my magic.

"Banish him!" I shrieked.

"I can't!" Kismet shouted back.

My eyes widened at her. I gritted my teeth, my arms quivering. I couldn't hold him much longer.

Oliver grunted, curling his fingers into a fist. When his hand opened, pebbles fell from his fingertips. In his palm was a sharp spearhead made from rock.

Oliver bounded forward. With a swift motion, he sliced the makeshift weapon along the gargoyle's throat.

I released my hold on Damien, my arms throbbing. Gasping for air, I watched Damien crumple. Inky blood pooled from his throat. Before I could ensure he died, Kismet snatched my hand and tugged. I stumbled forward to match her pace, and together, the three of us sprinted away from the enemy.

CHAPTER 4

WE RAN FOR SEVERAL BLOCKS. THE CARS WHOOSHED PAST us, and the buildings were a blur from the sweat that was stinging my tired eyes. When my chest ached and my breaths felt sharp enough to slice right through me, I stopped, doubling over and wheezing.

"Is he . . . dead?" I panted.

"He's Second Tier. So no," Kismet said breathlessly, flagging down a taxi driver. We piled in the backseat, and Kismet gave the driver an address.

For several minutes, we all panted heavily, our faces covered in sweat. My arms still shook. My shoulder pressed against Oliver, and I looked at him. His face was drained of color, and his eyes were wide as he stared, mesmerized, out the window.

Of course, I thought numbly. *He's never been in a car before.*

For a long moment, I watched him. Fear, shock, and confusion mingled in his eyes and swarmed in my chest through our blood oath. The longer I stared at him, the more subdued the emotions became. His face was still pale and a bit sickly, but I felt him take steadying breaths next to me.

At long last, he looked over at me, catching me staring blatantly at him.

"Are you all right?" he whispered.

His green eyes were much too close to me. His grass and gunpowder scent tickled my nose, and I swallowed, looking away. "Yes. Are you? This must be frightening for you."

Oliver shrugged one shoulder, but his eyes betrayed his uncertainty. "I'm just . . . adjusting to the time. What is this machine called?"

"An automobile. Or vehicle. But we call it *car* for short."

Oliver's brow furrowed. "Like a railway car?"

"Uh, kind of."

"I've heard of machines like this," Oliver said slowly, his gaze distant. "There's a motor company that formed in Massachusetts a few years ago—er, well, in my time. Their motorized vehicles looked similar, but this is still

. . ." He trailed off, shaking his head, his eyes filled with wonder and confusion.

I smiled. "I know it's a lot to take in."

"Yes, it is." Oliver looked at me, and our gazes locked. My mouth suddenly felt dry. My eyes fell to his hand, which was resting on his knee. His fingers twitched toward my leg, the movement almost imperceptible.

Maybe it was the lingering adrenaline, or maybe I was just crazy, but I was seized by the sudden urge to take his face in my hands and make out with him right there.

Instead, I crossed my arms and gazed out the window, trying to ignore the heat roaring inside my body. *Now is not the time.*

I stared at the skyscrapers out the window. The driver stopped frequently at traffic lights. *Will the gargoyle be able to follow us?* I wondered. Perhaps that was why we ran several blocks before getting into a cab—to ensure he didn't trail too closely behind us.

"He's long gone," Kismet muttered as if reading my thoughts. "He would've attacked us again by now if he'd followed."

A wave of relief swept over me, and I closed my eyes, trying to quell the shaking of my limbs.

After about ten minutes, we pulled in front of an apartment complex that was so fancy it looked more like a five-star hotel. Kismet paid the driver, and we all exited the taxi. Questions burned in my mind, but Kismet seemed intent on getting to her apartment first. I clenched my fingers into tight fists and followed her into another lobby. Though it was smaller than the lobby in the Council building, it had finer furniture—a chaise sofa, a crackling fireplace, mahogany end tables, a chandelier hanging from the ceiling, and an elegant crimson rug that looked like it belonged in some kind of palace.

Sheesh, how can she afford a place like this? I wondered. Judging by John's condescending remarks, Kismet didn't hold a position of much authority in the Council.

Perhaps her mysterious dark warlock fiancé footed the bill.

I yearned to ask her, but I knew we had to wait. Kismet waved politely to the man at the reception desk and led us to another elevator. She punched the button for the sixth floor. When the elevator doors opened, she led us down a hallway lined with gold carpet. Each door we passed had an ornate bronze knocker just below the apartment number. I watched as the numbers climbed higher and higher—610, 612, 614 . . .

At long last, we reached Kismet's apartment: 626. She inserted a key and held the door open for us, her face still a mask of indifference and apathy. I suppressed a shiver. The last time I'd seen her face like that was when El Diablo had been about to kill me and Oliver.

Oliver and I entered the dark apartment. The door shut behind us, and Kismet turned on the lights. I gasped, my heart dropping to my stomach.

All the furniture from my parents' home in North Grove—it was *here*. The same brown sofa Kismet used to sleep on as a raven. The same bookshelf with magical texts and encyclopedias my dad had studied from every night. All the photos of my family before my parents died. Baby pictures of me. The grandfather clock that ticked so loudly I'd thrown the remote at it years ago, shattering the glass cover. Mom had shrieked at me for an hour, and Dad had grounded me for over a month and made me work to pay for the repairs.

The memories brought a sludge of emotions that clogged my throat, making it hard to breathe. This apartment even smelled like them, though our home was hundreds of miles away.

My eyes felt hot. I rubbed my nose. "I—Kismet," I said thickly. "How?"

Kismet's eyes grew soft as she dropped her keys on the coffee table. "I knew you'd be coming back. I couldn't just get rid of everything. All those memories."

I shook my head, my face crumpling with incoming tears. "You didn't have to—you shouldn't have—oh, *Kiz*."

I rushed forward and embraced her. The sobs came freely then. I buried my face in her shoulder, inhaling her familiar scent of raspberries. Even mingled with sweat, the smell was still comforting. She hadn't smelled like that in Santiago or Manila. The scent made me feel safe. At home.

Her arms circled around me, holding me tightly. "I'm so glad you're home," she said weakly, her voice betraying tears too.

I pulled away and looked over my shoulder at Oliver, whose back was turned as he gazed at the family photos on the wall. Discomfort wriggled through me at the thought of him seeing my awkward preteen years. Here was my life, spread out for him to absorb. I wasn't sure how I felt about that.

"Oliver, this is Kismet Harrington," I said. "I know you've met her before, but she's a bit older than she was back then."

Kismet chuckled, and Oliver faced her and bowed his head. "A pleasure, Miss Harrington."

"Call me Kismet," she said with an awkward laugh.

"How?" I asked again. "You traveled with us, but where did you go? And how did you find me? How did you get permission to—?"

"Slow down, Desi," Kismet said, raising her hands.

"I'll explain everything. But first, you two need to bathe. You stink."

My mouth fell open in mock horror. "Rude."

Kismet smirked. "You'll find outfits and toiletries in the spare bedroom. Desi, you can use the bathroom in my room. And you're probably starving. I'll reheat leftovers while you guys get changed."

She disappeared into the next room. I swallowed and looked at Oliver as Kismet bustled noisily in the kitchen —dishes clattering, the microwave door slamming shut, the kitchen faucet running.

Oliver's eyes drifted around the room, lingering on the tall lamp, the giant television, followed by the computer in the corner: the modern technologies he wasn't accustomed to. Then, his gaze fell on me. The shock and awe were still evident on his face, but his eyes were alight with something else. Something that made my toes curl and my face feel hot.

"Right, well," I said, my voice cracking. "We should, uh . . ." I trailed off and pointed toward the spare bedroom.

I darted inside and turned on the light, inhaling sharply when I noticed my bed resting in the middle of the room. The same bed I'd slept in when I lived in North Grove. When I'd lain there restlessly until two in the morning before the spring equinox when I cast that spell.

I cleared my throat, gathering my clothes and towel before the memories suffocated me. I had just left the spare bedroom when I stopped short. Slowly, I turned back and found Oliver in the guest bathroom, standing stiffly in front of the toilet, his body frozen.

I pressed my lips together, trying not to laugh. "Need some help?"

Oliver whirled to face me, eyes wide. He pointed to the toilet. "What the devil *is* this?"

I laughed. "It's for, uh, relieving yourself. You know, urinating?" I showed him how to flush and demonstrated how to turn on the shower, all the while enjoying his awestruck and baffled expressions.

"Brilliant," he whispered, his lips widening into a smile.

My stomach churned at the light in his eyes, the pure wonder and amazement. My heart twisted, but I wasn't sure why. There was something about having him here mingling with the world I'd left behind. It unsettled me.

I left him and took the longest shower of my life, savoring the hot water and the delicious feeling of conditioner in my tangled hair. I scrubbed feverishly at my neck, which still felt sticky from the gargoyle's web.

When I was finished, I dressed in dark skinny jeans

and a T-shirt from some heavy metal concert I'd attended. When I looked at myself in the mirror, my stomach lurched. This was the same outfit I'd worn the night I met José. *Lilith, that was an eternity ago.*

I shook my head, ridding myself of the memory, and emerged from my room. Oliver was seated on a bar stool, dressed in cargo shorts and a faded T-shirt. Seeing him dressed in modern clothes made my head spin. I watched him chow down on lasagna while Kismet leaned against the counter, her arms crossed.

"So, are you going to tell us what's going on?" I asked, sliding onto the stool next to Oliver.

Kismet set a plate of lasagna in front of me, and I took three huge mouthfuls, moaning with pleasure.

Kismet laughed. "I figured you'd like that."

"It's delicious," Oliver said.

"Stop stalling, Kiz," I snapped before taking another bite. "What was that gargoyle thing? And why couldn't you banish him?"

Kismet sighed, drumming her fingertips along the counter. "There are aspects of my blood bond that . . . I can't quite escape from."

I stilled. "You're still bonded to El Diablo?"

Oliver stiffened next to me. I knew that name jolted him, making him remember who El Diablo really was:

Colonel Greenwood. Oliver's superior in the army and his mentor within the Council.

Also, the father he'd never known.

Kismet winced, her eyes closing. "Not exactly. I—" She groaned, rubbing her face with her hands. "Something changed when I became your Familiar. It dulled the tether between us, but it's still there."

"Where did you travel to? After he cast the spell?"

"I arrived just after the day you were born," Kismet said. "It's how I was sentenced to become your Familiar —because of unsanctioned time travel."

My jaw dropped. "*That* was your crime? But it wasn't even your fault! How could they do that?"

Kismet shrugged. "I knew it would happen. I probably would've fought it harder if I hadn't known. And how do you think I was able to interrupt your interrogation?" Kismet raised her eyebrows at me. "As soon as I was able, I reported the time travel to the Council to flag your arrival. I wasn't exactly sure when you'd come back, but I knew you would. I had to make sure you two weren't imprisoned or sentenced for it."

"If you reported this to the Council, then why did we rush out so quickly?" I asked. "Why was there a fracking gargoyle waiting for us?"

"Because Damien and John Dickers are on Levarret's payroll," she said darkly.

John Dickers—the man who had interrogated me. *That's why he looked so relieved when Kismet said a dark warlock lived here.* A demon working on the Council would certainly be on Levarret's payroll too. So had Kismet made that up? Or was she really engaged to someone who was working for Levarret?

Impossible. She can't be. She would never.

"Who's Levarret?" Oliver asked.

Kismet's face became stony and rigid. Her gaze darted to the floor.

I cleared my throat. "He's the Third Tier demon wreaking havoc in this time period. And . . . he killed my parents."

Oliver sucked in a breath and looked at me, but I couldn't meet his gaze. Instead, I asked, "If Dickers works for Levarret, why would he just let us go?"

"Because of Councilman Burke," Kismet said. "He works for Levarret too. I forged his signature on that form to buy us enough time to get out. John knew if the Councilman signed off on your release, then he could too. But it won't take long for them to realize what happened. In fact, if Damien's on the case, they probably already know."

"Won't they find us?" I glanced around, half-expecting the door to burst open to reveal the entire Council here to apprehend us.

"We're safe for now," Kismet said. "I gave the Council a false address when I was first hired. And I wasn't lying when I said there are powerful protective wards here. But eventually, they *will* find us. And we'll need to be ready. Now that you've escaped, Levarret will do anything to find you. It's why he sent Damien after you."

"*Me?*" I shook my head. "Why? What does Levarret want with me?" He *had* killed my parents, but I was a nobody. I wasn't a threat to him.

"Not just you. Both of you." Kismet's eyes flicked from me to Oliver.

I looked at Oliver, and his brow furrowed, his green eyes puzzled. Darkness crept into my chest. A sense of foreboding gripped my throat so tightly I couldn't breathe. Couldn't speak.

"Why?" Oliver asked, his voice hard.

The air grew still with anticipation. My insides felt numb. I somehow sensed the words before Kismet spoke them.

"Levarret is Matthias Greenwood. He is El Diablo."

CHAPTER 5

THUNDER ROARED IN MY EARS. FIRE BURNED BEHIND MY eyes, scorching me and burning my flesh until I felt nothing but the charred remains of my body. I felt El Diablo's fangs piercing my neck. His moan of pleasure sent revulsion and nausea churning in my stomach—the sickening sense of weightlessness and the blissful nothingness I'd felt when he drank my blood.

El Diablo. He was *everyone*. Everywhere. Matthias Greenwood. Levarret. A trusted mentor. An evasive demon lord. The scourge of Santiago. The doom of Manila. And now he was taking my time period from me too.

Kismet and Oliver were speaking, but I heard nothing but the deafening rhythm of my pulse.

My eyes fell on the heavy oak dining table that my

parents had found at an antique store after hours of shopping. I remembered arguments at that table when I'd skipped class. Laughter when Dad drank so fast that water spurted from his nose.

Matthias Greenwood had taken that from me.

"*Why?*" I screamed so loudly that Kismet and Oliver jumped. My fingers curled into tight fists as rage bubbled through me. "Why? What does he gain from their deaths?"

Silence fell. I didn't dare pull my gaze from that worn oak table. I knew as soon as I looked at Kismet or Oliver, I would burst into tears.

"Without their deaths, you never would've time traveled," Kismet said softly. "He needed you in the past so he could cast the time travel spell."

"He had Sofia for that," I said angrily. "She had all the information he needed."

"She never would've given it to him," Oliver said. "At least not all the pieces." He swallowed, his eyes closing. "I used the spell in front of him when he stabbed Desi. He knew the words because of me."

He's not allowed to feel more regret than me right now. It was a savage, selfish thought, but I couldn't help it. This moment— this anger and emotion belonged to me right now.

My nostrils flared, and I clenched my teeth so tightly

my head started throbbing. Sliding down from my stool, I began pacing up and down the room, parallel to the bar where Oliver sat. My legs itched to stretch and dance, but my fury was all-consuming. For the first time in years, I didn't want to dance. I wanted to give in to the rage.

"Desi, your parents' deaths were fixed points in time," Kismet said, her voice still infuriatingly quiet like she was worried about enraging me. I was already way past that. "If they'd been alive, you never would've time traveled. Matthias would've remained in Santiago and never would've come here to kill them in the first place. It's all part of one big circle in the timeline. Remove any vital event, and the timeline collapses. This was all—"

"Don't say it," I snarled, pointing a finger at her. "Don't say it was meant to be. This—this—" I choked on my words, my anger fizzling as realization set in. "This is *my* fault."

Oliver stiffened. "Desi."

I shook my head. "I picked this fight with him. *I* started it. I snuck into his prison and freed Sofia and those other Santeros. He retaliated, then I retaliated, and then he trapped us both in Manila. If I'd just fracking kept my head down and kept to myself in Santiago, then . . ." I trailed off, my face crumpling with grief as the agony consumed me. I stopped pacing and leaned against the kitchen wall.

"Desi, *stop*," Kismet said firmly, placing her palms on the counter and leaning over the bar to stare at me. "Listen to me. If you'd done that, if he never knew about you at all, then he never would've time traveled. He never would've become Levarret and killed your parents. And if your parents had been alive, you would never have felt the need to run away, the desire to escape from it all. Don't you see? It would've caused a ripple, undoing *everything*—"

"I. Don't. Care." I slid against the wall until I sat on the floor, propping my arms on my knees. Sudden exhaustion settled over me, but the pain and ache in my chest were so severe that I couldn't escape it. I couldn't find the rest my body so desperately needed. "I don't care about the damn timeline or these fixed events or *anything*. My parents are dead because I pissed off a Third Tier demon." I leaned my forehead against my arms, squeezing my eyes shut as if I could block out their faces. But there they were, smiling proudly at me as if I had some great potential to be a Hunter like them. When really I'd just brought about their downfall.

I heard movement but didn't lift my head. Oliver's outdoorsy scent mingled with the vanilla of whatever shampoo he'd used. I felt his body heat as he sat on the floor next to me.

"Your parents' deaths are on *him*, Desi," he said, his voice low and soft in my ear. "He's responsible for that, not you. I—I can't pretend to understand how you're feeling right now. But he took everything from me too. He violated my mother, cutting her off from her dreams and her way of living. She died of influenza because she couldn't afford treatment. He—he made me believe he was my mentor. He gave me opportunities within the Council, but it was all just to"—he broke off and exhaled —"to trick me. To put me in a position of power so he could *use* me. He knew. He knew all along that I was his son, and he waited until the perfect moment to play that card."

His warm hand touched my arm. I pressed my lips together as hot tears dropped onto my shirt. "This is what he does," Oliver said. "He rips apart people's lives because he has the power to do it. But you have a choice, Desi. You can drown yourself in grief. Or you can pick yourself up and *do* something about it."

Anger and devastation swirled within me, mingling with the buzz of my magic. My hands ached to stretch forward and Push, to blast something into oblivion. But with that urge came the horrifying reminder of what I'd done in Manila—the darkness in my magic, the shift from blue to black, and the pitiful howl of the werewolf I'd sacrificed.

I shuddered. I didn't trust myself anymore. Or my magic.

Slowly, I lifted my head. I didn't look at Oliver, but his presence next to me strengthened my voice. "What do you know?" I asked Kismet. "Tell me everything."

Kismet's brows creased, but she nodded, circling around the bar to sit next to us on the floor. I knew it was ridiculous for us to sit on the cold tile like this when we were surrounded by chairs, but somehow it made our discussion feel more intimate.

"I don't know exactly what year he arrived," she said. "But when I got here in 1983, I *felt* him. Our blood bond was still intact. I was sentenced and imprisoned, and all the while, he called to me. Thank Lilith I was cuffed the entire time, otherwise I might've been forced to go to him."

"What changed?" I asked.

"My curse," Kismet said, her sharp, blue eyes drilling into me, conveying some deeper meaning I couldn't see.

I shook my head. "The Familiar's curse?"

Kismet nodded slowly. "With the curse, my magic was reborn within *you*. My magic became light again, and I no longer felt him. Not while I was bound to you."

My head reared back. "'Bound to me?' What do you

mean?" The way she said it reminded me of the blood bond between her and El Diablo, but our relationship hadn't been like that at all. I'd ordered her around plenty of times, and she'd resisted easily. *Thank Lilith for that.*

Kismet crossed her legs and folded her hands in her lap. "Aurologists around the world have discovered that the Familiar's curse is the strongest bond between two souls. Stronger than a blood bond or any other blood magic out there."

My mouth fell open. "How?"

"From the research I've gathered, it's a combination of factors. One of those factors is time. It's the longest duration of any blood magic out there. The other factor is the way my powers are bound. They're tethered to yours." Kismet leveled her gaze at me. "I couldn't perform magic without you, and I channeled my abilities through your own. My magic was blue because yours was too. Those limitations were meant to keep me a prisoner, but it only strengthened the tether between us."

"So what happened to your blood bond?" Oliver asked quietly. "When the curse was broken, did it return?"

Kismet shrugged one shoulder. "Yes and no. I felt him again, but it wasn't as strong. Now it sort of serves as a blood oath, similar to what you two have."

I bristled, sensing Oliver's gaze on me. Heat seared along our blood oath, and I swallowed, focusing instead on Kismet. "So you can't find him? I mean, I found Oliver through our blood oath."

She shook her head. "I only feel certain emotions, but it's distant and vague. The farther away he is and the more power he gains, the less I'm able to sense him. It's like he's avoiding getting too close to me. Otherwise, I *would* be able to seek him out. Other limitations passed through too, like my inability to banish a demon who works for him."

I deflated slightly. A small part of me had hoped Kismet could point the way so I could end that son of a bitch once and for all. But even if she *had* known where he was, I was no match for El Diablo.

"But if you were sentenced to become a Familiar, why wasn't he?" Oliver asked.

Kismet shrugged. "He's Third Tier. His reaction time was probably better than mine since he'd been planning this. I'm fairly certain he would've fled as soon as he arrived, knowing the authorities would be after him. And, of course, it's helpful that the time travel spell seems to deposit people in an isolated location to avoid drawing attention."

My brain numbly registered something from her words. *That's why Oliver and I arrived in a bathroom.*

"The reason I'm telling you this," Kismet said slowly, drawing my eyes to her solemn expression, "is because the bond of the Familiar's curse is the key to everything. It's taken me years to understand it, and it isn't a proven theory, since so few have time traveled. But from what I can ascertain . . . the bond of the Familiar's curse is strong enough to pull two people *through time.*"

I stilled. My heart froze in my chest, and goose-bumps tickled my skin. When my heart resumed its beating, it thumped so loudly and erratically I was sure I would pass out. "Are—are you saying—"

"The bond you and I have is the reason we ended up where we did."

My eyes widened, and my back straightened. I glanced quickly at Oliver, whose face was pale, his eyes distant and thoughtful as he considered this revelation.

I shook my head. "But . . . we were bound for almost eighteen years. How did that bond influence the spell? How did it decide where to put us?"

"The theory is that the time travel spell sensed the greatest point of weakness along the bond. So when you first cast the spell in 2000, the spell put you in Santiago . . . right after I'd become a slave to Matthias."

I inhaled sharply. All this time I'd thought it was because of José's ancestors that I'd wound up there.

Kismet seemed to read the confusion in my face.

"There are other factors that influence the spell. Just like there were other points in time when I was weak and vulnerable. For instance, when I was an infant. Helpless. Defenseless. Unable to perform magic." She paused, her eyes moistening. For one strange moment, I thought she would burst into tears. Then she blinked and continued, "I believe this is why I traveled to the year you were born."

I swallowed, my head spinning. *I was weakest as an infant? Does this mean I won't ever be weaker than that? I won't ever find myself in a position like Kismet did, becoming a slave to someone else? Losing my free will completely?*

"Don't overthink it, Desi," Kismet warned. "It's not an exact science. Like I said, there are many other factors that influence the spell."

"But then why did we end up *here*?" I asked, gesturing to Kismet. "It doesn't look like you're in any mortal danger."

Kismet grew very still, her eyes guarded. Emotion flashed in her face before she smoothed her expression. "I sent for you."

I blinked. "You can do that?"

"I cast a summoning spell for you last week. I didn't think it would work, but I had to try." She shrugged one shoulder, avoiding my gaze. "I guess it was stronger than I thought."

I narrowed my eyes, watching her, waiting for her to spill whatever she was hiding. But before she could, Oliver spoke.

"What about when I cast the spell?" he asked.

Distracted, my gaze snapped to him and then back to Kismet. *Good question.*

"Did you have a Familiar?" Kismet asked.

"No."

"When did you travel to?"

"A week in the future."

Kismet nodded, frowning and wringing her hands together. "It's possible you would've traveled farther if you had that bond with a Familiar. I obviously can't say for sure, but perhaps that's why you didn't travel very far. Because every part of your soul was in one place."

I raised a hand. "Whoa, hang on. 'Every part of his soul'? You mean a part of my *soul* is with you?"

Kismet winced with a slightly guilty expression on her face. "Yes."

I thought of Elena and Guillermo and their bargain with the shaman in Manila—they'd sacrificed a portion of their souls in order to stay safe from blood rituals. When I'd found out, I was horrified. I didn't think anything justified severing your soul.

But it seemed I had done the same thing. Even if it was inadvertent.

"That's why it's stronger than a blood bond," Oliver murmured, stroking his chin.

"How can the Council *do* that?" I said. "How can they cast this curse and bind an innocent baby's magic to a criminal?"

Kismet flinched, and I regretted my words instantly. "They're aware of the research," she said in a strained voice. "They're looking for stronger evidence. But in the meantime, all sentencing of Familiars has been put on hold for the past year."

"What about El Diablo?" Oliver asked.

"Call him Matthias," Kismet said sharply. "El Diablo is the name he chose to inspire fear. If you call him by his mortal name, then he's just another man."

Oliver stared at her, his jaw rigid. He nodded. "What about Matthias? How did the Familiar's curse influence his spell?"

"That's what I can't figure out. I don't know what year he traveled to, and I don't know if he ever had a Familiar. But even if he *did,* that Familiar surely wouldn't be alive in this century."

"Do you think your blood bond with him pulled you to the same year—1983?" Oliver asked.

"It's possible. After all, *you* had a blood bond with him too, and you both traveled to roughly the same time when you cast the spell."

My eyes sharpened as they fell on Kismet. Her gaze was fixed determinedly on her knees as she picked at her fingernails. *What's she hiding?* "Kismet, you couldn't have possibly gotten all this information by yourself. Who helped you?"

Kismet shifted her weight, her gaze darting to me quickly before falling to the tiled floor. "You're right. I did have help. But before I tell you more, I need to know, Desi. Where do you stand?"

I felt the weight of her words, but uncertainty crashed through me. My mouth opened and closed helplessly.

"I mean, now that you know all this, what do you intend to do?" Kismet clarified.

Fire blazed within me. My magic surged forward, ready to be unleashed and to fight. Though a small part of me knew I needed time to process all of this, I couldn't deny the rage and determination thrumming in my body.

"I want to end him."

CHAPTER 6

I TOSSED AND TURNED IN MY BED, MY MIND FADING IN AND out of a strange dream. Something jolted my senses, and my eyelids fluttered open. The air smelled . . . different.

I jerked awake. A dark shadow crossed in front of my window, blocking the moonlight. A sinister chuckle sent ripples of fear through my body, freezing me in place. I couldn't breathe. Deep down, I knew I should scream to alert Mom and Dad to the presence of an intruder, but I couldn't do it. My limbs were stiff, and my throat was closed off. My body wouldn't obey me.

"You are nothing," a voice murmured. "A pitiful shadow of how I remembered you. It would be so easy to end you right now. But alas, I have bigger plans for you, child."

The intruder chuckled again, and the shadow moved. Moonlight streamed from my window, illuminating my room.

My eyes flitted frantically around my room, but I couldn't see him. Where had he gone?

A hand gripped a fistful of my curls. I gasped, my head throbbing, but another hand clamped over my mouth to silence me.

"Remember, Desiree," the voice growled in my ear. "You are mine.*"*

Something heavy smashed into my skull. The next thing I knew, Mom and Kismet were shouting my name. I woke up on the cold, concrete sidewalk, bathed in the yellow glow of a streetlamp. Kismet healed me, and Mom held me tight against her chest. They exchanged panicked remarks, but I didn't remember any of it. Then Mom gasped, the color draining from her face, and ran back into the house.

Something was horribly wrong. Where was Dad?

Amidst all the chaos, I couldn't shake the feeling of the intruder's whispers that raised the hair on the back of my neck. The feel of his breath on my skin.

My eyes flew open. I pressed a hand to my cheek, and my fingers came back wet. My chest constricted with sobs, and I covered my mouth. I sat up in bed. I hunched over and tried to rid myself of the terror of that night and the trauma that followed when I found out Mom and Dad had been killed.

It was *him*. Matthias Greenwood had been in *my* house, in *my* room. He'd threatened me. Whispered things to me. He could've killed me, but he knew he would need me later.

I'd been twelve years old. Only a child.

Bile rose in my throat, and I squeezed my eyes shut as if I could squeeze out the memory.

I often had visions—memories in my dreams from the connection to my parents and their light magic.

But this was different. I'd never remembered that night until now. It had always been a foggy haze. All I remembered was that I'd woken, something had hit me, and then I'd been on the sidewalk. But now, the gaps were filled. Somehow, my brain had put the pieces together. Now that I knew Levarret and Matthias were the same person, something had clicked.

With a shudder, I threw off the blanket. I wouldn't be getting back to sleep anytime soon.

I grabbed a jacket from the closet and slipped it on, shivering against the chill of night mingled with the air conditioning I still wasn't used to.

Carefully, I eased open my door. The whole apartment was dark and still. Kismet had promised that we'd meet with her mysterious friends first thing in the morning and make a plan for finding Matthias. After all Oliver and I had been through, we needed sleep first.

I rubbed my forehead. *Sleep. Yeah, that's not happening.*

My eyes closed, and in my mind, I saw the dark shadow and heard the taunting whisper.

I crossed my arms, feeling small and helpless. El Diablo had that effect on me—even more so when I remembered how I'd felt at such a young age.

Who was I kidding? I couldn't beat him. This was why I'd decided to turn dark—to gain enough power to stop him from hurting the ones I loved. But that was a mistake. I'd almost crossed a line I would've never been able to come back from.

Now that I'd realized that, what could I do? A light witch couldn't Ascend. I couldn't gain more power. But Matthias could.

Tiptoeing into the kitchen, I opened the fridge, wincing at the bright light that stung my eyes. I grabbed a bottle of water and chugged half of it. The cool liquid soothed the coarseness of my throat, but my raging fear lingered.

I leaned against the counter and focused on my breathing. In and out. Ordinarily I'd try to stretch or dance—ballet and yoga always soothed me. But I couldn't. I didn't know why. Something in me had changed, and dance didn't provide the same release it had before.

I set the bottle on the counter and stiffened as a flood

of foreign emotions filled my chest. Unease. Worry. Fear. Confusion. Irritation.

Oliver. He was awake.

I stared at the kitchen door, heart pounding as I realized he was lying on the couch just in the other room.

A knot formed in my stomach. If I slipped back into my room now, he would see me.

Was that a bad thing?

I swallowed, clutching the edge of the counter behind me. My mind was a jumbled mess and my body a torrent of fear. I needed my friend. Regardless of what had happened between us, I still needed him.

With a sigh, I left the kitchen and slid into the living room. The sofa creaked as Oliver shifted and turned.

My throat felt dry. I cleared my throat, and his movement stopped. "Can't sleep?" I asked.

Oliver sat up, and my breath caught in my throat. I stared at his disheveled hair, his sleepy and disoriented eyes, and—*Oh Lilith, he's not wearing a shirt.* My eyes flicked over the muscles of his chest and abdomen before I hastily glanced away, my cheeks burning.

This was a mistake.

"No," Oliver said, pushing off his blanket and swiveling around so he was sitting. He shivered and snatched a white shirt from the floor. A part of me was disappointed, but the more logical side of me knew it was better with him clothed. I wouldn't be able to think straight otherwise.

Oliver slid his shirt on and rubbed his arms. "It's so damn cold in the future."

I chuckled without humor. "It's called air conditioning. A system that heats and cools a building. It bothers me too. I'm so used to the constant heat in Cuba."

"Do you miss it?"

"A little." I shook my head. "I should be asking *you* that. I took you away from your home. From everything and everyone." I rubbed my nose and dropped my gaze. "I'm so sorry, Oliver."

"Desi." Oliver stood and crossed over to me. I stiffened at his approach, the nearness of his warmth, and the allure of his scent. He froze, sensing my apprehension. Hurt flashed across his face before it melted into regret. "Don't be sorry. I made the choice to stay with you no matter what. Even if I'd known what he—what Matthias was going to do, I still would've come here with you."

I wrapped my jacket tighter around my chest, uncomfortably aware of the fact that I wasn't wearing a bra under my T-shirt. Slowly, I sank into the armchair behind me, my gaze fixed on the floral carpet.

"I do miss it," Oliver admitted, sitting on the couch and leaning forward. He propped his forearms on his knees. "I'll miss Santiago and the coven. I'll miss the America I knew and the friends I made on the Council. But Desi, I'd already lost everything. My boss had deceived me. My job was a hoax. I had no parents, no siblings. I had Alba and the coven, but . . ." He shook his head. "I never felt like I fit in there. I was always seen as 'the American.'"

I snorted. I could relate to that. I sobered as I thought of Elena and how she'd become so much more to me than a fellow Huntress. She'd been my best friend. And I would never see her again.

Heat stung my eyes, and I closed them against the pain of that loss. I'd never gotten to say goodbye. She would never know what happened to me. I would never get to laugh with her about her crush on Guillermo or commiserate with her about my feelings for Oliver. We'd never get to hunt side by side again or face demons with our identical Telekinetic powers.

"Lilith," I moaned, covering my face with my hands. "This is so hard."

Oliver remained silent. My eyes filled with tears despite my best efforts to prevent them. I sniffed and dropped my hands, swallowing down my agony.

"I know," Oliver whispered.

I shook my head. "No, you don't." I heaved a shaky sigh. "I need to tell you something."

Oliver straightened, his eyes tense. "You can tell me anything."

It all spilled out. I told him about my blood ritual with the werewolf that helped me save Reyna, the constant helplessness and fear that drove me to turn dark, my agreement with Bay to let him train me, and how my magic had changed to black, cutting me off from the connection to my parents.

During my confession, Oliver's eyebrows lowered, his jaw hardening, but he said nothing. I omitted my kiss with Bay, but I sensed Oliver knew. He knew there'd been something between me and Bay. But I didn't want to draw attention to it.

Tears streamed down my face by the time I finished. I wiped my nose and cleared my throat, fixing my gaze on the floor because I was too scared to watch his reaction. Too ashamed.

Several moments of silence passed between us. Somehow it felt better to share this with someone. Even if I knew he was probably disappointed in me.

At long last, Oliver said quietly, "Do you remember that conversation we had in my mother's floral shop? About me being afraid my father was a demon?"

I frowned at the subject change but nodded.

"Well, the truth was, I wasn't so much afraid he was a demon as I was afraid he didn't love me. I didn't care if he practiced light or dark magic. In a way, I already knew he was a demon before he told me. And some demons have no choice, you know? A vampire who's Turned has no say in the matter—once the transfer has been made, he's a demon no matter what. Same with werewolves. So I always wondered if my father was one of those unwilling demons. What if it wasn't his fault?"

I grew very still, not daring to breathe. Oliver's gaze was distant, his eyes unfocused as he poured his deepest thoughts to me.

"I can't lie to you and say I've always been disgusted with Matthias," he went on. "In my darkest, weakest moments, a small part of me thinks he can still achieve some kind of redemption. And when I first found out who he was, I wanted to believe the best in him—that he'd been Turned against his will. That my mother never told him about me; otherwise, he would've reached out and found me. That he really *was* doing all these horrible things for the right reasons.

"But . . . eventually, I saw him for what he really was. A monster. Someone beyond capable of loving me or anyone. Someone so lost in his purpose and his thirst for power that there's room for nothing else in his heart."

I wrung my hands together on my lap, staring

breathlessly at Oliver. His eyes shone with tears, and the corners of his mouth pulled down.

His moist eyes rested on me. "I suppose my point in all this, Desi, is that even if you had turned dark, I still would've loved you. Just like I would've loved my father if he—" he stopped, his words cutting off as his eyes closed. A tear rolled down his face. "And if I end up like Matthias—"

"You won't," I said sharply.

"No, but if I *do*," Oliver insisted. "If I do turn dark, and I have a son, I want him to know that I *do* care. That I *do* love him. Even if our blood isn't connected and he's a light warlock, or if he's a dark warlock and I stay light, I need him to know that I will always be there for him. In all the ways my father wasn't. I may be doomed to follow Matthias's magic, but I am *not* him. And I'm determined to be different. To be better."

"You *are*," I said, sliding off the armchair so I knelt in front of him. I pressed my fingers against his clasped hands. "Oliver, you aren't doomed to follow his magic."

"You don't get it, Desi," Oliver whispered, his face crumpling. "I've felt the pull of dark magic all my life. It's how I always knew my father was a demon. There's always a part of me that yearns to follow that side of magic. It calls to me. And I know that one day, I won't be able to refuse. There will be a strong enough reason to bring me there just like there was for you. So I can't judge you for that, Desi." Oliver looked into my eyes. "I don't blame you, and I'm not even disappointed. In a way, I'm envious. Envious that you made that choice and came back from it. Now you *know*. You know for sure why you can't make that choice. But I don't. There are conflicting feelings in me warring for both sides. And I don't know which side will win."

I leaned forward. "But Oliver, you've made it this far. You're still a light warlock. Surely that means something —that you've resisted that pull your whole life."

Oliver shook his head. "The pull has grown stronger now that I know who my father is. Like that connection has solidified. I can't run or hide from it like I could before. It's staring me in the face. And I'll have to confront it someday."

I pressed my palm against his warm cheek. His light stubble scratched my skin, and he closed his eyes, leaning into my touch.

"I'll help you," I said quietly. "I'll help you face it. You aren't alone in this, Oliver. I'll be there for you, and we can fight this together."

His eyes opened, his green eyes swelling with heat and uncertainty. He lifted his head, staring at me so intensely that my stomach churned. "You'll be there for me . . . how?"

I swallowed, knowing what he was asking. As his girlfriend? As his friend? "I don't know yet. But I know I need you in my life, Oliver. No matter what we are to each other."

I clasped his hands again. For a long moment, we stared at each other, our gazes locked and our emotions churning through the blood oath. I felt connected to him in a way I'd never felt before. We were exposed; our vulnerabilities were stretched out in front of each other, their exteriors stripped and naked. Despite our uncertainty and conflicted feelings—despite the way that vulnerability slithered through me and made me feel weak—in that moment, there with him after sharing our darkest secrets, I felt whole. I felt understood.

A door slammed. I jolted awake, my mind a jumbled mess and my cheeks sticky with the usual tears, though this time I couldn't remember the dream.

I turned my head and froze. Oliver's face was right next to mine. He was reclined on the sofa, his head facing me, while I was sitting on the floor, curled up against the base of the sofa with my head propped on the cushion. Our hands were still clasped, though our grips had loosened with unconsciousness.

My cheeks felt hot as I watched him sleep. His face was stretched in blissful innocence. His slow, heavy breaths poured from his mouth and tickled my face.

Someone cleared their throat loudly.

I jumped, withdrawing my hand from Oliver's and bolting to my feet. Kismet stood in the doorway, arms crossed and eyebrows raised.

"I—we—we couldn't sleep," I said, gesturing helplessly between Oliver and myself as if somehow conveying that nothing scandalous had happened between us.

The corners of her lips twitched. She raised her hands in surrender. "No judgment here, Desi. This is the twenty-first century, after all. I wouldn't blame you."

I cocked my head at her, remembering her comment about living with a dark warlock. Before I could ask her about it, Oliver groaned and shifted. I took a few embarrassed steps away from him to put more distance between us, but the effort did nothing to subdue the flames in my cheeks. I pointed to him and then toward the kitchen. Then I stammered some excuse about getting ready before darting out of the room.

Cheeks flushed, I closed my bedroom door and leaned against it, exhaling heavily. Why was I so flustered? Oliver and I hadn't *done* anything last night. And besides, since when was I such a pearl-clutcher? A few months ago, I'd wanted to go all the way with him.

Get it together, Desi. I shook my head and forced the thoughts from my mind. One look in the mirror told me my curls were not to be reckoned with today, so I pulled them into a messy ponytail and changed into street clothes before emerging.

I stopped short when I found Oliver and Kismet speaking in low voices in the kitchen. My heart jolted, my eyes roving over Oliver's form. He wore a faded green polo that made my head spin with bittersweet memories. Thoughts of my dad wearing the same shirt circulated in my mind—sharing picnics in the parks, strolling through the mall as I gushed over ChapStick and pierced ears, and cooking pancakes on Sunday mornings. Mom and I had always made fun of him for wearing polos. *Why can't you wear T-shirts like a normal Dad?* I'd complained.

But now, seeing this polo again sent sharp stabs of longing through my chest. I would give anything —*anything*—to see my Dad wearing that polo again. Even just once more.

Oliver turned to look at me, his eyes questioning and curious. Wondering what was wrong. He was much taller and bulkier than Dad had been, and the shirt stretched beautifully over his torso and muscles, making him look hot enough for a GQ magazine.

Seeing Dad's polo on this beautiful boy who made my chest feel like mush was so conflicting that I had to look away. My shallow breaths shook me, my hands trembling as I accepted a piece of toast from Kismet. I felt Oliver's eyes on me and knew he must've felt my strange array of emotions through our blood oath.

"Hope it's okay I gave him your dad's clothes," Kismet said in a low voice, though I was sure Oliver could hear. "I didn't have anything else to offer him."

I swallowed. "What about that dark warlock you're engaged to? Surely he'd have spare clothes lying around."

Kismet's head reared back, her eyes tightening and her lips pressing together. I took a bite of my toast, staring determinedly at the counter in front of me.

I heard Kismet inhale, probably to explain her fiancé was just a farce for John Dickers's sake, when a high-pitched twittering sound interrupted her.

I stiffened, eyes wide as I gazed around the room to look for the source of the noise. It sounded like a dozen birds chirping, but the rhythm of their twittering was too precise and repetitive to belong to real birds.

"Damn," Kismet muttered, setting down her toast. "They're faster than I thought."

"What *is* that?" I asked, scrunching my face in distaste. My ears throbbed from the shrill sounds.

"Wards," Kismet said. "They warn me when unwanted visitors approach. Come on, we're out of time."

CHAPTER 7

KISMET DARTED OUT OF THE KITCHEN. AFTER exchanging a look, Oliver and I followed and found her packing a bag in the living room. Slinging the bag over her shoulder, she hurried past us toward the back window. Sunlight streamed through, peeking over the tops of adjacent buildings and casting a warm glow on the bookshelves along the opposite side of the room.

More high-pitched twittering echoed in the apartment, increasing in intensity. I resisted the urge to cover my ears.

"Do you think it's the Council?" Oliver asked.

"Undoubtedly," Kismet said as she eased open the window. A cool breeze hissed into the room. "I thought it would've taken them longer to find me. Sorry for the hasty exit." She swung one leg over the windowsill and shimmied through the window. Oliver and I followed suit. I rubbed my arms against the morning chill as we climbed onto the fire escape. I gripped the metal railings, my arms trembling with every step down the ladder. My heart thudded with each panicked breath I took. A deep inhale sent a sharp slice of cool air into my lungs. It was way too cold outside. What month was it anyway? This felt like winter in Santiago—maybe even colder. But in New York? It could very well be fall.

Focus, Desi. I hastened my descent down the ladder, peering briefly over the edge toward the dumpsters waiting at the bottom. *Good thing I'm not afraid of heights.*

I glanced at Oliver behind me, but he kept up with our pace. The chirping from Kismet's apartment echoed in the air around us until suddenly, it stopped.

We froze, glancing up toward the suspicious silence.

"They've made it inside," Kismet whispered. "Come on, we can't be here when they look out the window."

Metal creaked as we hastily shuffled down the steps. *Almost there. Almost there.* Only one more ladder.

Magic tickled my nose. "Duck!" I shrieked.

The three of us dropped to the metal floor. Just above us, the fire escape groaned ominously.

"Move!" Kismet shouted.

We scurried out of the way. A huge metal panel smashed to the floor where we'd stood.

I glanced upward, squinting, and saw a figure leaning over the railing of the fire escape. I expected it to be that gargoyle, Damien, but this one looked human. He stretched his hands toward us again. The surrounding metal shifted in response.

A Pusher. Like me. Though my heart raced a mile a minute, the adrenaline of facing an enemy sent waves of exhilaration through me.

I inhaled and stretched my hands skyward toward our assailant. Magic churned through my body, spinning, circling, and gaining momentum. I closed one eye like I was looking through the scope of a rifle. Zeroing in on my target, I aimed carefully and Pushed him.

His yelp pierced the air as my magic blasted him backward. Glass shattered, but I didn't wait to see if he'd get back up again. Kismet offered a half-smirk, and Oliver raised his eyebrows, clearly impressed.

At long last, we dropped to the bottom of the fire escape, and Kismet ushered us down the alley and around the back of the building. The sounds of traffic grated against my ears—horns blaring, cars whooshing past, and footsteps shuffling. I strained to hear shouts or smell the tingle of magic in the air. But the scents of downtown New York were too strong and confusing for me to hone in on anything magical.

Oliver and I followed Kismet, weaving between

alleys and buildings. The traffic sounds faded until I only heard our quick footfalls and faint music pumping from a nearby apartment. Excitement churned within me like my magic had just gotten warmed up. I glanced over my shoulder, but no one followed us. My disappointment startled me. Shouldn't that be a *good* thing?

Eventually, we emerged into a narrow alley where a lone taxicab was parked. I froze, my skin crawling with suspicion, but Kismet said, "It's okay, he's with me."

She sounds like a government spy, I thought, squashing down my apprehension as we all piled in the backseat of the cab.

The driver glanced at us from underneath a red baseball cap. Kismet slid him a wad of cash and said, "You know where to go."

The driver nodded wordlessly and shifted into reverse to back out of the alley. He snaked down side roads, working his way expertly back onto the main road. The cab bumped over potholes and uneven pavement.

"What's with the cloak and dagger, Agent Harrington?" I asked.

Kismet shushed me, but her eyes crinkled, and her lips twitched.

After twenty minutes, the cab pulled up to an abandoned mall. The parking lot was empty and riddled with cracks, through which weeds burst through freely. A garage-like metal door blocked the entrance to what had once been a department store.

I frowned at Kismet, but she muttered something inaudible to the driver before sliding out of the car. Oliver and I followed suit.

The cab drove off, and Kismet approached the sealed off store entrance. I pressed my lips together, shoving my questions aside, and followed her.

Kismet approached the shiny, silver door and pressed her palm to it. The surface rippled, and a blue glow emanated from her fingertips. I was reminded of when Elena had first led me to the magical realm in Santiago—she'd done something similar with the red door that served as a portal.

Lilith, I miss her.

I squashed the ache down. The metal door cranked and slid open, rising higher and bathing the dark store in a bright light.

Kismet entered, and Oliver and I followed. As soon as we crossed the threshold, the door slid shut, plunging us into darkness.

I blinked, my eyes adjusting and my heart racing. I raised my hands, but I couldn't Push an enemy I couldn't see.

"State your name and personnel number," a deep voice rumbled from the darkness.

"Kismet Harrington," Kismet said, her voice loud. "3427."

Fluorescent lights from the ceiling switched on, and I winced. After blinking several times, I gazed around the store, my mouth falling open.

Instead of mannequins and racks of clothes, we stood in a warehouse-sized bunker. Cots and bunk beds lined the walls, and in the middle of the room stood a crowd of people, all of them wielding weapons. Some were dressed in rags, and others wore business casual attire. I counted twenty individuals, and each one stared at Kismet with recognition in their eyes.

The man in front had short, black hair, brown skin, and a neatly trimmed goatee. He sighed with relief and lowered his athame. He strode toward Kismet, his long legs closing the distance between them in three steps before he embraced her.

"Thank Lilith," the man said. His deep voice told me he was the one who spoke earlier. "When you didn't check in, we feared the worst."

"I couldn't risk it," Kismet said, patting his arm and offering a half-smile. She gestured to me and Oliver. "This is Desi and Oliver. They're interested in joining the cause."

My heart thundered at her words, but I kept my face neutral as I looked at the man with interest.

"Teddy Meeks," the man said to us, grinning widely. "A pleasure." His gaze shifted back to Kismet. "Are you staying?"

Kismet nodded. "My home has been breached. Do you have the space?"

Teddy laughed, a booming sound that filled the room, and gestured wide with his hands. "Of course! Stay as long as you like."

Kismet pulled Teddy's arm, bringing him closer, and whispered, "Have you seen him?"

Teddy's smile vanished. Slowly, he shook his head. "He hasn't returned or sent word yet."

Kismet pressed her lips together and nodded. Her blue eyes flicked to me and Oliver and then back to Teddy.

I rubbed my arms and looked at the crowd behind Teddy, trying to find a common denominator among these enthusiasts for whatever cause Kismet referred to. But they seemed to have nothing in common. Some were old with graying or white hair. Others were as young as Oliver and me. Some looked wealthy, judging by their designer clothes, but others seemed borderline homeless. Were all these people here to stop Matthias? And why weren't they able to sleep in their own homes?

Kismet jerked her head toward the cots and bunk beds, and we followed her across the room past the crowd. Kismet nodded and waved to a few people. I wasn't sure how to respond, so I averted my gaze. But I still felt their curious eyes on me as we passed.

Kismet set her bag down in front of a bunk bed with clean, undisturbed sheets. Oliver claimed a cot near the bunks and sat down, resting his head against the wall.

"So, uh, no privacy?" I asked, raising my eyebrows at Kismet.

"There are other shops you can go to for bathing and other needs," she said, shrugging her shoulders. "It's not perfect, but it's safe."

"Safe from *what*?" I asked.

Kismet fixed me with a hard stare. "Don't be dense, Desi."

My face slackened. "Matthias? Is it really that bad? Bad enough for these people not to be safe in their own homes?"

"Yes, it *is* that bad," Kismet said sharply. "Why do you think I summoned you? We need you, Desi. War is coming."

A lump rose in my throat, and I crossed my arms to hide my shaky hands. "What can *I* do? I've faced Matthias before, and I'm no match for him. Not even close."

Kismet touched my arm. "You won't be alone, Desi. We need all the numbers we can get. Look around." She gestured toward the dispersing crowd; some ventured toward the beds, and others drifted toward the exit that led to the rest of the shops within the mall. Some sat in camp chairs and chatted animatedly together, while others sat quietly to read or rest.

"See her?" Kismet said, pointing to a girl about my age with bright purple hair and piercings all over her face. "Her parents work for Matthias. She dropped out of school and ran away, looking for refuge. If we hadn't taken her in, she probably would've followed in her parents' footsteps.

"And him." Kismet gestured to a frail old man resting in a cot, his thin wispy hair sticking up in different directions. "He used to work for the Council and was laid off when he found damning evidence of those on Matthias's payroll."

She pointed to a middle-aged man and woman, their heads hunched over as they whispered together. "Those two were criminals convicted of executing Matthias's top informants." Then, she gestured to a woman and two men dressed in suits. "And those three still work for the Council now, feeding us information whenever they can."

"And they're all here to bring down Matthias?"

Oliver asked breathlessly. His eyes were wide and awestruck as he gazed around the room. The excitement in his face made me feel strangely empty. I wasn't fully on board with this just yet, but it was clear he was ready to dive back into soldier mode.

Kismet nodded. "When you were a kid, Desi, only a few people believed in the threat of Matthias, and they were deemed conspiracy theorists. Like your parents. But now, people's eyes are opening. Which only means Matthias is about to make his move. He's lingered in the shadows for so long that when he starts to make himself known, we should all be paying attention."

"Desi?" a voice asked.

I looked up, frowning, and found two guys about my age approaching with wide grins on their faces. They seemed vaguely familiar.

"Merciful Lilith," I breathed, my heart jumping in my throat as I rose to my feet. "Cameron? José?"

My old friends beamed at me. Their hair was buzzed almost to their scalps, shorter than even Oliver's hair. I hadn't recognized them without their grungy, long hair and baggy clothes. We used to hang out and avoid our responsibilities and drink—well, *they* would drink. I despised alcohol. But back then, we'd been thick as thieves. It felt like ages ago.

Cameron swept me in his arms and lifted me off my

feet. I yelped, clutching his shoulders for support as he spun me in a circle. When he set me down, José grabbed me and pressed a wet kiss against my lips.

I froze, stunned, my eyes wide. I sensed Oliver rising to his feet behind me, but I didn't dare look at him. Hot jealousy rippled through our blood oath, and my stomach clenched.

"Uh, I—I can't believe you two are *here!*" I said, my face on fire as I rubbed the back of my neck and took a step away from José. "Where's Mia?" I looked behind them, searching for our dark-haired friend who always drank too much back in the day.

Their smiles vanished, and they exchanged a solemn look. "She's, uh, in rehab," Cameron said, rubbing his nose. "Last we heard, she's not doing too well."

My stomach dropped, and a sour taste filled my mouth. Mia—who'd never judged me for my past, who'd laughed with me and supported me with ballet and my decision to renounce all things magical, who'd made a mix tape of music for my dance routines—was in rehab?

"Lilith," I whispered. "I—I'm so sorry I wasn't here."

José shook his head. "Don't worry about it, *bella*. Kiz explained everything to us."

I raised an eyebrow at Kismet, who shrugged. "They volunteered to join our cause. All on their own."

I spread my arms, gaping weakly at them. "But—*why*?

Last I saw, you two were hellbent on drinking and partying 'til you died."

José nudged my shoulder. "Yeah . . . 'til you left."

I dropped my hands. "What?"

"When you disappeared, we thought Levarret had taken you," Cameron said, his blue eyes anxious. "We thought it was our fault. For encouraging you to come to Miami with us. We thought you'd been abducted on the road."

"*My* fault," José said, his dark brows pulling together. "I was the one who pressured you."

"We figured we should get our act together and do something," Cameron said. "You know, in honor of you. Then when Kismet's curse broke, she told us about these underground rebels, and we jumped on board."

A slow smile spread across my face. "This is *amazing*, guys. I'm so proud of you."

Oliver cleared his throat loudly behind me. I glanced over my shoulder at him. His bulky arms were crossed, his eyes burning with anger as he stared at José. The tightness of his jaw sent coils of discomfort racing through me.

"This is Oliver Gerrick," I said quickly, pointing to him. "He's, uh, a soldier from the Spanish-American War. We met in Santiago."

José and Cameron's mouths fell open in wide, goofy

grins. "Whoa!" José whooped. He and Cameron slapped hands, wearing equally amazed expressions.

"Dude, that's sick," Cameron said, stepping forward to shake Oliver's hand. "An honor to meet you, man."

Oliver frowned and shook his hand. "Likewise . . . I think."

I snorted and covered my mouth.

"Oh, Desi, I almost forgot." José stepped toward me, and I stiffened, my limbs locking up. *What do I do, what do I do, what do I do? Does he still think I'm his girlfriend?* I crossed my arms and leaned slightly away from him. He withdrew a pack of envelopes from his back pocket. "Kiz mentioned you'd be back soon, so I grabbed these from my abuela. They—well, she said you'd know who they're from."

I took the stack of letters from him, my hands trembling as I looked at my name written elegantly on each one. The handwriting was so familiar. *Alba.*

Heat flooded my throat. My eyes burned and blurred, distorting the letters from view. I swallowed and nodded, pressing my lips together. Slowly, I folded the letters and pocketed them, willing myself not to cry in front of everyone.

"Thank you," I said, my voice breaking. "Thanks so much."

Alba, Ramón, Guillermo, Elena, Sofia. Would the letters

tell me of their fate? Of Alba's child? My fingers itched to pull the letters out to read, but I didn't want to cry in front of all these witnesses. Perhaps I could find a moment alone in one of those adjacent, empty shops.

Before I could ask Kismet where I should go for some privacy, the air surged with magic. The surrounding rebels jumped to their feet and drew their weapons.

"What's going on?" I asked Kismet.

"Visitor," she said quietly, drawing closer to me. "Stay silent."

The lights shut off, and darkness surrounded us once more.

The metal door slid open, bathing us in a faint white light. A tall figure stepped forward. The door slammed shut, and Teddy said loudly, "State your name and personnel number."

"Bayani Matapang," a familiar voice said. "3428."

CHAPTER 8

MY LIMBS SEIZED UP. MY BLOOD CHILLED, AND MY mouth fell open. Tight, shallow breaths poured from my mouth. *Merciful Lilith. He survived!*

The lights flicked on, and Bay squinted, his face splitting into a wide grin.

I took a step, prepared to ambush him with questions, but then froze. Something was . . . different about him.

He stepped forward, clapping Teddy on the back and exchanging comments with some other rebels. My eyes narrowed as I tried to pinpoint what seemed off about him. He wore street clothes, which was unusual—dark jeans and a tight T-shirt. His hair was a bit longer than I remembered, falling forward into his face.

I gasped and staggered backward. Lines of gray

mixed with his usual black hair. Wrinkles formed around his eyes when he smiled at his comrades. Though he was still fit and bulky like I remembered, he was . . . *older.* Much older.

Sickness swirled in my stomach. *How long has he been here?*

"Desi, you all right?" José asked, nudging me again.

My mouth opened and closed numbly. I couldn't speak. It was all too much. My brain was on overload processing all these bombshells: Levarret's true identity, the bond between me and Kismet, this hidden underground rebel base, José and Cameron, letters from Alba, and now *this?*

I sensed Oliver behind me, and I stumbled backward into his chest. His hands slid over my arms. The warmth of his skin against mine grounded me. I inhaled through my nose and exhaled through my mouth, counting my breaths. One . . . Two . . . Three . . .

Bay strode over to us, and I swallowed hard. Then I realized he wasn't looking at me—he was looking at Kismet.

She surged forward, and they embraced, their arms pressed tightly against one another. Bay's brows pulled together, his eyes closing and his expression full of relief.

"Thank Lilith," Kismet said quietly when they drew apart. She pressed a hand to his cheek. "Is it done?"

Bay's eyes tightened, and he nodded. "It's done."

"Bay?" I blurted. I finally found my voice, and his name spilled abruptly from my mouth. I couldn't control it. My brain wasn't working right anymore. "You're—you're *here*?"

His gaze shifted to me. Excitement lit up his face, but he didn't seem surprised. Of course he wouldn't. Kismet would've told him I was coming.

"Desi," he said, his voice more gravelly than I remembered; I was so used to him saying my name with that smooth, charming timbre, but the years had changed him. He stepped forward and hugged me tightly against his chest. He smelled of the familiar sandalwood, but there was something else mingled with it—something that smelled a lot like Kismet.

He released me and looked me up and down, still grinning. "How are you?"

"Fine," I said, dazed. "How are *you*? What year did you come back?"

"1982—a year before Kiz," he said, nodding toward her. *Kiz.* Just what *was* their relationship? "We were both sentenced as Familiars."

Bay? A Familiar?

Then, I remembered what Kismet had said about the Familiar's curse pulling people through time. That was why. Whoever his ward was, that person had pulled him to 1982 just like I'd pulled Kismet.

I shook my head, still numb with shock. "I—I'm so sorry."

Bay laughed. "Don't be. Those years changed me for the better."

Those years. As if it hadn't been days since we'd seen each other. Since I'd watched Matthias stab him in the stomach. Since he'd turned me over to the Kulam coven.

His face sobered as if he could read my thoughts. He rubbed the back of his neck. "I forgot." His eyes closed briefly. "It's still fresh for you, isn't it? My betrayal."

I said nothing. My tongue felt heavy in my mouth.

"Desi, I'm so sorry," he said. "For everything. I was young and vulnerable, and I trusted Isko. He betrayed me just like I betrayed you. If I could go back and undo it, I would."

I nodded without really thinking.

"These past years have changed me, though," he went on, stepping closer to me. "I've been tortured by my past mistakes, haunted by the people I've hurt, and—"

"I—I can't do this," I said loudly, raising a shaking hand to stop him. Desperation poured through me as I looked at Kismet. "Where can I go to be alone? I just—I need a minute. To process everything."

Her blue eyes were guarded. Wary. Had she known what happened between me and Bay? Slowly, she tilted her head back. "The nail salon to the left. It's empty and has lots of places to sit."

I nodded and strode away, trying not to break into a sprint despite how urgently I needed to escape. My heart thumped heavily in my chest, each beat dragging me down to the depths of my suffocating emotions.

I tore away from the crowd and the shop that felt so stifling though it was the size of a football field. I sucked in deep breaths so hard it hurt, scraping my throat and lungs with each inhale and exhale. But in spite of my breathing, my brain kept begging for oxygen like I still wasn't getting enough. Like something was suffocating me.

And all the while, my mind kept racing with tormented thoughts: *Levarret. Matthias. Bay is alive and has been for almost two decades.*

And José, here and now, thinking he can just kiss me out of the blue without even asking?

And Oliver! I just told him about Bay convincing me to go dark. What will Oliver do, being around Bay and José? Lilith, Oliver's traveled one hundred years into the future—confused, disoriented, and completely isolated from everyone he knows —and it's my *fault.*

Oliver was here because of me, because he loved me and had pledged to be with me, but I couldn't even commit to him right now. I couldn't even sort through any of the thoughts in my head right now.

I should have cut him loose when he left for Manila. I should've ended things earlier so he could've been happy with Gwen instead of following me to this wretched future where his asshole father was taking over the world.

On and on my thoughts continued. And whenever I returned to my obsession over Kismet, or Bay, or José, or Cameron, or Matthias, it all circled back to Oliver. Whatever Matthias had done to me, he'd done worse things to Oliver. Whatever conflicted feelings I had for Bay and José, Oliver must have it so much worse. And no matter how overwhelmed or stressed I felt being in this time, he had every reason to feel even more so.

So why was I so wrapped up in my own thoughts, my own selfish doubts and uncertainties, my own anxiety and crippling fear? Why couldn't I shove all that aside for his sake?

My feet stumbled forward of their own accord, taking me out of the old department store to the wide walkways between shops. It was strange to hear nothing but silence instead of the usual chatter and buzz of shoppers floating around the mall. Here it seemed empty. Almost haunted.

Several shops had barred gates blocking the entrances, but I easily found the nail salon Kismet had mentioned. Most of the furniture had been emptied but there were a few lingering, dusty benches. The air still smelled of chemicals, and I wrinkled my nose before carefully sitting on a bench. I heaved a sigh, my nostrils tickling from the scents in the air.

Something bulky pushed against my back pocket. I shifted and remembered Alba's letters.

My heart stilled. How I longed to go back—to Santiago, to the coven, and to my life there.

With my throat tight, I pulled the letters out, my hands shaking. The papers were faded and dusty. They felt as fragile as if they might vanish into dust in my hands. Gingerly, I opened the first one.

Dear Desi,

By now I'm sure you've returned to your time. I know the transition must be jarring for you, but take heart. I see peace for you in your future.

My son is now six months old. We have named him Juan. He is a delight for our little family. With El Diablo gone, we feel confident in raising our son in a safe environment.

Sofia is well. She sends her regards and begs you not to

blame yourself for what happened to her. El Diablo would've come for her regardless of your involvement. In fact, your actions in Manila saved her life. According to Elena, El Diablo was so focused on you and casting the spell that he paid Sofia no attention, and she was able to escape.

Elena misses you deeply. She works too hard trying to distract herself. She won't talk to any of us but Guillermo. He listens to her and provides the quiet strength she needs to lean on at this time.

Thoughts and prayers for you and Oliver. We think of you often and wish you well.

Alba

A hard lump formed in my throat. I pressed my lips together, fighting back tears. I feverishly dug through the remaining letters, hoping to absorb every bit of Santiago and the coven like I could somehow transport myself back there.

The next few letters summed up their life in Santiago. I read about the birth of their second child, Manuel. My heart clenched seeing that name written out, reminding me of the friend I'd lost. Then, Alba wrote of Elena and Guillermo's wedding. My face split into a grin. *Way to go, Elena!*

My eyes scanned the current events as Alba relayed them: *the construction of a railroad in Santiago . . . the U.S. occupied Cuba again . . . a dangerous Second Tier demon causing skirmishes within the city . . . Cuban soldiers drafted for the Great War, which ended before they could fight.* My head spun as I struggled to remember what little I knew about Cuban history. When did Castro come to power? What about the Cold War? Were Alba and Ramón alive for that?

My heart jolted when I pulled out her next letter, dated 1919. My pulse roared in my ears as I read:

My heart is heavy as I write to you. Last week, a battle broke out between us and the demons. We knew it was inevitable; the tension only continued to mount even after we banished the Second Tier demon and supposedly neutralized the threat. But his followers retaliated.

Today, we suffered a great loss to our coven. A third of our numbers were killed—including Elena and Guillermo.

They died bravely, securing safety for the rest of us. They went down fighting, which is what I know they would've wanted. They were both strong warriors. May God be with them in the afterlife. Though they had no children themselves, I will ensure my children remember them always.

My eyes closed, my hand shaking so fiercely that the letter fell to the floor. Tears streamed down my face. Though deep down I knew Alba, Ramón, and everyone else had died years ago, knowing Elena and Guillermo had barely had twenty years together shredded my heart to bits.

I should've been there fighting with them. I should've been there.

My face crumpled. I dropped my head into my hands, sobbing freely. My chest ached, and my heart throbbed in bitter agony. Elena and Guillermo had had no children—no one to carry on their legacy or their name.

I raised my hands to my head and gripped a fistful of my curls, gritting my teeth. I groaned, and more choked sobs poured from my mouth. A pitiful wail escaped me, echoing in the large and empty shop. My chest quivered as I cried and cried.

When my throat was raw and my eyes heavy from the tears I'd shed, I heaved a shuddering sigh and bent to reach the letters I'd dropped.

I froze. Oliver stood at the entrance to the salon, his shoulders tight and his eyes tormented.

How long had he been there? Had he just stood there, watching me cry my eyes out?

Then I remembered our blood oath. He must have sensed my pain and anguish.

I hastily wiped my face and nose and shifted, trying to rise.

Oliver raised a hand and stepped toward me. "Don't. Please." In a few long strides, he was by my side, sitting next to me on the bench. He tucked a few loose curls behind my ear. I knew my hair must've been a disheveled mess, but all I could think about was Elena.

My lips trembled. My mouth stretched wide, preparing for more sobs. I covered my face and shook my head.

"It's all right," Oliver said quietly, placing his hand on my knee. "You don't have to speak."

I swallowed hard, my throat burning. Before I could burst into tears again, I snatched the letter from Alba and thrust it into his hands. His brow furrowed as he read, and I closed my eyes. I couldn't watch his reaction.

I felt him stiffen next to me. "No," he whispered. His arms tightened. "No!" His voice cracked.

More tears leaked out of my eyes. Silence fell between us. I wept quietly, and Oliver lifted a hand to his own face. I couldn't bear to look at him or see his tears. It was already too much for me.

The sorrow between us was almost palpable, like a living thing stretching and growing. It clung to us, smothering us. Claiming us for its own.

Despair clawed at my throat, threatening to drown me in tears again. I swallowed, and my chest burned.

At long last, Oliver said thickly, "They died alongside each other—the ones they loved. It's how I'd want to go."

I shook my head, my nostrils flaring. "They shouldn't have had to die at all. Elena wasn't even forty years old.

We should've *been* there, Oliver. If I hadn't—if I'd just *grown up* and turned down Bay's offer, I never would've been trapped by the Kulam coven, and Matthias never would've—"

"Desi, stop," Oliver said, turning to face me. His eyes were moist, but his cheeks were dry. Determination hardened his expression. "You don't know that we could've changed anything. If you'd refused Bay, that coven would've just come for you anyway. Isko had planned this from the beginning. He wasn't going to let you get away." He gently touched my shoulder. "And even if we *had* stayed in 1899, what if we hadn't been in Santiago when this happened? What if you'd been in America with me? This seems like it was a brutal battle. You can't save everyone, Desi."

"I am so *sick* of people telling me that the deaths of those I love are meant to be. That it can't be altered or changed." I threw my hands in the air. "We can fracking *time travel,* but we can't change anything important! What's the *point* of all this?"

I let my hands fall on my lap. My body sagged, hunching over. I had no energy left. Nothing.

"The point is to stop him from killing other people we love," Oliver said.

Slowly, I turned to look at him. "You're on board with this? This cause Kismet is fighting for?"

Oliver straightened. "Of course. Aren't you?"

I sighed. Exhaustion pulled at every inch of me. I just wanted to go to sleep and not wake up, not have to face this reality. "I don't know. Every time I get involved in fighting him, I just royally screw up. I don't trust myself or my magic anymore. My instincts led me astray last time." I dropped my gaze to my hands as I wrung them together.

Oliver covered my hands with his. "Your instincts are good, Desi. You told me you tried backing out at the last second with Bay. You realized it was a mistake."

"A lot of good that did."

Oliver shook his head. "But how can you say those things? You're a good Huntress—good enough that Kismet *sent* for you. She needs you, Desi."

Hearing Kismet's name stirred something inside me, some nagging feeling in my stomach that wriggled through my despair. My brows pulled together. "I'm not so sure that's why she sent for me—for us. She's hiding something." I shook my head, withdrawing my hands from his and trying to ignore the cold absence of his warmth. "I can't commit to this. Not yet. But I'll stick around as long as they'll let me. Because I need to help Kismet even if she won't tell me everything."

Oliver exhaled long and slow. "Desi, how can you even debate this? It's *Matthias* we're talking about.

We've been fighting him for a year, but now we aren't alone. There's a small army here, a band of rebels fighting for a cause that we were vastly outnumbered for during my time. How can you even consider refusing?"

I looked at him and the incredulity and firmness in his eyes. He had no qualms. No doubts. How I envied that. "It's so easy for you," I said quietly. "Once a soldier, always a soldier. But some of us . . . don't have much fight left in us."

"That's not true at all," Oliver said, leaning closer to me. "I watched you fight that gargoyle and the demon who chased us. I *saw* the thrill in your eyes. I felt the same thing. Don't try to deny it, Desi. You *love* being a Huntress."

"That's different! A single fight with a demon like that—it isn't the same. That was self-preservation and nothing more. I had no choice—it was fight or flee. But you're asking me to commit to a full-blown *war*, to risk myself and those I love again and again. This isn't just a one-time gig."

Oliver's brow furrowed, his lips pressing together as he no doubt puzzled over my modern jargon. "Well." He paused and took a breath. "If you decide not to stay, then I won't either."

My heart stilled, and I looked up at him. "Don't say

that. You believe in this. You should stay no matter what I decide."

Oliver smiled, his eyes soft. "I'll stay with *you*." His eyes darted down to my hands clasped in my lap. Heat rose in my cheeks, and I wondered if we thought the same thing: that our hands were no longer touching.

It was such a silly thing to be thinking about right now considering the heavy reality we were facing.

But I couldn't keep my heart from racing or my stomach from twisting as our gazes locked again. He leaned in.

I sucked in a breath, and he stopped mere inches from my face. His sweet breath mingled with mine, and his grass and gunpowder scent made me dizzy. I closed my eyes against the heat and yearning inside me.

"I'm sorry," I whispered.

Oliver withdrew slightly, his eyes flashing with hurt before smoothing into sympathy. "Don't be. You're going through quite an ordeal right now. I should leave you be." He stood.

Panic bubbled up my throat, forcing me to blurt out, "No!"

He froze and raised a questioning eyebrow.

My mouth opened and closed. I dropped my gaze to the dusty floor. "I, uh, don't want to be alone right now. I'd like you to stay. If you want."

His eyes softened, and he nodded. Bending over to sit again, he stopped, his eyes fixed on something on the floor. "What's this?"

I glanced down. "Alba's letters."

"Did you read all of them?"

"No. I stopped when I read about—" My words choked, cutting me off. I didn't go on. Oliver knew what I meant.

"Desi, look at this." His words were barely more than a breath, his eyes wide and transfixed. Slowly, he reached for a frail piece of paper with some kind of diagram on it. When he pulled it toward him, I leaned closer, squinting at it.

"It's a pentagram." I recognized the star shape and tried not to think of all the horrifying things that had happened—or almost happened—thanks to the pentagram. The letter was dated 1940. Together, Oliver and I silently read Alba's words.

There's talk of another great war in Europe, though Ramón and I aren't long for this world. I doubt we'll see the end.

I've scryed often for you, Desi, in my efforts to help you glean all the information you need in your time. And it seems God has granted me one last vision for you. I can't See as well as I could years ago, but hopefully it'll still be of some use to you.

The spell you seek is in the Grimoire. I've glimpsed it, but not in my language—in yours. My English isn't so good, but I could ascertain it was a spell to reanimate or reawaken the dead. It wasn't a typical necromancy spell—this one can serve more than one purpose. For instance, it can be used to banish someone who can't be killed.

This spell will help you defeat El Diablo.

CHAPTER 9

Oliver and I immediately returned to the rebels' main area to share Alba's information with Kismet. When we arrived, we found the crowd of rebels surrounding a tall, glowing figure. For one wild moment, I thought it was Gwen Peters, the Nephilim Oliver had been engaged to.

Oliver and I exchanged wary glances before we approached the group. Kismet noticed us first. She broke apart from the crowd and clasped my hands in hers, her eyes searching mine.

"Are you all right?" she whispered.

I offered a tight-lipped smile that I knew she could see right through. "I will be." My nervous gaze shifted around the room, but Kismet replied to my unspoken question.

"Bay left on an assignment. He's not here." She watched me, her eyes sharpening, and I looked away from her scrutiny.

Oliver cleared his throat. "We found something you need to see." He handed her Alba's letter.

Kismet scanned it, frowning, and then looked up at us. "I don't understand. Why would we need a spell to banish someone who can't be killed? Matthias is Third Tier, but he's not immortal. Demons of the Third Tier have been defeated before, and it'll happen again when we stop him."

She handed the letter back to Oliver. My eyebrows lowered. "So you're just going to dismiss Alba's information? Just like that?"

Kismet sighed. "I'm not dismissing it, Desi. I'm just saying we don't need it right now. Perhaps we will later. I don't doubt Alba's abilities, but it's possible she's Seen something we can't use just yet. And for now, our priorities are elsewhere."

Irritation prickled through me. I opened my mouth to object, but Oliver interrupted.

"What's going on over there?" he asked, pointing to the crowd of rebels.

"Someone from our team is reporting back intel," Kismet said, glancing over her shoulder at her fellow rebels.

"Nephilim?" Oliver asked.

Kismet shook her head. "Fae."

I stiffened, my blood chilling. I'd never seen a faerie before—well, at least not a pure-bred faerie. Bay was half-fae, but he lived among demons. Fae were myths even in the magical world. They kept to themselves, balancing light and dark magic together in ways demons and light casters never could.

Momentarily distracted from my anger at Kismet, I shifted my weight from one foot to the other, leaning over to catch a glimpse of the faerie. "Why? How? Aren't they in hiding?"

Kismet nodded. "Most are. But this one worked directly with Matthias and defected when she realized what his plan was."

My eyes shifted to Kismet and widened. "Fae . . . working with *Matthias*? I thought they didn't like to get involved."

Kismet frowned and shrugged one shoulder. "So did we. Our contact says she doesn't know why her family allied with him, but she claims the ties go way back."

My legs felt restless, and I rubbed my forearms. "I— can we meet her?" Perhaps she could provide answers about Matthias and what year he arrived here.

Kismet raised an eyebrow at me. "That depends. Have you made a decision about joining us yet? I can't exactly show the face of our deep undercover operative to just anyone."

I fixed her with a flat stare. "Kiz, this is *me* we're talking about. You really think I'll go rat her out to Matthias?"

For the briefest moment, Kismet's eyes flicked to Oliver, and my heart dropped to my stomach like a stone. I felt Oliver straighten next to me ever so slightly. He noticed it too.

"You don't trust him," I said tightly, my voice barely above a whisper.

"Can you blame me? He's Matthias's son! He performed a blood bond with him. He worked closely with him on the Council, which, if you haven't noticed, is completely corrupt now."

"And you think that's *his* fault?" I snapped. "Besides, *you* made a blood bond with him too!"

Kismet's eyes closed, and she rubbed her forehead. "Desi, I don't have time for this. I'm in charge of a delicate operation that could be dismantled from the slightest error in judgment. I'm not taking any chances. So if you'll swear in with us, then you're welcome to everything we have. But for now, you have to abide by our rules."

"Kiz, after *everything*—"

Kismet raised a hand to silence me, her gaze turning

to the crowd as Teddy lifted a hand to wave her over. "I'm sorry, Desi. We'll have to talk about this later."

Before I could object, she turned away and joined the crowd, who still obscured the mysterious faerie from view.

I raised my hands and dropped them on my thighs, my teeth clenching and rage boiling through me. After everything Oliver had done for us, how could she not trust him? *I* was the one who almost went dark, but he was solid as a rock! How could she do this?

"Desi, it's fine," Oliver said quietly.

"No it's not," I growled.

"She barely knows me. Even if I weren't his son, she still has every reason to doubt me."

I looked at him. His eyes were fixed pensively on the crowd of rebels, his brow furrowed and his gaze distant. "What is it?" I asked.

"There's something strange about the fae getting involved. You're right, it's not like them." He squinted as if trying to get a better look at the faerie.

"You want to talk to her," I guessed.

He nodded.

"Oliver, you should swear yourself in," I said. "I know you believe in this cause."

His gaze finally tore away from the crowd and fixed on me. "I won't do it without you."

"I wouldn't hold it against you, Oliver. You've already jumped through time for me. The least I can do is let you fight for what you believe in. This is *your* time now too."

"No, Desi, you don't understand." Oliver faced me and took my hands in his. "When Kismet says we need to 'swear in,' she means with a blood contract."

I grew very still. *Blood contract.* Like the one I'd signed with the Kulam coven.

This had to have been Bay's idea. The idea made me feel nauseous.

"And since we share a blood oath," Oliver continued, his gaze dropping to our clasped hands, "I'm worried that if I sign the contract, it'll somehow taint our connection. I don't want this pulling you in too if you aren't ready to commit to this."

"But our blood oath wasn't affected when I signed the blood contract with the Kulam coven." In Manila, Bay had required Guillermo, Elena, and me to sign a blood contract before working with him.

Oliver's eyes hardened for a brief moment before softening again. "Every blood contract is different and requires different things. I don't want to take any chances."

My mouth felt dry. I didn't know what to say.

Oliver's eyes met mine again, questioning me. He wanted an answer.

I opened and closed my mouth. "I—I don't know yet." Swearing to secrecy was one thing, but a blood contract was *permanent*. I knew firsthand that you were bound by the orders within the contract. Once I made that decision, I couldn't come back from it.

It seemed a lot like dark magic to me. And it didn't sit well with me at all.

Oliver nodded. "That's okay. It's a big decision. I won't rush you."

My heart fluttered, and my skin melted under his gaze. I sensed a double meaning in his words. Was he talking about the rebels or something else? Something just between the two of us? My face felt hot, and my stomach squirmed and wriggled.

Desperate for a distraction, I busied myself with arranging my small bag of clothes near my bunk bed, though I felt Oliver's gaze on me the whole time.

Over the next few days, Oliver and I were introduced to several other rebels and were peppered with questions about how we knew Kismet and why we joined the cause. Oliver and I kept fumbling with our responses, unwilling to share how we had time traveled. I also didn't want to commit to the cause just yet, so I just smiled and lied through my teeth about what a grand purpose we had, fighting this battle against Matthias.

Kismet wasn't around much. Though she was friendly when she saw us, she was still more distant than I remembered. Perhaps she'd changed more than I'd thought. Oftentimes, she gathered other rebels like Teddy to discuss something in private, always careful to do this away from me.

Away from Oliver.

Their secrecy made me burn with anger, and I tried to ignore the discomfort I felt with the whole situation. This hopeless cause of battling Matthias with such few numbers, the idea of swearing in with a blood contract, and the fact that Oliver was being judged for his lineage.

Kismet was such a hypocrite. She'd served Matthias for how many years?

I stayed by Oliver through everything. We trained, cooked meals, cleaned weapons, and went on supply runs with some of the other more trusted rebels.

After returning from a run to a nearby drugstore, I dropped our grocery bags, panting from the effort of speed-walking back to the abandoned mall. Another rebel smiled and thanked me before taking the groceries to shelve them against the wall with the other supplies.

Wiping sweat from my brow, I glanced at Oliver. He hadn't even broken a sweat. Of course.

"So, that was . . . fun," I said, gulping down a bottle of water. "What exciting lives these rebels live."

Oliver grimaced. "You wouldn't want an exciting life in this line of work. Exciting means war." Something hardened in his expression, sending chills up and down my body.

I sighed. Looking over his shoulder, I found José waving eagerly at me.

My heart sank. "Oh, no," I muttered.

Encouraged by our eye contact, José bounded forward and slapped Oliver on the shoulder. Oliver stiffened, his spine straightening so he towered over José. I'd been careful to avoid my ex-boyfriend as much as possible since we'd arrived, not wanting a confrontation between him and Oliver.

Or perhaps between him and *me*. Maybe I was just a coward.

"There you are, *bella*," José said with a wide grin. It was still so weird seeing that mischievous expression on someone with a military-style buzz cut. So unlike the José I'd known before.

I bristled at his nickname for me. It didn't feel appropriate now that we weren't together. But did *he* know that?

"Did you enjoy those letters I gave you?" José asked.

Oliver scowled and fixed a hard gaze on José. I easily read his accusation: *Those were private.*

I cleared my throat "Uh, yes. Thank you. Did—did *you* read them?"

José raised both hands. "Nah. Abuela made me promise not to."

"How is your abuela?" I'd never met her before, but she sounded like an incredible woman. Especially if she knew how important those letters were.

And because she most likely had *known* Alba in person.

José shrugged one shoulder. "She's all right. The crime has spread to her city, and it's taking a toll on her. She misses when things were easy. Safe."

I chuckled. "Don't we all."

José wiggled his eyebrows. "Reminds me of the old Desi, eh?" He leaned forward and rubbed a thumb along my cheek. His fingers were warm, but they felt so *wrong* touching me like that. I recoiled and backed up a step.

In a flash, Oliver stepped between us, staring down at José with fire in his eyes.

"Oliver," I warned.

"Don't touch her," Oliver growled. He towered over José by at least a foot. Anger blazed in his face, and his hands shook. I felt the crackling of his magic pulse through our blood oath.

"Oliver!" I said, grabbing his shoulder, but he wouldn't budge.

José's eyes widened, but the amusement never left his face. He raised both hands again, stepping backward. "Easy, man. It didn't mean anything. Desi and I go way back."

"*Oliver,*" I said through clenched teeth. "Step aside, or I will *Push* you away." I shoved his arm, and this time, he moved a few feet away. But he was still close enough to intervene if José stepped out of line.

José blew air through his lips and widened his eyes at me as if to say, *Can you believe that guy?*

I sighed, closing my eyes for a moment. "Listen, José. You and I aren't together anymore. Things changed when I left. I'm not interested in just picking up where we left off. I'm sorry. I—I should've been up front with you about it as soon as I first saw you."

José's expression smoothed into something unreadable.

I shifted my weight from one foot to the other. "So can you stop touching me like that? Please?"

José's glanced from me to Oliver. "You two—?"

"That's none of your business," I said stiffly.

José raised his eyebrows and pressed his lips

together, shoving his hands in his pockets. "Okay. I get it. I hear you loud and clear, Desi." He cocked his head at Oliver, his eyes curious. "Just, uh, keep your bodyguard under wraps, eh?" He chuckled to himself, shaking his head as he strode away, still swaggering in that infuriating way he'd always done before.

I exhaled, relieved José had taken that so well. I looked at Oliver. His fingers were clenched into tight fists. His hard gaze was still fixed on José across the room.

I touched his arm, and he broke his vigilant stare and turned to me. Anger still blazed in his eyes.

"I need you to let me fight my own battles," I said quietly.

Oliver's brow furrowed. "What do you mean?"

I sighed, rubbing my temples. "Am I weak, Oliver?"

Oliver's mouth fell open. "What? I—*no.*"

"Do you think I'm strong enough to handle myself if I'm attacked?"

Understanding flashed in his eyes, followed by resignation. "Yes."

I stepped closer to him. "Then I need you to trust me. As much as I love watching you play the hero . . ." I trailed off, lifting my hand to his face. He tilted his head to the side, leaning his cheek against my fingers. His face felt warm. Familiar. Safe.

A hot lump lodged itself in my throat, and I forgot what I'd been trying to say. With my hand on his face, all I felt was heat and longing. I wanted to touch more of him—his hair, his arms, his chest, his lips.

He lied to you. He was engaged to another girl when you almost slept with him in Santiago.

The nagging voice spread through me like a poison.

I swallowed, dropping my hand. Though I knew the voice wasn't being fair—I'd played my part in that disaster too by pushing Oliver away—I couldn't rid myself of it. All I thought of was how he'd lied to me. He'd planned on marrying someone else and hadn't told me when we'd been together.

My face flushed. I rubbed the back of my neck, avoiding his gaze, though I felt it burning through me. My eyes shifted instead to the dispersing crowd. A ripple of urgent murmurs swept through the rebels. They each pulled something small out of their pockets and whispered to each other, their faces taut with concern.

"What's going on?" I asked.

Oliver shook his head, frowning.

Then, Kismet hurried up to us, breathless and eyes wide. "I need your help."

I straightened. "Of course. What is it?"

"A Nephilim sent a distress call. He's in grave danger. Can you and Oliver go to him?"

My mouth opened and closed, and I shared a bewildered glance with Oliver. "Uh, yes," I said. "But what about you?"

"I have to stay with Persephone—the faerie," Kismet said. "She'll be arriving soon and needs round-the-clock protection. She defected from Matthias, so she's a target. If he comes here for her—"

"Right. I understand." I gritted my teeth and looked at Oliver again. He nodded.

"Thank you." Kismet glanced over her shoulder and waved at José.

My stomach dropped as he jogged back over to us, a wicked grin on his face. *Great.*

"Take these two to Dimitri's location," Kismet said to him. "Use the coin to pinpoint the location."

Oh, right, I thought. *He's a Teleporter.*

José nodded, looking perfectly at ease despite the situation. "Not a problem. You two ready?"

I raised an eyebrow. "Are you sure you can handle Porting *two* people?" When I last saw him, he had no interest in developing his powers—just like me.

"Porting?" José snorted. "You're in the twenty-first century now, Desi. It's 'Jumping.' And don't sweat it. I've trained a lot over the past year." He stretched both arms out to us. "Your carriage awaits, *bella*."

"Para de llamarme así," I muttered in Spanish. *Stop calling me that.*

José's eyes widened, and a surprised laugh burst from his mouth. He grinned and wiggled his eyebrows, as if to say, *You learned Spanish?*

I rolled my eyes but gripped his arm in mine. Oliver did the same. With a small *pop*, we vanished.

CHAPTER 10

MY STOMACH CHURNED, AND MY SURROUNDINGS SPUN sickeningly until finally we came to a stop in front of an alley—the kind where muggings and murders happen at the beginning of crime shows. A filthy dumpster sat at the end of the alley, and a figure moaned on the grimy ground. A faint white light flickered from his face like he was a light bulb that was about to go out.

"Lilith," I whispered. My heart stopped, my gaze falling to the open wound in his gut that poured blood on the ground.

I raced toward him, lifting my hands. But I didn't know what to do. I wasn't a healer. The Nephilim's jet-black hair was slick with sweat, and his eyes rolled back. Beads of sweat formed along his forehead, and all the color had drained from his face.

I was no doctor, but I knew he wouldn't last long.

In an instant, Oliver and José were by my side. For the first time since I'd known him, José's expression was grim. Solemn. His eyes were wide, but there was no fear, shock, or disgust in his face.

He'd been in situations like this before.

"Give me a cloth or something," I muttered, watching more blood ooze from the wound.

José shrugged out of his jacket and handed it to me. I rolled it into a ball and held it against the wound, pressing down firmly.

"Here," Oliver said, pressing his hands against mine. He looked up at José. "Can you Port him back?"

But José was staring at something behind us, his face pale. I followed his gaze, and my stomach dropped.

It was the gargoyle who had chased us earlier—Damien. He stood at the mouth of the alley, his broad, gray wings spread behind him and a bloody dagger clutched in his clawed fingers.

"I warned you," he growled, his dark eyes flashing.

Then he pounced. Wings flapping, he soared several feet in the air and flew toward us, barreling into José before any of us could react. José tumbled, grunting from the impact. Damien wrestled him to the ground, his sharp teeth inches from José's throat.

"Go," I told Oliver. "Help him! I've got it here."

"Hang on." Oliver moved my hands out of the way and pressed his palms against the man's wound. A blue glow surrounded the injury, and a layer of thick ice formed over the gash. "It won't hold for long, but it should help."

"I'll stay with him," I said, nodding toward José.

Oliver rose and bounded forward. He shot a jet of flames against Damien, who shrieked and jerked backward off of José. My energy seeped out of me, channeling itself into Oliver. An advantage of our blood oath was that we could share energy in battle.

The Nephilim next to me moaned, and I looked at him. His face looked even paler, if possible. His face crumpled in agony.

"Shh, it's okay," I whispered. "We'll get you out of here." I looked back at the fray. *Come on, José.*

José Ported to me and grabbed the Nephilim's hand. Then José cried out, his back arching, and slumped over sideways. A dagger protruded from his left shoulder.

A strangled gasp tore through me. I stood, shrieking in rage. My hands flew forward and I launched Damien backward into the brick building. He roared and collapsed against the dumpster with a loud crash.

Oliver hurried forward, and I rushed to José's side. His face was covered in sweat, his eyes closing against the pain. But he was alive.

"It's fine," he grunted. "Go kick his ass for me."

I held back a hysterical laugh and raised my gaze back to the gargoyle. When he righted himself, I flung him backward again and again. With each thrust, he howled until he stretched a trembling, clawed hand toward me. Thick, black smoke poured from his fingertips and covered my face, blinding and suffocating me. I tried to scream, but I couldn't suck in a breath. I lifted my hands to my face, but nothing was there. Flexing my fingers, I Pulled at the magic smothering me. It resisted, and I gritted my teeth, my lungs screaming for air.

Damien screamed, and I Pulled his black magic off me. Oliver had shot more flames at the creature. While Damien was down, I Pushed him, holding him in place. My arms shook as he thrashed against my grip.

I looked at Oliver. "Do it!"

"He's Second Tier!"

"I don't *care*! Do something so we can get out of here!"

Oliver glanced at Damien, then José, then back to me, his mouth opening and closing. Then, Oliver's jaw tensed, and he raced toward the gargoyle. A huge, jagged rock formed in Oliver's hand, and with a swift movement, he rammed it into the gargoyle's chest. Damien lurched, his black eyes wide. Then he fell, his head lolling forward and inky black blood oozing from the spear in his body.

I held Damien steady, waiting for him to come to, but his body remained limp. Lifeless.

Oliver's hands burst into flames, and he pressed them against Damien's body. *For good measure, I guess.* The gargoyle's wrinkly gray skin erupted into flames, and a nasty, burnt smell filled the air.

My arms dropped, and I doubled over, my limbs quivering and ragged breaths pouring from my mouth. "Can you . . . Port?" I asked José, too exhausted to look up.

"I don't think it matters anymore." José's voice was empty. Grave. I'd never heard him speak like that.

Ice hardened around my heart, numbing me with chills. *No.* I straightened and found José crouched by the Nephilim, whose eyes were wide open and vacant. The Nephilim's chest no longer moved with his breaths. Ice from Oliver's magic lingered on the wound, but a fresh puddle of blood surrounded him. He'd lost too much.

We were too late.

"No," Oliver breathed, horror etched in his face. He shook his head. "No."

After feeling for the Nephilim's pulse, José's eyes closed. His brows creased, and he pressed a palm against the Nephilim's chest. "Be at peace, *hermano.*"

Bile crept up my throat. My mouth crumpled, my eyes hot with tears. I rubbed my nose and looked away, but my chest heaved with sobs. He was alive when we'd arrived. We could have saved him. If only—

Oliver released an anguished yell, thrusting his fist into the wall. A heavy crash echoed in the alley as he summoned rocks in his hands to smash into the adjacent building. His face was tortured, a torrent of anguish and remorse.

I rubbed my forearms, staring numbly at the street in front of us. *What the hell are we doing?* We were only teenagers. We didn't even have our own lives figured out, so how were we supposed to save others' lives?

Ever since I embraced my powers in Santiago, I'd devoted myself to saving people. But that was what sent me down the darkest of paths in Manila.

I couldn't save anyone. I couldn't protect anyone. I was still weak and helpless just like Matthias wanted me to be.

Tears streamed down my face. What was I supposed to do? If my powers couldn't protect people, then what could I do here? How could I stop Matthias or *any* demon from taking lives?

José hissed in pain. "Ah, that stings. We should go before I'm too weak to Jump."

"What about—?" I asked.

"Hang on," José muttered. He gingerly slid his hands into the Nephilim's pockets, searching for something. I tried to squash the nausea in my stomach. It seemed so wrong. Like he was mugging a dead person.

"Got it." José removed a coin from the man's pocket.

"What's that?" I asked.

"A tracker. Every rebel has one. It gives our location and has a distress signal. This Nephilim alerted us when he was in peril. But the coin is tied to our life force, so if we die . . ." José trailed off.

"Then no one will know where he is," I guessed.

"Right. It's to protect the base if one of us is captured or if the coin falls into the wrong hands. That way no one can find us. But the coin takes twenty minutes to deactivate just in case the owner misplaced it or something." He sighed and pressed the Nephilim's eyelids closed. "Kiz will want to investigate his coin. See how and where he was first attacked." He looked at me with tormented eyes. "I'm not strong enough to Jump with you two *and* him."

"I can stay behind," Oliver said immediately.

José shook his head. "I don't even know if I'm strong enough to make it there and back. Besides, there could be more demons coming to ensure the gargoyle finished the job. I'll let Kismet know his location so she can send someone to . . . give him a proper burial."

I swallowed, my chest aching at the thought of just leaving this Nephilim's body here. My eyes stung with more tears, and I nodded.

Oliver and I crouched next to José, who remained on his knees. He sucked in several sharp breaths, and with a *pop*, we disappeared from the alley.

We appeared inside the rebel warehouse this time, ignoring the pretense of knocking and providing a password like before. In an instant, Kismet and several others surrounded us and examined José's wound. One rebel carted him off somewhere.

Kismet looked behind me and Oliver, no doubt looking for the Nephilim. "Where is he?"

I opened my mouth, but no sound came out. I couldn't speak. I couldn't even breathe.

"We lost him," Oliver said, his eyes tight. "The gargoyle from earlier attacked us, and the Nephilim lost too much blood."

Kismet's eyes widened, her face slack. She ran a hand through her long, blond hair and closed her eyes, her nostrils flaring. "Damn it," she moaned, covering her face with her hands.

"Who was he?" I whispered, finding my voice at last.

"His name was Dimitri," Kismet said in a strained voice, dropping her hands. Devastation pulsed in her eyes. "He was gathering intelligence for us, using his powers to cloak himself and get close to the enemy without being detected. Matthias must've put a tail on him." Her eyes sharpened. "Where's Damien?"

"Dead," Oliver said flatly.

"How? He's Second Tier. He can heal."

"I stabbed him. And set him on fire."

Kismet shook her head. "It doesn't matter. Unless you stake him or cast the banishing spell, he'll just keep coming back."

"Stake him?" I asked, frowning.

"Gargoyles are mutant forms of vampires," Kismet explained. She glanced from me to Oliver. "Are you two hurt?"

I shook my head.

Kismet sighed, rubbing the back of her neck. "Well, thank you for trying."

Those words sounded so stupid. We didn't deserve praise; we deserved to be kicked out for failing.

Maybe I didn't belong here. Maybe this wasn't the cause for me.

My eyes raked over the huge room until they fell on Bay. He was speaking in low tones with another rebel. Then his gaze lifted. My chest tightened, but once again, he only had eyes for Kismet.

He strode toward us, his eyes remaining on her. She

leaned into him, and he whispered something urgent in her ear. She nodded, her brows furrowed.

Discomfort twisted through me seeing them together. But it wasn't jealousy. I'd known when we kissed that he wasn't right for me. Plus, he was old enough now to be my father. That part weirded me out enough.

So why did I feel this way? Was I feeling possessive of Kismet? I couldn't place it, but it felt strange watching them like this. Like two of my worlds were colliding when they never should've been touching at all.

Bay's gaze rose to meet mine, and I froze. My limbs itched to run, to stretch, to *move*—but I stood there, motionless and locked in place by his stare.

"Can we talk?" he asked.

CHAPTER 11

I CROSSED MY ARMS, GLANCING AT KISMET OVER BAY'S shoulder. She didn't seem surprised to see him talking to me, but she looked wary. Watching to see what would happen.

I cleared my throat. "I thought you were on assignment."

Bay frowned, cocking his head at me. "I was. And now I'm not."

I shrugged, feigning nonchalance. But his presence here rattled me.

His eyes narrowed and roved over my face, scrutinizing me. Then he smirked. *Lilith, that smirk.* It was so familiar but so foreign. Wrinkles lined his eyes and cheeks when he smiled like that, but he was still so damn charming. "You don't like being caught by surprise. I forgot that."

I bristled. *Don't talk to me like we know each other. We're practically strangers right now.*

"My fae abilities allow me to Jump in here on occasion," he said. "I try to avoid it, though. Just in case."

Jump. So he was using modern jargon now. In Santiago, our coven called it 'Port.'

"You're *fae?*" Oliver asked loudly.

Bay and I stared at Oliver, whose expression was slack with shock. Then he looked to me, his mouth snapping shut. He ran a hand through his hair. "I, uh—sorry."

Bay chuckled. "Don't worry about it. I'm part fae, but I only have a limited amount of their powers." He looked back at me. "So. Can we talk?"

I felt Oliver stiffen next to me, and I waited for him to interject. But he didn't.

Good, I told myself, trying to ignore the churning in my stomach. I needed to be a big girl and face this. Sooner or later.

"Sure." I tried to sound casual, but it came out stiffer than I'd intended.

Bay stepped closer to me and stretched out his hands as if to wrap me in an embrace. "May I?"

I looked at Oliver. He was staring hard at the floor,

his gaze determined. His brows pinched, and his jaw tensed. I knew he didn't like this.

But he also knew I could take care of myself.

"Go ahead," I said. "Don't worry, Oliver. We'll be right back."

I really said it more for Bay's benefit—so he'd know I didn't intend to be with him for very long.

Oliver nodded tightly but still didn't look at me.

Bay held me against his chest. I was once again disoriented by his sandalwood scent mingled with Kismet's raspberries. *Oh yeah,* I thought. *They are* definitely *together.*

Then, black shadows rippled around me, obscuring Oliver and the other rebels from view as we were swept away.

When the shadows faded, we stood in an empty food court. Benches and chairs were still bolted to the floor, but each restaurant was vacant and empty like a ghost town. The air still smelled of fried foods, sending waves of nostalgia rippling through me as I remembered going to the mall with my parents and my friends. So many years ago. A million things had changed since then.

"Please, sit." Bay gestured to the nearest table and chairs.

"What is this, your office?" I snorted as I sank into a chair.

Bay smirked again. "Of a sort. This is on the other side of the mall. Most of the rebels don't fancy a walk this far, so it's just me and the Jumpers who come here."

I crossed my legs. "So what did you want to talk about?"

Bay sat across from me at the table, his expression sobering. "I tried to tell you this earlier, but I think . . . it was all just a little too much for you."

I bounced my leg in the air and chewed on my tongue, saying nothing.

"It's all well and good to give you a vague, blanket apology," he went on, "but I thought it might mean more if I told you my story and what I've been doing the last eighteen years."

I looked at him. His gaze was fixed on the dusty table, his eyes distant.

"I'm listening," I said quietly.

He swallowed and nodded, his brows creasing. "I, uh, arrived the year before Kismet did. 1982. The year that . . . Stefan was born. My ward. I served as his Familiar."

I grew very still, watching him.

"He lived in North Grove like you and your parents did, but his family were demons. His father was a dark warlock, and his mother was a werewolf. Since I was bound to him, my magic remained dark. And for eighteen years, I had to live with that darkness—the darkness I'd tried to ignore in Manila when Isko betrayed me. It festered within me, strengthening as Stefan's powers strengthened. I saw darkness with a different perspective—seeing it as Stefan saw it.

"He didn't want it. He tried to perform light magic at first, but then he felt disconnected from his parents. He couldn't bear to be separated from them or their blood, so he followed in their footsteps. But he often asked me about light magic. About what light casters do to protect people, about the code they follow and how to prevent themselves from going dark. And as I taught him what little I knew about light magic, I often thought of . . . you."

I couldn't move. Couldn't breathe. I sat there, frozen, as he told his story.

"I thought of your constant determination to protect those you loved at any cost. I taught Stefan everything I knew you believed in—light magic, using your powers for good, fighting those who oppressed others, helping mortals . . ." Bay shook his head, closing his eyes. "It was uncanny how similar you two were. And Desi, he did *all* those things. In his spare time, he was a Demonhunter. He monitored the streets and protected innocent mortals from demon attacks. He couldn't serve a coven because the light casters didn't trust him, and the dark casters saw him as a traitor.

"One day, I sensed something wrong in our bond. I found him knocked unconscious in his room holding a weapon that was covered in his father's blood. His father was dead, and his mother was missing. To this day, I still don't know what happened—if his mother was in on it, or if she was just kidnapped and then killed. He never heard from her again." Bay shifted and looked me in the eyes again. "But he was framed, and the demons came after him. His father had been a trusted leader among them, and this was one step too far. Stefan was a fugitive because of Levarret. Matthias. He didn't like Stefan interfering with his demons. So Matthias put a price on Stefan's head and sent him into hiding."

Bay's brows knitted together, his eyes tormented as he recounted the story. "Stefan ran away after that, and I helped him. He dropped out of school and changed his name. He found a job at a fast-food restaurant and kept a low profile until he turned eighteen. Then, I helped him disappear permanently. I don't know where he is now, but I pray to Lilith he's safe."

I finally found my voice. "Why are you telling me all this?"

Bay's tortured gaze met mine, and he leaned over the table toward me. "You almost went dark because of me. So you could protect people. Stefan made a similar choice, and it cost him everyone he loved. I saw firsthand the trauma he endured because he tried to do the right thing." His expression crumpled, his eyes closing again. "Desi, I can't express to you how sorry I am for manipulating you, for putting you in that position. I know it's no excuse, but I honestly thought Isko was just trying to recruit you. Not sacrifice you."

I swallowed, my throat filled with emotion. Heat stung my eyes, but I blinked it away. *I can't cry in front of him.* Fixing my gaze on the tiled floor, I said softly, "You hurt me, Bay. I thought I knew you. I pictured us training together, fighting alongside one another to protect people. I thought we had the same goals. I believed in you and your principles." I took a deep breath. "But all of it, all the time we spent together was just a big setup. And now I don't know what to believe. I just feel . . . lost." *Weak. Helpless. Unable to protect anyone.* He'd made me feel like some kind of hero when we rescued Reyna together and when I'd first performed the blood ritual. But now I felt like a fool.

Bay opened his eyes, which swam with sympathy. "I know. I'm sorry. If I could take it back, I would. But I promise you, you *will* find yourself again. I felt lost too after my mentor betrayed me, after my coven—my family—was killed. I found my purpose in Stefan. You can find yours too."

"How?" I shrugged helplessly. "I'm not a Familiar like you were. I'm not bound to protect anybody."

"Maybe not. But you still want to, right?"

I didn't answer. *Oliver. Kismet.* With all my heart, I wanted to protect them. I wanted to protect others too. But uncertainty tainted my resolve. What if I couldn't do it? What if I lost someone else like the Nephilim?

Would I go dark again if it meant saving others? I didn't want to put myself in that position. Not again.

I rubbed my nose and asked, "Is that why you joined the rebels? Because of what happened to Stefan?"

"Yes, but it was more than that. When I found out it was really Matthias, I—I *had* to get involved. Matthias took everything from me. He slaughtered my coven. He tried to kill me. He took me to this time against my will. Away from everything I knew. All our research tells us he was planning this for a *long* time, and I need to find out why. Why he used me and my coven—and *you.*"

"What happened after your curse was broken?"

Bay's eyes tightened, his gaze dropping. "I joined Kismet. We formed the rebels and have been working here ever since." He wouldn't meet my gaze.

"Do you love her?" My stomach churned, but my voice was level. Calm.

Bay looked at me. Certainty rang in his voice as he said, "Yes."

I sucked in a breath. I'd been expecting this, but it still came as a shock. "Does—does she love you?"

Bay cocked his head, frowning. "I think so. At least she tells me she does."

"Even though you're a dark warlock?"

Bay laughed, ruffling his salt-and-pepper hair. "Why would that matter to her? She was a dark witch once too."

"I just mean that almost all dark casters work for Matthias. Didn't she suspect you at first?"

Bay's smile faded. "Ah. Well, yes. It did take her a while to trust me. Every relationship has a learning curve. But our goals were aligned: to protect the world from Matthias. To protect those we love and those who are innocent. To allow people to live freely."

I uncrossed my legs and bent over, resting my arms on my knees and staring hard at an empty restaurant counter. "It sounds like a worthy cause."

"You don't seem so certain about that."

I sighed, dropping my head. "It's just . . . so much of a commitment. I'm not sure I can trust myself to make a permanent decision like that. Not after . . ." I trailed off. He knew what I meant.

"Desi, I know you have no reason to trust me or my promises, but I swear on my life that I will die before letting you go dark again. Kismet's magic is still blue, and yours will be too. We fight for magical beings everywhere—not just light and dark. So you'll see some gray area here. But this cause is a good one. We're the only ones fighting this. Without us, Matthias would have complete control over magic."

I said nothing. My jaw ticked back and forth as I considered his words. Something within me burned like a fire roaring to life for the first time in weeks.

"One day you'll have to choose a side, Desi," Bay went on. "You can't stay neutral forever. You're either with us, or you're with Matthias."

Rage pulsed through me. "I will *never* be with Matthias," I growled, turning my head to stare at him.

Bay raised an eyebrow. A challenge. "Prove it."

CHAPTER 12

WHEN BAY AND I RETURNED TO THE MAIN AREA, OLIVER was sitting on his cot, bent over with his forearms on his knees and watching the rebels carefully. Teddy was sparring with Kismet and two other rebels. The three who were on the Council were gone, perhaps maintaining their cover by going to work. The teenager with piercings and purple hair was facing a wall, flinging an athame into a dartboard and then Pulling it back with her magic.

I approached Oliver first. He stood when he saw me, then stiffened when he noticed Bay by my side.

"Let's do this," I told him. "Let's swear in."

Oliver's eyes tightened almost imperceptibly as they shifted from me to Bay. Confusion and hurt swirled through our blood oath, but he quickly smoothed his expression and nodded stiffly. "If you're sure."

"I am. It's time I stop hiding behind excuses."

Oliver's eyes were guarded, but he offered a small smile. "Good." He looked at Bay. "What do we need to do?"

Bay waved Kismet over. Her hair was pulled back into a sweaty ponytail. She wiped her brow and jogged up to us.

"They need a contract," Bay said to her.

Kismet's eyes widened as she panted from exertion. "Really? That's great! I'm glad you've come around."

I pressed my lips together. I didn't like the phrase 'come around' too much. It implied my hesitation was unfounded. I *knew* she was hiding something. A lot about this operation felt off to me. But I wouldn't find out anything by staying on the sidelines.

Besides, Bay was right. I was either with them or with Matthias.

Kismet held up one finger, indicating we wait. She disappeared for a moment, shuffling through the bags beside her bunkbed, and returned with two folded sheets of paper.

"Bay and I will both sign to ensure your side of the contract is adhered to as well," she explained, handing one contract to each of us. "These contracts swear you to secrecy about our operation. Even if under duress, you will not be able to disclose any information about us. It also prohibits you from using our operation against us or fraternizing with our enemies. Feel free to read through it, though, to make sure it's to your liking."

I started reading, but my eyes glazed over from the confusing legal jargon. I blinked a few times, skimming through the words and hoping that if anything unsavory was snuck in, it would stand out to me.

But who was I kidding? I wouldn't be able to spot that kind of deception.

One thing I *did* know: I trusted Kismet. Even if she was keeping secrets. How long had she kept secrets from me as my Familiar? She'd known about my time travel and that we'd met in her past, but she hadn't said anything. She probably knew that it would've altered the timeline. So I knew that whatever her reasons were, they had to be good.

I glanced at Oliver, who was reading through his with a furrowed brow. Perhaps he understood more because of his work on the Council.

At long last, he looked up and nodded, his face a hard mask of determination.

Bay pulled a long, thin knife from his belt and pressed it into his fingertip. He signed his name on both, and then Kismet did the same. She held the blade out to me first.

I swallowed. Alarm and panic raced through me at the thought of signing with my blood. Flashes of pain and my own screams rippled through me from when Isko had tortured me with the voodoo doll. I'd been unable to protect myself then because of the blood contract I'd signed.

No, Desi. This is different. Kismet would never do that to you.

My eyes shifted to Bay. *But he might.*

Bay's dark eyes tightened, and regret burned in his gaze so strongly, I almost felt it emanating from him.

Sucking in a breath for courage, I pressed the blade into my finger and signed my name. Oliver took it from me and followed suit with his contract.

Magic pulsed around us, piercing the air with ash, lime, and some other scent I couldn't place. Maybe magic smelled different in the future and I hadn't noticed it before.

The faint pain in my finger vanished, as did the blood dripping into my palm. Something in my chest squeezed, building in pressure and intensity. I gasped out, and then it released, funneling out of me like smoke.

"What was that?" I choked.

"Just a test we built into the contract," Kismet said casually, rolling up the papers and shoving them into her pocket. "Something to ensure your intentions were pure."

"What would've happened if they weren't?" Oliver said tersely.

Kismet leveled a hard look at him. "You wouldn't still be standing."

I suppressed a shudder and rubbed my arms to ward off the chill from her words.

Kismet ticked her head backward. "Come on. Persephone is waiting."

My eyes widened. "She's . . . *waiting*? For us?"

Kismet smiled. "I knew you'd join us sooner or later. She's been resting after her latest assignment, but I figured once you two signed, you'd want to speak with her right away."

"I—uh—*yes*," I sputtered, sharing an eager glance with Oliver. *Merciful Lilith, I'm about to meet a faerie.*

It shouldn't have been so exciting for me, especially since Bay was part fae and I'd already seen some of the amazing things he could do.

Perhaps that was why I was so excited; to see how much *more* Persephone was capable of.

Kismet and Bay led us out of the rebel warehouse and down the walkway of the mall. We passed the nail salon where I'd read Alba's letters, and we entered a shop with glass-encased counters. Though there was no merchandise, I could tell this had once been a jewelry store—the high-end kind where you bought engagement rings.

Kismet approached a door behind one of the counters labeled "Employees Only." She knocked three times and waited.

A high-pitched voice trilled, "Come in, Kismet."

Kismet pulled open the door to a small office, and a glittering glow blinded me. Squinting, I stepped forward, and a confusing array of scents assaulted my nose: lemon lime, cranberry, morning dew, and freshly mowed grass. It tickled my nostrils so severely, I almost sneezed.

Gradually, the glow subsided to reveal a creature sitting idly in an armchair. Her long, iridescent legs dangled seductively over the arm of the chair. Her skin was pearly white and glimmering, more so than any diamond I'd ever seen. Large, violet eyes blinked underneath inky black eyelashes. Her hair was hot pink and fell down her shoulders in thick ringlets.

My mouth fell open. I stood there frozen, completely mesmerized.

Kismet cleared her throat. "Seph. Tone down the glamour just a bit please."

A light chuckle echoed in my ears like the peals of a bell, and then the glow dimmed. Her skin didn't sparkle anymore. Her violet eyes shrank just a bit, making her look less like a Barbie doll and more like a person. Her hair pulled back into her scalp, surrounding her head in a pixie cut. The pink color remained, however.

Persephone dropped her legs and stood gracefully from her chair. She towered over even Oliver, and I balked.

"You must be Desiree and Oliver," she said, flashing a brilliant smile at us. Her eyes lingered a moment too long on Oliver. I glanced at him, and his eyes were wide, transfixed by Persephone. I could hardly blame him, but a twinge of jealousy surged through me.

I swallowed, finally finding my voice. "A pleasure to meet you, Persephone."

Persephone curtsied low, sweeping her arms to the side with all the grace of a queen. "The pleasure is mine. Please, sit."

I looked around and found four cushioned chairs facing her armchair, though I was certain they hadn't been there before. My legs felt like jelly as I slowly slid into a chair. Oliver followed suit next to me.

Persephone sat too, swinging one long leg over another. "So, what would you like to know?"

I opened and closed my mouth, still at a loss for words.

Oliver spoke first. "Why—why are you getting involved? Everything I know about the fae is—"

"That we stay out of it," Persephone said with a nod. "Yes, and for the most part this is true. But when a bargain is struck with a High Fae, then his descendants are bound by it, similar to a blood contract. And, sadly, my ancestor struck a bargain with Matthias that my family is forced to adhere to."

"But—but then how are you here, helping us?" I asked. "Aren't you also bound?"

Persephone's smile widened to reveal sharpened teeth that made her look like a predator. "No. Only those who are High Fae are bound. My kind are a bit primitive in their belief that only males may serve as High Fae. A curse—and a blessing, if you will. Were it not for this disappointing custom, I would not be able to join your little rebel cause."

"So what does your family do for Matthias?" Oliver asked.

Persephone flexed her fingers, inspecting her fingernails as they lengthened into long claws. "As I said, being a female has its disadvantages. I am not privy to all my father does, but I have heard him frequently mention another High Fae named Alastor."

"Seph doesn't know much about Alastor," Kismet chimed in. "But your parents did, Desi."

I blinked, startled, and turned to face her.

"In a sense, he was Matthias's predecessor. He was a Third Tier demon who waged many battles against the light casters. Your parents banished him when you were eight."

I frowned. "Alastor. The name doesn't ring a bell."

"Your parents didn't want to name him in front of you," Kismet said. "For faeries, names hold power, and your parents feared that if you used his name without thinking, you might accidentally summon him."

"Hold on," Oliver said, raising a hand. "A *demon* High Fae? Is that even possible?"

Persephone nodded grimly. "Yes. Though we practice both light and dark magic, the same rules apply to us as they do to you. If we perform enough blood rituals, we are marked by dark magic. However, unlike your kind, we can still return to light if we wish, though it is a difficult path."

My mouth felt dry. Flipping back and forth between light and dark? I was slightly ashamed of how appealing that sounded. *If I were fae, I could Ascend and then just jump back onto the side of light magic.*

"But fae are so powerful," Oliver said. "What did Alastor have to gain by Ascending?"

"From what I learned from Desi's parents," Kismet said, "Alastor was hoping to summon the demon king Asmodeus."

Silence fell between us. My brow furrowed as I glanced from pale-faced Oliver to Kismet's grave expression. Persephone's gaze dropped to the floor, and Bay's jaw hardened, his beefy arms crossed over his chest.

"Who is Asmodeus?" I asked.

"He's one of the lords of the underworld," Kismet said. "He rules an army of undead demons. If he is raised, his demon army will come with him."

My blood chilled. "Why did Alastor want to summon him?"

"I don't know," Kismet said with a shrug. "Perhaps he wanted to harness the army to do his own bidding."

"Or maybe he wanted to use the army to tip the scales in favor of demons," Bay said, raising an eyebrow. "Does that sound like anyone else we know?"

I leaned forward, clasping my hands together over my legs. "So . . . you're saying Matthias was in league with Alastor? And this bargain is why Persephone's family is enslaved by him?"

"Not enslaved," Persephone said sharply, "but bound to collaborate. We are not servants like with a blood bond. Yes, Matthias was in league with Alastor, but

Alastor was not *my* ancestor. Through his connections to dark magic, other members of the High Fae joined the cause as well. Including my ancestor, Fenrir."

Persephone took a breath, and her voice was slow and articulate as she continued. "I am told that there was an attempt to raise Asmodeus. Alastor gathered many of his allies, including Matthias. Together they formed an oath to serve and protect each other. Then they attempted to raise Asmodeus and his army. This attempt killed Fenrir and mortally wounded Alastor. Many of the High Fae withdrew at that point, but Fenrir's devotion was sealed with his blood. My family has been in service of Alastor's ally ever since."

The air chilled around us from her words. My insides felt hollow and empty. I rubbed my arms, trying to bring warmth back to me, but all I felt was darkness.

"Alastor's ally," Oliver repeated slowly. "So Matthias and Alastor were in league with each other. Do you think—"

"That Matthias will try to succeed where Alastor couldn't?" Persephone finished gravely. "Yes. Yes, I do."

My heart stopped. My breath caught in my throat, and I straightened, eyes wide. *Matthias is trying to raise Asmodeus. Merciful Lilith, how are we going to stop him from doing that?*

"Matthias is a Third Tier demon," I said, trying to

sound nonchalant, but my cracked voice betrayed me. "Third Tier demons have been banished before. I mean, look at Alastor—he was Third tier *and* High Fae. If he could be stopped, so can Matthias."

"That's the problem," Persephone said. "The battle against Alastor consisted of casters *and* fae. We allied together to stop him. But this is different. Many of the fae have withdrawn, swearing never to involve them-selves in the wars of casters ever again. There are some who still serve Matthias, but they do so begrudgingly. If Matthias invokes a war, you will not likely have any support from the fae, because we are so mistrustful of the bargains our ancestors made."

"So then why are *you* helping?" I asked, cocking my head at her, assessing her. "If you aren't bound, then what brings you to our side?"

Persephone narrowed her eyes at me. "I sense your distrust in me, Desiree. Faeries cannot lie, so I am unable to speak deceit to you. I am young for a faerie—I am only twenty years old. Many of us can live to be several hundred years old. The oldest of my kind are set in their ways and are unlikely to join any cause. But I am young, and all I have seen are my father's brutal acts in the name of Matthias's cause, the way my brothers are forced to follow and assist although in their hearts they loathe it. I know Matthias has a tendency to enslave others. It is bad enough that the High Fae are compelled to work alongside him, but I fear he will one day find a way to enslave my kind completely—that Asmodeus will provide this opportunity for him. I want to rid the world of his tyranny before this comes to pass."

The small room rang from the intensity of her words. I watched her, awed by her story and by the complicated past of the fae that I'd known nothing about. These impressive creatures were essentially immortal, but they'd remained so hidden that I'd only heard whispers of their existence. Yet Alastor and Matthias had drawn them out against their will. Any hope of allying with the fae deflated within me. Persephone was our only hope.

Kismet suddenly stiffened in her chair, her back arching and her face crumpling in agony. A strangled cry poured from her mouth. She hunched over, gasping for breath.

In a flash, Bay was by her side, his hands on her shoulders. "Kiz, what is it? What has he done?"

Matthias. I jumped to my feet, my hands curling into fists.

A sheen of sweat formed on Kismet's forehead. Panting, she cast her wide eyes from me to Persephone and then to Oliver. "Matthias, he . . . he's Ascended to the Fourth Tier."

CHAPTER 13

GOOSEBUMPS ERUPTED ON MY ARMS, AND MY HEART stopped for a full beat. I felt suddenly cold—so cold. My arms and legs were numb. Useless. I couldn't move. My mind roared with panic, a screaming torrent of fear and hopelessness.

Amidst the chaos circulating through my brain, my eyes shifted until they met Oliver's. His green eyes locked onto mine, his face a ghostly pallor, his mouth agape. Horror etched into his face, and, through our blood oath, I felt his emotions—they matched mine. Shock. Numbness. Terror. Despair.

Yet somehow as I watched him, the riot within me seemed to settle. So I held his gaze. It grounded me, bringing me back to earth and back to the reality before me.

I snapped back to the conversation, and Persephone and Bay's voices grew louder and clearer.

"I am telling you it's not *possible*," Persephone snapped, her eyes blazing. "No one has Ascended to the Fourth Tier in all of magical history."

"I'm not lying," Kismet growled. "I *felt* it."

Persephone raised her long, white hands. "I am not calling you a liar. I just think you are mistaken. Perhaps he merely formed a simple blood ritual."

"I believe Kismet," I said loudly. "Matthias was trying to Ascend back in our time—in 1898. He almost succeeded. I have no doubt that, with the resources and the time he's accumulated here, he's managed to finally make it happen." I swallowed and met all their grave expressions. "The question is, what do we do about it?"

Persephone threw her hands in the air. "It's *useless.* If a Fourth Tier demon has never existed, then we don't know how to banish one."

"A being who can't be killed," I whispered. A chill raced down my spine as I thought of Alba's letter. *This spell will help you defeat El Diablo.* I snapped my fingers, trying to recall her exact words. "The spell—Alba's spell. It's something to do with reawakening the dead, but it can also be used to defeat someone who can't be killed."

"What is she talking about?" Persephone snapped.

"A Seer from her time," Kismet said slowly, her eyes

thoughtful. "She Saw a spell in the Grimoire that could help us." She shook her head, closing her eyes. "We don't have time to thumb through every page in the Grimoire, though. Especially if it's not found with other necromancy spells."

"We need to *train*," Bay said firmly. "Not all of these rebels are Hunters. They've been training, but they need a lot more work. If we do manage to confront Matthias before he summons Asmodeus, it'll be brutal."

Kismet nodded. "You're right. Bay, you work on training the rebels. Persephone, you keep gathering information and see what your family knows about Matthias's Ascension and what his timeline is for summoning Asmodeus. We need to know how much time we have left. I'll keep recruiting, trying to sniff out those who defy Matthias and the Council but are too afraid to speak out. Desi, you and Oliver search through the Grimoire—"

I was already nodding. "Right. To find Alba's spell."

"No. To find the spell to summon Asmodeus."

I blinked. "What?"

"We need to know what's required to cast it," Kismet said, ignoring my confused expression. "If we can stop him from obtaining certain ingredients, we'll buy ourselves some time."

"Can't I look for both?"

"There's no *time*, Desi. If he's Fourth Tier, he could have enough power to cast the summoning spell right *now*."

"Kismet, we need to *destroy* him," I said, brows furrowed. "Stalling him won't work in the long run. But if we can find this spell—"

"Desi, if he succeeds, the whole *world* will be overrun by bloodthirsty demons," Kismet said, her nostrils flaring. "I'm not chasing some fairy-tale spell while he raises hell. Besides, even if this miracle spell *does* exist, who here is powerful enough to cast it? No, it's easier to thwart him from casting a spell than it is to try to defeat someone who's never been defeated before."

My mouth fell open in indignation, but Kismet had already sprung into action. She strode out of the small office with Bay right behind her.

I lifted my arms and let them fall uselessly against my thighs. I glanced at Persephone, who waved her long fingers, offering a sarcastic smile.

"Sorry, sweetie," she said. "Good luck to you both."

With an explosion of pink smoke, she vanished. I coughed as a sickly sweet perfume assaulted my nose. The smoke cleared, and it was just me and Oliver.

I growled in frustration, running my hands through my thick hair. "I can't believe this! She followed Alba's visions so carefully back in our time, and now she disregards it like some old wives' tale?"

Oliver pressed his lips together and watched me silently.

"What, you agree with her?" I snapped.

Oliver raised his hands in surrender. "I didn't say that. But there's some wisdom in preparing for the worst."

"Finding a way to banish him *is* preparing for the worst!"

"Desi, think about it. If we spend all our time searching for this spell and *don't* find it and then are unprepared when Asmodeus and his army rises from the underworld . . .?" He lifted his arms, letting his heavy question trail off.

My determination deflated, and despair coiled within me. "I can't just ignore Alba."

"I know." He stepped closer to me. "I'm with you, Desi. Alba's family. I'll follow her advice, even if she's . . . she's already on the other side." His eyes tightened, his Adam's apple bobbing as he swallowed.

Sorrow extinguished my anger in an instant. I looked at him—his pinched brows, his chin stiff as he resisted breaking down despite having seen me do the same thing.

His family was gone too. He was completely alone. I read it in his face and in the emotions from our blood oath.

I couldn't let him feel that way.

I closed the distance between us and took his hands in mine. His palms were large and covered mine easily. I laced my fingers through his and clasped them tightly. "I'm so sorry, Oliver. But you're not alone. I swear to you, I will be with you. I won't ever leave you. I'm *here.*"

Oliver offered a tight smile, his eyes guarded. He nodded as if to try to reassure me, but I still sensed his uncertainty and regret. Somehow, I knew what he was thinking: *You're here, but not in the way I want you to be.*

In that moment, a flash of longing burned through me so intensely it was painful. Flames scorched through my chest. I wanted to be *with* him. I wanted to be his. In every way.

I leaned in, embracing the heat of his body being so close to mine. Desire blazed in his eyes. My lips parted, my stomach churning with anticipation.

"Found it!" shouted a voice.

Oliver and I sprang apart. With my face on fire, I turned to the interruption.

Bay hauled the Grimoire and slammed it onto Perse-phone's empty armchair. He grunted and stretched his arms. "This thing is *heavy*." He glanced between the two of us, no doubt noticing our flushed faces and embarrassed expressions. "You two . . . all right?"

I cleared my throat. "Yeah!" I said too loudly. Then, quieter, I said, "Yeah. Just peachy. We'll get to work on this right away."

Bay raised an eyebrow, his black eyes calculating as they shifted between me and Oliver. He'd always been way too perceptive for my liking. That infuriating smirk spread across his face, and he nodded. "Great. Good luck, you two. Join us in the main area when you can to brush up on your training."

He strode confidently out of the room. I stared numbly after him, too afraid to look at Oliver.

What would've happened if Bay hadn't interrupted us? I'd wanted to kiss Oliver. Desperately.

And yet a tiny voice whispered within me, *As soon as you screw this up, he'll find someone else to be with.*

It was a nasty thought, but I couldn't push it from my mind.

I'll screw this up just like I did in Santiago—just like when he sought out Gwen because I couldn't give him what he wanted.

Deep down, I knew it wasn't true. He'd been blackmailed into the arrangement with her. But I couldn't quench the knowledge that *I'd* pushed him away from the start.

I had a bad habit of pushing people away. If I moved forward with Oliver, I would undoubtedly let him down again. I couldn't commit when I knew there was this part of me that withdrew instead of opening up. I still didn't fully know how to do that yet.

Maybe this was for the best. Maybe we weren't ready to dive back in.

Or rather, *I* wasn't ready.

"Desi?" Oliver asked quietly.

"Right, um." I cleared my throat and rubbed my nose. "Let's get started. I don't care what Kismet says—we can look for both spells and see what we find."

I finally looked at him. Regret flared in his eyes, but his expression was smooth. Composed. He'd arranged his features to hide the disappointment, but I still saw it. Still *felt* it.

He ached over our lost opportunity. And I was sure he read the doubt and uncertainty in my face and knew the moment was gone.

"All right," he said with a stiff nod.

He turned and dragged the large desk closer to the armchair. With a grunt, he hefted the Grimoire up and slammed it down on the desk. Puffs of dust floated in the air. I coughed, my eyes burning and my nose tickling.

Oliver looked at me, his face still impassive, and gestured to the armchair.

I sighed and sank into the chair, while Oliver took the smaller chair opposite me. The fabric still reeked of the sickly sweet fae smell. "Where should we start?"

"Necromancy," Oliver said at once. "Both spells are associated with it. Even if Alba said it wasn't directly related to necromancy, it's still better to check there first."

"Sounds good to me."

At first, my skin felt hot as we bent our heads next to each other and muttered together, searching through the old and worn pages of the text. But after a while, exhaustion pulled at every muscle in my body, and it became increasingly difficult to keep my eyes open. I blinked often, rubbing my eyes, and had to reread the spell names a few times to fully register their meaning.

How to raise a lost lover . . . Potion for animating a decayed corpse . . . Communing with spirits . . .

After over an hour of leafing through every page of the necromancy section, I groaned, throwing my hands into the air. "It isn't in here!"

Oliver rubbed the bridge of his nose. "It's possible the

spell won't outright say Asmodeus's name. I feel like I've heard him referred to as something else." He squeezed his eyes shut, his brow furrowed. His hand waved nonsensically in the air. "Something like demon overlord or demon general . . ." He trailed off, shaking his head.

Familiarity prickled along my skin, sending shivers down my spine. Suddenly alert, I straightened in my chair as the familiar rush of a memory burst in my head.

I eased my door open, careful to leave only a crack so the hinges wouldn't creak. In low voices, my parents discussed the events of their recent Demonhunt.

"Yes, but we don't know that for sure," Mom said. "He could be trying to summon anyone."

"No, I'm certain I heard him refer to the Demon Master. There's only one demon with that title."

Mom shook her head, her long curls bouncing against her cheek. "Demon Master could mean anything—anyone."

"Are you willing to take that chance?"

Silence. Then Mom said softly, "Of course not."

"Me neither. Let's pull out the Grimoire and see what we can find."

I gasped, my eyes wide as I fell forward. My arms slammed against the desk, my head dizzy from the shift back to reality. I often had visions—memories of my parents from our connection by blood, but usually it was in my dreams.

On the rare occasion I had a vision while awake, it was to convey something important.

"What is it?" Oliver asked, alarmed. His wide eyes searched mine. "Are you hurt?"

Breathless, I shook my head. "I'm fine." I looked up at him. "Demon Master. Asmodeus is referred to as the Demon Master."

Oliver's brow furrowed like he doubted this. For a moment, he stared at me, reading the certainty and conviction along our blood oath. Then his eyes lit up, and he lifted a finger. "We came across something like that."

Bending over, he hastily flipped through pages and pointed to a spell labeled, *To summon the Demon Master.*

I whooped in triumph, and Oliver flashed a grin at me. Heads bent close together, we leaned close and read the spell. The list of disturbing ingredients sent my stomach churning and reminded me of the disgusting elements I'd had to combine for the time travel spell last year.

My eyes flitted down the page. As I read, horror clenched my heart into a tight ball. *Merciful Lilith.*

With my throat dry, I looked up at Oliver. His face was a mask of hard fury. I couldn't speak. Bile crept into my mouth, and I covered my mouth with my hand.

I couldn't tear my eyes away from the words on the

page: *This spell demands a sacrifice from each faction of magic. Each magical being must offer themselves up willingly to the caster. The caster must then remove their hearts from their bodies and offer them as a sacrifice to the Demon Master.*

CHAPTER 14

I CLOSED MY EYES, SHAKING MY HEAD. *HE CAN'T DO THIS. He can't find that many willing magical beings to sacrifice themselves.* "No, he can't—" I choked on my words and swallowed. "Okay. How—how can we send Asmodeus back?"

Oliver was silent as he searched the spell. He sucked in a sharp breath and said quietly, "'To summon the Demon Master, the caster must offer a sacrifice of his own, such as a bargain of servitude. This will bind the Master to the caster's soul when he steps through the veil of the underworld. The only way to send the Demon Master back to the underworld is to banish the caster.'"

My eyes widened. "So we banish Matthias, we send Asmodeus back."

Oliver looked at me, his expression grim. "We need to find Alba's spell."

Determination surged through me. Sitting forward, I pulled the Grimoire toward me. "Yes. Good. And if we find a spell to banish him and use it *before* he summons Asmodeus—"

"Then we won't need to worry about sending Asmodeus back at all," Oliver said, his eyes alight with energy.

More silence fell between us as we flipped through pages. Like before, we emerged empty-handed and decided to try another section. My stomach growled, and my eyes ached, but I pressed on. After searching through *Necromancy*, we perused *Banishments, Demons and Other Dark Casters*, and even *Potions and Magical Ingredients*, but we couldn't find any mention of a spell that could defeat someone invincible.

"Her letter was too vague!" I said in frustration, pushing back my wild and frizzy curls. "Couldn't she have been more specific than 'it's a necromancy spell but not actually a necromancy spell?'"

"The spell wasn't in her native language," Oliver snapped. "Give her a break. We'll find it."

"You don't know that!"

"What do you want me to say, Desi?"

"I don't know," I moaned, burying my face in my hands.

"It doesn't matter anyway," Oliver muttered angrily. "Nothing I say to you ever makes a difference."

I dropped my hands, my temper rising. "What did you say?"

Oliver's brows pinched, and he opened his mouth, but a deep rumble shook the walls around us. Oliver teetered and lifted a hand to steady himself against the wall, his eyes wide.

"Earthquake?" I said uncertainly, my anger vanishing.

The ground quivered again, and a loud explosion crackled through the air, echoing against the walls of the mall.

My blood ran cold as I looked at Oliver.

"We're under attack," he whispered.

We bolted out the door, slamming it shut behind us. I almost turned back for the Grimoire, but no—it would be safer if it remained hidden.

We sprinted down the walkway, following the sounds of gunfire and shouts that hauntingly reminded me of the battles in Santiago and Manila. I shoved the traumatic memories from my mind and struggled to keep up with Oliver. A stitch formed in my side. I wheezed and puffed, my lungs burning.

The rebel warehouse came into view, and my heart

jolted at the sight. Every rebel was battling someone. Bursts of blue and black light mingled like sinister fireworks, filling the air with smoke and magic. Some people fired pistols, though I couldn't tell which side.

I patted my jeans and swore. Of course I didn't have weapons. I hadn't even bothered to ask Kismet for stakes and athame holsters. How stupid was I?

"You go . . . first!" I shouted at Oliver, hoping he'd know what I meant.

I felt his assurance through our blood oath. He stretched his arms. Huge bursts of wind poured from his palms, lifting him into the air like a rocket.

My jaw dropped as I stood there watching him fly. When had he learned to do that?

Oliver pulled energy from me, and I teetered as exhaustion claimed me. I blinked spots from my eyes and staggered off to the side to catch my breath. I'd be no use if a demon killed me right here.

Oliver launched himself into the fray and threw a fireball at an assailant. Then I stepped forward, drawing from Oliver's power through our blood oath. My feet pounded against the floor, adrenaline coursing through me. My hands lifted, Pushing away a vampire who bared his fangs at me.

I need a stake. We need more weapons, or we'll never win this.

A dark warlock blasted his black magic toward me, and I leapt away from it. Flame singed my hair as I just barely missed the assault. I eyed the demon angrily, my eyes narrowing. In his left hand was a long dagger.

I cocked my head and smirked at him. Lifting my hands, I grunted and Pushed him high into the air. He yelped and spun with the movements of my hands. I flexed the fingers of one hand to hold him in place. With my other hand, I yanked and Pulled the dagger from his grasp. It soared toward me. I dropped my hands and caught it. The warlock screamed as he fell to the ground in a crumpled heap.

The weapon, though foreign to me, brought me a strange sense of strength. I rubbed the ornate hilt, and my nerves soothed. *I can do this.*

I surged forward, swiping at a werewolf, dodging a blast of black magic, and then stabbing another vampire. Blood poured down my arms, but I knew it wasn't mine. Sweat trickled down my face. My chest swelled from the thrill of the fight. I felt unstoppable. Powerful.

I rammed the blade into another demon's chest and kicked him to the floor. Claws raked down my shoulder. I cried out, my back arching and needles of agony slicing through me. Sensing an attack, I ducked, sucking in sharp breaths to combat the pain. A gunshot blasted through the air. My ears throbbed from the noise, and I winced. Somehow I knew the bullet had just barely missed me.

Popping back up to my feet, I stared down my assailant and froze.

It was Matthias.

He lowered his smoking pistol, his lips curling into a smirk. He was older—*much* older. His brown hair was now almost all gray, and wrinkles formed around his eyes and mouth when he smirked at me. But power still emanated from him. So much power it almost suffocated me, filling my lungs and throat.

I almost stood there like an idiot while he fired again. At the last second, my adrenaline took over, and I tumbled out of the way.

"Too afraid to fight like a real demon?" I roared at him, rising back up to my feet. "Hiding behind that gun makes you an even bigger coward than I thought."

Matthias cocked his head at me, his eyes narrowing. "I don't see you lowering your weapon, Desiree."

I resisted the urge to flinch at the sound of my name coming from his vile mouth. "You're Fourth Tier now, buddy. Grow a pair and fight me like a man."

Rage burned in his dark eyes. Slowly, he slid his gun into a holster at his waist and spread his arms wide. "Make your move then."

My nostrils flared, and fury ignited inside me,

bringing me to life as if I'd been asleep until now. Fire roared in my chest, igniting something powerful within me.

He killed my parents.

I screamed in rage and bounded forward. Anticipating his flames, I leapt gracefully into the air, arcing my body away from his fire and spinning midair. I relished his shock for the briefest moment before flinging the dagger toward him. He dodged, but not quick enough. My blade sliced into his arm.

With a growl, he poured inky black smoke from his hands, the smoke so thick it obscured him from view.

Panicking, I pulled on more of Oliver's energy and tried Pushing the smoke out of the way. But it was too thick.

I dropped to the floor, breathing heavily. I could smell the tingle of his magic. He was close. Too close.

I closed my eyes. *Trust your senses, Desi. Smell him. Where is he?*

An array of scents tickled my nose. I couldn't pinpoint his. A hint of metal. Gunpowder. Sweat. Blood. Ash and lime.

There. I felt him right in front of me. I flexed my fingers and Pushed.

I heard him grunt and roll away. I bumped into legs and bodies as I tried to escape his blinding, black fog.

Something tight gripped my foot. I thrashed and kicked, but his hold tightened. Sharp pain knifed through my shin, and I cried out.

"Desi!" Oliver shouted from a distance. He knew I was injured.

And he could blow this fog away.

"Oliver, I need your wind!" I screamed.

More pain pressed into my leg. I gritted my teeth, tears stinging my eyes. If I didn't get away soon, Matthias would saw my leg off. I didn't want to know if he was biting me or cutting me with a knife.

Then, a storm burst above me, tousling my hair and whipping against my face. The fog dispersed, and I blinked, eyes watering. As the air cleared, I glanced over my shoulder and found Matthias, his hand surrounded by small daggers as he gripped my leg.

I cried out again at the sight of the blood soaking through my jeans. Squinting at him, I realized the daggers were his *claws*.

What the hell?

I didn't have time to wonder at this. Now that I could see him, I lifted a shaking hand and Pushed him away from me. He floated backward only a few feet.

I had to move.

Trying to rise, I bit back a scream from the agony in my leg. I couldn't put weight on it.

Move. Move. Move!

I felt his black magic behind me and dropped to the floor again. But when I tried to rise, my body wouldn't move. I was spent, unable to fight.

No.

"José, get her out of here!" Kismet screamed somewhere to my left.

"No," I said weakly.

A warm hand gripped mine, and with a *pop*, we vanished.

We landed on soft carpet.

I rolled, trying to rise, and shrieked, "Oliver!"

A hand clamped over my mouth. "Shut up, Desi."

I blinked and found José watching me with sharp, warning eyes. I clamped my mouth shut and nodded, my arms shaking.

Slowly, José dropped his hand, and I looked around. We were in a large hotel room with two king-sized beds. Several other rebels surrounded us, some sitting on the sofa bed and others pacing restlessly around the room. In the kitchen area, Teddy lifted his hand to the purple-haired girl's head to heal a nasty gash along her cheek.

"Where are we?" I whispered to José.

"A hotel across from Kiz's place," José said quietly. "It's our temporary safehouse for situations like this. As

soon as she gives the signal, I'll Jump to the next location with however many rebels are left."

"Left?" I repeated numbly. How many had died
already?

Oliver.

Then I felt him in my chest. A surge of relief,
possibly from knowing I was alive too.

Fight, Oliver. You can do this.

"Come on," José said, trying to raise me to my feet.

I winced, my palms sweaty, and shook my head. "I—I
can't."

"Just come over here to let Teddy look at you."

Pressing my lips together, I nodded and scooted
awkwardly on the floor toward Teddy. José gripped my
hand firmly the whole time, and I looked up at him
gratefully.

I couldn't believe this was the same guy who'd
skipped pretty much all of senior year, drank alcohol,
and partied like a frat boy.

"I've got her." With a grunt, Teddy hoisted me from
the armpits and leaned me carefully against the fridge.
"Hold still, Desi."

I nodded again, closing my eyes. A bright blue glow
burned through my eyelids, and warmth surrounded my
leg. A sharp pain stabbed through me, and I hissed. Then
it vanished, and the glow subsided.

Exhaling slowly, I opened my eyes and tested the weight of my leg.

No pain.

I sighed in relief. "Thank you so much." I touched Teddy's shoulder, offering a grateful smile. He inclined his head toward me.

Then, my eyes found José in a corner. Next to him was Cameron, who held a bloody tissue against his nose. I hurried up to them.

"Send me back," I told José.

José's eyes widened. "You crazy, Desi? No way. We stay here and wait for the signal."

"Oliver and Kismet are still there!" I cried. Cameron shushed me, his wide eyes darting around the room.

José touched my shoulder. "Look, I get it. I'm worried too. But I'm under orders. I can't just Jump around whenever I like. Stay here, and trust Kismet and Bay. They'll get out as many people as they can." He suddenly stiffened, fishing a hand into his pocket to reveal a silver dollar similar to the one he'd taken from the dead Nephilim. After squinting at it for a moment, he muttered, "Be right back," and vanished with a *pop*.

"How did Levarret find us?" Cameron whispered to me, his voice muffled from his bloody nose. "We were completely cloaked. *Double* cloaked."

"He's Fourth Tier now," I said gravely. "Maybe that comes with some uncloaking abilities."

Cameron's face drained of color, his expression horrified.

"You didn't know?" I asked.

Cameron shook his head, dazed. "We had just gotten back from an assignment when the attack happened." He closed his eyes, his brows pinching. "Fourth Tier. Holy *hell*." He pressed his hand against his forehead, his fingers curling into a tight fist.

Another *pop*, and José reappeared. My heart lurched as I looked at his companion—then despair filled me. It wasn't Oliver.

It was a woman I remembered from earlier who worked for the Council. Still wearing business attire, she sported a bad burn on her arm that had singed half her sleeve. Red welts coated her exposed skin.

"Go see Teddy over there," José urged.

The woman winced and nodded, ambling toward the other side of the room.

"How was it?" I asked, stepping toward José and resisting the urge to grab his arms and shake the truth out of him. *Is Oliver alive? What about Kismet? Is Matthias still there?*

He shook his head. "There's not much left. I didn't see Levarret, but there are some other demons still searching the area. It looks as if the rest of our guys have fled."

Cameron hissed in pain and shoved a hand in his pocket. He withdrew a small, orange object that he tossed back and forth between his hands like it was on fire. Then, the orange color faded to reveal another silver dollar.

José straightened and turned out his pocket until his own coin fell to the floor. Then he faced us, his eyes grim. "That's the signal. It's time to move."

CHAPTER 15

José Ported with me and Cameron, bringing us to a thick forest lit by the fuchsia rays of the setting sun. The crisp, chill air tickled my skin, and I shivered, rubbing my arms.

"Where are we?" I whispered. The woods felt so still that I feared disturbing them.

"I don't know," José said. "I just followed the coordinates from Kiz on the coin." He squinted. "There. I see a light."

I followed his gaze. A few yards away, faint lights glimmered, beckoning us forward. "Why wouldn't she send us directly to them?"

"Maybe she wants to make sure demons don't follow us," Cameron said. "Or maybe these guys don't take too kindly to strangers."

I swallowed. "Should we wait for the others?"

"No," José said. "It's safer to move while we're split up. You two go on. The others will be right behind you."

Before I could object, he vanished with another *pop*.

I gritted my teeth. Approaching a strange house in the middle of nowhere with no weapons? That was nothing. I'd just faced off with Matthias himself. I could do this.

A cold uncertainty crept inside me as I thought of those still fighting. Kismet. Bay.

Oliver.

I searched within myself for some emotion from Oliver, some communication—*anything.*

But our blood oath was silent.

No, I told myself. *I'd know if something was wrong. I'd feel his pain. I'd feel* something *from him.*

Perhaps he was unconscious. Or perhaps he was just calm. Emotionless right now. It could mean anything.

"Ready?" Cameron asked.

I nodded, and we stomped through the brush and foliage. Leaves and vines clung to our clothes, and I was grateful for the length of my jeans that protected against thorns. Within ten minutes, my limbs felt numb from the cold and the monotonous movement of my steps.

Gradually the lights grew closer, and a grand three-story mansion came into view. I stopped short, my mouth falling open. The manor stretched high into the sky, lined by mighty pillars and a wraparound porch that was filled with ornate potted plants. Shiny sports cars in a large, circular driveway winked in the light of the sunset.

"Hot damn," Cameron breathed. "What billionaire owes Kismet a favor?"

I chuckled wryly and continued walking, curiosity urging me forward.

As soon as we stepped onto the driveway, a warm, blue glow illuminated the manor like a forcefield. I tried to keep going, but my limbs were frozen stiff. Alarmed, I glanced at Cameron and found him stuck just like me and grunting with effort. Our bodies were bathed in blue magic that somehow trapped us there like prey waiting to be devoured.

A loud, electronic cawing sound echoed along the grounds, burning my ears. We'd tripped some sort of alarm.

"Easy," I muttered to Cameron. "Hopefully they'll be welcoming when they find out who we are."

And who exactly are *we*? I wondered. *Rebels, sure. But we're two teenagers in way over our heads with a fracking Fourth Tier demon.*

I wasn't sure *I'd* let us in if I owned a mansion like this.

A small *pop* drew my eyes to a tall, thin figure standing a few feet away from us. Long, gray hair fell over his forehead, and his dark eyes narrowed at us.

"Who are you?" he said in a raspy voice.

"We mean you no harm," I said. "Kismet Harrington sent us."

The man cocked his head at us, considering. "Your names?"

"Desiree Campbell and Cameron Fletcher."

The man's eyes widened, his face paling. "You're the Timecaster?"

"I, uh." My heart stopped, my blood chilling. A "yes" formed on my lips before I could stop myself. Clenching my teeth, I buried the response before I gave away too much information.

The man waved a hand. The blue glow surrounding the manor vanished along with the sharp bird noises. I exhaled, finally regaining control of my body. The tension in my limbs melted away, and I rubbed my chest, confused.

"Don't worry," the man said, striding toward us. "The effects will wear off soon."

"Effects of what?" Cameron asked, looking around nervously.

"The alarm system I have invokes a truth-telling

agent," the man said, offering an apologetic smile. "It's just a safety precaution to ensure you aren't enemies."

Truth-telling. It reminded me of the potion that was forced on me in Manila, which made me woozy and a bit giddy. But this was so different. My limbs felt like jelly, and my tongue felt a bit numb.

Imagining just how far the magical world had come since 1899 made me feel sick. It served as a blatant reminder that I was no longer in my time.

My time. Somehow, I wasn't shocked to realize I'd been comfortably referring to the nineteenth century as my own time. It had been my home. My everything.

"My name is Elias Caldwell," the man said, extending his hand to shake ours. "A pleasure to meet fellow comrades of Kismet. Will there be more of you arriving?"

"Yes," I said, trying to swallow down the numbness in my mouth. "We aren't sure how many, though."

Elias waved a hand. "Don't worry about it. Please, come inside."

He led us up the driveway and past the sports cars, which all looked brand-spanking-new.

"So, how do you know Kismet?" I asked, struggling to keep up with the stride of Elias's enormously long legs.

"Oh, I've known her for years," Elias said. "We were

both involved in a messy conflict with the Council a while back and have been allies ever since."

"So are you with the rebels?" Cameron asked.

"Not exactly," Elias hedged. "I try to remain neutral. Self-preservation, you know. I have no problem providing safe refuge to some friends. But the less you tell me about what you're up to, the better. I want as much plausible deniability as possible in case I'm questioned."

I widened my eyes at Cameron as a warning, and he nodded slightly. *Keep our mouths shut.*

"Do you live alone, Elias?" I asked, gazing up at the beautifully sculpted pillars and the iron balconies hovering over us as we stepped onto the porch.

"Yes, except for a small household staff. I'm a retired aurologist, so I've got deep enough pockets to live comfortably on my own for a while."

Aurologist. The word sent a prickle of recognition through me, but before I could focus on it, another blue glow flashed over us.

I stiffened, expecting to be frozen again, but my legs still moved forward. Apparently, once freed from his truth-telling prison, we were immune.

My heart lurched in my throat when I noticed two figures at the edge of the driveway. I squinted, but I couldn't make out who they were.

"Friends of yours?" Elias asked.

I looked at Cameron, who also squinted. "I can't tell from here," he said.

Elias raised his gaze to the newcomers, his brow furrowed. "Ah, yes. You're right. Well, you two head on inside. Megan will get you situated. I'll remain out here to ensure no unwanted intruders try to slip through."

He flashed us a grin and strode down the steps toward the frozen figures.

I lingered in the doorway, my body as stiff as if I'd been trapped by Elias's alarm system again. My eyes remained on the two figures. One stood a foot taller than the other. Could it be Oliver? Or Felix. I vaguely remembered him being really tall too.

"Desi?" Cameron said.

"Right." I jerked my gaze away. *Oliver can take care of himself. You're not his mother. Stop being such a worrywart.*

But I couldn't shake the guilt wriggling through me that he had willingly followed me here to this time only to be caught up in this battle and facing a deadly enemy. He was here because of *me*, and he could be injured or worse—

I crossed my arms, forcing the thought from my mind as we entered the foyer. The ceiling stretched high above us, adorned with elaborate paintings and sculptures. My eyes widened as I took in the grand spiral staircase, the decorative railing, and the impressive paintings on the walls that were taller than I was.

"Lilith," I breathed, awestruck.

"I never knew aurologists made *this* much money," Cameron said, wiggling his eyebrows at me. "Maybe I pursued the wrong career path."

I snorted and shoved his arm.

A figure appeared around the corner with her arms full of folded sheets. She had long, straight, brown hair and wide-set green eyes. Black headphones covered her ears, and her eyes widened when she saw us. She released the pile of linens, and they hovered in the air in front of her as she yanked her headphones off.

"Sorry," she said with a laugh. "I'm Megan. Are you guests of Mr. Caldwell's?"

I blinked at the girl. She looked to be about my age and wore jeans almost identical to mine. Imagining the maids and housekeepers of 1899 made my head spin. Of course there weren't household staffs here like there were back then—dressed all formally and addressing people by titles.

"Yes," Cameron said, clearing his throat. "He said you could help us?"

"Of course! Right this way." Megan nodded toward the staircase, and Cameron followed. I glanced over my shoulder at the figures of Elias and the two rebels. The blue glow had vanished, and they were walking toward us.

The sun glinted off one of the rebels' gold hair, momentarily blinding me.

My heart jerked forward in my chest, and a resonating burst of relief and excitement burned within me in response—I knew he saw me too.

"Oliver!" I cried, sprinting out the door.

Ignoring Cameron's objections, I raced down the steps toward the driveway. Oliver broke into a run too, his tall form drawing closer to me. My legs pumped faster and faster, my heart racing. *Thank Lilith. Oh, thank Lilith he's okay.*

I threw myself into him, and his arms wrapped around me, pulling me close against him. Laughing, I buried my face in his chest, feeling his rapid heartbeat and the joy emanating from our blood oath.

"I'm so glad you're safe," Oliver said breathlessly as he stroked my hair. "I saw you fighting him, and I just . . ." He trailed off and exhaled, his breath tickling my face.

I drew back and looked up at him. His eyes were filled with emotion so raw and vulnerable that I wanted to cry. A smear of black soot coated his forehead, and his left sleeve was ripped and bloody. I saw no cut on the exposed skin, so I assumed Teddy healed him.

"The blood oath," I said, touching his cheek. "Oliver, you would've felt something if I'd been in trouble."

His eyes closed, his brows pinching as he nodded. "I know. But still."

I couldn't blame him. I'd had the same irrational fears.

Which was utterly stupid because we both knew we could take care of ourselves. I hadn't been this torn up about him in Manila or even in Santiago.

Had I?

Behind Oliver was the purple-haired rebel I remembered seeing earlier. I smiled at her. "I'm Desi."

"Gina." She nodded at me, then lifted her hands. "I'm not really the hugging type, though."

I snickered and shook my head. "Yeah, don't worry. I'll keep my distance."

A chuckle from behind Gina drew my attention to Elias. His arms were folded as he watched us, eyebrows raised. "You kids go on in. I'll wait out here for the others." Amusement danced in his eyes, and he turned away from us to face the forest again.

Gina smirked and walked with us toward the porch. I kept my arm looped through Oliver's, though I longed to clutch his hand or wrap my arms around him again.

"What happened?" I asked in a low voice, glancing at him and Gina.

"Kismet had some kind of explosive vanishing potion," Gina said. "She magicked us away to the lower level of the mall and we snuck out that way. We couldn't use José, though, so we had to move on foot. Took more time."

"And Matthias?" I looked at Oliver.

His lips flattened, his jaw tense. "Gone."

"How many rebels did we lose?"

Oliver shook his head. "We don't know. Kismet sent us away and went back to search for survivors. I saw at least one go down, though. An older man with long hair."

"Les," Gina said solemnly, rubbing her nose. "He was a good guy. My first friend with the rebels." Her brown eyes tightened.

We climbed the steps of the porch and rejoined Cameron, who was chuckling at something with Megan. The linens were floating in the air again as she covered her mouth and snorted with laughter.

Cameron's crinkled eyes shifted to us, and his grin widened. "Ollie! You made it! And Gina, good to see you too." He slapped Oliver on the shoulder and winked at Gina.

Oliver wrinkled his nose. "Ollie?" I bit back a smile.

Megan straightened, the humor in her face smoothing as she returned to business. She pulled the floating linens against her chest again. "If you all will follow me, please? There are rooms prepared for you upstairs, and Mr. Caldwell has sent meals up already."

My eyebrows rose. "How?"

Megan flashed me a smile. "The security system isn't the only impressive magical technology he has access to."

We climbed the massive staircase together. I never left Oliver's side. We followed Megan down a long hallway lined with elegant paintings of waterfalls, mountains, and other serene landscapes. Decorative mahogany tables held the most intricate vases I'd ever seen—with swirling paint strokes and detailed carvings. I gave the tables a wide berth, knowing the vases were probably worth a fortune.

Megan stopped at a balcony railing that overlooked the foyer. "From here on out are the guest rooms. Take your pick. There's plenty of space, so you don't have to share a room if you prefer solitude. Your other friends will room upstairs once they arrive. If you need anything, push the button by the bed, and I'll be happy to assist you." She smiled warmly at us, her gaze lingering on Cameron before she headed back down the hallway to climb up to the third floor.

"Dibs on the one at the end," Gina said abruptly

before shuffling down the hallway and disappearing into a guest room.

Cameron laughed and saluted me and Oliver before he took the room opposite Gina's.

Then it was just me and Oliver. Our arms were still linked, and warmth coursed contentedly along our blood oath. The longer we stood there, the more awkward I felt. Heat crept into my cheeks, and my mouth felt dry. Suddenly, I didn't know what to do with myself. I wanted to pull away from him but draw him closer at the same time.

"I suppose we should pick our rooms?" Oliver asked quietly.

"I suppose we should." But neither of us moved. I didn't want to leave him just yet.

"I know it probably isn't appropriate," Oliver said, his voice barely above a whisper, "but do you think . . ." He trailed off, his lips tightening and his eyes fixed determinedly on the painting behind me.

I cleared my throat. "Oliver, I would really appreciate it if you came with me into my room. You know, to make sure there isn't an assailant lying in wait for me there. For my protection." I raised my eyebrows at him.

Oliver laughed, his stiff expression melting away. "Very well. For your protection, of course."

We entered the room next to Cameron's, and I

gasped. It was bigger than my entire apartment back in Santiago. A king-sized bed with a canopy and lavender drapes rested on one end of the room. At the other end of the room was a beautiful, white sofa and chaise facing a large coffee table with a tray of meat and potatoes that made my mouth water and my stomach growl.

Oliver and I exchanged eager grins before we bounded forward. Oliver stretched out on the sofa, and I immediately started devouring the meal. A moan of pleasure escaped my mouth, and Oliver chuckled.

"You seem hungry," he said with mock seriousness.

I nudged his ribs. My mouth full, I said, "You want some?"

"I'm fine, thanks." His gaze drifted over the room. "It feels like we're in a castle."

"I know. Who knew Kismet had such wealthy friends?"

A comfortable silence passed between us as I ate and Oliver relaxed, his gaze softening as he stared out the window. I knew neither of us wanted to talk about Matthias, so I kept quiet, focusing only on the fact that we were both here. Alive. Unharmed.

I dabbed my mouth with a napkin and sat back, sighing. "I'm sure you have an equally satisfying meal waiting in your room too if you want to go look."

Oliver's expression sobered, and he sat forward,

shaking his head. "No, I, uh . . ." He cleared his throat and looked at me, brows furrowed. "Why did you run to me?"

I blinked. "What?"

"Earlier, when you saw me with Gina and Elias. Why did you run to me?"

"Because I was excited to see you." I frowned, unsure what he was getting at.

"Right. Of course." Oliver stood and paced the length of the room as he rubbed his chin.

"Oliver, what's bothering you? Tell me."

"I just—" He ran a hand through his hair. "I just don't know where we stand." He gestured between us.

Something cold slithered in my chest, but I cocked my head at him, feigning confusion. "What do you mean?"

"I mean, in Manila, you said you needed time, and you keep withdrawing from me. But then just now, I thought maybe—" He wouldn't look at me. "I just need to know if there's someone else."

My head reared back, and a surprised chuckle burst from my lips before I could stop it. "What? How could there be someone else?"

Oliver finally stopped pacing and faced me, his eyes tormented. "Are you in love with Bayani?"

I rose to my feet. My brows pulled together, and my mouth twisted. "Bay? He's like twice my age now!"

Oliver rolled his eyes. "Desi, you know as well as I do that in our time that's perfectly appropriate."

I shook my head, crossing my arms. "*No.* Absolutely not. It was just jarring seeing him after he . . . betrayed me. In Manila."

Oliver lifted his arms, letting them fall on his thighs. "But you trust him. You feel *something* for him, right?"

Irritation prickled through me. "Oliver, whatever you're getting at, just *say* it."

"You told me you couldn't commit to joining the rebels, but then you speak with Bayani for ten minutes, and suddenly your mind is made up. So forgive me for not believing you when you say his betrayal was on the forefront of your mind."

My brows lowered. "I'm not lying to you, Oliver."

"Really? So this isn't some kind of payback for me lying to you about Gwen?"

Hot anger boiled in my chest at the sound of her name. "No," I said through clenched teeth, "but if it *were*, it would be everything you deserved."

Oliver's eyes burned, and his nostrils flared. "You know, I don't get it. I mentioned marriage to you, and you rejected me. I had every right to pursue another, but you distanced yourself from me even after I ended the arrangement with Gwen and pledged myself to you. But Bayani—he turns you over to his coven of Kulam warlocks to sacrifice you for a blood ritual. And after one conversation, you not only forgive him, but you trust him enough to sign a blood contract and join his cause?"

I clenched my fingers into fists. "Those two circumstances are different."

"Different how?" Oliver spread his arms, his eyebrows raised with mock surprise. "By all means, please explain."

I shook my head, stepping closer and jabbing a finger at him. "Bay didn't break my heart. He didn't lie to me about being engaged and then come to Santiago and kiss and flirt with me while his bride-to-be waited for him back in America! And not only that, but Bay showed me a side of himself I hadn't seen before. A side that made me realize demons have a reason to fight against Matthias too. You're a light warlock, Oliver. I expect *every* light caster to want to fight him just like my parents." Tears filled my eyes, and I swallowed. "You knew when we first met that I had no desire to follow in my parents' footsteps. I needed a reason to fight besides, 'it's my duty.' And Bay provided that reason."

Hurt and confusion flashed in Oliver's eyes. "So my reasons weren't good enough?"

I threw my hands in the air. "I didn't say that at all! If my own parents had been here to convince me to fight, I would've told them the same thing, Oliver! It's not about who I love more or who I trust more. It's about my *personal* reasons for fighting, and I don't owe that explanation to you!"

"No, but you sure as hell owe me *something*," Oliver snapped, stepping toward me. "I'd move heaven and earth for you, Desi! Can't you give me something? Either cut me loose or stop being a coward and *be* with me!"

"I'm not a coward!"

"Then *tell* me! How can you forgive Bay but not me?"

"Because Bay isn't the one I'm in love with!" I shouted.

Oliver froze, his eyes wide and his mouth open. "What?"

I gritted my teeth. Tears spilled down my face, and I dropped my gaze from his. It was out. I couldn't take it back now. "I love you, Oliver. And I'm afraid. Afraid of opening myself up to you again, of trying to heal and fix myself so I don't push you away like I did before. I forgave Bay because I don't fear death as much as I fear . . . losing you." My voice cracked at the last word, and my eyes closed. My heart throbbed like an open wound, exposed and raw. Here I was, spread out before him. An easy target. All he had to do was say one word and I'd be crushed. Pulverized beyond repair.

It was thrilling. And terrifying.

But Oliver didn't speak. Instead, he closed the distance between us and caught my face in his hands. His eyes burned with desire as he brought my lips to his. My trembling hands pressed against his chest. Our kiss deepened, our mouths opening wider and our bodies drawing closer together. Fire raced through my chest, and something within me roared, taking over completely.

My brain shut off, and my hands moved on their own. My fingers yanked the fabric of his shirt so forcefully I heard it rip. The sound only aroused me further. I drew back, panting, and rolled his shirt up to his shoulders, exposing the muscles contracting along his chest and abdomen with his heavy breaths.

I expected him to stop me. To roll the shirt back down and step away from me.

But he didn't. He lifted his shirt up and over his head, dropping it onto the floor. His eyes were alight with energy and disbelief as if he surprised even himself.

I stared at him. The air between us seemed to crackle with electricity. "We can stop," I whispered, though my body yearned to keep going. "We don't have to—"

"I want to." Oliver drew nearer until I was close

enough to kiss his bare shoulder. My eyelids fluttered closed. "I want to do this with you, Desi. I love you."

Heat swelled within me. I wanted to share this with him. I wanted him to be my first. First love. First time. "I love you too."

Then desire took over, and we were kissing again. Our fingers fumbled with our clothes and pants, our chests pressed together, and our mouths were a clash of tongues, teeth, and moans of pleasure. Heat and desperate longing churned through our blood oath, only fueling the flames between us. My body ached for him—to be joined with him and cross that threshold with him.

A heavy pounding on the door stopped my heart, though it still thundered against my chest. Oliver pulled away for a brief moment. My vision blurred, and I blinked, momentarily disoriented. Somehow we had fallen onto the bed together, and my shirt was off.

Uncertainty raced through me. Oliver and I stared at each other. His eyes were wide with shock but still wild with that energy that made me burn up inside.

Maybe whoever it is will just go away.

But the pounding continued, and Kismet's voice jolted me off the bed. "Desi, it's me! Open up, *now!*"

I scrambled back into my T-shirt and ushered Oliver against the wall and out of sight from the door.

Smoothing back my hair, I took several deep breaths and pulled open the door.

My blood ran cold at the sight of Kismet. Her outfit was drenched in blood, and her hair was a mess of sweat and ash. Her eyes were haunted and vacant, and devastation crumpled her expression. Her lips trembled as she said, "Persephone—she's dead."

CHAPTER 16

ALL WARMTH FLED FROM ME. MY HEART DROPPED TO MY stomach like a stone.

"What? How?" I whispered.

"Matthias. He promised her brothers freedom from their bargain with him if they gave her up." Kismet raised a shaking hand to her forehead. "Seph alerted me through her coin, but by the time I got there, it was too late."

"That's how he found us at the mall," I said numbly. "He was looking for her."

Kismet nodded, her face crumpling. The wild passion from earlier left me, and I felt cold inside seeing my strong mentor so weak. So tormented.

I opened my arms and embraced her. Her sobs pressed against me, muffled by my shirt.

In my whole life, I'd never comforted Kismet as she cried. Not once.

It shook me to my core. My insides felt like jelly, and my heart was swollen with sympathy. But somehow, I remained composed on the outside, rubbing her back and holding her tightly. I wondered if this was how *she'd* felt comforting me as a child all those years ago.

Oliver stepped forward from behind me. Thankfully, he was fully clothed again, though his shirt was ripped at the bottom. "I'm so sorry, Kismet."

Kismet didn't register any surprise that he was there. She just nodded and wept further into my shoulder.

I had so many questions. Did Persephone give Matthias any information? Did this mean Matthias no longer had fae working with him? Did he know where we were now? But instead of asking these questions, I let Kismet grieve the loss of her friend.

"It was my duty to protect her," Kismet moaned. "I promised her she'd be safe. I promised her I'd never leave her side."

"You thought she was safe with her family," I said quietly. "There's no way you could've known."

Oliver ran a hand across his face, his eyes grim. "Lives are often lost in battle. It doesn't make it any easier, but she served a noble cause. The best thing we can do to honor her is to carry on, fighting in her name. Fighting for justice."

My heart swelled at his words. I looked at him and saw the fierce soldier I'd known in Manila and Santiago. The man I'd fallen in love with.

Yes, love. I was in love. Openly, gloriously in love.

Oliver's eyes warmed as they met mine, but we only shared a brief moment before he turned to Kismet again. "Do the others know?"

Slowly, Kismet shook her head.

"I'll go relay the news." And then he was gone, closing the door softly behind him.

"That was kind of him," Kismet said thickly, pulling away from me at last. "I don't think I could bear telling another person right now."

I carefully guided her over to the sofa and sat down next to her. "Kiz, I've never seen you torn up like this."

Kismet wiped her nose, her puffy eyes darting away from me. "I've been a bit more . . . emotional than usual."

I raised an eyebrow, my gaze dropping to her belly and back up. *Not* visibly *pregnant. But she could still be pregnant.* I didn't dare ask, though.

"We lost three others in battle today," Kismet said. "It's a miracle the rest of us got out. I think Seph's death was just one too many for me. The failure of it all crashed down on me. I'm sorry to dump it on you."

I squeezed her hands. "Don't apologize, Kismet. You were there for me my whole life. Let me return the favor."

Kismet offered a watery smile. "I'm glad you and Oliver made it out." She shook her head, her expression filling with despair again. "But we couldn't grab the Grimoire before we fled. I'm sorry."

I stiffened. I'd completely forgotten. "Kismet, we found the spell to summon Asmodeus." Quickly, I filled her in on the requirements of the spell and how to send Asmodeus back once he was summoned.

For a long moment, Kismet stared over my shoulder, her eyes calculating and her sorrow melting into determination.

Then she was on her feet. "We have to go to the Council. *Now*."

"What?" I jumped up, gaping at her. "Matthias *owns* the Council!"

"Not all of them. And if we present this to them and they actively *refuse* to protect all magical beings from the possibility of being sacrificed, they'll be outed as co-conspirators to Matthias's treachery." A hopeful smile lit up her face. "So either they'll reveal themselves or they'll have to help us."

"Yeah, *or* they'll arrest us on the spot," I said incredulously. "Or execute us. We're not exactly the most trust-worthy informants."

"All we need to do is provide them with the spell and evidence that Alastor was planning this alongside Matthias all those years ago." Kismet's gaze sharpened as she thought. "I'll have to get back to my apartment and dig through your parents' files."

"Kismet." I grasped her shoulders. "You aren't going anywhere. You're covered in blood. You just lost several comrades. Take a minute to cool off and think this over, and then we can act."

Kismet swallowed, her gaze still far away, but the light in her eyes flickered and then vanished. "I—" She stopped, her mouth clamping shut. Then she deflated. "You're right. Of course you're right." She covered her face with her hands.

I frowned and looked closely at her. "Kismet, where's Bay?" From what I'd observed, he was her partner in this operation. He should definitely have been privy to our conversation.

"I, uh, I don't know," Kismet said quietly. "I saw him Jump, and I know his coin is still active. So he isn't dead. But I—" She shook her head, her expression crumpling again.

Oh, Lilith. I knew exactly how she felt. That was why she was so torn up.

But she didn't need to break down again. She needed a distraction.

"Okay," I said, taking her hand and leading her out of the room. "Let's get you cleaned up and fed and then we'll make a decision. Together."

Darkness poured in from the windows, highlighted by feeble rays of moonlight. After ensuring Kismet was taken care of, I bathed and found a surprising array of dresses exactly my size in the wardrobe next to my bed. Frowning at the lack of pants, I picked a frilly yellow dress that reminded me of a similar outfit I'd borrowed from Alba in Santiago.

I crept downstairs to the sound of low voices. My footsteps softened along the stairs as I listened.

" . . . probably wouldn't have happened if we'd just been here all along." The bitter voice sounded like it belonged to Gina.

"Don't be stupid," Cameron snapped. "Elias made it clear he's trying to stay neutral. Kiz obviously used this place only as a last resort."

"But his wards—"

"Would've failed just like ours did. Levarret is *Fourth Tier*. Not much can stop him."

"Which means we can't stay here long," rumbled another familiar voice: Teddy. "Don't get too comfortable here. With every passing minute, we put Elias in more danger."

"What kind of magic does he have anyway?" Gina asked. "He's a Jumper, but he can do other things too."

"He's an aurologist," Cameron said, and I could practically hear him shrugging as I continued descending the staircase. "He has access to all kinds of magical technology. Maybe he found a way to inject himself with some serum to give him more powers."

"Now who's being stupid?" Gina scoffed.

"We need to be productive while we're here," Teddy said, interrupting their arguing. "Megan, do you know if Mr. Caldwell has a Grimoire?"

"I don't believe he does," came Megan's soft voice.

"Damn," Teddy said with a sigh. "Our options are limited then."

"He has a vast collection of research on certain spells, though," Megan said. The tilt of her voice indicated she was trying to be helpful. She struck me as the type who didn't like disappointing others. "I can see if he'd be willing to let you take a look."

"That would be wonderful. Thank you."

At long last, I arrived at the end of the hallway, which opened to a small bar. Teddy, Cameron, and Gina sat on barstools, and Megan sat reading in an armchair in the corner. They all looked up at my arrival. Teddy raised a glass full of amber liquid.

"Good to see you again, Desi," he said with a tired smile. "Glad you're okay."

"Likewise," I said, sliding into a barstool alongside Cameron. "Who else is here?"

"Felix, Kendall, José, and Tess," Teddy said, wincing. "We lost the others."

My blood chilled, and I closed my eyes. Though I'd hardly known them, their loss still struck me like a blow.

"To fallen comrades," Cameron said, lifting his glass. Gina and Teddy clinked theirs with his, and I lifted a hand in acknowledgment. I wasn't too fond of alcohol.

"Where do we go from here?" Gina asked after sipping her drink. "Does Kismet have a plan?"

All eyes shifted to me. Perhaps they heard her banging on my door earlier.

My face burned as I thought of Oliver and me shouting . . . then undressing. What else had they heard?

Clearing my throat, I said, "I don't know. She was covered in blood when I saw her, so I forced her to take care of herself first. We can make a plan later."

Discomfort flicked between us. Gina and Cameron shifted in their seats. Teddy's eyes tightened, his jaw hard as he gazed distantly through the dark window in front of us.

My gaze slid to Megan, who continued reading quietly as if she couldn't hear us. She'd mentioned Elias's research on spells. Perhaps he had information about the spell to banish Matthias.

Sliding off my stool, I carefully approached her. She looked up at me with a ready smile. Eager to please.

"Hi," I said, sitting on the sofa across from her. "Thanks for all your help."

Megan's smile widened, and dimples appeared in her cheeks. "Of course."

"So, uh, where is Elias—er, Mr. Caldwell now?" I asked nonchalantly, glancing around as if I might find him peering around the corner.

"He's sleeping, thank goodness." When I frowned, she added, "Most nights I find him holed up in his office working."

"Working? I thought he retired."

"He did. But he still works to develop new technology."

I cocked my head at her. "What exactly is an aurologist?"

"He studies how magic relates to the soul. He harnesses the connection between one's aura and one's powers to create something new. Like this." Megan released the book in her hands, and it floated a foot in the air.

My eyes widened. I'd thought that was strange when she'd done it earlier. I just assumed she was a better Pusher than I was; in all my life, I'd never managed to get things to hover in the air without lifting my hands.

"You're a Pusher?" I guessed, pointing a finger at her.

Megan nodded. She lifted her right arm, revealing a thin metal band along her wrist. It reminded me of the dampeners from Manila that had rendered me power-less. But this looked like a darker metal, and it was thicker too. More like a handcuff than a bracelet.

"Each cuff is tethered specifically to the caster's aura," Megan said, a hint of pride in her voice as she rubbed the metal on her wrist. "Mr. Caldwell has to do extensive research on the subject first before binding them to the cuff. It doesn't work right with anyone else."

"What else can you do with it?" I asked, awestruck.

"Not much," Megan said with an embarrassed chuckle. "My aura isn't marked with anything signifi-cant. I can move things around the room without touching them, and I've been practicing Pushing without seeing, but it's proven difficult."

Pushing without seeing. That would be incredible. The first thing I'd learned when developing my powers was that I couldn't Push something I couldn't see or smell.

"How long have you worked here, Megan?" I asked, leaning forward.

"Since Mr. Caldwell retired five years ago."

I raised my eyebrows, impressed. Perhaps she was older than I'd thought. Or Elias had seen some real potential in someone so young. *I* probably wouldn't have said no to an opportunity like this. Especially with the perk of getting to use Elias's technology.

With a sharp gasp, I finally connected the pieces. Kismet had mentioned how aurologists had studied the effects of the time travel spell. She must've been working with Elias. I was certain of it.

"Are you okay?" Megan asked, brows furrowed.

"What?" I said, distracted. "Oh, yeah. I'm fine. Just peachy." My heart raced. My legs itched to sprint away, find Elias, and ask him the millions of questions I had about time travel, auras, Familiars, and Timecasters. What did he know about Matthias? Did Elias have theories about why Matthias ended up where he did?

I swallowed down my questions, my legs bouncing uncontrollably. With a groan, I stood and hitched my right leg in the air. The strain in my leg was an embarrassing indicator of how out of shape I was. But still I stretched, reaching my hand to clasp the toe of my shoe. I held the pose, my leg quivering from the stretch. Slowly, I counted to ten, dropped my foot, and lifted the other to repeat the move.

"Wow, you're flexible," Megan said. "A dancer?"

"Yeah," I said with a grunt, dropping my leg and bending at the waist to touch my toes. "Ballet and yoga relax me. Or at least, they used to."

"What relaxes you now?"

"Honestly? I don't know." Panting, I straightened, my body feeling slightly less jittery. "I thought it was Demonhunting, but I don't really trust my instincts anymore."

"Maybe you need another outlet," Megan said.

"What do you mean?"

"I mean, maybe you need to find some kind of target practice that doesn't involve an actual magical being. Like Demonhunting with inanimate objects." She flashed a grin at me.

Though she was joking, something inside me rattled at her words, perking up as if recognizing the answer I'd been searching for.

A loud cawing sound echoed in the foyer. My heart lurched, and Megan jumped to her feet. Her hasty footsteps pattered down the hallway until I heard her knock softly on a door.

"Yes, I know!" came Elias's muffled voice.

I glanced at Cameron, Teddy, and Gina, who all

looked up in curiosity. Together, we wandered toward the foyer. Elias emerged from down the hall, his gray hair ruffled and his eyes slightly bloodshot.

"You all wait here," he said tiredly. "If I'm not back in ten minutes, come after me." His voice held a hint of humor, but I knew he was serious. At this hour, who could it be?

Then I realized: it was Bay. It had to be.

I had to go get Kismet.

I raced upstairs to the hall of guest rooms. Oliver opened his door, which was across from mine, and looked at me sleepily, his gold hair mussed and distractingly sexy. He was shirtless, wearing nothing but cargo shorts.

"What's going on?" he asked, his voice low and husky.

"Someone else has arrived," I said. "I think it might be Bay. Is Kismet in her room?"

Oliver nodded, eyes widening. "I'll get dressed."

I offered him a soft smile, which he returned before closing his door again.

I knocked several times on Kismet's door. After a moment, she opened it, blinking in confusion. The darkness behind her indicated that she'd slept, though lines and pink patches on her face made me wonder if she'd accidentally fallen asleep reading or something. *Typical Kismet. Never resting unless her body forces her to.*

"Someone's here," I said quietly.

Her expression sobered, and she nodded before closing the door.

The cawing alarm stopped, and I raced down the stairs. Though I was certain it was Bay, a strange sense of fear rippled through me. *What if it isn't? What if it's Matthias? Or someone else who's discovered our location?*

Teddy, Gina, and Cameron stood by the open front door, squinting in the darkness. Each of them clutched a small weapon behind their backs: Teddy a pistol, and Cameron and Gina an athame.

"Stand down!" Elias called from afar. "This one's on your side. I think."

I think. If it were Bay, he would've known for sure.

Apprehension raced through me. *Who is it, who is it, who is it?*

At long last, Elias climbed the steps of the porch, his brow furrowed as he beckoned to the two figures behind him. One was a tall, gangly teenager with dark red hair that fell past his ears. And the other was—

I gasped sharply, staggering backward. It was a were-wolf. The large creature stood at about two-thirds the boy's height, despite being on all fours. Light gray fur glinted in the moonlight, and yellow eyes narrowed at us as the wolf drew nearer. Though it was clearly suspicious of us, I noticed the wolf's lips were closed, concealing its fangs. I'd never seen a werewolf do that before. From what I understood, the need to bare teeth was ingrained in them as a reaction to being threatened.

Gina and Cameron raised their athames, and Teddy lifted his gun. "Who are you?" Teddy demanded, his deep voice so menacing I almost shuddered. "Why have you brought a werewolf here?"

"My name is Stefan," the boy said and then gestured to the wolf. "This is my mother, Isabel. We—we're looking for Bayani. He was my Familiar."

CHAPTER 17

A SHOCKED SILENCE RIPPLED OVER US. SOME OF US exchanged surprised looks.

"Stefan?" asked a faint voice from the staircase.

I turned to find Kismet, her face pale and her hair pulled up into a messy bun. A few steps behind her stood Oliver, who wore a green sweater. His hair was still slightly disheveled.

Stefan's almond-shaped blue eyes raised to Kismet and sharpened with recognition. "Kismet!"

Kismet squinted, then her eyes widened. She flew down the staircase and embraced Stefan tightly. "Lilith," she said with a chuckle. "I almost didn't recognize you with your hair so long. It's so good to see you."

Stefan grinned, pulling away. "It's been a long time. Where's Bay?"

Kismet glanced over her shoulder at us as if Bay had magically shown up without her noticing. "He's, uh, on assignment right now. He should be back soon." Her gaze fell to the wolf, and she stiffened. "What—Stefan, who's this?"

"This is my mother, Isabel," Stefan said, rubbing the back of his neck. His eyes darted around at the shocked and confused gazes of his welcome party.

"Stefan, you can't bring her here," Kismet said through clenched teeth. Isabel released a low growl.

Then, I remembered what Bay had said: Stefan's father had been killed, and Stefan's werewolf mother had vanished. Had she killed his father?

Fear coursed through me, swirling in a sickening spiral within my chest. In an instant, I felt Oliver's presence behind me. His scent and warmth soothed my terror. I reached a hand behind me, and he laced his fingers through mine. I closed my eyes, and he squeezed my hand.

"Can we come in?" Stefan asked. "I promise I'll explain everything."

Kismet's eyes tightened, but she looked past him to Elias.

Elias waved a hand. "Oh, sure. But stay on the back porch, please. I don't want wolf hair all over my carpet."

A few minutes later, we all gathered on Elias's

fine patio furniture with candles burning between us and insects chirping through the screen. I sat nestled against Oliver's side in a love seat. We weren't holding hands, but we were close enough to leave my skin burning. I smelled something soapy mingled with his grassy scent, which meant he'd showered. I swallowed, not daring to turn my face to look at him. *There are more important things to focus on right now.*

Stefan sat in a chair with Isabel curled up at his feet. Her sharp, dark eyes were vigilant like she was his protector.

Stefan blew air through his lips. "Lilith, where to start? I, uh, grew up with Bay as my Familiar. Both my parents are—were demons. I tried my hand at light magic, but the separation from them . . ." He trailed off, his eyes closing. "I couldn't bear it."

In a way, I could sympathize with him. I'd almost turned dark, cutting myself off from the connection to my parents forever. If the situation were reversed, I wasn't sure I'd want to switch to light magic either.

"But I caused some trouble with Levarret's demons," he went on. "One day I was doing my homework, and someone knocked me out. When I woke, I found my father murdered. My mother had vanished. I assumed she'd been taken captive. For years I lived on the run, trying to hide from Levarret. But I found Mom a few weeks ago. Or rather, *she* found *me*.

"She had been working with Levarret, as everyone suspected, but as a double agent. The night my father died, he'd figured out who I really was. That I wasn't really his son. And he threatened to tell Levarret. Dad fought Mom, and she killed him in self-defense. Then, fearing he'd already told others, she left a trail to lure Levarret and his followers away from me. Only it didn't work as well as she'd hoped. Levarret's guys still managed to track me down."

Kismet raised a hand to stop him. "'Who you really were'? What does that mean? Jack wasn't your father?"

Stefan shook his head, his expression grim. "No." His face paled, and he swallowed. "The news is still fresh to me, and it, uh . . ." He shook his head again, looking so ill I almost looked around for a bucket to hand him. "It hurts to say it aloud."

"You're Levarret's son," Oliver whispered gravely.

The air froze around us. Even the insects quieted for a full beat, highlighting the intensity of the moment.

Stefan's eyes flew to Oliver, and a dozen emotions crossed his face: surprise, gratitude, fear, and . . . confirmation.

My hand flew to my mouth. My blood chilled. Levarret's son. *Matthias's* son.

Stefan and Oliver were half-brothers. Separated by almost a century.

I looked at Oliver. His jaw hardened, his eyes blazing. He knew exactly what Stefan was going through. The disgust. The horror. The pain in acknowledging the monster who was his father.

"Merciful Lilith," Kismet breathed, her eyes wide. She stared at Isabel in accusation. "How?"

"She can't speak," Stefan said with an apologetic grimace.

"I know," Kismet snapped, waving a hand. "I just don't understand it. She was Levarret's lover?"

Stefan nodded, still looking ill. "Their relationship was off and on. Dad—or, Jack—entered the mix soon after Mom ended things with Levarret. It was supposedly a mutual break-up. Mom says that Levarret claimed he was bored with her, and she was frightened of him enough to realize they had no future together. He didn't hunt her or wish her harm, so she was able to keep her position on the Council and everything. She married Dad, and he believed her when she claimed the baby was his.

"I never noticed." Stefan shook his head, his expression crumpling. "When I tried light magic, I felt cut off . . . but it was only from my mom. I never shared a connection with Dad—with Jack. I just thought they were somehow the same. Like the connection I felt through her was shared by him too.

"After Dad found out and was killed, Mom rejoined Levarret and was questioned about me. Levarret *knew*. He knew I was out there somewhere. Mom claimed that I'd attacked her and that she feared for her life. She didn't know where I was, but she swore to help him find me so we could be reunited as a family. Her goal was to give Levarret false information in his search for me."

Stefan ran a hand down his face, suddenly looking exhausted. "All those demons who found me, who made it so I had to change my name and relocate over and over—they weren't hunting me down. They were trying to bring me to Levarret. So we could have some kind of sick father-son reunion." His mouth twisted in a grimace. "And eventually, Mom's cover was blown. He figured out she'd been lying to him. I think something changed when he Ascended to the Fourth Tier. He can sense lies now, or at least that's what Mom says." He shuddered. "Knowing I was in danger, she found me, and we tracked you all to your hideout and then to this place. Mom says she smelled Bay here."

I stiffened and looked at Kismet, who shook her head. "We come here often. It's possible his scent has lingered from a previous visit."

I looked at Isabel in curiosity. Her eyes were closed

as Stefan scratched behind her ears. I didn't know much about werewolves, but I knew their condition differed depending on how they were bitten. Some were stuck in werewolf form all the time, and others only shifted with the moon's rising. Judging by Stefan's story, I assumed his mother was the latter.

"What does Levarret want with you?" Oliver asked, his voice sharp.

Stefan blinked. "I don't know. Maybe he wants me to join him?"

Suspicion sharpened Oliver's eyes, and his nostrils flared. I knew what he was thinking: Matthias wasn't sentimental. He'd almost sacrificed Oliver to give himself power.

Matthias didn't care about reuniting with his lost son. Which meant Stefan had some kind of value to him.

I looked at Oliver with a question in my eyes. He shook his head ever so slightly. He didn't want to tell Stefan they had the same father. At least not yet.

"What about Kyle?" Kismet asked, leaning forward to rest her forearms on her knees.

"He's safe," Stefan said. "He's my half-brother. Mom sent him overseas to live with Dad's second cousin. As far as we know, Levarret hasn't found him or even sent anyone looking for him. Whatever Levarret knows about me, he knows Kyle's not important to him."

"How old is Kyle?" I asked quietly.

"Fifteen."

I swallowed. His entire family had been torn apart. Stefan's too. And they were both so young.

"So why do you need to see Bay?" Kismet asked.

"Oh, right," Stefan said with a quick shake of his head. His red hair flopped over one eye. "I know you two were looking into some kind of . . . research between auras and a link between two souls. Well, Mom heard Levarret speaking with one of his men about a spell of blood and bone. A spell that could undo him."

Oliver stiffened next to me, and I felt recognition and alarm floating along our blood oath. "Lilith. I know what spell you're talking about! I came across it when we searched through the Grimoire. A spell to . . . to . . ." He snapped his fingers.

My eyes widened. "A spell to awaken a soul." We'd passed right over that spell because it hadn't mentioned necromancy or banishing someone who couldn't be killed. "It's to commune with lost spirits or something like that. You need blood or bone of the victim's descendants and ancestors."

"That's the one." Stefan pointed his finger at us.

"How can that spell undo him?" Teddy spoke at last, crossing his arms as he leaned against a wooden beam of the patio.

"I don't know," Stefan said. "Levarret caught Mom eavesdropping after that. She thinks that's what made him originally suspect her. A few days later, she had to flee."

My heart racing, I glanced at Oliver. Our eyes were alight with the same energy. *We know what spell it is.*

We just needed a Grimoire. Or perhaps access to Elias's research. If the spell involved the soul, an aurologist would most certainly have information about it.

"That's why he wants you," Oliver said, his eyes darkening. "Because with your blood, someone can defeat him."

"He wants to *kill* me?" Stefan asked, horrified.

Join the club, I thought.

"If he has no progeny, then no one can defeat him," Oliver said grimly.

Which means Oliver is a target too. I squeezed his hand next to me.

"It doesn't matter," Kismet said sharply.

I stilled, my eyes shifting to her. Indignation roared within me, and I stared at her through lowered brows. "What do you mean, 'it doesn't matter'?"

Kismet stood, determination blazing in her eyes. "I mean, we stick with the plan. This doesn't change anything."

I jumped to my feet too. "What plan?"

"We go to the Council and reveal Matthias's plan in hopes they will enact protection protocols for the other magical beings."

"Who's Matthias?" Stefan asked blankly.

"We can't risk *everything* on this sliver of hope that the Council will listen to us raving about something they have no reason to believe!" I cried. "Things are different now! We know he is actively hunting Stefan and—" I cut myself off, clamping my mouth shut. I dropped my hand, realizing I'd subconsciously gestured to Oliver beside me.

"Why is he hunting you?" Stefan's wide eyes moved to Oliver.

I sucked in a breath. Before I could speak, Oliver said, "I'm his son too."

Cameron gasped, and Gina's eyes grew wide. Teddy's jaw hardened as he stared at Kismet as if accusing her of keeping this a secret.

"Lilith," Stefan breathed, his face paling. "When—how old are you?"

Oliver chuckled without humor. "Nineteen. But, uh, I'm not really—it happened—"

I almost snorted. What was he supposed to say? *I was born over a hundred years ago, so don't worry about who my mother is.*

"I already said it doesn't *matter*," Kismet snapped. "We're not pursuing this."

"Why not?" I snapped.

"Because it won't *work*."

A hushed silence fell between us. Something within me deflated, but still I persisted. "How do you know?"

"We still don't know why he was pulled to this time," Kismet said, rubbing her forehead. "If he *is* connected to someone else's soul, that connection could save him. We don't have time to hunt down every person he's been in touch with since he cast that spell in Manila. Now's our chance to act. If we can convince the Council to side with us, we can stop him *before* he summons Asmodeus. But if we waste time running around on this wild goose chase, and he manages to summon the Demon Master, then all our work will be for nothing!"

The atmosphere rang with her words. My pulse roared in my ears, and my fingers clenched into fists. I wanted to yell back at her. I wanted to scream, *If all we do is delay him, he'll keep trying until he succeeds! We have to end* him! But I knew the clock was ticking. The immediate action would be to stop him *now* to buy ourselves more time to banish him later.

Suddenly, a loud cawing sound echoed through the manor. I stiffened, my gaze shifting to the house. Then, the cawing multiplied, layering sound after sound until it was a piercing screech penetrating through the air. An endless, shrill alarm.

We all covered our ears and shouted incoherently at each other. I read the shock in Kismet's face, the confusion in Teddy's, and the panic in Oliver's.

Then, Elias arrived at the doorway to the living room and waved his hand, indicating that we should follow him. Our ears still covered, we filed back into the house and toward the front door. Teddy and Kismet dropped their hands to draw their weapons. Oliver laced his arm through mine, and though a part of me irritably thought, *I can take care of myself,* another part of me was grateful for his warm presence next to me.

Apprehension pounded a rhythmic beat in my chest, hammering against my ears. When we reached the front door, Elias threw it open, and I sucked in a sharp gasp.

A crowd of at least fifty people were frozen in mid-air, their bodies highlighted by Elias's blue magic as they tried to move toward us.

CHAPTER 18

"LILITH," ELIAS BREATHED, HIS FACE PALE. THEN HE chuckled nervously. "Good to know my wards are intact in case an army attacks."

"We go out together," Kismet said, her fierce eyes shifting to each one of us. Though it sounded like a command, the look in her eyes gave us the option to refuse.

Slowly, we all nodded. I stared numbly at the crowd of newcomers, and a small part of me registered relief that not one of them was a figure in flames. Though the last I'd seen of Matthias, he'd had no qualms about wearing his human form.

Oliver's fingers gripped mine tightly as we descended the stairs to the circle driveway, following the bobbing of Kismet's blond head in front of us.

Each step took an eternity. I kept waiting for the figures to break free of Elias's enchantment, but it held them steady as we approached.

Then Kismet burst into a run, sprinting away from us. My heart lurched in my chest. I stretched a hand to stop her but then froze when I saw who it was.

Bay.

He stood in front of the crowd, his shirt torn. Blood stained his arms and face, but his eyes were bright as they focused only on Kismet.

Kismet bounded into his arms. Though he couldn't embrace her, his face softened, and his brows pinched. Concern and relief mingled in his expression. Kismet half sobbed, half laughed into his shoulder.

"You're alive," she cried. "Thank Lilith, you're alive."

The rest of us caught up to Kismet, and Elias's wary gaze shifted to the frozen figures behind Bay. "Friends of yours?" he asked casually, though the tightness in his eyes betrayed his fear.

"Yes," Bay said, his voice unsteady. "They're with me."

Elias waved a hand. The blue glow of his magic vanished, releasing Bay and the crowd behind him. Bay relaxed, stretching his arms to gather Kismet against his chest. As I watched them embrace, these two people who were connected to me in such complicated ways, I felt nothing but gratitude. No unease. No discomfort seeing them together.

Perhaps it was when I fully committed to Oliver that I let go of Bay completely. Or perhaps I'd finally been convinced Bay wasn't as dark as I'd feared.

Whatever the reason, I'd moved past it. A small smile spread across my face as Bay and Kismet shared a passionate kiss.

Oliver cleared his throat next to me, obviously uncomfortable with this public display. I nudged his ribs and raised my eyebrows as if to say, *We've done a lot worse.*

A blush bloomed across his cheeks.

"Where the hell have you been?" Kismet demanded when she drew away, shoving Bay's shoulders.

Bay stumbled backward and laughed. "Gathering reinforcements." He gestured behind him. His comrades were mostly men who had dark hair and angular eyes like Bay. Filipinos. I was inexplicably reminded of the Filipino rebels fighting in Manila back in 1899.

Here I was, about to face another war side by side with descendants of the same people I'd fought alongside over a hundred years ago.

"What?" Kismet said. "I don't understand."

"All my connections in Manila came through. I called

in favors and rallied those who'd been on the sidelines all these years."

Kismet shook her head, speechless.

Bay laughed again. "What did you think I was doing when I traveled overseas so frequently?"

Kismet shrugged. "Research? I never dreamed all those people you'd reached out to would show up *here* in person!"

"Indeed," Elias said stiffly. "A warning might have been nice."

Bay grimaced. "Sorry. I worried sending word would be too dangerous if Matthias intercepted it."

Elias waved a hand, rolling his eyes. "Don't worry about it. I have the space, though some of you may have to share a room."

As soon as I heard Kismet excitedly telling Bay how we now had a big enough force to stand against the Council, I slipped away from the crowd to find Elias. I knew I didn't have much time. Kismet had to catch Bay up with the chaos of Stefan and Isabel, but it wouldn't be long before the rebels would assemble and gear up to leave for the Council.

I started with the closed door that Megan had

knocked on when Stefan arrived. I rapped quietly on the door a few times, biting my lip in anticipation.

"Yes, yes, come in," muttered a distracted voice from the other side.

I opened the door to a room surrounded by towering shelves, file cabinets, computers, boxes of papers and books, and a small sofa bed in the back corner. A wide window bathed the room in moonlight. Elias was crouched in front of a small laptop, his gray hair sticking up at odd ends.

"Oh. Desiree." He straightened. "I thought you were Megan. What can I do for you?"

"Megan mentioned that you had research on various spells," I said, my heart thrumming nervously in my chest. "I was wondering if I could look through what you have."

Elias offered a tired smile, stretching his hand toward the cluttered mess around us. "Help yourself. What spell in particular?"

"A spell to awaken a soul."

Elias stiffened, his shoulders squaring. His hands hovered over his keyboard. Then, he turned to face me, his eyes alight. "That's an interesting spell. What do you intend to use it for?" His tone was conversational, but his eyes were guarded.

I swallowed. "To banish Matthias."

Recognition flared in his eyes. "And how do you know this spell can achieve that?"

I hesitated. I couldn't exactly tell him I'd been communicating with a Seer from the nineteenth century. "I don't know for sure. That's why I was hoping to find more information about it."

Elias stroked his chin, watching me with a mixture of amusement and curiosity. I bristled under his scrutiny, feeling like I was being tested somehow.

I must've passed the test because he clapped his hands and bounded forward, grinning eagerly. "The fascinating thing about this spell is the translation," he said, digging through boxes and opening file cabinet drawers. "The word *awaken* comes from the Latin word *resurget*, which actually translates more literally to *rise*. The more devout witches of the time named the spell in relation to one rising to the heavens—sending a soul heavenward to its maker."

My eyes widened. "Witches believed in heaven?"

Elias shrugged one shoulder, still feverishly flipping through pages and folders. "Some did. Some believed that all practitioners of magic, whether they practiced light or dark magic, were God's chosen ones and would inevitably rest with Him in the afterlife. No matter their deeds on Earth." He wrinkled his nose.

"So . . . whoever wrote this spell believed a man like

Matthias would end up in heaven," I said, my tone flat. *If that's true, I'd rather go to Hell.*

Elias scoffed and waved his hand. "Pay them no mind, Desi. It's the translation error that points us in the right direction. Ah!" He withdrew a thick manila folder and bustled over to me as eagerly as a child on Christmas morning.

"This is all the research I've gathered on the spell over the years," he said, heaving the thick folder onto a desk. Dust puffed up from underneath the folder, and he coughed, waving a hand in front of his face. "You're lucky this spell is so connected to souls and auras; otherwise, I might not have anything on it at all!"

I smiled uncertainly. Luck had nothing to do with it. I was learning more and more that everything was connected. Though it hurt my head to think of *how* everything was connected, I knew there was some mysterious force at work pulling together the threads of these events until we were all stitched in one eternal quilt.

Perhaps there *was* a God out there orchestrating all this. Though I felt less comfortable believing in a deity than in a collection of spirits from the great beyond, guiding and directing my path.

Mom and Dad. I certainly hoped they were involved in this.

Before Elias could open the folder, a gentle knock sounded at the door.

"Sorry, sir," came Megan's soft voice, "but you're needed in the parlor. Kismet and Bayani have something urgent to discuss with you."

Damn. If they needed to talk to Elias urgently, then that meant my time was almost up. I looked pleadingly at Elias, whose expression filled with equal disappointment. He heaved a sigh, glancing from the folder to Megan and then to me.

"Desi, you're welcome to take this and study it," he said, carefully placing the thick folder into my hands. "Please take care, though. Years of research have gone into it."

I nodded eagerly, tracing my fingers along the dusty surface of the folder. "Thank you, Elias." My voice cracked, and something stirred in Elias's eyes. He offered a thin-lipped smile and squeezed my shoulder before ushering me out of his office and locking the door behind us.

I hauled the folder into my room and plopped down on the elegant carpet, exhaling slowly. When I dumped the contents onto the floor, my eyes widened. It looked like at least a hundred pages.

Blowing air through my lips, I started leafing through the pages, searching for something helpful. My eyes glossed over phrases like *Latin translation,* and *connection to auras,* and *different with light and dark magic.* Elias seemed to dissect every part of the spell between how it affected First and Second Tier demons to how the communion of one's soul with another was achieved. As far as I could see, his notes were focused more on communicating with those beyond the grave— not *sending* someone to the grave.

My eyes started to itch, and exhaustion tugged at my body. How long had it been since I'd slept?

A light knock sounded at the door. "Come in," I said, distracted.

Oliver poked his head in, frowning when he found me on the floor. "What are you doing?"

"Uh, looking through Elias's research," I said, looking back to the papers. "Do you need something?"

When Oliver hesitated, I looked back up at him. His cheeks flamed, and his eyes darted to the floor. He rubbed the back of his neck. "I . . . wanted to apologize. For—for how inappropriate I was earlier. I never should have—have come into your room with you. And I should've stopped us before—" He faltered, closing his eyes, his face full of shame.

I stood, heart racing. "No, Oliver, *I'm* sorry. You told me before that you didn't want to—you know—before marriage, and I shouldn't have pushed you. I'm sorry." I wrung my hands together.

"Desi, no! You have nothing to apologize for. I was— I would've—" He stopped, but desire blazed in his eyes, and I understood him perfectly. He would've gone all the way.

"I would have too," I said.

Oliver's mouth opened and closed. Then he said weakly, "Why?"

I frowned, cocking my head at him. "What do you mean? Because I love you."

Fire burned in his eyes. He strode closer to me, grasping my fingers in his. "I love hearing you say that," he whispered, pressing his lips against my fingers.

A shiver of pleasure rippled through me from the feel of his soft lips against my skin.

"I love you too, Desi," Oliver said. "But what I don't understand is that if you love me and want to make love to me, then why—why don't you want to marry me?" His brows creased. "Is it because of my bloodline? Because you'll be joining yourself to the son of a demon?"

I smiled and pressed my hand against his cheek. Light stubble tickled my fingers. "No. Of course not. I just—" I shook my head. What argument did I have? For

Oliver and the customs he was used to, it made perfect sense for us to marry.

So why was I faltering at the prospect? I was nearly nineteen. Though I was young, I knew I'd never look at another man the way I looked at him.

So why do you hesitate, Desi?

I exhaled a puff of air in exasperation. I couldn't find the words. I couldn't think straight. So instead I stood on my tiptoes and brought my lips to his. He uttered a small noise of confusion but cupped my face in his hand, his mouth moving slowly and tenderly with mine.

"I don't know," I finally whispered when we pulled away. "There's so much uncertainty right now. I—I want to, Oliver. I do. I just have to sort through my thoughts and figure things out. Can we wait until we're settled? Until we find our place in this time, and Matthias is gone, and we can focus on us?" I gestured between us and rested my hand against his chest, feeling his rapid heartbeat.

Oliver nodded, his eyes sympathetic. "Yes. Of course." His eyes crinkled with his warm smile, and I felt understanding and agreement flowing through our blood oath.

Relief blossomed through me. Every time we talked about marriage, it usually ended with one of us hurt or confused. For once, it was nice to have a mature conversation where we both disagreed but came to a resolution together.

We're fracking bona fide adults now. The thought frightened me.

"I could use your help," I said, glancing at the open bedroom door.

Half his mouth quirked up in a knowing smile. "Doing something scandalous, are we?"

I shoved his shoulder and gave him my best "come hither" look. "Don't tempt me."

He snorted, but a blush crept into his face again.

My smile faded. "I know Kismet explicitly told me not to, but I've been researching Alba's spell."

Oliver sobered too. "Are you sure that's a good idea? Shouldn't we be helping everyone prepare?"

"This *is* helping them prepare. Look, if I find this spell and if we can't convince the Council, we'll need a back-up plan anyway."

Oliver's mouth pressed into a thin line, but he nodded. "All right. I'll help." But his eyes tightened, filling with an unreadable emotion that pulled at his expression.

Sensing his uncertainty along our blood oath, I raised my eyebrows. "What is it?"

He shook his head. "Nothing."

"Oliver, *tell* me."

He sighed, gazing toward the window. "It's just—you have this mission. This goal. And I envy that." He exhaled. "Lately, it's been really hard for me, feeling so purposeless. Before, I held a leadership position on the Council, and I was a corporal in the army on the path to becoming a sergeant. I—I had a mission. A calling. I followed orders and gave orders. But now?" Oliver shook his head. "Now, I'm floundering like a fish out of water. I have no idea where I'm going or what to do. I just feel . . . lost." He ended with a helpless shrug.

My heart cracked and throbbed, wounded by the devastation in his face. *It's all my fault.* I gently stroked his hair. "Well, if you were still on the Council—still a corporal—what would you do right now?" I gestured to Elias's files.

He looked at me, eyes wide and eyebrows drawn together. "If confronting the Council would provide us with more reinforcements, then we focus on that. Stopping Matthias from summoning Asmodeus would win a battle for us." He gestured to the papers on the floor. "This will help us win the war. And it will go much faster once we have the time and the men to work the task along with you." His lips pinched, almost apologetically. "Focus on one battle at a time."

My heart plummeted. I thought about arguing. But what did I know about warfare? Oliver and Kismet had better instincts than I did. Besides, the last time I'd felt certain about what to do to stop Matthias, I had almost become a dark witch. I suppressed a shudder. I didn't want to go down that path again.

Reading the conflict in my face, Oliver rubbed my cheek with the back of his hand. "Desi, if this is important to you, I'll drop everything and work on it with you."

I shook my head. "If I were your subordinate, what would you tell me to do?"

Something warred in his eyes, and he grimaced. "I'd tell you to follow orders."

I stiffened. *Even if those orders involved shooting unarmed Filipino rebels as they fled a burning building?*

As soon as I thought it, regret swarmed within me. That hadn't been his fault. Not entirely. So I nodded, swallowing down my retort. "You're right. Of course you're right. Kismet needs me right now."

Shoving down the burning curiosity in my chest, I exhaled and slid Elias's extensive research under the sofa and out of sight.

CHAPTER 19

FOR THE NEXT FEW HOURS, I HELPED STRENGTHEN ELIAS'S wards and cast cloaking and protection spells on the rebels. It wouldn't protect us from a direct blow, but if we were ambushed, it was our best bet.

Discomfort wriggled in my stomach when I thought of Elias's manuscript of notes waiting for me in my room. But every time I thought about it, I squashed the thought, reminding myself that I couldn't trust my instincts anymore. Kismet had years of experience with Matthias. She knew the best route to take.

And I trusted Oliver with my life. If he were my commanding officer, I would follow him straight into battle.

So I obeyed orders. I helped clean and distribute weapons, rehearsed the plan with my comrades, and relayed information between groups. Since there were so many of us, we agreed that only a handful of us should approach the Council in case they were hostile. If the Council received us, the second group, led by Bay's friend Raul, would join us to serve as witnesses in our case against Matthias.

Kismet handed out enchanted silver dollars to those of us who didn't have one. If Raul's group, Group B, didn't receive a communication from our group, Group A, within half an hour, they were to assume the worst. Kismet gave explicit orders that Group B should immediately withdraw to Elias's manor—as well as any of us in Group A who could get away. But I noticed a few furtive looks between Cameron, José, and Gina that indicated they wouldn't follow orders—they would try to rescue us. Seeing that determined glint in Cameron and José's eyes made my heart swell. I couldn't believe how far they'd come.

Per Kismet's orders, once the meeting was over, I collapsed in bed for an hour or two to regain my strength. Much too soon, someone gently shook me awake. The sun shone in my eyes through the window, and I mumbled incoherently, stumbling into a fresh set of clothes, and loaded my weapons in their holsters. I glanced sleepily at my reflection in the mirror. My long curls resembled more of a shoulder-length mane than anything flattering. Though it was a relief to wear jeans and sneakers, my tank top almost made me feel naked.

I lived in the nineteenth century for far too long.

But as I stared at the uncertainty in my eyes, I realized I hadn't spent *enough* time in the nineteenth century. I wanted to go back, to live there for longer than just a year. That was where I felt I belonged.

I tied my hair back into a ponytail and sighed heavily before emerging from my room.

The crowd of rebels had gathered in the foyer, murmuring gravely to one another. Thick tension filled the air, swarming around me like the stifling humidity of Cuba.

My eyes immediately found Oliver, and I weaved through the crowd to get to him. Before I could, a small hand gripped my wrist.

"Desi," Megan whispered, guiding me to the hallway away from the crowd. "I wanted to give you something." She pressed a black cuff into my hand.

My eyes widened as I inspected it. The cool metal felt soothing against my warm skin, and it thrummed with magic. Something deep within me palpitated in response to its energy. "Megan, is this—?"

"It isn't one of Mr. Caldwell's," Megan said with an apologetic grimace. "He was busy working on cuffs for the Jumpers. This one is something I fashioned myself using his research. I've been fiddling with the technology for a year now and finally made a breakthrough."

I remembered what Megan had said about the cuff she worn—that it was linked to her soul and enhanced her abilities as a Pusher like me. I swallowed, my chest burning. "Megan, I—I don't know what to say. You didn't have to do this."

"You don't have to wear it if you don't want to. There might be some kinks and glitches I still have to work out. Plus, I haven't been able to conduct a thorough study on the subject—uh, *you*. But I kept thinking about you and your desire for an outlet, and . . . I don't know, I thought it would help if you had something connected to your aura." She shrugged. Her dimples ignited with her shy smile.

"No, this is perfect. Of course I'll wear it. We'll need all the help we can get." I wrapped my arms around her, hugging her tightly. My eyes felt warm. I couldn't believe this girl, this *stranger*, had been thoughtful enough to make something like this for me. "Thank you. So much."

Megan drew away, her lips tightening. "Be careful, Desi." She squeezed my arm and disappeared down the hallway.

The cuff in my hand throbbed like it had a soul of its own. Slowly, I slid it onto my wrist. A burst of energy and awareness coursed through me. My insides bonded to something otherworldly, my body now tethered to the world beyond and the souls that awaited me. I saw my parents' faces, Manuel, Alba, and Elena. A deep presence hummed in my chest, a power source finally switching on after remaining dormant for all these years.

I inhaled a sharp gasp. Tears pricked my eyes, though I had no idea why. I sensed Oliver behind me before I saw him.

"Are you all right?" he asked.

I swallowed, wiping my cheeks and turning to him with a smile. "Yes. You?"

He scanned my body, his eyes lingering for a second too long on my bare shoulders. I resisted the urge to cover myself with my arms. "I'll be fine when this is all over."

I took his hand. "It will be. Soon." My chest burned with more certainty than I'd ever felt. *It'll be over soon. And we can focus on our future.*

José rubbed his hands together eagerly and said, "Who's up first?" I noticed a black cuff wrapped around his wrist that was identical to mine. Of course he'd be wearing one of Elias's special cuffs. He had the toughest job of all: Porting all of us to our destination.

Bay lifted a hand and said, "Aldo is a Jumper as

well." He gestured to a skinny, middle-aged man, who nodded politely. He, too, wore a black cuff on his wrist.

"Each Jumper can take three passengers," Kismet said loudly. "They will take you two blocks away from the Council's headquarters. Group A, wait for the rest of our party to show up before you go inside. After that, Group B, you'll know what to do."

Several rebels shifted around, some muttering hastily to each other. Many wore fierce, determined expressions. Some, like Cameron, even looked excited.

Not a single person looked afraid. Every pair of eyes blazed, alight with the knowledge that this cause was worth fighting for. Worth dying for.

Did I believe that?

I looked at Oliver. That same fire burned in his eyes too.

Perhaps I believed in this cause enough to lose my own life. But not enough to lose Oliver's. If I had to choose between stopping Matthias and saving Oliver, I knew which one I'd pick.

I squeezed his hand, and his hard green eyes fixed on me, softening slightly at the concern in my expression.

"We stick together, right?" I whispered

Oliver smiled. "I swear I won't leave your side, *dulzura.*"

Warmth spread through my chest, and I nodded. *We can do this.*

José grabbed Cameron, Gina, and another rebel by the arms and Ported with a small *pop*. The other Teleporter, Aldo, did the same. Several tense minutes passed as José and Aldo popped in and out, in and out. Magic rippled in the air like a warm breeze, tickling my nose until I sneezed. I clasped Oliver's hand tightly in mine, my palm coated with sweat. He didn't seem to mind. We didn't look at each other, but we stayed close enough for our arms to touch, our bodies straight and stiff. Just his warmth next to me kept my knees from buckling.

We can do this.

At long last, José, his face pale and sweaty, stretched his hands toward me and Oliver. Despite his fatigue, he still managed to wiggle his eyebrows and offer a smirk, which I ignored.

Oliver and I looped our arms through his, and with a *pop*, we vanished. We appeared in front of a street corner I recognized. Across the street was the small bookstore I'd arrived in over a week ago, just moments after Matthias had cast the time travel spell.

That feels like months ago. It seemed like I was a completely different person now.

We hovered in the shadow of an alley between shops, squeezing up against the brick wall with the other rebels. Cameron winked at me, and Gina jerked up her chin by way of greeting. We wanted to keep the element of surprise on our side, so we had to stay hidden until we were all ready to barge into the Council. Kismet had kept reminding us: the goal was to provide an impressive number of witnesses *without* violence.

But I was doubtful. Deep down, I feared Matthias's ties were too strong within the Council. They wouldn't listen to us.

With my free hand, I fingered the cool metal of the cuff on my wrist. Electric energy surged through me, swelling within my chest. Power sparked just under my skin, waiting to burst out.

After the remaining rebels had Ported, Kismet and Bay healed José and the other Teleporter before signaling for Group A to proceed.

My hand still clutched Oliver's as I followed the crowd. We strode down the sidewalk, weaving through the throng of passersby, trying *not* to give away our intent to disrupt the corrupt bureaucracy of our magical world.

You know. Same old, same old.

Anxiety welled up in my throat as we approached a monstrous, glass building across from an almost identical building, both glittering in the sunlight. I couldn't even see the tops of the buildings—they seemed to pierce through the very sky.

Definitely not in North Grove anymore. Or Santiago.

I heard Oliver exhale next to me. I ran my thumb along his knuckles, hoping to reassure him.

Following Kismet's lead, we entered the building, ignoring the receptionist at the counter, who watched us with wide eyes. A second too late, the receptionist dialed frantically on her phone, but we'd already made it to the elevators.

Oliver and I filed into one elevator with Gina, Cameron, José, Kismet, Teddy, and a few of Bay's friends I didn't know. Bay and the others took another elevator.

Kismet waved her hand, and the same strange Venn Diagram symbol from my first visit appeared. She pushed the button, and the elevator shuddered with movement.

Oliver groaned slightly, his eyes closing. I knew he still wasn't used to this strange new technology. Even my own stomach churned from the motion.

Once we got to the right floor, the elevator doors finally split open, revealing several figures, one of whom I recognized: John Dickers, my interrogator. The one who was on Matthias's payroll. Men and women surrounded him, each wearing designer clothes that were probably paid for by Matthias's wallet and each wearing a stern scowl.

We rebels stepped out of the elevator, gathering in the lobby and facing off with the dozen or so members of the Council who were waiting to greet us.

"Really, Kismet?" asked the man in front—a tall, wiry fellow with smooth, white hair. "You come barging in here with an army?"

"Not an army," Kismet said, crossing her arms. "But witnesses who will testify to Levarret's plan to summon the Demon Master."

A few Council members behind the white-haired man shifted, eyes darting around.

"Surely, you don't expect us to believe these tales," John Dickers scoffed, adjusting his glasses on the bridge of his nose.

"He's Fourth Tier!" Kismet shouted angrily. "How does this not concern you all? No one should have that much power!"

"He's posed no threat to us," the white-haired man said. "He hasn't made any attack. But *you*, Kismet, have shown hostility toward the Council. It was unwise of you to show up here."

Just then, the elevator dinged behind us, and the rest of our group filed out, filling the space behind us. The white-haired man clenched his jaw, his eyes sweeping over the crowd as if counting how many of us the Council would have to fight.

"Councilman Burke, we have *proof*," Kismet hissed, stepping toward him.

The white-haired man—Councilman Burke—stiffened. "What proof?"

Kismet raised her wrist, revealing another cuff just like mine. "My soul is still tethered to Levarret's. This device will channel his thoughts, granting you access to the link I share with him."

My blood chilled. Every member of the Council in front of us froze, eyes wide and faces pale. Some looked terrified, and others looked deeply curious. It made me wonder how many people here actually *did* work for Matthias—and how many were just blind to what he really was.

Councilman Burke lifted his chin, his dark eyes sharpening. "Very well."

Kismet drew closer to him and offered her hand like a handshake. Oliver tensed next to me.

Councilman Burke clasped Kismet's hand in his. Then, his body lurched forward, his back arching and a frail moan escaping his lips. His arm quivered in Kismet's grasp. She closed her eyes, her brows pinching and her face taut. Beads of sweat formed on her forehead.

I sucked in a breath. My eyes found Bay as he moved closer to Kismet, pain flickering in his eyes.

If Burke's on Matthias's payroll, will this really matter? I wondered.

Of course it would. This was *proof*. Enough people were here with us to rally to our defense.

Then why did my insides tremble with trepidation?

Something wasn't right.

Oliver's hand shook in my grasp. I looked at him and found his face covered in sweat. His eyes were wide. Frantic.

"What is it?" I whispered.

"I don't—I don't have my powers," he said quietly.

I stilled. My eyes shifted to Kismet and Councilman Burke, their hands still locked and faces stiff. What were they seeing? Could they be snapped out of it?

I wiggled the fingers of my free hand. Something churned within me, but when I focused on it, I realized the feeling was foreign to me. It was from the cuff, not my abilities.

My breaths sharpened. With a slight movement, I flexed my fingers toward a vase on the table by the elevators.

Move, I willed it. *Tip over. Fall to the floor.*

Nothing happened.

Kismet cried out. Sparks erupted from the cuff on her wrist, and her body convulsed violently.

"Kismet!" Bay roared, moving toward her.

Shock stiffened me, lacing through my heart. I stepped forward to help Kismet, but Bay got to her first. Oliver clasped my hand tightly, and I went still, my heart thrumming madly in my chest.

Bay grabbed Kismet's free hand, his arms shaking when he made contact. His body seized, and he grunted, faltering a step in his effort to pull her away from Councilman Burke. In a flash, one of Bay's Filipino comrades was at his side, helping him drag Kismet away.

Councilman Burke's white hair stood straight up, but his face was smooth. Confident. He flicked his wrist as if shaking his hands free of dirt.

"You left me no choice, Kismet," he said in a strained voice. "He warned us that you were coming. He warned us of that lunatic Caldwell's tech and gave us measures to counteract it. It seems you weren't as fortunate."

Bay staggered toward the elevator, half his body limp and dragging on the floor. Several other rebels rushed to his aid, helping carry Kismet's unconscious form.

My heart lurched when I saw her. Smears of black soot covered her hands, and her hair was prickly and frizzed, fanning around her face like an ethereal mane.

I dropped Oliver's hand and unsheathed my athame. Several others next to me drew their weapons as well.

Councilman Burke chuckled. "Don't think you'll fight your way through. We're armed to the teeth with soldiers who can take you down in an instant. But if you come quietly, we can come to an arrangement."

Like hell. My gaze flicked over the expressions of my fellow rebels. I read the determination and fire in their eyes.

We would not go quietly.

Teddy shouted a fearsome battle cry and surged forward.

But before he reached anyone, before the Councilman could lift his hands to electrify one of us again, before I could fling my athame toward our enemies, a deep roaring sound outside stopped us.

It sounded like a low-flying plane. But then it grew louder. My ears throbbed from the thrumming of the engine.

Then, the building exploded around us.

CHAPTER 20

"Desi, we just want you to be prepared."

I stared wide-eyed at my parents' grim expressions. Even my Dad's usually warm, humorous eyes were taut. Afraid.

I clutched my teddy bear closer to my chest. Kismet ruffled her wings, bowing her feathery head.

"Prepared for what?" I asked in a hushed voice.

"This demon we've been hunting." Mom glanced briefly at Dad. "He's planning something terrible. And if he succeeds, our lives will change forever. If he succeeds, things will get bad. Really bad. We need you to promise that if that happens, you'll listen to us. No matter what. If we tell you to run, hide, or flee, you have to do it. Even if we tell you to flee with Kismet and leave us behind, you do it. Do you understand?"

My heart throbbed with fear, and my eyes burned at the thought of running from my parents. Weren't they supposed to keep me safe? Without them, what would I do? How would I protect myself? Kismet was only a human for one hour every day. I couldn't depend on her.

"Desi, it's important that you understand this," Dad said, leaning closer to me and tucking a stray curl behind my ear. "We don't know if this will happen. We hate to frighten you, but we want you to be ready."

I swallowed, my lower lip trembling. "This demon—can you stop him?"

Mom and Dad shared another glance. Even Kismet grew still as if waiting for their response.

"We hope so," Mom said at last. "He's strong, but we've faced demons like him before."

I took Mom's hand. "I believe in you. I know you can do this."

Mom's eyes warmed, shining with tears. "Thank you, sweetie."

"We feel stronger knowing you believe in us." Dad gathered both of us into his chest, pressing us together in a warm embrace.

Smoke tickled my nose. My head throbbed. I was so tired. So foggy. I didn't want to open my eyes.

More smoke poured into my face, choking me and suffocating me. Coughing, I shifted, but an explosion of pain darkened my vision. I lifted my hand to my head, and it came back moist with blood.

I couldn't see anything. The air around me was filled with . . . snow?

Snow in September?

I coughed again, tasting charcoal on my tongue.

Not snow. *Ash.*

Puffs of ash surrounded me like a dust storm. The air was so thick I could barely see my hand in front of my face. I spread my hands around me, trying to feel for something to indicate where I was. I couldn't remember what had happened. Teddy charging forward, the members of the Council ready for our attack, and then—

Something exploded. Something struck the building.

I waved a hand in front of my face, trying to clear the air. "Hello?" I croaked, my throat scratchy. "Can anyone hear me?"

A low moan resonated from a few feet away. *Oliver? Oh please, don't let him be dead. Please be alive!*

I tried to rise, but my leg buckled. Slices of fire rippled along my leg, nearly blinding me with anguish. I groaned, lowering to the floor again. I couldn't walk.

"Are you hurt?" I asked. "Who's there?"

Another moan, then a cough.

"It's me. It's Desi!" I shouted, my voice cracking. "Who are you?"

"Burke," grunted the voice. "Henry Burke."

I stilled. Councilman Burke. The man who was about to arrest us. The man who worked for Matthias.

Heat swelled around me. Sweat formed on my brow.

Flames. The building was on fire.

"Are you hurt, Desi?" Burke asked.

My heart lurched in my throat. This man shouldn't be concerned for me at all. He was my enemy—he worked for Matthias.

"Desi, are you hurt?" he asked again, sharper this time.

"I—yes. Yes, my leg. I can't walk."

"Is anyone else over there with you?"

I squinted through the smoke, trying to make out any shapes. My blood chilled when I found a pair of legs motionless nearby. *Lilith, no! Please don't be Oliver.* I squinted and scooted forward. The pain in my leg blinded me momentarily.

Whoever it was wore ballet flats and a pencil skirt. It was a woman's legs. A sliver of relief wormed through me, followed immediately by shame and grief. "Yes," I said numbly. "At least one other person. She—she isn't moving."

"Can you crawl, Desi?"

I shook my head. "I—I don't know. I can't see!"

I lifted my hands, wondering if I could Push the smoke away. I froze. Nothing happened. Faint magic flickered within me from my cuff, but my powers were gone.

"My magic, it's not working!" I shrieked, tears spilling down my face.

"I know. Mine isn't either."

I inhaled a shuddering breath filled with dust and coughed again. "What?"

"Something happened to all of us moments before the explosion. I felt it. Something siphoned our powers. Shutting them off. Like some kind of cloaking spell."

How? Who would do that?

Matthias. He would. But he had allies in the Council. Would he really disarm them like that?

I wondered if he had anything to do with this explosion. It wouldn't have been the first time. He'd caused a U.S. ship to explode in 1898, inciting the Spanish-American War—all so he could hide behind the mortals' battle while he waged his own.

"Can you move?" I asked.

Burke groaned again. "No. There's debris—a hunk of concrete on my leg. I've lost all feeling there. I won't make it out of here alive."

Something like regret climbed up my throat. Regret for this man who worked for Matthias?

I didn't know what to say.

Heat seared my face. Was the fire spreading?

We had to get out.

Gritting my teeth, I slid forward, wincing when my hands met jagged shards of glass. My leg pulsed, throbbing, but still I dragged myself forward, not sure which way I was going. For all I knew, I was heading toward a dead end.

But I was scooting away from the flames. Slowly, the heat subsided.

"Something exploded in the building," Burke said suddenly. He sounded farther away. I'd scooted in the opposite direction.

Which meant he was near the flames.

"What was it?" I asked.

"I don't know. A bomb maybe?"

My mouth felt numb. A bomb. How many had died from the explosion?

I had nothing to say, so I focused on scooting forward, my body trembling and my muscles throbbing.

A loud buzzing sound made me freeze. The buzzing deepened and intensified like some kind of motor. Then a deafening boom met my ears, and the ground beneath me quivered. I ducked my head and kept close to the floor, worried about toppling over and rolling onto debris. Chunks of concrete rained down from the ceiling. I covered my head, yelping as sharp rocks sprayed on me. Something heavy struck my elbow, and fresh pain blossomed from the injury.

A crash echoed nearby, and Burke cried out with a strangled sound.

"What? What happened?" My heart thrummed, and fear wracked through me.

"I don't—I don't know," Burke moaned. "Another bomb, I think. But . . . this can't be a coincidence." His voice sounded weak.

Horror spread through me, clutching at my heart and chest like sharp claws. This had Matthias written all over it. We had to get out now. Before another bomb went off.

I tried shifting. Prickles of pain shot through my arm. I blinked through the dust clouding the air and found a bloody gash on my elbow. I groaned, trying to sit up. "Are you hurt?"

"My body is . . . pinned down . . . I can't—" Burke choked off with a rattling gasp.

"Do you know what happened to the others?" I asked, still trying to slide along the floor. My hands pressed into more broken glass and shards of concrete, and I hissed.

"I heard—I heard screams." Burke's voice choked on sobs. "Some fell from the building to the streets below. I heard a few people on this floor too. Moaning. I couldn't tell who it was. But if there are others here, they're—they're gone."

Panic welled in my chest, almost as suffocating as the dust in the air. Oliver. Kismet.

Kismet had been unconscious when it happened.

Fire burned in my chest as I asked loudly, "What did you do to Kismet? When you took her hand?"

Burke moaned. I couldn't tell if it was from pain or regret. "Levarret gave us some kind of . . . interference. Some signal to disrupt the power from Caldwell's cuffs. It short-circuited."

"You electrocuted her?" I roared.

Burke sobbed again. "No. It was—it was only supposed to be a shock. He said it would only be a shock. I didn't know."

"I don't believe you."

"Please, Desi. I wouldn't lie to you. Not now, when I'm facing death. Levarret promised us he wouldn't harm us—or you. But he's the only one who knows the grand scheme. The only one who knows the horrors of what's happening here."

"What horrors?" I asked, my blood icing over at his words.

"He said—he said he'd been privy to some . . . attack. That his spies told him something would happen soon. He kept talking of a 'convenient interruption.' Something that would take care of the rebels for him."

I stilled. Bile crept up my throat. So he knew the building would be bombed?

"I didn't know it was *this*," Burke cried. "I didn't know he would just let us die along with you."

My stomach churned. Revulsion rippled through me. Though it was disturbing that Matthias would just leave his allies to die, it didn't surprise me.

"Fenrir," Burke said, his voice slurring.

"What?"

"Fenrir," he said, a bit louder. "The faerie. You need to know—" He broke off coughing

I blinked. Persephone's ancestor. "What about him?"

"He—he—Familiar." Burke gagged and wheezed. Flames crackled, and the smoke thickened in the air around me.

I scooted farther from him, but I had to know what he meant to tell me. "What about him?" I shouted.

"Familiar . . . Levarret . . ." Burke's voice faded. Then he fell silent.

I waited, desperate for more. What Familiar? Levarret was a Familiar? Or Fenrir?

But Burke didn't speak again. And deep down, I knew he was gone.

My throat filled with emotion. Tears stung my eyes. *It's just from the heat. From the smoke.*

But I knew better. Burke had just died. And I mourned his loss.

Weeping, I slid farther across the floor until my knee rammed into something sharp and solid. Crying out, I crumpled, reaching forward blindly with my hand until I met the jagged edges of something concrete. Something too heavy to move.

My head spun. It was getting harder to breathe. I lifted my shirt to cover my nose. It helped, but I still wasn't getting enough air.

I would pass out soon.

Skirting around the edges of the chunk of concrete, I clenched my teeth against the pain stabbing through my head, leg, and hands.

Keep going. Keep going.

The warmth from the flames subsided, and the smoke thinned. I coughed twice and shouted, "Hello? Is anyone there? Can you hear me?"

"Desi?" a faint voice called.

I coughed again. "Yes, it's me! Where are you?"

"Downstairs! I made it downstairs." It was a man. I couldn't tell who, though.

"Are you by the stairwell?" I called.

"Yes. But I can't—I can't Jump, Desi. I can't get you out."

José. I hated myself for it, but my heart sank. It wasn't Oliver.

Shaking the thought away, I forced myself to feel relief. Relief that one of my friends was safe.

"Is anyone else there with you?" I shouted. My heart stopped for a full beat as I waited for his response.

"Yes. Gina and Kismet. One of Bay's guys is here too." José stopped, and a high-pitched wail filled the air. With a start, I realized it was him. He was crying. "Desi—Desi, Cameron's gone."

Ice filled my stomach. *Cameron's gone.* My friend. My friend was dead.

He hadn't mentioned Oliver. Or anyone else. What if they were gone too?

I bowed my head, caving in and succumbing to the terror and despair. Sobs poured from my mouth. I screamed and wept, my tears mingling with ash on my face. My head roared with agony. The pain was blinding, taking over my brain and pulsing in nauseating waves.

I would die here too. But if Oliver was gone, wasn't that a good thing? At least we'd be together.

"Desi." José's voice was broken with more sobs. "Desi, can you get to me? We can help you. I hear first responders. They're in the building, trying to get people out. Just—just climb down to us. You can do it." He faltered. He sounded weak and unconvinced, but I knew he didn't have much stamina left.

Neither did I. It would be impossible for me to climb down stairs I couldn't see, on a leg I couldn't move.

"Just come down here," José said again. "Come to me, and—and as soon as my powers come back, I'll Jump. I'll get you out."

But neither of us had any idea when that would happen. Or *if* that would happen.

Blackness filled my brain. I slumped sideways, succumbing to the darkness.

"Desi?"

For the briefest moment, José's voice pulled me back. "José," I said weakly. "If you get out . . . if you see Oliver, tell him I'm sorry."

Then I blacked out.

CHAPTER 21

Desi.

Ugh, I thought. *Leave me alone. Let me sleep for ten more minutes.*

Desi, wake up! Now!

The urgency of the voice in my head startled me awake. A disorienting fog settled in my mind, beckoning me back to sleep. My head throbbed, and my body ached everywhere. Smoke filled my lungs. I took a breath and coughed, choking on ash.

Climb, Desi.

Climb *what?* I couldn't see anything through the smoke.

Magic flickered from within me. I faintly wiggled my fingers, but it wasn't *my* magic.

It was my cuff.

My eyes widened. Oliver? Kismet shared a blood oath with Matthias, and she'd used the cuff to see into his thoughts. Maybe my cuff was doing the same thing with Oliver. I'd heard his thoughts before, but each occurrence had been brief.

Suddenly alert, I scooted forward. *What do I climb?* I asked, desperate to hear the voice again.

There's a chunk of concrete a few feet away from you, the voice instructed. *You'll have to scale down it like you're rock climbing.*

With my mind an incoherent mess, I couldn't identify the voice. I couldn't even tell if it was male or female. In my head, it just sounded like *me*.

But it had to be Oliver. It had to be.

My brain exploded with pain as I shuffled forward and met a sharp, jagged edge. I hissed, gingerly reaching a hand forward to feel the sharp surface of the concrete.

That's it, the voice said. *Climb on top of it.*

I stilled. What if this was a trap? What if this was Matthias, luring me to my death?

I almost laughed. I'd die here anyway. I had nothing to lose.

So I climbed.

Agony flared in my leg, and I cried out.

"Desi?"

I ignored José's voice and scooted up onto the

concrete surface, gasping for breaths that wouldn't come. My head spun. My arms sagged with exhaustion.

Keep climbing, the voice instructed. *The concrete will lead you to the stairwell.*

Gritting my teeth, I slithered forward, trying to avoid moving my injured leg. But every shift of movement sent a burst of pain rippling through me, crumpling me and bringing me closer to the edge of blackness.

I can't give in, I thought. *If Oliver's alive, I have to get to him. I can't give in.*

I wriggled on my stomach across the concrete slab, stretching my hands forward to avoid objects that might skewer me. I dodged debris and rubble, following the voice that guided me and alerted me to where the edges of the concrete were so I wouldn't roll off it.

Stop, the voice said after I'd crawled for several tense minutes. Sweat poured down my neck. *Now turn around. Legs first, you'll drop from the concrete.*

I clenched my teeth, and tears rolled down my face. *I can't,* I thought. *I can't put weight on this leg. It'll end me. I know it will.*

Someone will be there to catch you. You have to trust me, Desi.

I swallowed back hysteria. My face was a sticky mess

of tears and soot. I nodded, though I knew the crazy voice in my head couldn't see me.

Lips pressed together, I shifted until I was facing toward the way I'd come. My eyes burned from the smoke. Heat tickled my skin, and I knew the flames were getting closer.

Closing my eyes, I slid my legs off the concrete. They hovered mid-air. The weightlessness sent panic through my chest. I was dangling off a cliff—off of nothingness. If I let go, I would fall into an unknown abyss.

Trust me, the voice said again.

"Okay," I whispered.

And I let go.

I was free-falling, plunging into darkness to my death. My stomach dropped, and my arms floated upward.

Then strong arms caught me, wrapping around my chest and cradling me. My leg seared briefly, but I opened my eyes, barely making out a muscular figure holding me.

Thank Lilith. It is *Oliver.*

I leaned my head back, too weak to even speak. My savior carried me, his arms swaying gently back and forth.

A strange scent tickled my nose.

I bolted upright. It was sandalwood. And raspberries.

No.

I tried squirming out of his grip, but Bay said, "Hold still, Desi. We're almost there."

"No," I croaked, coughing. "No! Where's Oliver?"

Bay hesitated. "I don't know."

"No," I said again, my chest constricting and my heart shuddering. *Where is he? Oliver, where are you?*

"Desi!" Kismet shouted.

And then I knew. It had been *her* voice I'd heard. *She'd* been guiding me.

Disappointment crashed through me. Of course. She was my Familiar. Our souls were bound. Of course the cuff would keep us connected.

I closed my eyes, searching inwardly for Oliver, for some faint emotion or feeling. Some evidence he was alive.

Our blood oath was silent. Frighteningly silent.

No, not just silent.

Empty. It was nothing but a void. I'd never felt anything like it since we'd performed the magic to bind ourselves together. Sometimes I'd felt silence when he slept or didn't feel much emotion. But never this throbbing absence, this gaping hole like a vital organ of mine had disintegrated into ash.

My mouth crumpled, opening wide in a silent scream. Sobs poured through me. I wept loudly, burying my face into my dusty hands I choked on more soot, but I didn't care. He was gone. *Gone.*

A hand pressed into my shoulder. If I'd had more strength, I would've knocked it away. I didn't want to feel anything. I didn't want anyone's comfort. I just wanted to black out again, to surrender to this nightmare.

Footsteps echoed, but I barely registered the sound.

"Can she walk?" An unfamiliar voice—one of Bay's friends perhaps.

"No," Bay said. "Are the stairs intact?"

"Somewhat. There are first responders in the stairwell, though. If you can make it part of the way, they can help you get her down."

"Good. Let's move."

"Oliver," I wheezed.

The others fell silent.

"Oliver," I said louder. "I'm not leaving without him."

More silence. Then Bay said, "Sorry, Desi. I'm not giving you a choice."

I tried shoving Bay's arm, but my limbs wouldn't move. Instead my head lolled backwards, my eyes closing.

Just take me, Death. Take me away from here.

Don't you dare, Kismet said in my head.

Fire roared in my chest at her intrusion. *Get out of my head!*

Kismet said nothing else.

I swayed in Bay's arms, and the motion sent ripples of pain shooting up and down my body. But I welcomed it. With each slice, burn, and ache, I felt closer to Oliver. The more pain I felt, the more I thought I might die and join him. There was still hope. Still a chance for us to be together.

Gradually, the smoke cleared. Though my lungs still rattled and throbbed, I could suck in cleaner gulps of air. Loud exclamations and shouts met my ears. Footsteps bustled. The warmth of other bodies pressed around me.

The next few minutes were a blur. I must have passed out again. Hands passed me along like a hot potato. I smelled something plastic and unfamiliar. Something sterile like rubbing alcohol. A small object was pressed against my face. I resisted at first until I realized it helped me breathe.

When I opened my eyes again, I was outside, squinting at the snow.

No. Still ash. Dust. Scraps of paper. The road was a sea of white and gray. People screamed and sobbed, their faces and clothes powder-white. Police officers and paramedics darted past me.

I closed my eyes again, searching once more for Oliver. *Are you there? Please, I'm begging you. Just give me some clue that you're alive.*

Nothing.

I wept again. My body was caked with soot, tears, and sweat. I felt like I wore a second skin with this nasty paste covering my entire body.

"My powers are back," José whispered in my ear. "I'm taking you back to Elias's now."

I frowned, shifting my fingers. Something familiar pulsed through me. My magic was back too. But how? Why?

Then a loud sound hissed behind me, followed by the crumbling of rocks. My wide eyes scanned the area and rested on the building we'd just exited. Plumes of inky black smoke poured from the top where the explosion had happened. Sections of the building collapsed like the tower was caving in on itself. Panicked shouts surrounded me. Ash and debris cascaded from the building.

The building was falling.

The tower crumbled like it was made of dust. My heart lurched in my throat as I watched unblinking, unable to look away. The horror of it all pierced right through my heart like an icy knife.

"We're getting out of here," José muttered.

A small *pop*, and the air whooshed around me.

We arrived on the porch of Elias's manor, though the image of the building crumbling was imprinted on my mind forever. The tower had seemed so impenetrable. So magnificent and grand and almost indestructible.

But it had just collapsed. Like it was nothing. Like the earth could swallow it whole in an instant.

Like it never existed.

My eyes watered, and I blinked to clear the moisture. Dizziness swept over me, and I staggered. Jose's arms caught me, but the blackness crept into my vision until it took over completely.

I woke up tucked in a bed. My sweaty hair clung to my forehead. I sat up slowly and noticed I was no longer covered in dirt and dust. My head prickled with a dull ache, but it was nothing I couldn't handle. Carefully, I tried moving my leg.

It was fine. Completely healed.

I blinked, squinting against the sunlight that streamed through the window. I was in fresh clothes. My hair, though sweaty, smelled like peach shampoo.

Who the hell bathed me?

My eyes raked around the room. *My* room. The guest room at Elias's house.

Then the pieces snapped together.

"Oliver!" I shouted, whipping the blanket off and

stumbling toward the door. My freshly healed leg ached slightly from the movement. "Oliver!"

The door opened before I could reach it. Kismet stared at me through red-rimmed eyes. She was dressed in clean clothes too, but she looked like she'd been crying for hours. Tears and snot covered her face.

My heart dropped like a stone.

She burst into tears and grabbed me in a tight embrace. My throat burned, and I closed my eyes against the agony of her sorrow.

"What happened?" I choked, trying to extract myself from her arms. "I heard something about . . . bombs going off?" The image of the building collapsing seared through my brain, and a fresh wave of horror lanced my heart.

Kismet shook her head. "No. Planes—planes struck the towers."

I stiffened, and a chill raced down my spine. *Planes.*

"They're saying it was a terrorist attack," Kismet said thickly, wiping her nose. "A plane hit the pentagon too."

Lilith. My eyes widened, my blood running cold. "Who did it? Are we—are we under attack?"

"I don't know. They're saying this was an act of war, but nothing has been decided yet."

"How many of us got out?" I whispered.

"Bay, José, Paolo, Gina, Teddy, and Julio."

My brow furrowed as I tried picturing each person's face. I didn't know Paolo or Julio; they must've been Bay's friends from Manila.

Kismet exhaled a shaky breath. "All of Raul's guys are fine. They were in Group B and were outside when—when it happened."

I waited to hear more—to hear Oliver's name—but that was it. That was all who'd survived.

Something in me broke. Shattered. My strength left me, and I teetered. Kismet caught my arms, but I still fell, my mind receding somewhere far away to the blackest of holes.

Oliver was dead.

CHAPTER 22

THE NEXT FEW DAYS WERE A GRAY BLUR OF TORMENT. People popped in and out of my room to check on me, but I barely spoke. Barely ate. Barely moved. I was lifeless; simply existing.

The numbness—the raw, gaping abyss in my chest—took me back to six years ago when I'd lost my parents. The throbbing agony mingled with the void of depression. The loneliness. The anger, guilt, and disbelief.

My mind was a torrent of shattering emotions that I was powerless to control.

After the first day, I shed no more tears. My body was dried up, shriveled to nothing more than dust.

My fault. My fault. The words pulsed through me like a rhythm, a song I couldn't escape. It was my fault Oliver was gone. I brought him here to this time because of my connection to Kismet. I fought to keep him here even when John Dickers suggested Oliver be sent back to his own time.

Oliver was here because he pledged to stand by me.

I should've let him go. Should've let him marry Gwen. He would've been safe. He would've lived a full life and had children and grandchildren.

José came to my room often. He sat by my bed and said nothing, his broken gaze fixed on the window or the carpet. Sometimes, he read a book to himself. Sometimes, he wept quietly. His visits ranged from twenty minutes to a few hours, but we never spoke.

For some reason, I preferred his company over anyone else's. The others were constantly trying to *fix* me. To get me out of bed. To get me moving and eating. It pissed me off.

But José—he knew what I endured. He endured it too. He lost friends. Friends like Cameron. And perhaps he needed to escape from the others too and commiserate with me. Be numb with me.

I vaguely wondered what he did when he wasn't with me. Did *he* eat and exercise and do other productive things? Or was he a lethargic mess, confined to his room like me?

But I was never curious enough to ask.

At one point, an unfamiliar woman entered my room

after knocking politely. I didn't answer, of course. Anytime someone knocked, I always hoped that my silence would encourage them to leave.

It never worked.

This woman had graying burgundy hair that fell just past her shoulders. Her wide-set blue eyes were rimmed with yellow. A werewolf.

She offered a tentative smile, seating herself in the armchair next to my bed. "I'm Isabel. It's nice to meet you in person, Desi."

I blinked sleepily at her. Isabel. Of course. Stefan's mother. I'd only seen her in wolf form. For a moment, guilt spread through me. I hadn't even bothered to ask about Stefan and his mother and how they fared during all this. But the guilt left me almost instantly as the depression within me swallowed it up.

"I can't pretend to imagine what you're going through," Isabel whispered, her eyes shining. "And I realize we don't know each other, so it's hardly my place."

Yeah, I thought bitterly. *So leave me alone.*

"But I killed my husband. The love of my life."

I stilled at that, my heart stopping for a full beat.

"The man I loved more than anything in the world," Isabel said in a strained voice, "tried to kill me for keeping something from him." She sucked in a shaky breath. "And I had to choose: my life or his."

I swallowed, my eyes warming. If I'd been in her situation, I would've easily chosen to end my own life first.

"I know what you're thinking," Isabel said, dropping her gaze to her thin fingers clasped on her lap. "You would give your life for his. This devastation is too much to bear. I felt the same in every way but one: my son. I knew that if Jack had succeeded in ending my life, then he would've done the same to Stefan. Jack's anger and horror at what I'd done and who I'd been with, the monster he thought lived under his roof . . ." She trailed off, shaking her head. "It took over everything else. Any love he had for us was overpowered by his hatred and fear. He feared Levarret above all others. Feared his retribution and feared him finding out and thinking Jack had something to do with hiding Stefan's true identity."

Isabel sighed and leaned forward, her moist, blue eyes widening, her expression clearing. "You're young, Desi. I don't want to disregard your emotions. I know this is probably the most powerful grief you've ever known."

I didn't know if she was right. I was so much younger when I'd lost my parents, and that pain had dulled to a bearable ache. Perhaps it had been stronger back then. Perhaps it was the same.

"But you still have a life. You may not have a child yet, but perhaps you will someday. One day you'll have someone to care for as I do. It might not be a child of your own—perhaps a student or a niece or nephew. But people *need* you, Desi. And even if you don't know them yet, you have to be strong. You have to carry on—for them."

She didn't wait for my response. With another sad smile, she stood, wiping a tear from her cheek before she left the room.

I remained motionless under the covers, staring blankly at the chair she'd occupied. She was right; I didn't understand right now. I couldn't possibly fathom the idea that I had to get out of bed to go care for some child I'd never met before.

All her words did was remind me of my parents. And how they *hadn't* chosen to live for me. They'd given that up. They'd made the opposite choice, putting my fate into my own hands. Leaving me alone.

I knew it wasn't fair, but at that moment, I hated Isabel. She'd unknowingly reopened that wound.

I lost track of the days. Sometimes I slept, but my dreams were plagued with visions of Oliver's lifeless and empty gaze, his body sprawled among the debris. I often woke in the night with tears on my face and couldn't get back to sleep. I dreamt of my parents too. Their screams. Matthias's laughter. It was like everything I'd tried to squash from my thoughts, every haunting fear or memory, came flooding back to me in my weakest state.

I couldn't stop the dreams.

Dad stroked my cheek, and I stirred awake, blinking sleepily at him. "What time is it?"

He smiled, and his eyes crinkled. "Early. I thought you might want to get a head start."

"A head start on what?"

"Our hike! Did you forget?"

I rubbed my eyes, thinking. Then my face broke into a grin. "Oh! Yes, let's go! Now!"

Dad laughed as I flew out of bed and hunted for my best outdoor clothes. All I'd wanted to do was go camping with Dad. He suggested we start with a hike. I was secretly hoping he'd already packed our overnight things in the car and would agree to camp tonight if the hike went well.

I was determined to impress him with my endurance. I was going to dominate this hike.

"There's that look," Dad said when I emerged, dressed and ready to go.

"What look?"

"There's fire in your eyes. When you get like that, you're unstoppable, Desi."

My eyes opened, finding Kismet sitting next to my bed. Fresh tears poured down her face.

I didn't need this. Not now.

Wiping tears from my own face, I turned away from her and squinted against the sun pouring through the window.

"You don't have to talk," Kismet whispered. "Just listen."

I blinked at the window, waiting. *Just get on with it. Whatever lecture you want to dump on me.*

Kismet cleared her throat. "I . . . haven't told anyone this. It's extremely private, and lives depend on it, so please—please keep it to yourself."

I grew very still. My breaths sharpened, and my brain buzzed. *What has she been hiding?*

Kismet hesitated for a long moment. I almost turned around to face her again, but then she spoke. "I got pregnant last year."

My eyes widened, and my heart lurched in my throat. I whipped around to look at her, my chest churning with more energy than I'd felt in days. "What?" I croaked.

Kismet nodded, her gaze fixed on the floor. "It wasn't long after you left. Maybe a few months. Bay and I had just gotten together and left North Grove." She paused, her eyes closing as she cried softly.

She lost the baby, I thought, horrified.

Kismet shook her head as if reading my thoughts. "It's not what you think," she said, sniffing. "I, uh, I had the baby. A b-beautiful little girl. My darling angel." Her voice raised in pitch, practically a squeak as she sobbed again, covering her face.

My eyes burned with more tears. I didn't want to cry, dammit. I swallowed, but emotion lodged in my throat, burning through me.

"I-I feared for her life," Kismet went on. "Feared what would happen to her if Matthias found out. When I started showing, I went away. Told the rebels I was going overseas to r-reach out to some connections. Bay helped me with my cover story, constantly telling the rebels how I was doing and what country I was in. All the while, I stayed locked in our apartment with the lights off, keeping up the appearance that no one was home."

Kismet paused and wiped her nose. "Bay wanted me to leave, to stay with someone, but I had no one to turn to. And I didn't want to leave him. We had to be together on this. Him and me.

"After I had my baby, Bay told the rebels he was joining me in Manila, and we stayed home with our child for a few weeks. Bay stayed up with her in the nights, cuddling her. We both knew it was temporary, so we drank in every moment."

Kismet's face crumpled again as more tears poured down her face. My pillow was moist with my own tears. I closed my eyes, trying to block out the grief in my heart for her.

"When she was a f-few months old, we gave her to C-Cameron's mom. Even Cameron didn't know about it. His mom swore to protect our baby girl and even signed a blood contract to prove her loyalty."

Kismet sucked in a deep, shuddering breath. I opened my eyes to look at her. Something huge filled the space between us. Something tense. Monumental.

There was more to this story.

I held my breath, waiting.

"I lied to you," Kismet whispered. "And I'm so sorry. With Oliver, I didn't know . . . I couldn't be sure. It was my baby girl, you know? I had to take every precaution, and he—he was Matthias's *son*. I'm so sorry I didn't trust him, Desi."

My head throbbed when she mentioned Oliver's name. Agony coursed through me in waves, threatening to drown me. Instead I focused on something else she'd said. "Lied to me how?"

"I told you that I summoned you here. To this time.

That wasn't entirely true." She paused. "The day you arrived in New York City was the day I gave my baby up."

I frowned, not quite comprehending. Then my eyes widened as I remembered what she'd said to me about the bond between us: *the time travel spell sensed the greatest point of weakness along the bond.*

So I arrived in Santiago in 1898 when Matthias had enslaved her. And then I arrived in New York City in 2001 after she gave up her child to someone else.

"That was when you were weakest," I breathed.

Kismet nodded, weeping again. "It felt like cleaving my soul in two. Like someone had torn off a limb or stolen a vital organ. It felt worse than when I lost Richard all those years ago. Even worse than when I became Matthias's slave. It's completely altered me. My magic hasn't been the same. I haven't been able to perform even the simplest spells." She shook her head, wiping her face again. "Desi, I wouldn't wish this pain on anyone. But I had to tell you the truth. That's why you were brought here. I didn't—didn't know. I didn't realize my grief was strong enough to pull you here. But once it did, I started to hope." She looked at me, her eyes alight with something unreadable. "I started to hope for a better world for my baby. With you and Oliver here, with the rebels growing, I thought we actually stood a chance against Matthias. A chance to defeat him once and for all. And then my daughter could live without fear. She could have a safe and normal life."

I couldn't breathe. I just stared at her, shock numbing my entire body.

"I don't want to put this on you, Desi," she said, sniffing. "I don't want to burden you with my sorrow when you have so much of your own. But I figured you deserved the truth. You deserved to know why you were brought here. You deserved to know that it was *my* fault Oliver—" She broke off, her eyes closing again. "I'm so sorry," she whispered. "So sorry."

I closed my eyes too as more tears trickled down my face. *It's not your fault. It's mine.* I wanted to say the words, but I didn't have the strength.

Kismet had a daughter. A baby girl. With Bay.

Perhaps the baby had Bay's dark skin. And Kismet's blue eyes. I was certain she was beautiful.

"I-I'd love to meet her," I said in a strained voice. "If you'll let me."

Kismet covered her mouth, her moist eyes crinkling as she half laughed and half sobbed. Then she leaned forward, grasping my hand and squeezing it. "I would love that more than anything." She hesitated before saying slowly, "Desi, if anything should happen to me and Bay, we both agreed that we want you to raise her."

I blanched, sitting up so fast my head spun. "What? *Me?*"

Kismet's eyes widened, and a hysterical laugh burst from her lips. "Yes, *you.*"

I shook my head. "No. I can't! I can't raise a kid! Hell, I can't even take care of myself!"

Kismet raised both hands and shushed me gently. "Relax, Desi. It's only a hypothetical. We've had to take every precaution, and we've both considered the fact that we might lose our lives in this fight with Matthias. Cameron's mother isn't exactly young. She can't do this long-term."

I continued shaking my head like a bobblehead.

"You don't have to answer right away. Just . . . remember that Bay and I don't have any family here. Our daughter will go into the foster care system if we can't raise her."

My head stopped shaking. *Foster care.*

She would be an orphan.

Then Isabel's words came back to me: *One day you'll have someone to care for as I do. People need you, Desi. And even if you don't know them yet, you have to be strong. You have to carry on—for them.*

My mouth felt dry. I couldn't speak.

"Just think about it," Kismet said, rising from her

seat. "Take your time processing all this. And I hope and pray that someday you'll forgive me."

Her footsteps were quiet as she slipped out of the room, leaving me sitting in bed with my mind a scrambled mess of emotion.

CHAPTER 23

SOMETIME JUST AFTER DAWN, MY GROWLING STOMACH urged me out of bed. My chest still throbbed with numb agony, and my mind spun with images of Oliver, Kismet, and a generic baby girl's face. But my body ached to move. To do something.

It was a huge relief. But it also devastated me. It felt like I was moving on from Oliver's death—that I'd accepted it.

Knowing that most of the house was still asleep, I crept quietly down the stairs and poked my head into the kitchen. Empty.

Sighing with relief, I strode in, my bare feet slapping quietly on the polished tile. I made a sandwich and sat at the bar, munching quietly and staring determinedly at the stainless steel fridge doors as I tried to drown my thoughts in the mundane.

Soft footsteps jolted me off the bar stool. I swallowed the last bite of my sandwich and started to leave, not wanting to talk to anyone just yet, but I froze when Megan emerged from the hall. She was wearing her headphones again, which blared some rock music that I could hear from across the room. She hummed absently until her eyes found mine. Her face paled, and she hastily removed her headphones.

"Desi!" she breathed, eyes wide. She fumbled with something in her pocket, and the music turned off. "I didn't think anyone was up yet."

I shrugged one shoulder, rubbing my arms. I really just wanted to get back to my room.

To my dismay, Megan set her MP3 player and headset down on the bar and approached me, pressing her lips together. "I heard what happened. It's so terrible. Too terrible for words. I'm so sorry."

I nodded. Warmth stung my eyes, and I swallowed.

Megan's gaze fell to the black cuff still wrapped around my wrist. She took my hand, her eyes lighting up. "How did this work for you?"

I smiled, grateful for the change in subject. "It saved my life. Thank you."

Megan beamed. "Really? I'm so glad!" Her smile faded. "But—how? The others said their magic wasn't working. That someone had cloaked the building, cutting off their powers."

I nodded, rubbing a thumb along the cool, metal surface of the cuff. I hadn't had the heart to take it off. I kept hoping Oliver's voice would creep through, strengthened by the magic within the cuff. Like Kismet's had.

"I'm not sure how it works," I said. "But I heard Kismet's voice. It must've been the bond we share." I closed my eyes. "It was the strangest thing, though. For a moment I thought it was *his* voice. Oliver's." His name caught on my throat, choking me.

Megan frowned. "Oliver? Why would it be Oliver's voice?"

I cocked my head. "Our blood oath. It's only happened once or twice, but sometimes I could hear him speaking to me through—" I stopped.

Megan's face had completely drained of color. She dropped my hand, her eyes wide as saucers. Her mouth grew very small.

Panic raced through me. "Megan, what's wrong?"

Her mouth opened and closed. She looked like she might pass out. "I—I'm so sorry, Desi. I didn't know about the blood oath."

I shook my head, confused. "It's fine, Megan."

"No, it isn't." She darted away from me and toward

the armchair she usually occupied by the bar. A thick book was wedged between the cushions. She removed it and feverishly flipped through pages, muttering to herself. "This is why we conduct a thorough study of our subjects. I was so stupid, thinking I could manage this in such a short amount of time." For a moment, her gaze lifted to meet mine, her expression tormented. "I'm sorry for being so reckless, Desi. I never should've given it to you."

I slowly approached her. "Megan, what's going on? Why is this such a big deal?"

Before she could respond, I hissed in pain. Something hot seared through the pocket of my pants. My shaking fingers withdrew the silver dollar that glowed orange. It scorched my palm, and I dropped it on the counter with a clatter. Squinting, I leaned closer and watched the engravings on the coin shift until they resembled a series of numbers like coordinates.

Hasty footsteps drew my attention to the banister. I vaguely recognized Kismet's blond hair. Just behind her was José. They both darted to the front door.

My mouth fell open, alarm pulsing through me. Kismet grabbed her jacket, and her eyes found mine, widening in surprise. "I, uh." She gestured vaguely to the front door. "Someone needs our help. Be right back."

José didn't even look at us as they rushed out the

door. From the other side, I heard a faint *pop* from the Teleportation.

A small nagging in my gut made me feel guilty for not volunteering to help. But Kismet knew best. She and José could handle it.

Frowning, I turned back to Megan. Her gaze had dropped to the page she'd opened to, and her finger slid along the page. "Here it is. Come here, I can fix your cuff."

"Why does it need fixing?"

Megan rubbed her forehead with a shaky hand. "I only took into account your bond with Kismet. I didn't realize there was anything else tethered to your aura. The cuff enhances certain connections within you. But if it isn't calibrated for those specific connections, it can block them out completely."

Something thrummed in my chest, roaring in my ears. A rushing sound filled me like the flow of a waterfall.

"May I?" Megan asked, reaching for my hand.

Numbly, I stretched my hand toward her. I couldn't think. Couldn't breathe. What was wrong with me? My body seized as if reacting to some kind of danger I didn't know about.

The tip of Megan's tongue stuck out as she concentrated on releasing the cuff from my wrist.

It popped open, and my body sagged from its absence. The steady hum of power within me faded. I hadn't even realized it had been there. Like a constant companion. Suddenly, I wanted to go to sleep again.

But then, something blared in my head, loud and incessant, as if I'd taken earplugs out of my ears.

Desi, a voice whispered in my head.

My heart stopped.

Desi! Are you there?

I staggered backward, my breaths ragged as they ripped through me. Sobs poured from my lips. I covered my mouth with my hand.

"What's wrong?" Megan asked.

Ignoring her, I turned and sprinted for the front door, nearly ripping it from its hinges in my haste.

Desi, I feel you. You're alive. Thank Lilith you're alive. Oliver's voice in my head strengthened when I reached the porch. His essence resonated within me like a beacon.

Oliver, I'm here! I'm coming!

Following his emotions along our blood oath, I flew down the stairs and raced down the driveway, weaving through Elias's fancy cars. I kept running, my tangled curls flying and my bare arms prickling from the chilly air. My heart thundered in my chest, pulsing so powerfully I thought it would burst from my body.

Wind whipped at my face, combining with my tears to burn my eyes. *Please, please, please.* Oliver's presence roared within me, growing louder and more intense as my legs pushed on and on. *Almost there.* I could practically feel him. Where was he?

"Over here!" a voice shouted.

My wide eyes scanned the forest surrounding Elias's home until I found three figures approaching. I hurried toward them, recognizing José, who was limping with Kismet's arm around him.

And next to them was Oliver.

CHAPTER 24

"Oliver!" I screamed, my throat burning. Frantic sobs burst from my lips.

Oliver was dressed in an oversized, white T-shirt and baggy jeans. His arm was in a sling, but his eyes locked onto mine as he started running too.

All I could do was cry. My face was a sticky mess of tears and snot. I finally reached him, slamming into his chest and wrapping my arms tightly around him. I buried my face in his shoulder, my tears soaking his shirt. His familiar grass and gunpowder scent filled my nose, mingled with something sterile and an odd tobacco smell. My fingers grabbed a fistful of his hair, nearly clawing at the back of his neck in an effort to fuse his body to mine so we would never be separated again.

"W-what happened?" I moaned, drawing back only a few inches to scrutinize him. Small cuts covered his face, and his eyes were bloodshot and red-rimmed, but otherwise he looked fine.

Torment and anguish filled his gaze as he stroked my hair with his good hand. "I thought—I thought you were dead," he croaked.

My mouth crumpled as I sobbed again. "*Me*? No, I—we couldn't find you! The blood oath . . ." I gazed at the marks left on my wrist from the cuff. My eyes closed.

Why the hell hadn't I just taken it off?

"I know. I couldn't sense you, either," Oliver whispered, pressing his forehead against mine. "Lilith, Desi. I—I can't believe you're here." His voice broke, his own eyes filling with tears. His expression looked so pitiful and devastated that I clutched his face in my hands. I brought my lips to his, peppering kisses all over his mouth and cheeks.

I would never be able to stop touching him. I would never let him out of my sight again.

Over Oliver's shoulder, I noticed José, whose face was pale and clammy. My eyes fell to the bloody gash on his leg. "What happened?" I asked.

"Demons were waiting for us, trying to attack Oliver," Kismet said, helping José hobble forward. "Thank Lilith we were able to Jump at all. José couldn't get us all the way to the door, but he still got us out alive." She cast a grateful look in José's direction. José ignored her, his jaw tight and his eyes hard as they fixed on the manor ahead of us.

Reluctantly extricating myself from Oliver, I wrapped José's other arm around my shoulders and helped Kismet lead him to the front door. Teddy was already waiting for us with his medical kit, and he helped José into another room.

I turned to Kismet, breathless. I couldn't wipe the stupid grin from my face. "How—how did you find him?"

Oliver lifted his silver dollar. "Thanks to the exceptionally tight pants of your time, this stayed in my pocket during—" He stopped, his eyes darkening.

During the terrorist attack.

"What happened to you?" I whispered, touching his cheek. "Where did you go?"

Oliver shook his head, pocketing the coin again. "It was the strangest thing. I—I *fell* from the building. I was trapped under rubble, trying to break free, when the floor collapsed from underneath me. I couldn't use my magic, but when I fell, I didn't think. I lifted my hands and summoned a gust of wind to carry me, and it *worked.* I—I think it was just the *interior* of the building that was cloaked. In mid-air, I had access to my powers again." He swallowed. "Without my instincts, I'd probably be dead. I'm just glad my body reacted before my mind could catch up."

"Thank Lilith you've got killer reflexes," I said with a shaky laugh.

Oliver nodded absently. "My reaction time was still sloppy. I hit the ground hard. Some civilians found me and brought me to the hospital. They had to operate on my arm and kept talking about a loss of movement. I couldn't even lift my hand." Anguish flared in his eyes as he looked at me. "You don't know how many times I tried to get up and run back to you, Desi. I was prepared to dig through every piece of rubble to find you. But my arm . . ."

Regret climbed up my throat, and I squeezed the hand of his uninjured arm.

"The medicine of your time is incredible," Oliver said, his mouth lifting in a half-smile. "The surgery was successful, and they kept me for a bit longer to monitor me just in case. Then I sensed it. The magic in the air emanating from my coin. I followed the scent to my bloodied jeans in the hospital room. I think it was some kind of . . . alert?" He looked at Kismet for confirmation.

She nodded. "It emits a warning before it deactivates. If it isn't reunited with its owner, it shuts off as a safety precaution."

"Right. Well, thank you for adding that feature, Kismet. It saved me. I didn't know what to do. I had no idea where Elias's manor was or how to find it without a Teleporter. Once I found the coin, it took a few tries, but I figured out how to send the distress signal.

Then, just before Kismet and José arrived, a demon attacked me."

My blood chilled. "Matthias."

Oliver nodded. "He probably wasn't expecting me to be in a mortal hospital. But I'm certain once he found me, he figured taking me out would be an added bonus. Without me, that banishing spell is useless."

My stomach churned, my heart jolting with recognition. *That banishing spell.* The spell to defeat him. To end this horrible feud.

A faint voice echoed in my head. Councilman Burke's final words. *Fenrir. Familiar. Matthias.*

I opened my mouth to tell them about this, but Kismet spoke first. "We're relieved you're alive, Oliver." She rubbed his shoulder, her eyes finding mine. Remorse burned in her gaze, and I knew what she was trying to convey to me. *I'm sorry I doubted him.*

My lips pressed together in a thin smile. I wasn't sure if I forgave her—I wasn't even sure if I was angry with her. It was so hard to sort through my emotions. At the present, gratitude and sweet relief surged to the fore-front, overwhelming everything else.

I wasn't mad at her. At least not right now. I clasped her hand in mine before helping Oliver inside.

"Are you hungry?" I asked.

Oliver shook his head. "Just tired. I couldn't sleep for days." His expression hardened, and he squeezed my hand in his.

I knew what he was thinking. I hadn't slept much either, thinking he was dead.

"Let's get you to Teddy, and then you can sleep," I said.

"I'm really all right."

"You're in a sling, Oliver. It'll be better when your body isn't aching. You'll rest easier."

Oliver sighed but nodded, his expression resigned. I guided him into the dining area where a small crowd of rebels surrounded Teddy as he healed José. A few people grasped Oliver's uninjured arm or clapped him on the back, expressing their relief that he was alive. Oliver smiled weakly at each person, but I could tell he was exhausted and just wanted to be alone.

At long last, Teddy gestured for Oliver to join him on the couch. Oliver pulled me over with him, keeping my hand firmly gripped in his. I knelt on the floor by the sofa while he sat across from Teddy. Teddy closed his eyes, his hands hovering in front of Oliver's injured arm. He murmured a spell, and his hands glowed blue. Oliver stiffened and grunted, his hold on my fingers tightening. Then the glow faded, and Oliver exhaled, his body deflating.

Oliver flexed his arm, his eyebrows raised as he rolled his shoulder with ease. The sling fell from his arm. "Incredible. Thank you, Teddy."

Teddy smiled and nodded before rising from the sofa. I looked around at the rebels lingering nearby, their eyes eager as they no doubt awaited the miraculous tale of Oliver's survival.

I cleared my throat loudly. "Let's get you to bed." I gripped Oliver's elbow and helped him up. Though he didn't need my assistance anymore, we linked arms as we climbed the staircase to the bedrooms.

Oliver didn't object when I entered his room with him. When I closed his door, the strange tobacco scent emanated from him again. I wrinkled my nose. "Where did you get those clothes?"

Oliver chuckled wearily. "I had nowhere to go and no clean clothes. The hospital attendants brought me these from their Lost and Found." He sniffed his shoulder and grimaced. "It'll be nice to wear my own clothes again."

I laughed.

We stood there, facing each other. Heat churned between us. My breath lodged in my throat, making it hard to focus. His green eyes burned with pain and longing.

He stepped toward me. "Desi, I—" He stopped, his eyes closing. A single tear raced down his cheek.

My heart shattered, and I closed the gap between us, pressing my palms gently against his face. "I know. I'm so sorry. But I'm here—*you're* here. It's all over." I kissed him. His lips were salty with tears.

I meant to kiss him once and then pull back—to give him space to rest and recover—but then he crushed me against his chest, his lips moving urgently over mine. His hot breath tickled my mouth. Our kisses deepened, our mouths desperate, exploring everything—lips, teeth, and tongues. Like we wouldn't get another chance to. Like our lives depended on it.

A low moan rumbled from his throat, igniting fire within me. I pulled back, panting, my eyes closing as I rested my forehead against his.

"We're here," I whispered, brushing my fingers against his cheek. "We're safe."

We held each other for a moment, sharing breath. Sharing relief that we were here together. Alive.

"I should let you rest," I said, though I didn't pull away.

Oliver's hands tightened at my waist. "Please. Please, stay with me."

His eyes shone with need and painful desire.

Something powerful resonated within me, filling my bones and my muscles with a certainty I'd never known before. *I'll stay with you forever. Always and forever.*

Oliver stroked my hair out of my face. "I love you, Desi," he murmured. "I love you with my entire soul."

I looked up at him. "I love you too." Then that same surety churned through me, resonating like the clear chime of a bell. *I'm yours, Oliver. Always.*

I smiled. My chest felt weightless. My skin erupted with goosebumps. I knew exactly what I wanted.

Him. Forever.

I had no doubts. No uncertainties. No qualms with pledging myself to him. I knew what it felt like to lose him. To lose that chance to be with him.

I didn't want to waste another minute.

I opened my mouth to tell him but stopped at the sight of his bloodshot eyes. His face was worn and haggard, his body slack with exhaustion.

"I'll let you get changed," I whispered, turning away. We could talk later.

Oliver caught my arm.

Before he could protest, I said, "I promise I'll stay. I'll

just be over there averting my eyes." My lips twitched. "You know, like a proper lady."

Oliver laughed, his face brightening and his eyes crinkling. My cheeks warmed as I crossed the room, flopping down on the sofa and facing the window. The bright morning sun peered through the curtains. I closed my eyes against the comforting warmth, basking in the feeling of being at home. Oliver was here. We were here together. *This* was home.

"All right," Oliver said.

I stood and found him dressed in a T-shirt and sweatpants. The sight almost made me laugh. I'd never seen him dressed so casually before.

Well, that wasn't true. I'd seen him half-naked before.

I squashed that thought down before it set me on fire.

We looked at each other. An awkward silence filled the room.

"Are you . . ." I trailed off and gestured to the bed.

Oliver swallowed and nodded. Something stirred in his eyes. "Desi, I—I'm afraid that if I try to sleep, I—" He closed his eyes, his jaw tensing. "I was in a dark place when I thought you were dead. I'm scared I'll go back there. That I'll forget you're actually here."

Regret laced through me. I stepped toward him. "I'll stay with you. I won't leave. I'll be here the whole time, I promise." If anyone understood how it felt to suffer from horrific nightmares, it was me. I would want the same thing.

Oliver nodded, though his brows still creased. His eyes filled with such sorrow that my heart broke all over again. I wrapped my arms around him and buried my face in his shoulder. A low, satisfied sound rumbled from the back of his throat. "I could sleep just like this," he murmured.

I laughed, closing my eyes and relishing his familiar smell and his warmth. "Come here."

I tugged him toward the bed. I sat down, scooting over to the edge of the mattress to leave room for him.

Oliver's eyes widened, and a blush exploded across his face.

I raised my hands. "Completely innocent, I swear. I wouldn't—not now."

Oliver closed his mouth, then opened it again. He nodded, though his face was still red. Slowly, he slid into bed next to me, leaving several inches between us.

We lay like that for a long time, avoiding eye contact. After a while, I heard his breathing slow, so I scooted closer to him. His hand reached out for me, and I rolled into him so his arm was around me. Burying my nose in his chest, I curled up against him and placed a hand on his stomach.

I knew I wouldn't sleep much since I'd recently woken up. But this was heaven for me. I traced faint circles on his chest even after his deep breathing indicated that he'd fallen asleep. I peered up at him and found his face relaxed and his eyes closed. His expression was innocent and completely at ease. Nothing distressed him.

I didn't remember falling asleep, but hours later, I felt Oliver shifting next to me. He groaned and stretched, then rolled to face me, blinking sleepily.

I smiled, resting my head in the crook of my arm. "Good morning." I glanced at the window. "Uh. Afternoon maybe? Evening?"

Oliver chuckled. "This is quite scandalous, you know. Sharing a bed when we're not married." His voice was low and husky.

I laughed too. "Not yet at least." The words were out before I could stop them.

Oliver grew very still next to me. "What?"

I swallowed. "Nothing."

"What do you mean, 'not yet'?" Oliver propped his head up, his eyes wide as he stared at me. "Desi, do you —?" He stopped, his mouth clamping shut as he looked at me. Desperation burned in his gaze.

I sucked in a breath. "Oliver, I—I want this. *This*. To

share your bed, to share everything with you. I want to be your wife. If—if you still want me to."

Oliver stared at me for a long moment. Then, slowly, his eyes widened, his face splitting into the most heart-stopping smile I'd ever seen. His eyes crinkled, and pure delight gleamed in his face.

"I—I—are you sure?" he asked.

I nodded, grinning. I took both his hands in mine. "Oliver Gerrick—"

"No, no, stop right there," he growled, fixing me with a stern look that was overshadowed by his joy. It made me laugh again, watching him try to be serious when we both couldn't stop beaming. "You're not taking this opportunity away from me."

My mouth closed, but more giggles burst from me. I couldn't stop myself. I was giddy. Absolutely twitterpated.

Oliver climbed out of bed and circled around to my side before dropping down on one knee. I sat up, my heart lodging in my throat. He gazed up at me, his eyes brighter than the sun. For a moment, I just looked at him, drinking it all in: Oliver wearing baggy clothes, his face still haggard, his hair mussed, and his eyes lined with red but shining and brilliant.

It was the most beautiful thing I'd ever seen.

"Desiree Campbell, you are my life," he whispered,

his eyes glistening with tears. "My everything. I want nothing more than to be by your side for all eternity. I love you with all that I am. Will you"—he paused and swallowed—"Will you marry me?"

My heart throbbed at those words, my body pulsing with a resounding *yes*. This was right. This was perfection.

"Yes. Yes, I will."

CHAPTER 25

WE AGREED NOT TO TELL ANYONE WE WERE ENGAGED. AT least not yet. Everyone was still grieving. In a way, we were too. But knowing we'd be married soon shined a light amidst the darkness of the terrorist attack.

I watched Oliver's face harden as each of the rebels recounted what had happened to them in the towers. I recognized the flare of determination in his face when Kismet spoke of the Islamic extremist group who had hijacked the planes and targeted the U.S. Oliver was a soldier. He wanted to fight back.

Every time I saw that look, I took his hand. I had to remind him there were bigger things to focus on. Sure, if he enlisted in the army again, he would make a differ-ence and save lives. But he was crucial to stopping

Matthias from murdering hundreds, maybe even thousands of people.

I hadn't told Oliver of Kismet's baby. I would tell him eventually, but it didn't need to be right now.

But thinking of her baby—tucked away safely in North Grove with Cameron's mother—made my heart twist. I thought of my own parents and the anger I felt after their death, thinking they'd abandoned me and left me on my own. I couldn't imagine how Kismet's daughter would grow up. How that would shape her thoughts and affect her life.

After a few days of resting, recovering, and tending to our wounded, Kismet approached me. I was huddled on the couch, watching Megan tweak my cuff, while Oliver sat on the floor with his back against my legs.

Kismet cleared her throat, and Megan looked up, blushing. "I'm sorry! I'll just—" She hastily gathered up her textbooks, notes, and my unfinished cuff and bustled out of the room.

I almost insisted that she stay, but the grim set of Kismet's eyebrows and the tightness in her eyes stopped me.

"What's wrong?" I asked, sitting up straighter.

She glanced warily at Teddy, Gina, and José, who drank silently at the bar. José's eyes were red again.

"I think it's time we tried things your way," Kismet whispered.

I frowned at her for a moment. Then, my eyes widened.

She wants to try to banish Matthias.

I looked at Oliver, and understanding flashed in his gaze. He nodded at me.

"What happened to stopping him from summoning the Demon Master?" I asked quietly.

Kismet's eyes closed, regret crossing her features. "It's too late for that. We don't have the manpower to monitor every magical being. It's only a matter of time before Matthias coerces them to sacrifice themselves for his spell. We need to stop him. Permanently."

I nodded. "All right."

I stood and led Kismet and Oliver to my room. Reaching under the sofa, I withdrew Elias's dusty notes about the spell to banish Matthias.

Kismet's brows knitted together, but she said nothing when I pulled out the folder.

"I didn't get much opportunity to look through it," I admitted, glancing quickly at Oliver. "But this is everything Elias has regarding the spell."

"You found it?" Kismet breathed, trailing a finger along the worn papers as delicately as if they were an ancient artifact.

I nodded. "I think so."

"Then let's see what we can find," Kismet said, her eyes glowing with that fierce determination I knew so well.

Fearless Kismet was back.

Many of the rebels were too shell-shocked and traumatized to be of much use, but we gathered Teddy and Bay as well as two of Bay's friends—Raul and Paolo—to help us sort through Elias's research. Together, we spread the papers out on the floor of my bedroom, the atmosphere silent except for the rustling of paper and the occasional scribbling of pens.

It was exhausting. Elias examined the effects of the spell on every kind of magical creature. I had to leaf through notes on werewolves, shapeshifters, Nephilim, and witches before I finally found vampires. I shifted, my backside numb from sitting for so long, and a loose sheet of paper fell from my stack.

I froze when I looked at it.

The effects of the spell in regards to fae and fae-born.

My eyes widened, my heart lurching in my throat as I remembered Councilman Burke's warning: *Fenrir the faerie. Familiar. Matthias.*

I dropped my stack and snatched the loose sheet, my eyes frantically scanning over Elias's curly handwriting.

The fae have their own definition of things. Those

inducted into the beliefs and rituals of fae are known as "fae-born" and are treated with the same rites and respect as if they were biologically fae.

The souls of the fae are also bound in different ways. Mentors, teachers, instructors, and other educators share a bond with their students that links their souls together similar to that of a Familiar's Curse.

Essentially, a fae teacher imparts a sliver of his own soul upon his pupil, thus making the student fae-born. Those who are fae-born, regardless of what magical species they are, possess that mark on their aura. This spell will be more difficult to cast with those who are fae-born.

"Bay," I said quietly, not looking up from the paper. "What do you know about those who are fae-born?"

I felt the others around me grow still, watching me.

"Not much," Bay said, rubbing the back of his neck. "It didn't happen a lot in my time. Nowadays, many faeries still take on pupils and induct them into their society, but I don't know anyone that applies to."

My pulse roared in my ears. The pieces were sliding together, but I still couldn't put my finger on it. "And what do you know about Fenrir?"

He paused. "Fenrir—Persephone's ancestor? The one who worked with Matthias and Alastor? All I know is that Fenrir was famous among the fae. Known for his legacy of teaching other species the ways of the fae."

My heart thrummed in my chest, resonating as the answer gleamed like a beacon within me.

"Merciful Lilith," I whispered, my blood chilling.

"Desi, what's wrong?" Oliver asked.

My wide eyes snapped to Bay, who frowned at me. "Was Fenrir a Familiar?" I asked.

Silence. Then Kismet swore, covering her mouth with her hand.

"In a sense, yes," Bay said, still confused. "The Familiar's curse doesn't work the same way among the fae, though."

"But if he creates someone who's fae-born, doesn't that mark him in the same way the curse would? Doesn't that bind him to someone else in the same way?"

A chilling shock settled over the room. Bay's face paled. Oliver sucked in a sharp breath. Teddy's mouth fell open.

"Fenrir . . . was *Matthias's* mentor," Kismet said in a hushed voice. "Matthias is fae-born."

Bay's face turned a sickly shade of green. He looked like he might puke. "No. That's not possible."

"Fenrir was alive for hundreds of years," Kismet said. "He was alive when Matthias was *born*. If Matthias had the right connections, he could've been trained under Fenrir. It would explain the bond they shared and why

Persephone's entire line was bound to work for him against their will."

"We would've known," Oliver said, his brows furrowed. "Surely, we would've known! Fae smell different. They—they have different powers. Kismet, you and I worked alongside him. How could we not know?"

"*I* should've known," Bay growled. "I'm part fae!"

My eyes fell to the paper on my lap, searching for an answer within Elias's notes. "No, none of us could've known," I said. "It says here, 'Fae-born only retain their fae-given powers if they live among other faeries, though their souls are still marked as fae.' He obviously didn't live with the fae, so no one could've known unless they examined his soul."

"So—so his connection through time was Fenrir," Kismet said, her brows pinching and her face tight as she concentrated. "Fenrir's most vulnerable moment was most likely right before he died—when he and Alastor tried to summon Asmodeus. That was . . . 1980. Just before you were born, Desi."

A knot formed in my stomach, my head spinning as I tried to sort out the timeline. *Alastor, a demon High fae, rises to power with Fenrir helping him. Matthias time travels and joins them in 1980. They try—and fail—to summon Asmodeus, the demon lord of the underworld, who has an undead army at his disposal. Fenrir dies when their attempt fails. Alastor continues his dark reign until my parents banish him in 1991. Matthias takes up the mantle after that, killing my parents in 1995 and continuing the task of summoning Asmodeus.*

Lilith, it was all so confusing.

"What does this mean about the banishing spell?" Paolo asked in a low, rumbling voice. I wasn't sure I'd ever heard him speak before. His jet-black hair and brown skin matched Bay's, though his eyes were wider and his nose smaller.

"Hang on," I muttered, searching Elias's notes. "For the spell to be successful, one must account for the fae mentor as the subject's ancestor and supply their essence as part of the spell's ingredients. A fae-born is considered separated from his own family's bloodline and adopted into the fae line," I read.

"So . . . we need Fenrir's essence," Teddy said slowly.

"Or Persephone's," Kismet said, her blue eyes sharpening. "They share the same bloodline."

I remembered Kismet at my door, her outfit soaked in Persephone's blood. I pointed to her. "Do you still have your clothes from—from that night?"

Her eyes tightened. She nodded. "Yes, I think so. I'll go check." She dropped her stack of papers and left the room.

"I found something here," Raul said, swiping his long,

black hair out of his eyes. "'For banishing a magical being, if the subject has offspring, you must include their essence in the ingredients. The spell is not effective unless the subject's progeny is connected by blood. Specifically, the progeny and the subject must practice the same brand of magic.'"

I frowned, trying to make sense of Elias's words. "Brand of magic?" I repeated.

"Yes," Raul said. "Like light or dark magic."

So Matthias and his two sons would both have to practice dark magic so their blood is connected.

I remembered the realization I'd had in Manila when I decided to go dark and work with Bay: that I would've lost my connection to my parents by practicing dark magic. A family was connected by blood only if they practiced the same magic.

My heart lodged in my throat. A shiver brushed along my spine. My hand snatched Oliver's instinctively. "No."

"Desi," he whispered.

"*No*," I almost shouted. "You are not going dark. Not for him."

Bay shifted uncomfortably. "There are dark casters in this room, Desi. It's not a damnable offense."

"He's Matthias's *son*," I growled. "Being connected to that monster by blood? Can you imagine the risk?"

Bay's eyes darkened. "Yes, I can, actually. Stefan takes that risk *every day.* And he's fine. Oliver will be too. Stop mothering him, Desi. There's more at stake here than injuring your boyfriend."

I blinked, my head rearing back. *How can he say that?*

I glanced around at the others—hoping someone shared my indignation—only to find averted gazes and awkward fidgeting.

I swallowed. Even Oliver wouldn't meet my gaze, though I felt his thumb tracing circles along my knuckles as if to comfort me. Had I embarrassed him? The tension in the room told me I'd definitely embarrassed myself—probably both of us.

My eyes closed, chagrin warming my cheeks.

Raul cleared his throat. "That's not all I found." He glanced briefly at Oliver. "It's not good."

What the hell could be worse? I didn't dare voice it—I didn't want to jinx it.

Paolo took a breath and said, "'Exercise caution when including the essence of the subject's progeny. If the spell is used to banish another, the progeny is at risk as well.'"

I lifted a shaking hand to my mouth, my eyes closing to ward off the grief threatening to consume me.

So, in an attempt to defeat Matthias, we would be

risking Oliver and Stefan's lives as well. *I might lose him for real this time.*

"No," Bay said, his gaze firm. I knew he thought of Stefan. "There has to be a way to protect them."

"Here," Teddy said, his brow furrowed as he scanned a paper on his knee. "Blood magic can be used as protection for those involved in the spell," he read.

I exhaled in relief. "Well, that's perfect, then. Oliver and I share a blood oath."

Teddy shook his head. "No, it says here, they're only fully protected if they perform blood magic with someone of the same brand of magic. So that they're also connected by blood."

A hard lump formed in my throat. My voice strained, I said, "So hypothetically speaking, if we did this right, then Oliver would not only have to go dark, but he would have to bind himself to another demon to ensure he was protected when we cast the spell?"

Oliver's eyes met mine. He squeezed my hand.

If it means saving his life, I'll go dark for him, I vowed. *I'll go dark to solidify our blood oath. I don't care what it does to me.*

"Not necessarily," Teddy said, and my gaze snapped back to him. "It says here certain blood rituals may exceed the brand of magic."

"Like what?" I asked, breathless.

"Blood bonds, the blood rite of handfasting, and a blood sacrifice."

Blood bonds, I thought, frowning. Well, that was out of the question—that would mean Oliver or I would be enslaved and forced to do the other person's bidding.

Raul blew air through his lips. "A blood sacrifice is hardly an option. Won't that kill him?"

"Not always," Bay said. "Sometimes they survive."

I stiffened, thinking of the werewolf I'd sacrificed in Manila alongside Bay. We hadn't killed it, but it had surely died after I'd drained its magical essence. My memory turned to that night I'd watched Bay sacrifice the Second Tier vampire. Right after the ritual, he staked him. Even after losing his magic, the vampire had survived the ritual.

I swallowed and tasted bile. *No. Not an option. Not at all.*

"What is handfasting?" Oliver asked.

"It's a marriage rite performed by a high priestess," Teddy said.

My mind climbed out of the dark hole of who I was in Manila. Teddy's words echoed in my head, piercing through the hazy, panicked fog of my thoughts. Slowly, I turned to look at Oliver.

Time froze around us. Suddenly, it was just the two of us alone, sitting next to each other. Nothing else mattered. Our gazes locked. Heat churned between us, circulating like an electric current. I heard nothing but my own roaring pulse and felt nothing but his hand gripped in mine.

His eyes bore into mine, probing me with a question: *Do you want to?*

I knew what he was really asking: *Do you want to get married right away? Do you want to use our marriage as part of the spell instead of hosting a huge, glorious celebration once all this is over? Do you want to marry a dark warlock who might be overcome with bloodlust and follow in his father's footsteps?*

But I didn't care about any of that. I would plunge myself into the deepest abyss, curse myself with the darkest spell, and pledge myself to the unholiest of demons if it meant protecting Oliver.

"Let's do it," I whispered.

CHAPTER 26

"Do what?" Bay asked, eyes narrowed.

I stilled at the suspicion in his voice. Clearing my throat, I decided to change the subject. "What can Stefan do to protect himself?"

"Protect myself from what?"

We all turned to the doorway where Stefan stood, his red hair covering one eye. His brows furrowed at the six of us huddled on the floor like some weird study group.

My mouth opened, then clamped shut as I noticed Bay's eyes widen.

"Stefan, what are you doing here?" Bay asked.

Stefan rolled his eyes. "I kind of live here. At least for now. What are *you* doing? And why do you look so guilty?"

At that moment, I understood Stefan completely. All

those years of hating my parents and Kismet for trying to shelter me—for treating me like I couldn't protect myself. They might've had a point, but hiding things from me hadn't been the answer.

"He should be here," I said firmly, matching Bay's glare. "He's vital to what we're planning."

The others remained silent during my staring contest with Bay. Though my insides squirmed at the lethal glint in his eyes, I remained composed, staring him down.

At long last, Bay groaned, dropping his head. "Fine. Get in here, Stefan."

Stefan bounded forward eagerly like a dog and sat cross-legged next to Bay. While Bay filled him in, I looked at Oliver again. His eyes met mine as if my gaze pulled at him like a magnet. Warmth softened his face, and he squeezed my hand. A breathless excitement filled my chest, and his own anticipation floated along our blood oath.

We're getting married.

"That's easy," Stefan said, drawing my attention away from Oliver's smoldering eyes. "I've made a blood oath with my brother, Kyle."

My eyes widened. "W-what? Really?"

Stefan nodded. "We wanted a way to stay in touch in case of emergencies. To make sure we were all right without risking communication that Levarret can track."

I raised my eyebrows, impressed. That made a lot of sense.

"And Kyle's a dark warlock," Bay verified.

Stefan nodded, and Bay exhaled with relief.

"That just leaves you, Oliver," Teddy said, his eyes traveling from me to Oliver as if he knew something had passed between us.

My palms grew sweaty, and I chuckled nervously. I looked at Oliver. *Tell them now?*

He nodded.

"Do, uh, any of you know a high priestess?" I asked, unable to contain my grin. "Because Oliver and I would like to perform the rite of handfasting."

A stunned silence greeted my words. I'd expected an explosion of commotion and excitement, congratulations, and cheers.

Not this. Stony-faced shock. Horror.

My smile slid off my face. Uncertainty bubbled up inside me as I met Oliver's gaze. Darkness crept into his eyes, and I felt his doubt running through our blood oath. His panicked eyes said, *This is a mistake.*

Alarm fluttered in my chest. What was a mistake? Marrying me or announcing it to everyone?

"Be very careful about what you're doing, Desi,"

Teddy said slowly, his eyes blazing as he glanced between us. "This isn't some spontaneous Vegas wedding that can be annulled. Using a high priestess and performing the blood rite is more permanent than you think."

Oliver frowned, no doubt confused about the Vegas reference, but I stiffened and said, "Are you implying we haven't thought about this? That we're just deciding this on a whim?"

"That's exactly what he's implying," Bay said harshly. "Two seconds ago, you didn't even know what hand-fasting *was*."

"For your information," I said hotly, "Oliver and I got engaged a few nights ago. And it just so happens our marriage can protect him too. That's not a whim; that's just an added bonus."

"Then let me describe this 'added bonus' in terms you'll understand," Bay snarled, leaning forward, his black eyes flashing. "Oliver will be a demon. A bona fide demon, who's connected to his father by blood. You, in turn, will share this connection in your blood. You'll feel Matthias, Desi. You'll be connected to him."

I suppressed a shudder at his words and gestured to Stefan. "You just told me Stefan was bound to him by blood and he was fine! I don't see you making the same argument on behalf of him or his brother."

"A handfasting rite is different," Teddy said in a clipped tone. "A blood oath can be severed if you perform blood magic with another being. But a handfasting rite can only be broken if one of you dies. So if he turns on you and decides to join his father, Desi, you are still bound to him. You can't escape it. You will be chained to a monster forever."

"Desi," Oliver said weakly. The regret and doubt in his face was almost too much for me to bear.

"No." I sliced a hand through the air, cutting him off. My eyes turned back to Teddy. "I *love* him, Teddy. I'll be by his side through thick and thin, light and dark. I don't care about the risk. This will keep him safe."

"It would be better if he performed a blood oath with someone like me," Bay said. "Something like that can be broken easily if need be."

The idea of losing my blood oath—losing that connection to Oliver—sent shards of ice slicing through my chest. "*No!* As much as I appreciate your lack of faith in us, I don't trust a single one of you to give a rat's ass whether Oliver lives or dies. We're doing this. We're getting married."

"What?" rasped a horrified voice from behind me. Slowly, I turned to find Kismet staring at me, her face drained of color.

Oh Lilith, not her too. My tongue felt like sandpaper in

my mouth at the sight of the terror in her eyes. Despite the fact that she didn't know or trust Oliver very well, my heart plummeted to my stomach. I'd wanted her approval. Her blessing.

"Kismet," I protested, but my voice cracked, shattering my confidence.

"Can I speak to you alone, Desi?" Kismet growled.

As one, the others stood and bustled out of the room. I swallowed back fear and snatched Oliver's hand before he could leave.

"He stays," I said.

Kismet's nostrils flared, her eyes on fire.

"He *stays*!" I shouted, unwavering under her steely gaze.

Resignation flared briefly in her eyes before the fury took over again. She flexed her fingers over her shoulder, and a gust of wind slammed my door shut. I flinched.

Kismet stepped toward me. "I can't believe you would agree to this."

I stared at her, willing my brain to function properly. She knew how I felt about Oliver. Could this really be that much of a shock?

Kismet went on. "If Matthias succeeds—if he and Asmodeus reign with their demon army, not only will you be united with a demon through handfasting, but you'll be connected to Matthias's bloodline! As will *everyone* in your household! If you have any children, they'll be connected too!"

My blood ran cold. I gaped at her, speechless, while Oliver stiffened beside me.

"I'm sorry, Desi, but I won't stand by and let this happen," Kismet said. "Oliver will perform a blood oath with Bay—"

"Kismet, *no*—"

"And that's the end of discussion!" she bellowed.

"Kismet, this is *my* life! You're not my mother, and you don't get to choose who I marry. You don't have any say at all!"

Kismet rubbed her forehead, and for a moment, she *did* look just like Mom when she was exasperated with me. Kismet opened her mouth, to argue, but I interrupted.

"I love him, Kismet. I'm going to be with him no matter what happens. You can't change my mind on this. If someone told you that you couldn't be with Bay, would you just give in?"

Agony flared briefly in her eyes. She pressed her lips together into a tight line. "You can be married civilly if that's what you really want. But joining yourselves in a blood rite . . ." She trailed off, shaking her head.

I drew closer to her. "This is *my* life," I said again.

"My choice. And I choose Oliver. This is what we both want, and it might save his life. Please, Kismet."

A thick silence settled between us. Resignation flickered in Kismet's eyes. I could see her processing my words and giving in.

Then Oliver, who had remained silent, finally spoke up. "Desi, she's right. I can't ask you to do this. I don't know what I was thinking. Let me perform the blood oath with Bay and then we can be married properly when this is all over. We can have a big wedding—a celebration instead of some horrific demon ritual."

My chest caved in, crumbling to dust as I looked from Oliver's remorseful gaze to the agreement in Kismet's eyes. *No.*

Just the other night, I *finally* realized my feelings for Oliver. I'd pledged myself to him and taken this step toward a lifetime commitment. And it felt *right*. More right than anything else in my life.

But now it was being snatched away, vanishing through my fingers like sand I couldn't hold onto. Because a part of me feared that if we waited until after all this was over, it would never happen. Matthias could kill us all.

Dread clawed its way into my chest, clutching my throat and cutting off my breaths.

I closed my eyes and felt Oliver's hand take mine. I

wanted to shake it off, but the warmth of his skin on mine was like a soothing balm.

"Desi, do you remember what I spoke to you about last week?" Kismet asked softly. "About what I'd ask of you if Bay and I die?"

I stared at her until my eyes widened. I felt Oliver looking at me questioningly. Slowly, I nodded.

"It's something you both need to think about," Kismet said, "if you decide to marry."

I swallowed as her eyes drilled into mine. "But—but we aren't even sure that's going to happen. Kiz, what if you *survive* this whole ordeal? Then it won't matter!"

Kismet's lips tightened. "The odds are against us, Desi. My chance of survival is low."

I scrutinized her—the wary edge to her gaze and the twitch in her jaw. She wasn't telling me everything.

My blood chilled. "You know something."

Her eyes widened a fraction. But she said nothing.

"Kismet."

Kismet sighed, closing her eyes. "I know the date of my death. Alba thought it was pertinent. That I should get my affairs in order." She paused and took a breath. "It's soon. Very soon."

I staggered back a step. The world tilted around me, but miraculously I stayed upright. My grip on Oliver's hand tightened. "*What?* No, it can't be true!

And even if it were true, how could Alba tell her that? It seemed like a monumental piece of information to give away. The Alba I knew was always so guarded about sharing her visions.

Kismet seemed to read the incredulity in my face. "Think of it this way, Desi: if I knew for certain my death would bring about Matthias's downfall, I would fight with everything I had. But if I was constantly trying to survive, to save myself and risk letting him escape and continue killing and gaining power?" She shook her head. "It's better that I know. Alba knew I'd stop at nothing to bring him down. And this gives me the fuel to do that."

She's going to die. Kismet is going to die. I swallowed, my throat dry. "Does Bay know?"

"Yes."

The devastation in her eyes made my heart stop. I sucked in a sharp breath. "He'll die too." It wasn't a question.

Kismet's eyes welled with tears, confirming my suspicions.

Oliver was frozen next to me. The blood drained from his face. Confusion flickered in his eyes, but his stony expression indicated that he understood the gist of our conversation.

Kismet and Bay were going to die. Soon.

A low, resonating boom shook the manor, and the walls rattled. My eyes flew open, meeting Kismet's perplexed gaze.

"What was that?" I asked.

Kismet opened her mouth, then Elias's alarm sounded. The sharp, cawing noise echoed throughout the mansion.

"That can't be good," Kismet muttered, racing out the door. Oliver and I followed, our hands still entwined.

Other rebels flooded out of their rooms, joining us as we hurried downstairs. A crowd had already gathered at the porch with Elias standing in front. The tightness of his shoulders and trembling of his fists made my heart lurch.

What's going on?

I pushed my way through the crowd of rebels, standing on my tiptoes to get a better look. When I finally managed to peer over José's shoulder, my heart dropped to my knees.

An army of over a hundred demons stood at the threshold of Elias's property. In front of them—his entire body lit on fire—stood Matthias Greenwood.

CHAPTER 27

Matthias and the demons were frozen, their bodies glowing from Elias's blue alarm system. But the air prickled with magic like crackling static. Matthias was too strong. He would break through soon.

"This is all my fault," Kismet whispered next to me, her eyes wide and horrified. "We stayed here too long. We should've moved on days ago."

"No sense in thinking like that now," Elias said, his tone cheery despite the grim expression on his face. He looked over his shoulder and snapped his fingers. "Megan! My goggles and gloves, please."

Goggles and gloves? I thought, bewildered.

"Right away, Mr. Caldwell." Megan's light voice echoed in the foyer behind us.

"What can we do?" Oliver asked, looking at Elias.

"Fight like hell," Elias said, his jaw tense. "This is my home. I like it here. It would be great if I didn't have to move. Or, you know, die."

I would've laughed, but my heart palpitated so intensely I thought I would pass out.

An entire army. There's no way we'll survive this.

"José, get Stefan and Oliver out of here," Kismet said.

"What?" Oliver and Stefan said together.

"It's you he wants!" Kismet snapped. "If he kills you, we can't perform the spell."

Oliver and Stefan started arguing at once.

"You can't just send us away—" said Stefan.

"*No*, I'm staying!" said Oliver.

I looked at Oliver—the determination blazing in his eyes and the strong edge of his jawline as he clenched his teeth.

I let go of his hand. "Go."

He stared at me, anger flaring in his face.

I pressed my palm against his cheek. "Be safe. Please."

"Desi—"

José grabbed Oliver's arm. With a small *pop*, they vanished.

I tried to quench the sting in my chest from his departure. Fury and bitterness swarmed along our blood oath. *Forgive me, Oliver.*

"Ah, perfect," Elias said with a grin as Megan handed

him heavy, black goggles that looked like some kind of virtual reality mask. His black gloves were more like gauntlets than anything meant to keep his hands warm.

Another *pop*, and José reappeared, searching for Stefan.

"Stefan!" shrieked a voice behind me. Isabel.

Alarmed, I scanned the porch for him. Then, Isabel burst free from the crowd, sprinting down the stairs. I squinted and found Stefan surging toward the demon army.

"What the hell is he doing?" I cried.

"It's not him," Elias said darkly. He hastily slid the giant goggles on his face and donned the massive gloves. Wiggling his fingers, he cleared his throat and stretched a hand toward the demons.

"What do you mean?" Kismet said.

Suddenly, a fluttering sensation swarmed within my stomach. Then, Elias pointed a finger, and a flash of white lightning lit up the sky.

Matthias doubled over, his fiery form crumpling slightly. As he did, Stefan abruptly halted just a few feet away from him. Stunned, Stefan turned to look at us, his face ashen.

Isabel caught up to him and snatched his hand, drawing him back to the porch.

"What *was* that?" I asked Elias.

"Mind control," Elias said. "Must be a fun side effect of being Fourth Tier."

"No, what was *that*?" I asked, pointing to his gloves.

"These? The goggles let me see people's auras. The gloves let me strike them."

"Strike their—?"

"Auras, yes."

I blinked, dazed. "How does that even work?"

"Another time, I'll show you," Elias promised, stretching his hand again.

But this time, Matthias was ready. Though his body was still frozen in place by Elias's security system, a wall of fire rose from the ground, obscuring him from Elias's line of vision.

"Damn," Elias muttered, briefly lifting his goggles and rubbing his brow with his forearm. Then, he replaced the goggles over his eyes. "Come on, team. Let's move in. They'll break free of my enchantment any second now anyway." He looked at Kismet and widened his eyes. "Get out while you can."

Kismet's nostrils flared. "Not a chance." Her eyes shifted to José. "Take Stefan and hide yourselves until this is over. We'll send word when it's safe. We need you both."

José nodded, his eyes blank. Indifferent. With a *pop*,

he vanished and reappeared next to Stefan in the driveway.

Then, a huge ball of fire flew toward Stefan and Isabel. They leapt to the side to avoid the flames, and José tumbled to the ground along with them.

A few rebels roared and then we soared down the stairs, flooding toward the demon army. Another ball of fire flew toward Stefan, but I lifted my hands and Pushed it back against the demons. It slammed into Matthias's wall of flames and disintegrated.

Blasts of blue magic soared toward Matthias's fiery barrier, but nothing could break through. Elias still wore his goggles and gloves, sending bolts of lightning across his yard.

"We have to get through his fire!" Kismet roared.

"I'm on it," Bay said. He disappeared in a puff of black smoke.

Inky darkness crept toward Matthias's wall like long, dark fingers. It climbed higher and higher as if Bay's magic were vines. Cracks and holes appeared among the flames. A roar pierced the air and then the wall vanished, revealing Matthias's stiff form still engulfed in fire.

Tendrils of smoke swirled in the empty space next to Kismet and then Bay reappeared. A charred gash lined the left side of his neck, but he waved away Kismet's concerned look.

My stomach clenched. *They both could die today.*

More magic tickled the air. Crack. Splinter. *Boom.*

Elias's blue enchantment fizzled. The cawing alarm subsided, leaving an ominous silence in its wake.

A lump formed in my throat. *This is it.*

Matthias tilted his fiery head at us. I could almost feel his smirk.

Then, he surged forward.

Shouts and screams echoed around me. Lightning struck from Elias's gloves. Blades slashed. Shots fired. Blood spilled.

I took a deep breath and pushed my legs forward. *Get in there, Desi.*

I felt so rusty. So unprepared.

But I had to do this. I had to survive. For Oliver.

I wiggled my fingers. I had no weapons, but I felt my power surging within me. *I can do this.*

Just then, a dark warlock lunged for me, and my legs slid into splits. I arced backward, avoiding his blade and swinging my hands to the side. With a Push, I knocked his legs out from under him. He yelped, and I snatched his dagger and rammed it into his chest.

Something behind me raised the hair on the back of my neck. In a flash, I whirled, swiping my new weapon and slashing the arm of a man with yellow eyes. Were-wolf—in human form. He grinned at me, baring sharp-ened teeth, and flexed his hand. Long claws protruded from his fingernails.

My eyes widened. This werewolf could shift at will.

He swung his claws toward me. I dodged his blow and sliced into his leg. He stumbled and raked his claws into my shoulder. Blood ran down my arm. White-hot pain seared into my flesh. My head throbbing, I lifted a hand to Push him, but I was too slow.

The werewolf kicked me, and I fell. The dagger flew from my grip. He pressed his boot into my chest, cutting off my air. A massive weight crashed through my chest. Had he just broken a rib? I tried to lift an arm, but the force of his foot on me was too much.

But I didn't need my arms.

My legs flew up in my usual stretch. The toe of my shoe nudged his upper thigh.

The werewolf stiffened, glancing over his shoulder.

Taking advantage of his hesitation, I leaned forward and sank my teeth into his leg. *Taste of your own medicine, bastard.*

He gasped, and the weight of his foot let up just a fraction.

I lifted my hand and Pushed. He soared backward.

While he was still in the air, I lifted both hands and

caught him with my magic, spinning him around until he moaned and howled, his limbs flailing.

"Vile demon of unholy crimes,
I banish you 'til the end of time!"

I shouted the banishing spell, slicing my hands through the air. With a burst of blue magic, he vanished.

Panting, I glanced at the surrounding chaos. Three demons fought Bay, who kept Porting back and forth to evade them. Teddy took on two demons at once. Gina and Kismet stood back-to-back, facing a throng of at least six demons. Elias continued zapping auras, but his shoulders sagged, his form crumpling from the effort. A dozen or so demons fought to get to him. It wouldn't be long before they did.

We can't win this.

My eyes found the blob of fire a few yards away from me. Matthias.

And on the ground, his face covered in blood, was Stefan.

I spotted the dagger and grabbed it again, clutching it tightly in my hand as I sprinted forward. Stefan moaned, scrambling on the ground as he tried to move away from Matthias.

Matthias lifted a fiery hand. I raised my own hand and Pushed him.

With an "oof," Matthias staggered backward. But to

my dismay, he remained on his feet. He was too powerful.

Recovering quickly, I flung my dagger forward, embedding it into his chest. He didn't even wince.

Lifting a hand, I Pulled it back, then launched it forward again. And again.

At last, he grunted, but it was mingled with laughter. "Your efforts are useless, Desiree. I'm Fourth Tier now. That pitiful blade can't do anything."

My fingers clutched the hilt even tighter in my sweaty palm. "It can still slice your throat. Tell me, how long would it take for you to heal if I sever your head from the rest of your body?"

Matthias's white eyes narrowed into slits. He shot jets of fire at me, but I ducked, swinging my legs around to kick him in the face. Flames scorched through my sneakers. I hissed but pivoted back toward him, slashing into his neck.

He groaned, stumbling back a step. Then, hot agony sliced through me. I gasped. Pain rippled in my chest, and I fell to my knees.

Matthias held a quivering arm in the air, holding me steady. Somehow his magic froze me in place and squeezed the breath out of me. White-hot daggers pricked my skin. I clenched my teeth. Dark spots danced in front of my eyes.

"Desi!" Stefan grunted, trying to rise.

A woman shouted, and Matthias's fiery grip loosened. I slumped sideways as Isabel aimed a pistol and fired into Matthias's face. His head swung backward momentarily, but he pivoted back, shooting a ball of fire into Isabel's chest. Isabel crumpled, smoke rising from her charred chest.

"Mom!" Stefan cried, crawling toward Isabel's limp form.

Matthias laughed and stepped forward, pinning Stefan to the ground with his magic. Stefan screamed. The sound ripped into my eardrums. I numbly turned my head, trying to lift my arms or do something. But pain paralyzed me. I couldn't move.

Lightning flashed, and Matthias flew backward into the concrete of the driveway. His flames were momentarily extinguished, exposing his human face—the ordinary graying hair and mustache.

A burst of blue magic assaulted Matthias. I glanced around to see Teddy and Paolo advancing. Paolo's black magic slithered forward like a snake. The onslaught of magic sent Matthias stumbling backward toward the forest. Then, a high-pitched whistle pierced the air.

The surrounding demons flocked toward Matthias, blocking him from view. And the battle continued. Teddy and Paolo were suddenly outnumbered. The other rebels rushed to their aid, but Matthias had too many men.

Paolo went down, blood blossoming from his chest. More gunshots filled the air. Elias's lightning bolts struck the demons, but it wasn't enough.

Stefan's shrill scream broke through the hazy fog of my pain. I wriggled forward on the ground, my chest throbbing.

There was Matthias, standing over Stefan and pointing a gun pointed at his head.

"I'm truly sorry," Matthias said. "It was never meant to be this way."

He pulled the trigger.

At the same moment, a large force barreled into Matthias. The gun wrenched sideways as the shot fired. Stefan yelped, covering his head with his hands.

I blinked, squinting at our ally. Then, my mouth fell open.

John Dickers. The man who supposedly worked for Matthias. His glasses askew, Dickers surged forward, lifting his hands and firing wisps of black magic into Matthias's face.

Suddenly, a stampede of men and women drew my attention to the forest. My eyes widened as I tried to make out distinct features, but they were all a blur of bulletproof vests and weapons that glinted against the afternoon sun.

Then, gunfire peppered around me. My ears throbbed and ached from the cacophony of noises. I sucked in a breath and pushed against the ground. My arms quivered, but slowly, I sat up, trying to ignore the pounding in my head.

Dickers. And that woman, too, looked familiar. She worked on the Council. She'd been there during the terrorist attack.

These people were on the *Council.* The Council that was supposedly owned by Matthias.

Hope burned in my chest. Ragged breaths poured from my mouth as I watched the members of the Council rush to our aid. Demons fell to the ground. Bursts of blue and black magic filled the sky like fireworks as demon after demon was banished.

One by one, Matthias's soldiers were picked off. Kismet and Bay killed a dark witch. Teddy sliced his athame into a werewolf. Gina twisted the arm of a gremlin-looking creature until the arm snapped, and the demon howled and writhed.

We were winning. Impossibly, we were winning.

I lifted a hand to Push a dark witch who advanced toward Kismet. The energy drained from me, and I slumped sideways again.

Then, a shadow appeared over me. Another were-wolf. He grinned down at me, revealing his jagged teeth. He leaned in, his putrid breath making my stomach roil. I waited until his clawed hand was inches from my chest. Then I summoned all my strength to bury my blade in his throat. He choked, gargling blood, and fell over, motionless.

A dozen rebels surrounded Matthias. Matthias roared, his arms swinging wildly. A few rebels fell over, but Matthias was still outnumbered. The rebels closed in on him.

Then Matthias burst into flames again, sending several people flying. With another explosion of fire that shook the earth, he vanished into thin air, leaving puffs of smoke trailing after him.

CHAPTER 28

PAIN THROBBED IN MY SHOULDER, FLARING RHYTHMICALLY like a warning bell. I blinked through the hazy fog in my mind, trying to register what happened.

"Is he gone?" I asked no one in particular.

"He's gone." Elias lifted up his goggles to look at me. Deep red grooves were etched into his face, and a trail of blood lined his jaw. "But he'll be back."

"We can't stay here." Kismet approached, wincing when she stepped on her left leg. A bloody gash stretched from her upper thigh to her kneecap. "I'm sorry, Elias. We overstayed our welcome. We shouldn't have involved you like this."

Elias waved a hand, though his eyes blazed. "Think nothing of it, Kismet. Besides, these assholes attacked *my* home. I'm on your side now."

Kismet's expression cleared, her eyes blank. "I—you'll fight with us?"

Elias shrugged. "Sooner or later, you have to pick a side, right? It's either you or him. I choose you."

His words prickled my mind. Bay had said something similar to convince me to fight with the rebels.

Suddenly, a throaty scream pierced the air. My limbs tensed, sending aches up and down my body. I looked around, expecting to find another demon attacking us.

Then, I saw Stefan with tears streaming down his face. Bay held Stefan's arms behind him as if to keep him from bolting into the forest.

"No!" Stefan cried. "They took her! They *took* her!"

My heart froze. "Isabel?" I whispered, looking at Elias. "She survived Matthias's fireball?"

Elias's face was ashen as he nodded. "Yes. I saw her get up just before—" He broke off, his mouth clamping shut.

My blood ran cold. Matthias took Isabel.

I couldn't feel my limbs anymore. I couldn't move anything except my eyes as I gazed numbly around the scene before me. Demons and rebels alike lay motionless on the ground. Stains of blood covered the corpses. Though some moaned and shifted, others were disturbingly still.

How many had we lost today? I tried to see if I

recognized anyone. Then my heart stopped. There was Paolo, his dark eyes wide and vacant. I hadn't known him well . . . but I'd still known him.

"Kismet," I said weakly, trying to rise. My arms trembled in my effort to push myself up to a sitting position. "Where do we go now? Where's Oliver?"

"The—the hotel room," Kismet said, still staring at Stefan. "It's our safe spot when we're in between hideouts." She blinked and shook her head, finally looking at me. Her brows pinched, and her eyes moved up and down my body. "Lilith, Desi!" She rushed over to me, her eyes falling to the wound in my shoulder. I closed my eyes, but I still heard her hiss. It didn't make me feel any better. The wound seemed to pulse under her scrutiny. "We need to get you to Teddy."

"Teddy didn't make it," Elias said quietly, pointing a finger. I followed his gaze, but he gestured to a body I couldn't see. I squinted and barely made out Teddy's army-style combat boots.

My heart dropped to my knees. My eyes felt hot, and I closed them against the grief. Fierce, loyal Teddy. He didn't deserve to die this way.

None of us did.

Kismet exhaled a shaky breath, her eyes moist. She blinked, pressing her lips together. I saw in her face the effort to keep her sorrow at bay. "We—we need a place to go. Elias, do you . . ."

"I know a place," said a familiar voice.

My tired eyes shifted to John Dickers. One lens of his glasses was cracked, and his gray hair stuck up in odd directions. A trickle of blood oozed from his nose, and scorch marks lined one sleeve of his shirt.

Kismet stared at him, speechless.

"The Council sides with you, Kismet," Dickers said, wiping his nose on his sleeve. "Levarret left his allies to die. He cloaked the building, knowing we were inside when those planes hit. We don't affiliate with someone like that. Someone with no loyalty."

Kismet stiffened. "Loyalty. You want to talk to *me* about loyalty?" She stepped toward Dickers, her nostrils flaring. "These rebels *died* because of your loyalties!" She jabbed a finger toward the bodies on the ground.

Black spots danced in my vision. "Kiz," I said weakly. "Argue later. Please."

"How do we know we can trust you?" Kismet said, glaring at Dickers. "This could be an elaborate trap to lure us right to him."

"We lost comrades today too," Dickers said stiffly. "We don't take that lightly, Kismet. Besides, do you have a better alternative?"

Silence confirmed his assumption.

Kismet swore under her breath. "Fine. I'll alert José. With Elias's cuff, he should be able to transport our wounded."

Then, my eyes closed as I succumbed to the pain. I felt a strong pair of hands lift me. Low murmurs surrounded me, but it was as soothing as a lullaby. I welcomed the rocking motion as someone carried me. The hushed whispers were like white noise. A small *pop* told me I'd been Ported somewhere. Then, something soft pressed into my cheek, and I drifted off to sleep.

A light snore woke me.

My heavy eyelids slid open, and darkness surrounded me. Faint moonlight filtered in through the curtains, illuminating my small bed and a figure that was slumped in an armchair next to me.

Oliver.

I sat up and winced. My upper arm still throbbed. Grimacing, I peered under my shirt and found bandages covering my forearm. I frowned. Kismet was a healer— why hadn't she healed me? Even Bay had healing powers. I knew Teddy had been the resident healer, but he wasn't the only one who could've done it.

Then, I remembered what Kismet had said about

giving up her baby—that she couldn't even perform simple spells anymore. Perhaps Bay suffered the same way. It would explain why Teddy had taken full responsibility for healing the rebels.

Teddy. He was dead. Killed by Matthias and his demon army.

I sat back against the headboard, and my throat filled with emotion. My eyes felt hot. I rubbed my chest, trying to breathe, but all I could think of was all the lives we'd lost so far.

And all the lives we'd continue to lose until this was finished.

Swallowing, I turned my gaze back to Oliver. His head was propped on the arm of his chair, his arms crossed as he snored softly.

My mouth lifted in a small smile. His face was blank. Free of tension. I wanted him to stay like this forever— undisturbed by the horrors surrounding us. Innocent. Safe.

I shifted to my good side and directed my gaze to the window. The pearly glow of the moon made me think of Isabel. What was Matthias doing to her right now? And what would *we* do to get her back?

My stomach growled, and I glanced at Oliver, not wanting to wake him. Perhaps I could slip out and find some food.

But where *was* I?

The room was small, filled only by a bed, a wardrobe, Oliver's chair, and a trunk. A faint sterile smell tickled my nose, but I assumed that was from my bandages. Then, my eyes found a large door across from my bed. At first glance, it appeared to be a closet. But when I squinted, I made out a small lock on the knob. And it seemed a bit big to be a closet. The door was slightly ajar, revealing tiled floor on the other side.

It was a bathroom. Like the kind you'd find in a hospital room.

We were in a *hospital*. Granted, there were no machinery, IV drips, medical instruments, or whatever normally filled a hospital. But at one point, this place had probably been filled with people who were sick and dying.

The thought made me shudder.

Just then, another rumbling growl quivered through my stomach. I closed my eyes against the ache of my hunger and slowly slid the blanket off to climb out of bed. My arm bumped Oliver's chair, and a flare of pain shot through me. I hissed, gritting my teeth.

Oliver jolted awake, sitting up so fast I almost toppled over in shock.

"Desi!" he said in surprise, his voice low and husky.

"I'm sorry," I whispered. "I didn't mean to wake you."

"What are you doing up?" Oliver ran a hand through his messy hair. "You should be resting."

"I *was* resting. But I'm too hungry. You get some sleep. I'll be right back."

Oliver jumped up and beat me to the door. "Let me get it for you. Don't exert yourself."

I chuckled lightly. "I'm fine, Oliver." I gazed around the small room. "So, uh, where are we?"

Oliver cleared his throat. "Some safehouse that the Council owns. They said it was for witness protection or something like that. 'Off the grid.' Whatever that means." He shrugged.

"And the others?" I asked in a small voice. "How many did we lose?"

"Kismet said we lost half our rebels in that fight."

My eyes closed, and grief consumed me. In a strained voice, I asked, "Stefan, is he . . ."

"He's fine, all things considered."

A lump formed in my throat. "Matthias will kill his mother."

Grim defiance shone in Oliver's eyes. "Not yet. Not if he still wants something from us." When I frowned at him, he said, "Me and Stefan. He wants us dead. As long as his offspring are living, we can be used for the spell to banish him."

Terror swirled in my chest. Oliver would always have a target on his back. Always.

Oliver rubbed his chin, gazing fixedly at the floor. Something unreadable haunted his expression.

I stepped toward him. "What's wrong?"

He lifted his hands and dropped them, then scoffed. "I'm just . . . so *useless*. I let you fight out there—I let you almost *die* out there. Stefan's mother was kidnapped. All while I hid here like a coward."

"You are *not* a coward," I said sharply. "Besides, you didn't 'let me' do anything! I *forced* you to go! Oliver, you're too important."

Oliver snorted. "You mean my *blood* is too important. That banishing spell is the only reason I'm here."

"No, you're here because you want to fight Matthias just like everyone else. You're here because I love you. And because you love me."

Oliver's eyes softened. "You're right. It's just hard staying behind and watching everyone else go into battle. I'm a soldier, for Lilith's sake." He ran a hand down his face. "I can't do *anything*. I can't fight with the rebels, I can't fight for this country. Do you have any idea what that terrorist attack did to me? I was ready to jump up and enlist as soon as I found out it was an act of war."

He groaned and crossed his arms, shaking his head.

"I've always known my duty and my place. And I just—I *can't* sit here and do nothing! I can't! Not while my country, my *people* are suffering. Not while there are people out there intent on taking lives. And I don't just mean Matthias."

His nostrils flared as he dropped his gaze. "The attack on the towers jolted me awake, Desi. I *have* to do something. I have to do my part to rid this world of evil —whether it's Matthias or someone else."

The wild, tormented look in his eyes broke my heart. I stepped closer to him and pressed my hands against his cheeks. My fingers toyed with the blond strands of hair that poked over his ears. It was the longest I'd ever seen his hair. He usually kept it high and tight.

"We each have our roles, Oliver," I said quietly. "You're on the sidelines right now, but it won't be like that forever. You'll do your part just like the rest of us."

"By becoming a dark warlock," Oliver whispered.

The truth of what he would have to do twisted through my stomach like a knife. My throat clouded with despair. *Oliver will become a demon.*

I somehow hadn't processed it until now. A small part of me had thought that if he just performed a little bit of black magic like I had, it would be enough.

But no. I'd come back and cemented my bond with my parents, who were light casters. In order for Oliver to be bound to Matthias's bloodline, he had to fully transition to dark magic.

I wasn't sure how I knew that. But I did.

"Oliver, you don't have to do this." I blinked tears from my eyes and looked up at him. "We'll find another way."

His eyes softened, and he tucked a stray curl behind my ear. "This is the only way. It'll be fine, Desi."

"But this is so permanent! There's no coming back from this! Do you really want to be a demon for the rest of your life?"

Oliver went still. His eyes remained fixed on me. "Perhaps not, but it's better than death. And even dying in the line of duty is a noble end."

I shook my head. "Oliver, this isn't some messed up heroic soldier thing—"

"Yes, it is," he said firmly. "We're at *war*. This is the fight I have to face. You said so yourself: I'll have to do my part. I felt uncertain and helpless before while you were all back there, fighting for your lives. But in *this*, I have no doubts, Desi. This is my purpose. This is my contribution to the battle. I have to do this."

I closed my eyes, tears streaming down my face. I wanted to argue with him, but my throat closed, cutting off my words.

"I'll be fine, Desi." Oliver swept a tear off my cheek.

I looked up at him. "You will?"

He rubbed his thumb along my lower lip. Shivers of pleasure coursed through my body. "I promise," he said.

His throaty voice cut through my terror, igniting something within me that made me want to make out with him right then and there. My heart raced, and a strange boldness took over me. "Then marry me."

Oliver stilled.

I put my hands on his shoulders. "Marry me, Oliver Gerrick. If you promise that you'll be all right after you go dark, then you have nothing to be afraid of. We can bind ourselves together permanently. Don't you want that?"

His Adam's apple bobbed as he swallowed. "You know I do," he said in a strained voice.

"Then let's do it."

He closed his eyes. "Desi—"

"You can't perform a blood oath with Bay, not now that we know . . ." I trailed off, choking on the words. *Now that we know Bay will die.*

Oliver's eyes tightened. He understood my meaning.

"What if it happens before we banish Matthias?" I breathed, stroking the hair above his ears. "You'll be at risk, Oliver. I—I can't take that chance."

"You'd rather take that chance with *your* life, then?" Oliver asked, his voice hard.

"It's not the same thing," I snapped. "It's not a guarantee you'll become like him. Becoming a demon doesn't automatically make you a monster. Look at Stefan."

"Stefan still has a family. He's still bound to others by blood. *I'm* not. Matthias is the only bloodline I have left."

"Not if you marry *me*," I whispered, standing on my tiptoes to press a kiss to his lips.

He groaned against my mouth, though his arms wound around my waist. "Desi—"

"Please, Oliver. Are you going to make me beg for this?"

The corners of his mouth twitched. "That would be thoroughly enjoyable."

I resisted the urge to roll my eyes. Instead I batted my eyelashes, giving him my best damsel-in-distress look. "Oh, please, big, strong Corporal Gerrick." I kissed his cheek. "Please, won't you take me as your blushing bride?" I kissed his nose. "Your delicate housewife?" I kissed his chin. "Your beloved ball and chain?"

He burst out laughing, ducking his head and covering his mouth. I snickered too, though the motion made my arm flare in pain.

Eventually, our laughs subsided, and we gazed at each other, our expressions sobering. So many questions flowed between us, and I could practically read each one from his face. *Could you marry a demon? What if I hurt you? What if I surrender you to Matthias? What if I become an unforgivable monster?*

"I will love you," I whispered, "no matter what. No matter who you become. No matter what magic you practice. I will always love you."

Moisture glistened in his eyes. He pressed his lips together into a thin line.

I took his hand and raised it to my lips. "Do you love me, Oliver?"

Agony flared in his eyes. "With all my heart."

"Do you want to marry me?"

"More than anything."

I kissed him then, drawing him into me. He curled his arms around me and hoisted me off my feet. I squealed and wrapped my arms around his neck, clinging to him. He laughed again, kissing me over and over. His soft lips moved over mine, his movements achingly slow. His tongue flicked along my lower lip, and fire burst inside me.

Please say it. Please do this for me.

He drew back, his eyes burning. I knew he heard my thoughts.

Please, Oliver.

The heat in his eyes mingled with delight, and I knew his answer before he said it.

"Yes, Desiree. I'll marry you."

A wide grin spread on my face. Exhilaration poured through my body until every inch of me tingled, and I threw my arms around his neck and covered him with eager, sloppy kisses. At first he chuckled, but then he kissed me back, his lips moving urgently, passionately, and desperately. My body ached for him. Yearned for him. I tugged at his shirt until his chest pressed against mine. I felt his own heart racing alongside mine.

We kissed and held each other until the fire along our blood oath was too intense for us to ignore. Though my heart screamed for more, I tore myself away from him, knowing it would mean so much more to him if we waited. For a moment, we both grinned at each other, breathless and beaming.

Oliver cleared his throat, his face beet-red. "I, uh, just need to go cool off for a moment."

He ducked out of the room, and I giggled to myself, forgetting my hunger entirely.

CHAPTER 29

Despite my assurances that I was fine, Oliver insisted on sleeping in the armchair next to my bed. I couldn't even pretend to be upset about it. Long after he'd fallen asleep, I just watched him, giddily imagining how I would be sleeping right next to him soon. How easy it would be for me to scooch up close to him, bury my face in his chest, or fiddle with his hair while he slept.

When I awoke, I was surprised I'd slept at all. My mind had been racing, too alert for any thought of sleep. I groaned, blinking against the warm sunlight streaming through the window. When I rolled over, I found José reading a book in the armchair next to me.

I jumped, eyes wide. "I—José! Where's Oliver?"

Without looking up, José said, "Kiz and Bay wanted

to dive into his demon initiation right away."

Alarm raced through me. "So, where did they go?"

"Some Council dude said they have prisoners awaiting execution. They're going to use them for some ritual, I think. Oliver didn't want me to wake you, but he wanted someone here in case you needed anything."

A lump hardened in my throat. So Oliver had just . . . left? Part of me had wanted to be there for him during the process.

But maybe Oliver didn't want me to see him transform.

Still, my heart twisted thinking of him diving into this dangerous territory without me. Perhaps this was exactly how he'd felt yesterday when he stayed behind while I fought.

I watched José. His gaze was fixed determinedly on his book, but his eyes weren't moving; they were glossed over, staring at nothing. Red circles lined his eyes, and shadows creased his face.

He looked terrible.

"José, are you all right?" I asked quietly.

José snorted without looking up. "Don't worry about me, Desi."

"José." I sat up.

José reluctantly lifted his eyes to meet mine. Something cold stirred in his expression. "What?" he snapped.

My head reared back. I'd thought he was still grieving over Cameron's death, but the hostility in his face shocked me. "Did I do something to offend you? I mean, I know I was pissed at you when I first got here, but . . ."

José chuckled without humor, shaking his head. "You only think of yourself, Desi. That much hasn't changed."

Stung, I gaped at him. "What?"

"You have no idea what you did to me when you left last year. No idea what Cam and I went through trying to find you. Then my abuela tells me all this mumbo jumbo about some higher calling, some greater purpose she grew up hearing about and how important it was to hold onto those letters for you. And I just was so impressed. So proud to know you, Desi. So excited that you'd be coming back.

"I waited for you. I joined the rebels for you, knowing you'd need help when you got here. And when you did, you—you arrived with some guy I've never met, and you never left his side. Then I tried acting normal, like we were back at your place in North Grove, like nothing had changed, and you bit my head off for it. Your new boyfriend threatened me. And suddenly I'm the bad guy?"

His eyes hardened, and he dropped his gaze. His nostrils flared. "Then, I lost my best friend, and I just couldn't keep up the ruse anymore. I couldn't pretend everything was fine because it's *not*. I'm just some pack mule for you guys here. Just some mode of transportation and nothing more. I have no value here. No purpose. And without Cam, I don't even know what the hell I'm doing. But do you care? No. You only care about your soldier boy toy."

I stared at him, speechless. His words pierced through me like a dagger tearing through fabric. Everything I'd known about José shattered. I remembered telling Oliver in Santiago that José was probably already dating other girls. That he'd long since forgotten about me.

If I'd known this—that he pined for me and waited for me—would I still have gotten together with Oliver? Would I still have remained in Santiago, or would I have tried harder to get back?

I'd never loved José. I knew that for certain. But never in my wildest dreams had I thought he loved *me*. Or even cared enough about me to feel this hurt.

My heart thumped madly in my chest. I had to fix this. But the hatred burning in his eyes was so intense I almost broke just looking at him. "José, I—I'm so sorry. I just—we weren't even exclusive, though! We agreed from the start that we could see other people if we wanted to. I didn't think we were serious."

José closed his eyes and sighed. "Yeah. I know. That was on me. But I thought you knew me well enough to know that sometimes it's just a face I wear. That the laid-back José is who I am when I don't know how to be —like when I'm around you."

I raised an eyebrow, my mouth still hanging open. "What, was I just supposed to read your mind? To know you wanted to be something more when you never told me?"

José rolled his eyes. "Of course not, Desi. I never wanted to push that on you. I wanted *you* to want more. But you never did. So I never asked."

I shook my head, biting back a retort. *So you're mad at me because I don't feel something stronger for you? How is that fair?*

"I just—you never even gave me a chance," José said, staring at a hole in his jeans. "You never let me prove to you that I was different. That I wasn't the same José. And, I don't know, I guess I just fell into the old habit of pretending I didn't care. Hoping that maybe if I faked it, I would start believing it." He closed his eyes. "I was wrong."

A heavy silence fell between us. I had no idea what to say. He was pouring his heart out for the first time since I'd known him. And with all the chaos surrounding Oliver, his bloodline, and his transition to dark magic—

plus Kismet and her baby and her and Bay's impending deaths . . . José's feelings had been the last thing on my mind.

And I hated myself for it.

If José had magically vanished, wouldn't I have tried to find him? Wouldn't I have worried? Wouldn't I have half hoped we'd go back to normal when he got back? Even if I hadn't loved him, he'd been my normal. My safe zone. Maybe José had craved that safety too, especially after losing Mia to rehab.

My eyes stung with tears, and I sucked in a shuddering breath. "I'm sorry, José," I said again. "I should've considered your feelings. You're right, I don't know what you went through when I left. But you don't know what *I* went through in 1898, either. It was all just . . . so much. And it weighed on my mind so heavily that I couldn't really think about anything else. Even so, I'm— I'm really sorry."

José's dark eyes met mine, and I almost cowered from the intensity of his gaze. I'd never seen him look at me like that before. Focused. Intense. Like he'd been half asleep the whole time, but here and now he was finally awake.

"Tell me," he said, leaning forward to prop his arms on his knees. "Tell me what you went through."

So I did. I dived into my story, starting with what

happened when I arrived in Santiago, when I met Oliver and the coven, and when we went underground to free the demon prisoners. I stumbled over the part where El Diablo tortured me and drank my blood, then blushed when I told him about my growing feelings for Oliver.

The more I talked, the dryer my mouth felt, but I didn't care. Each word lifted some small weight off my chest, and the longer I spoke, the better I could breathe.

José's expression cleared as he listened. Occasionally, his eyes danced with amusement, like when I talked about peeing in front of Oliver because there were no bathrooms. To see life in his eyes again spurred me forward, and I found myself grinning as I talked about my Demonhunting adventures with Elena and Guillermo, about when I first met Bay, and about the love I felt for Tala and her daughter Reyna.

I told him everything. Even the ugly parts—even when Oliver lied to me about being engaged. Or when I sacrificed the werewolf in a blood ritual so I could save Reyna. Or when Bay betrayed me, and I almost died.

During my monologue, something altered between us. Like the barriers we'd both put up finally crumbled down, and a mutual understanding of friendship grew in its place. I didn't mind sharing my secrets with him. And after a while, he'd leaned forward so far that our hands were clasped. But there was no heat. It was as if I clutched the hand of my best friend—as if Elena and I were talking, commiserating together, and she'd taken my hand to console me.

Thinking of her and everything I'd left behind brought me to tears. And eventually, José's eyes also glistened with tears when he dived into his side of the story. The late nights casting sloppy locator spells that sometimes didn't work. The constant Porting to the locations we'd frequented together as he tried to find me. The conversations with his abuela about what happened to me. Mia's downhill journey with alcoholism. When she left for rehab, it was only José and Cameron left. Joining the rebels with Kismet finally gave them a purpose.

I let him talk. For hours, we just talked. Despite how much I missed Oliver and longed to be with him, it was kind of a relief to relax and feel nothing. To just share stories with someone without that knot in my chest, or the butterflies in my stomach, or some intense emotion racing through me. To just *exist*.

After a while, José helped me down the stairs to the cafeteria to finally grab some food. Gina looked up and smiled at us from the table where she was making sandwiches.

Suddenly, an array of strange emotions filled my chest. I stilled and grimaced as they sliced through me like knives. Pain. Darkness. Regret.

Black magic.

Shadows swirled within me, threatening to suffocate me.

I swallowed, closing my eyes and focusing on breathing. It was Oliver. But what was he doing?

"Want a sandwich?" Gina asked me.

I shook off my dark thoughts and forced a smile. "Sure, thanks."

Gina handed me a ham sandwich. I devoured it in no time and fixed myself another while Gina and José talked and joked like old friends. But I couldn't join in. The emotions I'd felt from Oliver had jarred me out of my peaceful bubble from spending the morning with José. I was suddenly reminded of the horrors we had yet to face.

The door swung open, and Kismet entered. She looked around the room until her eyes settled on me. "Good, you're up. Oliver's been prepped. He's ready."

My eyes widened. "Ready?"

She nodded. "He's made three sacrifices so far. He's ready for the full coven now. I thought—I thought you'd want to know."

Anxiety swirled in my stomach. *That explains those emotions.* I couldn't imagine what he was going through right now. "A full coven?" I repeated numbly.

"When demons are first initiated, they usually have a

ceremony with a full coven to ensure the dark magic sticks. At least, that's what Bay tells me. It cements the transition. Pulls the caster over to the other side permanently."

I swallowed, thinking of Guillermo. He'd intentionally stayed on that cusp between light and dark magic so he could perform both. But people like Bay and his Kulam warlocks welcomed the transition.

Imagining the two—Guillermo fighting the pull of dark magic and Bay embracing it—was like two worlds colliding. And somewhere in between was Oliver.

"Does he—can I be there?" I asked quietly.

Kismet's eyes tightened. "He says if you want to, you can."

I stared at the tiled floor for a long moment, my head reeling. Would I want to see this? Would I want to see him endure this change?

It would be better than reuniting with him and suddenly find him a demon. No, I needed to see it happen. To register this change just like he would. We needed to do this together.

I took a deep breath and stood from the table. I felt Gina and José watching me, but I looked only at Kismet as I strode toward the door. "All right. Let's go."

CHAPTER 30

I trembled down to my very bones as Kismet led me through the door and into the parking lot. Cracks covered the pavement, filled with wild weeds and roots. I expected to see other buildings or something resembling a city, but there were only a few small cabins and a large building about the size of a library.

"What is this place?" I asked Kismet.

"It started as some sort of camp for casters with disabilities to safely train together," Kismet said over her shoulder. "It kind of fizzled, though, once the light and dark casters started attacking each other. When a child died, they shut it down. Now they use it as a safehouse."

When a child died. I swallowed numbly.

The more I learned about the Council, the more I despised it.

I followed Kismet silently as we weaved through overgrown bushes and tall grass. We stomped through the foliage toward the library-like building. Upon closer inspection, the large, screened windows and wood-paneled exterior reminded me of some type of mess hall.

"Is that where . . . it'll happen?" I asked, my throat dry.

"Yes. We needed somewhere covered for the vampires to participate."

I suppressed a shudder. *Vampires.* How would Oliver feel about that?

That's a stupid question, Desi, I chided myself. *He probably hates this whole situation.*

I smoothed my expression, determined to be strong for him. I would compose myself. I would hide my disgust and support him through this.

Because I love him. No matter what. That much I knew.

I clung to that certainty as we climbed the steps and entered through the creaky swinging door. The sound of it slamming shut brought waves of bad memories as I remembered participating in a girl's camp as a kid in North Grove. The smell of burnt hot dogs and marshmallows, the sound of camp songs, and the jeers and laughter from the girls when I woke up with my hair frizzed like a lion's mane.

It hadn't been pleasant. But I would've much preferred to be back in that memory than facing this.

I looked around the room and noticed that heavy shutters had been bolted against the windows, plunging the dining area into darkness. A series of candles cast an eerie orange glow around several hooded figures. The candles formed a pentagram, and runes had been etched into the floor beside each one.

The air reeked of dark magic. I hadn't smelled it this strongly since I was in Manila.

Goosebumps erupted on my arms, and I rubbed them to ward off the chill.

As my eyes adjusted to the darkness, I squinted at the figures surrounding the pentagram. They wore black cloaks just like the demons I'd encountered in the nineteenth century, though these demons' hoods were lowered. I recognized Bay, and Raul, and a few more of Bay's comrades, whose names I didn't know. A pair of white-faced men watched me with gleaming red eyes. Vampires. With a jolt, I also recognized John Dickers and several others from the Council.

I wasn't sure if I felt relieved or horrified that they were all willing to participate in this.

In the middle of the pentagram, also wearing a black cloak, stood Oliver. His stony gaze was fixed away from me toward the window shutters on the wall opposite him. His face was smooth. Stoic. But I noticed the tightness in his eyes and the rigid lines of his jaw. I felt the horror and fear rippling through our blood oath.

He was struggling to maintain a brave face. On the inside, it was killing him.

I tried to send him comfort through our connection. I wasn't completely sure how it worked—sometimes he heard my thoughts, and sometimes he didn't. I didn't seem to have any control over it.

I clenched my fingers into fists and thought over and over again, *You can do this. I'm here for you. I love you.*

After the third repetition, he turned to look at me. His eyes remained hard, his expression unyielding, but a spark ignited in his gaze. I knew in that moment that if he broke his concentration, his facade would shatter completely. He would break down.

So I offered a hesitant smile that I knew was unconvincing. But still, his eyes softened just a fraction.

"Just stay by me," Kismet muttered, grabbing my elbow and pulling me off to the side, several feet away from the pentagram. "No matter what happens."

I nodded numbly. I'd never seen a ritual like this before. I'd seen Bay perform a blood ritual twice—once for himself and then for me. But I'd never seen it with a full coven. Though Matthias had gotten close to performing one with me and Oliver.

The memory sent chills racing up and down my spine.

"Is everyone ready?" John Dickers asked, his voice deeper than I remembered.

A few demons nodded, but most of them blinked at him, their expressions blank.

"Very good," Dickers said, obviously satisfied. "Raise your hoods."

The demons obeyed, obscuring their faces in complete shadow. Even Oliver. Seeing his face smothered by blackness sent my heart skittering in my chest.

Relax, I told myself. *It'll be fine.*

I know, Oliver thought back to me. *I love you.*

I stiffened. Somehow, he'd heard me.

"Draw your blades," Dickers ordered from under his hood.

Everyone, including Oliver, drew a dagger from the folds of their cloaks. I tensed, and Kismet squeezed my arm.

"Spill your blood," said Dickers.

The demons slid the blades along their palms. Blood dripped onto the floor. I clenched my teeth so hard my head throbbed. The air around me thickened with black magic, suffocating me. I struggled to breathe.

Relax. It'll be fine. This time I was reassuring us both, unsure if he could hear or not.

"Whenever you're ready, Gerrick," Dickers said quietly.

I waited, holding my breath. My heart pounded painfully in my chest.

Any minute now, the man I loved would become a demon.

Though I was several feet away, I could almost feel Oliver drawing a breath. Then he spoke, his voice loud and unwavering.

"Blood of my blood, I summon this power.
Spirits commune with me this hour.
Accept this transition and the power therein,
And enhance my soul and magic within.
Dark souls who reside among the First Tier,
Embrace my blood and empower me here."

My pulse roared so loudly in my ears that I barely heard the other demons as they chanted, "Blood of our blood. Blood of our blood."

Dark energy swirled in my chest so thick and stifling that my chest caved inward as if cowering in fear. Blackness consumed me, draining the light that remained and obscuring it like inky darkness. What little light peered through the shutters was shadowed by the black magic pouring from each demon's palm. The magic floated toward Oliver's figure and blocked him from view. I clenched my fists, my fingernails digging into my palms.

I squinted, trying to see Oliver through the smoky, black magic that spun around him like a funnel cloud.

Where is he? It'll smother him!

Kismet rubbed my arm. I clutched at her fingers, focusing on her warmth for comfort. But the black magic in the air filled my nostrils, choking me. I couldn't breathe. My eyes closed against the darkness, and my parents' faces filled my mind. I focused on them, and I could breathe again. But it was like sucking through a tiny straw.

Then, a deep abyss opened up in my chest, clouding my mind. I remembered the thrilling power from when I'd sacrificed the werewolf in Manila. The addicting energy. The feeling of being unstoppable. Unbeatable. Invincible. I slaughtered those vampires who'd kidnapped Reyna like they were nothing more than insects.

I swallowed, but the thoughts persisted, racing through me and drawing me closer to that darkness I feared.

Kismet's fingernails dug into my arm, and I gasped. The pain sent a bolt of clarity through my mind. I looked at her, and even in the dimness of the room I made out her concerned eyes as they drilled into me.

I knew without a doubt she'd felt me falling and had brought me back.

I exhaled long and slow and patted her hand on my arm. *Thank you.* Though the darkness crept in on my mind like clawed fingers gripping me, I remained lucid. In control. I squinted through the circle of hooded figures, trying to see Oliver.

The black magic faded, revealing a figure within. It looked like he was struggling—trying to fight off the smoke surrounding him. But then, suddenly, he stopped, stiffening. His spine was straight, and his head whipped back so far that his hood fell. I couldn't make out his expression, but his eyes were closed, and his mouth was wide open. I couldn't tell if he was trying to scream or if he was in shock.

My heart stopped for a full beat as I watched him succumb. Then, at long last, the magic faded and dispersed, leaving the charred scent of darkness in its wake.

My rapid heartbeat thundered in my chest, and my pulse slammed against my eardrums. Oliver remained arched back, his eyes still closed. But an eerie calmness took over his features. His mouth had closed, and his eyebrows lifted almost with a sense of peace.

Then his eyes opened, and I sucked in a breath.

They were all black.

That glistening green I loved so much was gone.

There were no whites in his eyes. Only darkness and death.

Then, he yelled as if injured. His head dropped in his hands, his fingers shaking as he raked them through his hair.

I stepped toward him, but Kismet held me back. Panic flooded my throat. *What's happening? He's hurt. I have to help him!*

Oliver swung his head back and forth as if trying to shake something off him. The tendons in his neck stood out. His fingers clenched into fists by his side. His jaw ticked back and forth, and he slowly opened his eyes. They weren't black anymore. But his eyebrows drew together, his face pale and covered in sweat.

"Get out of my head!" he roared, covering his face with his hands.

Matthias. My blood ran cold.

Oliver clawed at his scalp, his fingers scratching like he could peel Matthias's influence from his head.

He's going to hurt himself.

I had to do something. Perhaps I could still reach him. *Oliver? Can you hear me? It's going to be okay. I'm here.*

Nothing changed. Oliver still struggled, running his hands over his head and face and looking deranged and unstable.

Oliver, look at me. I love you. You can do this.

He didn't register my words at all. Then, in horror, I realized why: we no longer practiced the same brand of magic.

Our blood oath was still intact, but it wasn't as strong as it had been before. I searched within myself and felt the briefest flicker of agony, whereas moments ago, I felt his panic as clearly as if it had been my own.

A lump rose in my throat. Long, red marks formed on Oliver's face from his fingernails.

None of the cloaked figures moved at all. Why weren't they doing anything?

I couldn't just stand there. I shifted, and Kismet tightened her grip on my arm. I turned to look at her, gritting my teeth. "Let. Go."

I would Push her away if I had to.

She seemed to read the determination in my face. She released me, and I bolted forward, shoving the demons aside to get to Oliver.

As soon as I stood in front of him, I could *smell* the difference. The scents of rot, ash, and lime mingled with his familiar grassy scent, filling my nose and clouding my throat. I resisted the urge to cough and grabbed his hands before he could scratch himself again.

He stilled at my touch, his wild gaze fixating on me.

Blackness swirled in his eyes, but I could still make out the green just behind it.

His hands were cold and clammy, but I pressed them to my lips. "I'm here, Oliver."

He froze, watching me. His hair stood up in different directions, and sweat coated his face. Labored breaths poured from his mouth, but he remained motionless. As if waiting for something.

Slowly, I drew closer and pressed my palm against his cheek. My thumb grazed up and down, tracing the space between his nose and lips. He closed his eyes, his expression softening.

"It's all right," I whispered. "I'm here. You're okay."

"I—I hear him, Desi," he moaned, his voice breaking. He sounded so pitiful that my eyes stung with tears. I couldn't bear to see him this way.

But I had to endure it. I had to be strong for him.

"Can you tune him out?" I asked softly.

Oliver shook his head. A single tear trickled down his cheek when he opened his eyes to look at me.

Of course not. Matthias won't let him go that easily. Not now that he knows they're connected.

I thought of my own connection to my parents. How almost every night for years, I dreamt of them and woke up in tears. I'd hated it for so long—hated the reminder of that loss and grief.

But it had never stopped. Eventually, I'd had to embrace it. Now, I didn't know what I'd do without that connection.

"Then don't fight it," I said firmly. "Let him in. He can't reach you here. He can't hurt you or me. You only share a connection. But he can't control you. Not like when you were bonded."

I wasn't absolutely sure of this, but I figured Kismet or Bay would've warned us if it were a possibility.

Of course, Matthias was Fourth Tier now. Who knew what he was capable of?

"Let him try to take you," I said, my voice rising. "Let him do his worst. You're *strong*, Oliver. You are *not* him. You're a soldier. A fighter. Remember why you did this: to defeat him."

Oliver inhaled a long, even breath through his nose. Then, he exhaled through his mouth and looked at me. "I am strong," he whispered.

I nodded, running my hand through his disheveled hair. "Yes, you are."

His eyes grew distant. He stared right through me, and in that moment, I knew he was focused on Matthias's words in his head. Then, a smooth serenity took over his features. Half his mouth quirked up in a satisfied smirk, but there was something almost feral about the look. Like he was a predator now, honing in on his prey.

"I am strong," he said again in a deep growl.

The sound jolted me. It didn't sound like him. He was different. A manic glint flashed in his eyes, and I knew what he felt: the power.

Oliver breathed out, his smile widening. Lifting a hand, he summoned a ball of fire that lit up the room. I squinted against the brightness and then stared, mesmerized.

Wisps of black magic floated within the flame, mingling with the shades of orange and red. The darkness looked like long, thin fingers clutching his magic. Like a monster had taken hold of him.

He was a demon now.

CHAPTER 31

I'M NOT AFRAID. I'M NOT AFRAID OF HIM, I KEPT TELLING myself as the darkness from the ritual faded.

The demons surrounding us lowered their hoods. Some muttered to each other. Others vanished in a puff of black smoke. I felt Kismet's gaze on me from across the room, but I could only stare at Oliver.

Inky blackness still swirled within his green eyes, making them look darker than his usual olive color. He stared at something beyond me, and a dark hunger stirred in his expression. I resisted the urge to shudder. Swallowing down my fear, I took his hand.

He stiffened and looked at me, the intensity of his gaze spearing right through me.

"Are you all right?" I asked quietly.

He stared at me for a long moment as if seeing me

for the first time. His eyes bore through mine, and the blackness within gradually faded. A soft smile spread across his lips. In that moment, he was my Oliver again.

"Yes. Thank you for being here with me, Desi."

Relief blossomed in my chest. "Of course." I tried to ignore how my stomach twisted and served as a reminder that something was off. That something was wrong. Instead of focusing on it, I pretended everything was normal and let Oliver lead me across the room to where Kismet and Bay stood, whispering in hushed voices.

"How'd I do?" Oliver asked, still smiling.

Bay nodded. Approval glinted in his eyes. "Very well. You fought harder than other initiates I've seen. Most succumb to the darkness right away."

"What's the alternative?" I asked.

Bay rubbed the back of his neck and exchanged a wary glance with Kismet. "It depends on the demon and the power of his transformation. The mildest initiations don't change much within the caster. The strongest will alter them completely. Some fight it, and some don't. Some find a gray area where they can still be themselves but work alongside the darkness when needed. It seems this is the direction Oliver's pursuing."

I frowned. He said it as if Oliver hadn't succeeded. Like there was still a battle for him to face.

"Which were you?" Oliver asked.

Bay grinned. "I found that gray area. And I can help you find it too, if you want."

Something dangerous flashed in Oliver's eyes, but it vanished instantly. His lips tightened. "We'll see."

A tense silence fell between us. I cleared my throat and looked at Kismet. "So, now what?"

"We start compiling ingredients for the spell," Kismet said. "I've sensed some alarming emotions from Matthias lately. I'm worried he's getting closer to summoning Asmodeus. We can't waste any more time."

A stone dropped in my stomach. *Oliver and I need to get married.*

Why did that make me so afraid? I squeezed his hand in mine, trying to reassure myself that this was what I wanted.

Kismet's eyes narrowed. She knew something was on my mind.

"Well, we should head back, then," I said, glancing at Oliver and forcing a smile. Without looking at Kismet, I led him toward the door.

We returned to the safehouse, marching wordlessly through the foliage. Oliver's hand felt cooler than normal in my grasp. I couldn't escape the tightness in my chest or the sharp pain in my gut. Every footstep echoed through me: *Wrong, wrong, wrong.*

"You're quieter than usual," Oliver said softly.

I blinked and rubbed my nose. "Just shaken from the ritual. It was . . . hard to watch."

Oliver nodded. "I know. I'm sorry. I don't know what I would've done without you there, though."

You would've succumbed to the darkness. That much I knew.

"Should we tell the others?" he asked.

I looked at him. "Tell them what?"

"That we're getting married."

The churning in my stomach intensified. "I . . . don't know."

"You still want to, don't you?"

"Of course," I said immediately. I'd worked so hard to convince him, I couldn't back down now. "I just don't know how they'll take it."

"We'll have to tell *someone*. I don't know any high priestesses. Do you?"

I chuckled without humor. "Nope."

An awkward silence passed between us. He felt like a stranger. We hadn't had a conversation this stilted since the day we met.

"It was so bizarre, feeling him in my head," Oliver whispered.

A chill raced down my spine. "I don't envy you."

"He wasn't speaking to me directly—I just . . . *felt* him. It's hard to describe."

I nodded. "I understand. Well, not exactly. I'm connected to my parents, but they're dead, so it's different." The lump in my throat hardened. My eyes burned, and I blinked away tears.

"I forgot about that," Oliver said quietly. He stopped and turned to look at me. Though shadows lingered in his eyes, they were almost back to his normal olive green. "What is that like? How do you cope with that constant presence?"

I swallowed. "I mostly feel them in dreams. Memories. Sometimes, I'll black out for a minute and have a kind of vision. Something important they want to convey to me." I sniffed. "I hated it at first. It was a constant reminder of what I'd lost. But in Manila, when I almost went dark . . ." I trailed off, shaking my head. "I realized it would sever that connection. And I couldn't do it. I needed them. I still do."

Oliver said nothing. I glanced sideways at him. His eyes hardened, his mouth forming a thin line. His jaw tensed as he stared, unblinkingly, at the vast parking lot in front of the safehouse. The cool, distant edge in his expression seemed so foreign to me. There was no warmth.

He seemed so foreign. Not at all like my Oliver.

I probably said the wrong thing. Talking about how much I needed my parents could only remind him how much he needed to separate himself from Matthias.

Oliver offered a tight-lipped smile, though his eyes were cold. "Well, I'm just glad he's not in my head anymore."

He's not? I looked at Oliver, uncertainty stirring in my chest. I couldn't imagine Matthias would give up so easily.

I opened my mouth to reply, but Oliver strode purposefully forward, so I let the subject drop.

A small crowd of rebels waited for us in the atrium, their eyes wide and expressions nervous. No doubt that word had spread of Oliver's decision to become a demon. Gina and José stood in the front. When they saw Oliver, José's face paled, and Gina sucked in a sharp gasp.

I stiffened, looking at Oliver. Shadows haunted his eyes again, darkening his expression. A strange vibrant energy lit his face, but the same easy grin sprang to his face when he saw José and Gina.

José recovered first and clapped Oliver on the shoulder, though his smile was tight and his eyes were wary.

"What—what was it like?" Gina asked in a hushed voice.

Bile rose in my throat. I couldn't live through this

again. The strange, unsettling feeling in my stomach only intensified until I felt nauseous.

I excused myself, ducking away as Oliver recounted the horrifying tale of his transformation. He didn't even look up as I left.

Heat burned in my throat. What was wrong with me? I'd known this would happen. So why did I feel this way?

Maybe I just have to get used to it. It only just happened. I need time to process it.

I climbed up the stairs and almost ran straight into Megan.

"Oh!" she said, smiling. "You're back. How's Oliver?"

"Fine," I said quickly. "He's downstairs if you want to see him."

"Oh, no," Megan said, lifting her hands. "I've seen my fair share of demons fresh from their transformation. I'd rather not."

I cocked my head, my heart pounding. "Really? What don't you like about it?"

Megan shifted her weight from one foot to the other. "It's those early stages that are frightening. The time when they think they have it under control, but they don't."

My blood ran cold. "Have you—I mean, what usually happens? How do they get past that phase?"

Megan shrugged. "I'm not entirely sure. The only demons I've met were Mr. Caldwell's clients. But Mr. Caldwell once told me that a newly-formed demon has to learn the hard way who's in control: himself or the darkness."

I shuddered, closing my eyes. I didn't need to hear this.

"Sorry," Megan said, grimacing. "You probably don't want to talk about it."

I took in a slow, even breath, glancing around at the damp stairwell surrounding us. The space was too cramped; I couldn't stretch or dance here.

"I need a distraction," I blurted. "What are you working on right now?"

"Would you like to see?" Megan said, her eyes alight.

I nodded, and she led me upstairs to her room. It was a bit more cluttered than mine; boxes of files and tiny gadgets surrounded her bed, crowding the room. After an apologetic look toward me, she helped me navigate to the armchair by the bed and gestured for me to sit.

"Mr. Caldwell is resting from the ordeal with his goggles," Megan explained, pulling out a notebook from one of the boxes. "I've been helping him to design something less . . . taxing."

I scanned her notes, glancing over words like *aura, power source,* and *imprint.* "What do you mean by *taxing?*"

"How much do you know about aurectomies?"

My mouth twisted. "Uh, nothing. But it sounds really unpleasant."

Megan laughed, plopping on the squashy mattress across from me. "It's the process of removing part of one's soul."

My eyes widened. "Oh, yes. I've heard of that. Like as a form of payment?" I thought of Elena and Guillermo and the bargain they'd struck with a Filipino shaman in order to protect their souls.

Megan nodded. "Most casters, even dark ones, don't perform aurectomies anymore, but the science of it is still there. In order to harness the powers of the soul, payment is required. So, for the goggles to function properly—"

"Elias had to sacrifice part of his *soul?*" I whispered, my heart lurching in my throat. "Why would he do that?"

"We were under attack," Megan said matter-of-factly. "He probably figured it was better than death."

My throat tightened. I wasn't so sure.

"Anyway, we've been researching ways to fuel the power source without weakening the wearer of the goggles."

"What have you found so far?"

It was a relief to dive into something new and take

my mind off Oliver's transformation and the strangeness between us. For the next hour, Megan and I went over her notes and research. Several aurologists had attempted to use rare gems, blood, and even the auras of other people to power their technology, but it was all unsuccessful. Megan's face lit up as she explained it all to me, gesturing enthusiastically with her hands as she spoke. My eyes fell to the black cuff on her wrist, and I frowned.

"Megan, about those aurologists who tried using other people's auras to power their devices," I said, pointing to her wrist. "Were the subjects . . . I don't know, *alive* at the time?"

Megan nodded. "Auras are useless without a host."

I drummed my fingers on my knees. "What kind of magic did the subjects use? Dark or light?"

Megan rubbed her chin. "I'm not sure. Why?"

"Well, maybe it functions like the bond between two souls. Maybe it's strengthened when the victim and the one wearing the goggles both practice the same brand of magic."

Megan's eyes widened, her gaze distant. Then, she raised a finger and pointed to me, her mouth stretching into a wide smile. "That's an interesting theory! I think I have some research on that."

My spirits lifted as she sifted through another box,

dumping a huge stack of notes on my lap. Together, we studied in silence, occasionally asking a question or making a comment.

Since Oliver's demon ritual, my mind was spiraling. I had to push aside that fear and unease and force my thoughts elsewhere, and this provided the perfect outlet.

For the rest of the day, I freed my mind of Oliver, his black magic, and the battle we had ahead of us. I even forced away thoughts of our upcoming wedding. Megan and I paused briefly for sandwiches that she had in a small cooler—claiming she knew she'd forget to eat if it meant having to leave her room—and then continued our research.

It comforted me to immerse myself in something as fascinating as aurology. I hadn't felt drawn to anything like this since I first started dancing. And this time, it was different; it directly related to myself and my magic. Ballet had been alluring because it was separate—a way to escape from being a witch. But this, here and now, felt important. Monumental. It was tied to everything. The weight of that importance settled comfortably in my chest like a warm compress. A reassurance that this was where I was meant to be.

Ever since Kismet had revealed that the link between our souls was the cause of my time travel, I'd been painfully curious about how the science behind it worked. I recognized that same fire in Megan. She *loved* this stuff.

And I could see why.

At the end of the day, Megan showed me her latest experiment: a large metal monocle. It looked like Elias's goggles severed in half so it only covered one eye, and it had a strap that reminded me of a pirate's eye patch. She pulled out a small box of tools and began tweaking while I peered over her shoulder. Occasionally, a zap of electricity jolted through the device, and we both jumped and then giggled.

Before we could test it out, someone knocked on the door. Megan rose to answer it while I inspected the monocle.

"There you are," said a familiar voice.

I looked up, and my stomach dropped. Oliver. Of course he'd been looking for me.

"Sorry!" Megan said, cringing. "I didn't mean to kidnap her for so long."

"Don't worry about it, Megan," I said, rising from the chair and stretching my stiff muscles. "I enjoyed it. Can I join you again tomorrow?"

Megan grinned. "Of course! Thanks for your help, Desi."

Once Megan's door shut behind us, Oliver frowned at me. "Are you sure you should offer to help her again tomorrow? Won't we be busy with . . .?" He trailed off, gesturing between us.

I shrugged, not meeting his gaze. "Maybe. But like you said, we need a high priestess, don't we? We should probably worry about that first."

Oliver caught my elbow, stopping me before we reached the stairwell. Without thinking, I flinched away from him, recoiling from the strange coolness of his skin.

Oliver jerked backward like I'd shocked him. "What's going on?" he asked, his voice quiet.

I couldn't avoid his gaze any longer. I looked up into his eyes. The shadows still swirled within them as if taunting me.

"Nothing," I lied, knowing he'd see right through it. "I just needed a distraction for a while."

"A distraction from . . . me?" His voice tightened.

"No," I said quickly. "Just from everything, you know? We're going through a lot. I needed to dive into something else." I lifted my arms uselessly. I couldn't speak correctly around him anymore.

Oliver took both my hands in his, and I gritted my teeth. It felt like a stranger touching me. I hated to admit it, but he didn't feel like *my* Oliver.

"Desi, you can talk to me," he whispered. "I'm still the same person."

No, you're not. I shoved the words down my throat and nodded. "I know. I just need . . . time."

"How much time?" His tone sounded strained. Hurt.

I met his eyes again. "I don't know."

"Should I talk to Bay? About performing a blood oath instead?"

A tense silence hung between us. The "no" came to my lips, but it stopped there. I couldn't say it. My vision blurred with tears, and I closed my eyes.

"Desi," Oliver said, wiping a tear from my cheek.

I gasped and drew away from him before I could stop myself. Something like anger flashed in his eyes.

"*Talk to me,*" he said fiercely. The intensity in his voice frightened me. It sounded like several voices layered together.

My blood chilled. I stepped back from him again. "I should—I should go. I need to find Kismet."

I turned from him, but he gripped my wrist so tightly I hissed in pain. "Oliver."

His eyes were all black now. I suppressed a scream, my voice lodging in my throat.

"You're not going anywhere," he growled, still using that foreign voice.

This wasn't him. This was Matthias.

CHAPTER 32

I WRIGGLED MY WRIST, BUT OLIVER'S GRIP WAS unyielding. "Let me go!" I cried.

"Desiree." With his free hand, he swept my hair out of my eyes. A shiver ran down my spine.

I slapped his cheek. "Let *go!*"

A dangerous fury ignited within him, and he grabbed my other arm with his hand, pinning me in place. I jerked against him, but it was no use. A quick glance around the hall told me we were alone. But if I screamed, surely someone would come investigate.

Desi.

I stilled. My eyes flew to Oliver, but the darkness still filled his face, distorting him into something dark. Something disturbing.

Yet I heard the voice again. *Desi!*

I blinked, my head rearing back. *Oliver.*

I'm still here, Desi. Help me!

My mouth opened and closed. The Oliver looking at me bared his teeth like a predator. Matthias had taken over.

But how could I get *my* Oliver back?

Without thinking, I leaned forward, pressing my lips to his. He froze, his body stiffening. A sharp inhale of breath broke our kiss, but I pushed myself onto him, drawing his mouth in for another.

Kiss me, dammit. Kiss me!

And then his arms wound around me, pulling me closer. A small tendril of warmth passed between us—a shadow of the Oliver I once knew. It strengthened until my stomach exploded in a swarm of butterflies. My skin felt hot under his touch. That glorious, grassy gunpowder scent filled me once more.

He moaned against my lips. I touched his face, my fingers roving over his cheeks, his nose, and his ears. He was mine again. All mine.

"Desi," he murmured, his voice returning to normal. He tried to pull away, but I kissed him again, easing his lips open until I felt his tongue emerge.

Oh, Lilith.

Oliver swept me up in his arms and crushed me against his chest, hoisting me up until my legs lifted off the floor. He broke our kiss and cradled the back of my head. I pressed my nose into his shirt. Tears sparked in my eyes as I buried myself in him, surrounding myself with the Oliver I'd longed for.

"You're back," I said in a strained voice. My eyes closed in relief. I hadn't been crazy. Here he was, and I still loved him. We were still the same.

Oliver panted in my ear, drawing away to look at me. Confusion and doubt crossed his features. "Was I gone?"

I searched his eyes. They were all green again, glistening with unshed tears.

I swallowed and nodded. "What do you remember?"

Oliver's gaze grew distant. "I remember returning here. Talking with the other rebels. Then . . ." His brows furrowed. "I don't know. It's a bit hazy after that."

"You just—you just attacked me," I choked, tears spilling from my eyes. "You were *him*, Oliver."

He stepped away from me, his eyes wide. Horror struck his face, and he ran a hand through his hair. "What?"

I pressed my lips together, willing myself to stop crying. I was only making this worse.

Oliver paced in front of me, running a hand down his face and breathing heavily. "But you—you brought me back?" He pointed at me, uncertain.

I nodded. "I think I caught him by surprise."

"Him." His eyes darkened. "Matthias."

I held my breath, waiting for that blackness to take over, but it didn't. Oliver stared at the wall behind me. "He's still there. But I see him now. Crouched in the corners of my mind. I thought he was gone before, but . . ." He shook his head. "He's with me. I think he always will be."

I shook my head, my expression crumpling. The threat of more tears loomed behind my eyes.

Oliver looked at me, his eyes tortured. Regret and grief pulsed from him in tangible waves, feeding off my own sorrow. I read it in his eyes: *We can never be together.*

"No. *No!*" I took his face in my hands and kissed him again. But this time, he remained still. Gently, he grasped my hands and stepped away from me.

"Desi, I can't," he whispered. His eyes opened, revealing the same captivating green I loved. But agony flared in his eyes so bright it blinded me, shattering my heart. "I can't." He dropped my hands and left, vanishing in the stairwell. The sound of his heavy footsteps echoed along with the rapid beating of my heart.

After Oliver and I parted, I went to my room. For the next hour, I sat on my bed, drumming my fingers along the edge of the mattress. Waiting. The sky outside darkened with impending dusk.

Oliver would come to me when he was ready. I just had to give him time.

But my heart stampeded inside me like a wild stallion, raging and panicked.

How can I just sit here? How can I possibly leave him alone right now? I thought of when he struck that bargain with Matthias and performed the blood bond—how he'd hidden it from everyone because he thought he could handle it on his own.

In a flash, I was on my feet, striding toward the door.

You're not alone, Oliver, I thought fiercely. *Whether you like it or not.*

Sorrow pulsed through our blood oath in waves. Though the intensity of it pierced my heart, a small part of me was relieved to feel him there at all. It meant he was still in control.

I followed the energy of his emotions, climbing up the stairs to the next floor and rushing down the hallway.

I paused between two doors. Oliver's emotions still burned within me. I closed my eyes, focusing on him and honing in on his presence.

This one. Certainty raced through me. I stared at the door in front of me and raised my fist to knock. Then I stilled.

He won't let me in.

So instead, I lifted my hands and Pushed it open.

A loud *crack* indicated I'd broken the lock. As I suspected, Oliver had barricaded himself in his room.

He sat on the edge of his bed just like I had earlier. He turned from the window to stare wide-eyed at me as I surged toward him. Tears streamed down his face, and he hastily wiped them away before jumping to his feet.

"Desi, what the hell?" Shock and anger flared in his face.

"Sit down." I shoved his shoulders until he plopped back down on the bed, his face slackening in shock. "I gave you time to wallow; now it's your turn to listen." Fire roared in my veins, strengthening my resolve. I paced in front of him, my limbs restless. I flexed my fingers and shook my hands, trying to rid myself of this anxious energy.

"I'm going to be your wife," I said. When he opened his mouth to object, I raised a hand to silence him. "Don't interrupt. I *am* going to marry you, Oliver. And as your future wife, I need to stick by you in *everything*. Not just the good parts but the bad parts too. The dark, the ugly, and the horrifying. No matter *what*, Oliver." I stopped and stared at him, my teeth clenched. "You're mine. Forever. Whether you like it or not. Do you understand?" I stepped toward him and placed my hands on his shoulders. He looked up at me, eyes wide and shining. In that moment, he seemed so innocent, like a heartbroken child seeking comfort.

"I don't care if we haven't exchanged vows or blood yet," I said, my voice softening. I stroked his face, brushing loose strands of blond hair out of his eyes. "I'm with you until the end. I'm here, bonded to you forever." I pressed my palm against his chest, feeling his rapid heartbeat. "We are one, Oliver. Let me in. I don't care how dark it is. The whole mess with Gwen and your engagement—"

Oliver flinched.

I rubbed his shoulder and offered a sympathetic smile. "That whole situation stemmed from you keeping secrets. You hid things from me because they weren't pretty. Because you didn't want to hurt me. Because they made things difficult. You don't have to do that anymore, Oliver."

I took his hands in mind. "No matter how dark, or nasty, or ugly something is, I will face it *with* you. I played my part in that mess too. I pushed you away. But not anymore. I'm here with you. Nothing you say or do will turn me away. I swear to Lilith, I will fight for you— even if Matthias claims you, even if Asmodeus himself enslaves you and drags you down to Hell. *I will fight for you*. Do you hear me?"

I gently placed my hands on his cheeks, bringing his

face closer to me. He had to understand this. I had to get through to him. He wasn't alone anymore. And until he could honestly tell me he no longer loved me, he would *never* be alone again.

Hope glistened in his eyes. Another tear raced down his cheek. "Desi—"

"No," I snapped, pressing a hard kiss to his lips. I pulled away and put my hands on his shoulders. "You're not hearing me. I'm not leaving until we figure this out together."

The corners of his mouth twitched. "Stars above, you're the most beautiful thing I've ever seen," he whispered.

I froze. *I wasn't expecting that.* Heat churned in my stomach, climbing up my chest and bringing painful desire along with it. I swallowed, my throat dry.

Oliver's hands clutched my waist. "Remember when I was the one trying to get you to open up when we first met? I goaded you into arguing with me." Amusement danced in his eyes.

I didn't move. I stared into his gaze, assessing. His eyes were still moist, but they were him. They were all Oliver.

I relaxed. "Look how far we've come."

"You've come much farther than me," Oliver said bitterly. "I haven't changed much, have I?"

"That's not true." I traced a finger over his upper lip. His breath hitched, and his fingers pressed more firmly into my waist. "We're not arguing now, are we?"

"Not in the slightest," he said, his voice so low and husky that my bones quivered and my toes curled.

Lilith, I wanted him so bad.

I dropped my hands and took a small step back, clearing my throat. A blush rose in my cheeks. I sank into the armchair across from him and placed my sweaty palms on my knees. *Change the subject. Now is not the time.*

I kept my gaze directed to the floor and said, "So, now that we're on the same page—what's it like? Is he still in your head?"

Oliver nodded. "Yes. It's still not as strong as before. Right after the ritual, I think—I think he withdrew on purpose."

"He wanted you to think you were still in control," I said quietly.

Oliver took a shaky breath. "Yes."

I looked at him, frowning. "But you *are* in control, right? At least right now."

"Ever since you told me that I"—he choked on the words, his eyes closing—"I attacked you, yes. I've felt him fade in and out, but he's only a presence. He was strongest about a moment before you barged in here."

"Maybe you woke up or something. When you realized what was happening."

"It feels that way. But I'm afraid of overconfidence. I don't want to let down my guard again."

Now that I was certain the heat had left us, I figured it was safe to approach him again. I sat next to him on the bed and took his hand. "Then don't. But don't push people away either."

I leaned my head on his shoulder, and he pressed a kiss against my forehead. "I won't."

Just after sunset, Oliver and I went downstairs to the cafeteria, where the rest of the rebels were eating dinner. My heart surged with confidence. With everything in my soul, I knew this was right. And no one would stop me.

I clutched Oliver's fingers tightly in mine. Several rebels looked at us curiously as we walked by. But my eyes were on Kismet and Bay, who were eating in the corner of the room. They were huddled together, jotting down notes and poring over the Grimoire they'd gotten from the Council. I had no doubt they were compiling a shopping list of ingredients for the banishing spell.

Kismet's gaze lifted to meet mine, her brows pinching. "Desi, what's wrong?"

I took a steady breath. "Oliver and I need a high priestess."

Kismet went still. Bay stiffened, his brows lowering.

"We're going to perform the handfasting rite," I went on, giving Oliver's hand a squeeze and focusing on the reassuring warmth of his skin. "If this makes you uncomfortable, then I suggest you make other arrangements . . . for what we previously discussed. Because if you can't get on board with this decision, then perhaps I'm not the best person to . . ." I trailed off, trying to find the right words without giving away her secret. "To do what you're asking of me." *Damn.* I started off strong but ended up bumbling through my speech like an idiot.

Kismet blinked at me. Something unreadable stirred in her eyes. She set down her sandwich and clasped her hands together on the table. "Are you absolutely sure about this?"

Her calm demeanor startled me. No anger. No defiance. "Yes," I said, a little too loudly. I cleared my throat and tried again. "Yes, we're sure. One hundred percent."

Kismet nodded, her jaw ticking back and forth. She exchanged a look with Bay. His brows remained lowered, his eyes fixed on Oliver, but he sighed and then looked at Kismet.

They stared at each other, communicating wordlessly for a moment.

Kismet looked back at me, the corners of her mouth creasing in a small smile. "Well, you're in luck. I just so happen to be a high priestess."

CHAPTER 33

WHILE KISMET AND BAY WENT TO GATHER INGREDIENTS for the ritual, I paced my room, trying not to explode as the same thought kept circulating through me again and again:

I'm getting married.

I had no doubts. I knew with all my heart that I wanted to be with Oliver. But terror clawed at my chest. The fear of committing myself so wholly to one person. Of being crushed the same way I was after my parents died. The raw, open vulnerability of leaving your heart in the hands of another.

It was beyond frightening. And it made my insides quiver.

I left Oliver to get ready. We both agreed to keep it simple—it wasn't like we had access to formal attire anyway. A plain white dress lay on my bed, borrowed from Megan's wardrobe. It was simple. Pretty. It definitely didn't scream "wedding dress," though.

It just didn't feel real.

I never imagined myself having a huge wedding. I wasn't that type of girl. But it was still a special event. I wanted this day to stand out. I wanted to be able to tell my children something more than, *Oh yeah, I just threw on a dress and we got married.*

My heart ached for my parents to be here. I knew if they were here, I would feel complete.

A light knock sounded at the door. I froze, my heart lurching in my throat. *It's Oliver. He's dressed and ready to go, and I haven't even processed this yet!*

While internally screaming, I strode to the door and opened it.

Kismet stood in front of me holding a large cardboard box.

I blinked and stepped by to let her in.

"Bay's getting set up downstairs," she said, hoisting the box onto the armchair with a grunt. "There's a small chapel that patients used to use when they couldn't attend church services." She straightened and eyed me up and down. "Oh good! You aren't dressed yet. Come here." She opened the box.

Frowning, I approached and peered inside. I sucked in a breath.

Inside was an array of items: silk flowers, a tiara, a veil, a small, black jewelry box that almost certainly held a ring inside, and, underneath it all, a shimmering, pearly white fabric.

My heart stopped for a full beat, my eyes glued to the fabric. I knew exactly what it was. Carefully, I dug my hands inside the box and shifted the items around, pulling out the gown. It unfolded, cascading to the floor.

Mom's wedding dress.

Decorative beads and lace crisscrossed along the bodice. It was sleeveless, and much shorter in length than I anticipated. When I held it up, it only fell to my knees.

"They were married on a beach," Kismet said, reading the surprise in my face. "Jenny said she wanted something simple. She didn't even wear the veil, though she kept it. Said it was her mother's."

A lump lodged in my throat. I blinked back tears and stared breathlessly at the gown. The skirt flared outward like a summer dress. Though it made the delicate bodice seem ostentatious, I thought it was perfect. No train to trip over but still elegant. A weightless wedding dress.

It was a relief, to be honest. I'd always hated those heavy, restricting dresses.

I sniffed and looked at Kismet. Her own eyes were moist too. She drew in a shaky breath. "Want me to help you?"

Swallowing, I nodded, at a loss for words. Though I could've certainly managed on my own, it was a comfort having Kismet there with me. I slipped out of my jeans and T-shirt and slid into Mom's dress. It fit a bit loosely on me, since Mom had been much taller. It also settled in awkward places around my chest, but I didn't care.

I was wearing my mother's wedding dress. It was as if she were here with me.

Then, unbidden, a memory overcame me.

"Why are you outside?" I asked, pointing to the picture of Mom and Dad standing together in the sand.

Mom smiled. "It's where we wanted to be married. We've never been particularly religious, and we have a certain fondness for nature. It made the moment more special."

I cocked my head, squinting at the photo. I couldn't make out the details of her dress. "You aren't wearing a veil. Or a crown. You don't have any flowers either."

Mom laughed. "I know. We'd planned on all those things, but when the time came, it just felt like . . . too much. So we simplified it. And it was absolutely perfect."

My heart warmed. The longer I stared at the picture, the more I saw. The crinkling around Dad's eyes from his wide smile. The blush in Mom's cheeks. The way they clasped each other as if desperate to hold on for one moment more.

The pure happiness emanating from the photo made me smile too. And I understood what Mom meant. Maybe if they'd had a huge wedding they wouldn't have been this happy. And then it wouldn't have been worth it.

"One day, you'll get married too, Desi," Mom said, stroking my hair out of my eyes.

I wrinkled my nose and stuck out my tongue. "Yuck. That's for grown-ups."

Mom's eyes twinkled. "I know. But one day, you'll be a grown-up. And I can't wait to see what kind of wedding you choose to have."

I stared thoughtfully at the photo a moment longer. My heart longed to get married someplace magical like a princess in a castle. But something within me resonated with the image of my parents on a beach. The simplicity. The ease. The care-free, relaxed atmosphere. Nothing like those tense wedding planning shows I saw on TV.

Yes, I decided. That was what I wanted. Something simple. Effortless. Happy.

I gasped. Tears streamed down my face.

"What is it?" Kismet asked.

I shook my head and choked on a sob. "Nothing," I said thickly. "I just feel her here. I feel them both."

Kismet rubbed my shoulder. "I know. Me too."

The tears flowed harder, overwhelming me. My chest shook as I wept. Kismet gathered me in her arms, and I sobbed into her shoulder. I couldn't stop. I didn't know if I was happy or sad. Maybe a bit of both. Delighted that I had this piece of my parents to hold onto. Devastated that they weren't here in person to see it happen.

When I finished crying, Kismet helped reapply my makeup and offered me her sandals to wear. They were much better than my grubby sneakers.

I stared for a long moment at the veil and tiara still sitting in the box. Then, I smiled and lifted the veil over my head. Grandma died when I was three, and I didn't remember much about her. But even so, it was nice to have her here with me too. It felt wrong to waste the opportunity.

Kismet adjusted the veil over my curls and stepped back, beaming. "Beautiful," she breathed.

My heart fluttered with anticipation. My chest felt weightless. *I might faint.*

"One more thing." Kismet dug inside the box and withdrew the jewelry box. When she opened it, my eyes burned with more tears. I blinked fiercely, trying to remain composed.

My parents' wedding rings were nestled together inside. Mom's princess-cut, white gold engagement ring and both their bands.

I covered my mouth, trying to stifle more sobs. This was too much. It was too perfect. Oliver had no family here and no heirlooms to pass on. I'd worried about finding a ring for him but had pushed the thought away, thinking we'd get to it later.

But here was a set of rings waiting to be worn.

"I don't"—I paused and swallowed—"I don't know if he'll want Dad's ring."

Kismet rolled her eyes. "Of course he will, Desi." She closed the box and carefully slid it into her pocket.

I nodded numbly. It still felt awkward pushing my parents' entire wedding memorabilia on him like this. I wrung my hands together, trying to ignore the erratic beating of my heart. "Kiz, do you—do you regret it? Not marrying Bay?"

Kismet's expression sobered, and something unreadable stirred in her eyes. She hesitated for a moment and then a shy smile spread across her face. "Actually, Bay and I eloped a few days ago."

My eyes widened. "*What*? Why didn't you say anything?"

"We wanted to do it in secret. We worried that if we made it a big deal, it would attract too much unwanted attention." Kismet shrugged one shoulder, but she was beaming. "I contacted a fellow high priestess, and she met us out here to perform the ritual." Slowly, her smile spread, lighting her face with an angelic glow.

I laughed in disbelief and embraced her again. "That's amazing! I'm so happy for you, Kismet."

Kismet rubbed my shoulder and pulled away, sniffing. "You ready?"

I exhaled through my mouth. "Yes."

Kismet looped her arm through mine and led me to the stairwell. My heart drummed a nervous rhythm with each step I took.

When we emerged in the cafeteria, we passed by a few rebels, who raised their eyebrows at us. But we ignored them and continued down the hall to the small door that led to the chapel.

We stopped, our arms still linked.

My breaths wouldn't stop shaking.

"So you're a high priestess?" I whispered.

Kismet snorted, no doubt seeing right through my stalling tactic. "Yes. I joined a holy coven when I was pregnant. It helped me commune with the spirits and feel at ease. It was monumental during childbirth."

I raised my eyebrows. I'd never pegged her for the religious type.

"It's not what you think," she said with a sigh. "It's less religious and more . . . spiritual. More like I'm united with the powers within me. The source of our magic."

"How come you never mentioned it?"

Kismet paused. "I didn't want anyone to ask questions. For all anyone knew, I was traveling overseas and making connections with other rebels."

I nodded.

"And I never told you because—well, because I thought you'd laugh at me."

I stared at her. "How could you think that? Kiz, you're like a mother to me."

A blush filled her cheeks. "That means nothing. You laughed at your mother all the time."

I nudged her shoulder. "I might not have understood right away. But I couldn't laugh at something like that."

Kismet rubbed my arm and smiled. "Shall we?"

I nodded again. Knots formed in my stomach, and Kismet pulled open the door.

A dozen pews filled the small room, separated in the middle by an aisle. At the front—near where an altar would've been—stood Oliver and Bay, surrounded by a circle of candles. Oliver was dressed in a white, button-up shirt and a black bowtie along with black slacks. His hair had been slicked back.

His eyes met mine across the aisle.

My chest exploded in a torrent of heat and desire. His eyes widened, his jaw slackening. Awe and admiration shone in his eyes. His gaze never drifted from mine as Kismet and I strode slowly down the aisle. I clung to her with trembling fingers, relying on her to keep me upright. Oliver's stare could've melted me into a puddle right then and there.

When we finally reached him, I saw tears on his face. I swept them away with my thumb, and he brushed a kiss against my fingertips.

"You're breathtaking, Desiree," he whispered.

Warmth radiated in my chest. My cheeks burned. "Thank you."

Kismet positioned herself behind the podium where a small bowl rested. "Draw your blade."

I suppressed a shudder at her words, thinking of Oliver's blood ritual. Instead, I focused on Oliver as he pulled out a small pocketknife and looked expectantly at Kismet.

"Spill your blood," she said.

Oliver ran the blade along his palm and then looked at me, his eyes apologetic.

I offered my hand and nodded. Oliver pressed the

knife against my palm. I hissed, watching the blood run down my hand.

"Enjoin your hands," said Kismet.

We clasped our bleeding hands tightly together. I looked at Oliver, my heart lurching at the intensity of his gaze. His eyes were all green. No shadows. No hint of demon. He was just my Oliver.

Kismet raised her hands so they hovered over the bowl. Her eyes closed as she uttered the spell:

"Spirits above, I bid you draw near,

Bind this blood and seal it here.

Entwine this couple in body and soul,

Strengthen their bond and make it whole.

Link them together, every word and breath,

And bind them forever until parted by death."

A ripple of magic tingled the air. The hairs on my arm stood on end. Heat churned between our hands.

"Go ahead, Oliver," Kismet said softly.

Oliver's eyes met mine before he spoke.

"Blood of blood and magic between us,

I forge this bond and pledge myself thus.

I offer my soul in complete unity,

To thee as my wife for all eternity."

A burst of energy filled my chest, tickling my throat and nose. I held Oliver's gaze, though my heart quivered. My stomach somersaulted again and again until I was sure I'd puke.

"Desi, your turn," Kismet whispered.

I released a shaky breath, my eyes never straying from Oliver's.

"Blood of blood and magic between us,
I forge this bond and pledge myself thus.
I offer my soul in complete unity,
To thee as my husband for all eternity."

Fire scorched my palm, but I held onto Oliver's hand, gritting my teeth against the pain.

Kismet said in a loud, clear voice, "As a high priestess of the holy coven of New York City, I declare you husband and wife through the handfasting blood rite."

My eyes filled with tears. Oliver was already weeping, his eyes vibrant beneath the moisture. His tears fell to the carpeted floor, and he laughed, wiping his nose with his free hand.

Kismet pulled the jewelry box from her pocket and opened it up. Then she handed me Dad's rings and gave Mom's rings to Oliver. She sniffed. "Here are the rings."

Oliver's eyes widened as he stared at the rings in my hand. "Are those—?"

"My dad's rings, yeah." I bit my lip. "Is that okay?"

More tears streamed down his face. "Damn it," he muttered, impatiently wiping them away.

I kicked him lightly. "Don't swear in the middle of our wedding."

We both laughed.

"Yes, that's more than okay," Oliver said quietly. "As long as you think it's what they would want." Something like regret shone in his eyes, and I knew what he wasn't saying.

As long as they'd approve of you marrying a demon.

I lifted my chin and stared him down. "They would want me to marry someone I love. So yes. They would certainly approve."

Oliver smiled and released my hand. Brief shock registered within me when I noticed our palms were no longer bleeding.

"Desiree Campbell, with this ring, I thee wed." Oliver slid Mom's rings onto my finger.

I suppressed a giddy laugh and said, "Oliver Gerrick, with this ring, I thee wed." I slipped the ring on his finger, relieved that it fit him perfectly.

We looked expectantly at Kismet, who shrugged as if to say, *My part's done.* She clapped her hands. "You, uh, may kiss the bride."

Oliver and I chuckled. He drew me in, his hand pressing against my back. I gazed up at him, memorizing his features. The crinkles in his eyes were just like Dad's from his wedding photo. The olive color of his eyes glistened like the sea. The desperate desire in his gaze made my stomach churn.

He kissed me gently at first. Then, he gained momentum, his mouth roving over mine, easing my lips open until I felt his tongue. I wrapped my arms around his neck, pulling him close. Heat exploded within me. Magic churned in my chest, thrumming as if with approval of our union.

Of our bond. As husband and wife.

CHAPTER 34

My stomach twisted and somersaulted like an acrobat as I climbed the stairs hand-in-hand with Oliver. We didn't speak, but tangible heat flowed between us. A premonition of what was to come.

Don't think about it. Just be with him.

Each breath rattled in my chest. The movement within my stomach intensified to the point of nausea.

Just what I need: to puke on my wedding night.

We reached the third floor, and Oliver held the door open for me. I made the grave error of meeting his gaze as I swept past him. His eyes scorched through me with an energy that was almost painful.

The spinning in my stomach escalated.

He clasped my hand again as we strolled down the hall like it was the most normal thing in the world. His palm was sweaty against mine, and I took comfort in that; it meant he was nervous too.

We paused in front of his closed door. The jagged edge of the door frame indicated it was still broken. I swallowed down my embarrassment.

Oliver took a deep breath, then raised his eyebrows at me. "Are you ready, Mrs. Gerrick?"

This isn't helping. A terrified chuckle burst from my lips. Oliver snorted, blushing furiously.

We were such a mess.

Oliver suddenly grabbed my waist and hoisted me up in his arms. I gasped, clinging to him in surprise. He offered me a wide grin, his face still beet-red. While carrying me, he kicked the door open. I looked around the room, my jaw dropping.

Rose petals littered the floor, and dozens of lit candles outlined the tiny room. Though the bed was small and squishy and the walls bare and bland, the atmosphere took my breath away.

"Did you do all this?" I whispered, glancing at him as he set me back on my feet.

His blush deepened. "Yes. Well, I didn't light the candles. Fire hazard, you know. I asked Gina to take care of it . . ." He trailed off, rubbing the back of his neck. He cleared his throat and quietly closed the door.

My heart lurched, and I swallowed. *Relax, relax, relax.*

How were we so awkward? How many times had we made out and started to undress each other like it was the easiest thing in the world? Yet here we were, unable to do what we both so desperately wanted to.

In a way, I could understand the difference. The other situations had been spontaneous. It had felt natural. But this was forced—like we'd scheduled an appointment for sex or something.

Stop it, Desi. Just bring that heat back. You know it's there.

I turned to face him, and his eyes met mine. That same passion and desire built in his gaze, stirring something within my chest.

Slowly, I took his hand. His skin was warm against mine. I focused on that, trying to block out the swarm of butterflies in my stomach.

"You'll"—he swallowed—"take the lead on this?"

I blinked. "What?"

His eyes closed, and he swore under his breath. "I, uh, I just . . . I've never done this before."

My eyes widened. "Neither have I," I said slowly. Comprehension dawned, and a hot blush erupted on my cheeks. "Lilith, Oliver! You think I'm not a virgin?"

Oliver's mouth opened and closed, his eyes filling with horror. "I—I—well, I just assumed—you were so willing to do this with me back in Santiago like it was nothing, and I—" His mouth clamped shut.

I covered my mouth, shame creeping in on my thoughts. *Merciful Lilith, all this time he thought I was sleeping around with other guys?* "Oliver, *no*! How could you think that? Remember in the demon caves in Santiago when I said it was my first night alone with a man?"

"I thought you were joking!"

I rolled my eyes. "Well, I *was,* but it was still true! No, the reason I wanted to do this with you was so we could share it together. A first time for us *both*. That's what you mean to me. It's what you've always meant to me."

Oliver stared at me, his eyes still wide as saucers. "You—you're a—"

"A virgin, yes."

A long silence passed between us.

"So that day in Santiago, you wanted us both to make love for the first time?" he asked with a frown.

I clutched my hands in front of me, my gaze fixed on the floor. "Yes."

Oliver ran a hand down his face. "I—wow. I wish I'd known that."

My gaze flew to his. "Would that have changed your mind?"

He grimaced. "Probably not. But a big part of why I

was uncomfortable was due to my . . . inexperience. I figured you presumed me to be like all the other soldiers dallying with women here and there." He shook his head. "*All* of them did it. I didn't want to draw attention to the fact that I didn't."

Something softened in my chest, and I stepped toward him. I placed my palm against his face. His cheek felt hot. "If you can still love me thinking I'm some hussy—"

Oliver barked out a laugh.

"Then I can still love you despite your 'inexperience.' We're in this together, Oliver. I've already embraced every side of you—the good and the bad. Nothing about you could turn me away."

He exhaled, leaning his face toward my hand. He caught my fingers in his and brought them to his lips, planting soft kisses along each one. A shiver of pleasure rippled through me.

"Come here," he murmured, grabbing my other hand to pull me against his chest.

I gasped when his hands snaked around my waist, lowering until they rested on my rear. I uttered a noise, half squeal and half laugh.

"I suppose I can do this now," he said in a low, throaty voice, raising an eyebrow at me.

My breath caught in my throat. *Lilith, he has no idea how sexy he is.*

I leaned in and kissed him. His lips captured mine, moving slowly and gently. Heat pooled in my stomach, begging for more. My fingers slid down to his collar, pulling at the buttons on his shirt.

Oliver followed my lead and tugged at his bowtie until it fell loose and drifted to the floor. Together we eased his shirt off, and I stood back to admire him—my husband.

I could officially lust after his body and not feel guilty about it.

I trailed my fingers up and down his abdomen, the hard planes along his chest, and the powerful muscles in his arms. I lingered over the scar on his arm from the athame wound in Santiago. Back from before I knew he was part-demon. Before we fell in love.

My eyes met his, and he offered a half smile. "I'm sure you have scars too."

I bit my lip, raising my eyebrows. "Want to see?"

Hunger stirred in his eyes. Slowly, he nodded.

I turned around, and he fiddled with the back of my dress. "I'm still getting used to these zipping things."

I snorted and covered my mouth. I'd forgotten zippers hadn't become mainstream in his time yet.

"They're called *zippers*, and they're extremely convenient."

"Hmm." Oliver's fingers brushed against my bare back as he unzipped my dress. My skin tingled from his gentle touch.

I slid the straps off my shoulders and let the dress fall to the floor. My heart thundered in my chest as I turned to face him.

His lips parted, his eyes wide. So much affection burned in his gaze that I wanted to look away—but somehow, I couldn't. His eyes roved up and down my body, and I resisted the urge to cross my arms and hide from him.

Just like he was all mine, I was all his too.

"You're so beautiful," he whispered, stepping closer to me. His hands brushed my bare shoulders, trailing down to my stomach.

I closed my eyes, my whole body shuddering with pleasure under his touch. His fingers lingered over the long scar on my chest from where Matthias had stabbed me. I opened my eyes and found his gaze hardened with fury, but only for a moment. His fingers continued, running along my arms and pausing at the crisscrossing scars from the shapeshifters' attack in Santiago, then the fresher wounds on my other shoulder from the were-wolf at Elias's manor.

"Does it still hurt?" he whispered.

"Not right now," I said, my voice practically a moan.

Something in him ignited, and he drew me against his chest again. His mouth was on mine, then he slid down to my neck, running his lips and tongue over my skin.

And then I was there. No more awkwardness. No more nervous anticipation. We were both enveloped in the heat—the fiery passion we'd kept contained for so long. My whole body burned like an all-consuming flame.

Momentary awkwardness returned as we fumbled and hesitated, uncertain exactly how to do it properly. But the heat never left. We checked in with each other often, pausing during the points of discomfort and making sure not to lose momentum or inflict any pain.

Then, I reached the moment where no amount of pain could touch me. All I felt was him—skin and fire and passion. They took over my brain, spiriting my soul away in an out-of-body experience that sent me spiraling.

It was a blur after that. I woke up cradled in his arms, though I didn't remember falling asleep. Exhaustion tugged at my sore muscles, but I focused on the feel of his skin on mine. That musky scent I knew so well mingled with something new—something intimate that no one else would ever get to smell.

I smiled, burrowing my face in his shoulder. In seconds, I fell back asleep and only woke when sunlight streamed through the window.

I shifted, my muscles stiff from sleeping in such an awkward position. The twin bed didn't allow for much space. But even if we'd had a king-sized bed, I would've wanted to curl up as close to him as possible.

Oliver groaned sleepily, inhaling so his chest pushed against my back. He hummed, a low, throaty sound that made my stomach clench. Carefully, I rolled to face him. He blinked at me, his hair mussed and breathtakingly sexy.

"Good morning," he said in that deep, husky, I-just-woke-up voice.

My heart started racing again. "Good morning, husband."

Oliver's eyes crinkled, and he leaned closer to press a kiss to my forehead. Then, he drew back and stared at me, gently sweeping my mess of curls out of my face.

"Your eyes are the most beautiful thing I've ever seen," he whispered. "Like two shining lakes that reflect my soul."

My heart stopped, my breath lodging in my throat at his words. I swallowed. "Your eyes are like a lush forest."

Oliver smiled. He leaned in to kiss me, but a rapid knocking sounded at the door.

"Lovebirds!" came José's impatient voice. "Breakfast!"

I sighed, closing my eyes for a moment. As José's footsteps faded away, I looked at Oliver. "We should probably . . ." I trailed off and moved to get up, but his arms grounded me, holding me in place.

Frowning, I looked at him. His eyes glinted, and that familiar yearning shone blatantly in his gaze. My heart stirred in response. How could I say no?

He read the consent in my face and grinned, rising until he was on top of me. He pinned me down with his powerful arms framed on either side of me.

"You're impossible," I breathed before he drowned me in kisses.

CHAPTER 35

Cheers and whoops greeted us as we entered the cafeteria hand-in-hand. My face burned, and I couldn't help but grin. Oliver rubbed the back of his neck with his free hand, his face red all the way to his ears.

"What's going on?" Stefan asked, looking up from his oatmeal to frown at us.

I blinked, suddenly realizing he hadn't been staying here with us. A quick look at Bay's guarded expression told me he must've found some super-secret hideout to keep Stefan safe. A ripple of irritation flared inside me. Wasn't Oliver just as important to protect?

My irritation died when I recognized the haunted look in Stefan's eyes and the darkness creeping in on his expression. With a jolt, I remembered his mother had been kidnapped. How had I forgotten?

"These two got married last night," Kismet said.

Stefan choked on his food. "*What?* Aren't you guys still teenagers?"

"Yes." I grinned at him, providing no other explanation.

Stefan didn't respond. His gaze dropped, and he became very fascinated with the food in his bowl.

As soon as Oliver and I grabbed our food, Kismet slid into the seat next to us without preamble.

"I need your blood." She stared at Oliver.

Oliver raised his eyebrows. "I, uh, what?" He shook his head. "Oh, right. The spell."

Kismet nodded, then grimaced. "Sorry. I'd love to give you some time to, you know, enjoy married life for a bit, but . . ." Something like grief passed across her face, and for a moment I saw what she wasn't saying: that she never got to enjoy married life. She never got a honeymoon or anything. And she probably never would.

A knot formed in my stomach. I couldn't enjoy my food anymore.

Kismet cleared her throat. "But we don't have any time to waste. The Council has been alerted to several kidnappings within the demon community. So far, the Nephilim are untouched, but it's only a matter of time before Matthias gets his hands on a magical being from every faction to perform the spell."

Oliver took another bite of food and nodded. "Yes, of course. I'll do whatever I can to help."

"Thank you. With Stefan here, we'll have all the ingredients we need for the spell. Also, Bay's been tweaking the locator spell to see if he can use it with your and Stefan's blood. Try and find out if Matthias fathered any more children." Her mouth twisted. "Lilith help us if he has. Hopefully you and Stefan are the only ones."

Oliver's eyes darkened. "I agree."

Kismet's gaze shifted to me. "Desi, Elias has asked for your help with his technology to make sure it functions properly before we seek out Matthias."

My heart lurched. "*Me*? Why?"

Kismet smiled. "I don't know. But he obviously sees some potential. Can you help him?"

My mouth opened and closed. Heat rose in my cheeks. "I—uh—yes, absolutely."

"Great." Hope shone in her eyes. "Oliver, meet us in the mess hall when you're finished. With any luck, we'll have the spell ready by nightfall, and we can end this once and for all."

Before either of us could say anything, she jumped up and left the room with a bounce in her step.

"She's cheerful," Oliver muttered.

I looked at him. The darkness hadn't left his eyes, but

it was different from when Matthias had possessed him. This time, it was his own bleak thoughts that took over.

I touched his hand. "What's wrong?"

"It seems as if she thinks she can change it." He looked at me with sorrow in his eyes. "Her fate."

A lump lodged in my throat. "Can't she?"

"In all the years I've known Alba, I have never heard of her visions not coming to pass."

My heart stilled at his words. *So no matter what we do—no matter how successful we are—Kismet and Bay will still die.*

Was that why Kismet was so optimistic today? Because she thought she could change that outcome?

"Oliver, I need to tell you something," I whispered, my heart racing. "Kismet, she—she had a baby last year. And we—"

"I know." Oliver's eyes softened.

My mouth fell open. "You do?"

He nodded. "She told me right before the ceremony. She didn't want me going through with the marriage without knowing."

My mouth remained open, then clamped shut. *Wow.* "That was . . . really thoughtful of her."

Oliver raised an eyebrow. "Why didn't you tell me sooner?"

"I would have! But everything happened so quickly,

what with your blood ritual and the aftereffects and then the wedding, and I just—" I sighed, covering my face with my hands. "I'm sorry. There's just a lot to think about right now."

Oliver turned in his chair to face me, leaning forward. His hands gently framed either side of my face, holding me as delicately as if I were fine china. "I understand, Desi. It's like you told me last night: nothing about you could turn me away. This is just something we'll have to face together when the time comes."

My face warmed. He pressed a soft kiss against my mouth, drawing me closer against him. I placed my hand on his knee, sliding my fingers up and up until he stiffened and broke the kiss with a gasp.

I laughed at the mixture of shock and arousal in his eyes.

He leaned even closer. "Don't tempt me," he growled.

My insides churned, and a small, devious part of me begged him to retaliate. I pushed the thought from my mind and jerked my head toward the door Stefan had just exited through. "You should probably get going."

Oliver closed his eyes and sighed. "You're right." Before I could react, he swooped in and ran his tongue along my lower lip, then jumped up from his seat.

I sucked in a sharp breath, watching him stride away from me, his shoulders shaking with quiet laughter.

A few minutes later, I tracked down Elias and Megan in what appeared to be a small staff lounge on the second floor. A counter and sink lined the left side of the wall along with a gaping hole where a refrigerator had once been.

Elias and Megan were huddled in the corner, surrounded by boxes and thick textbooks. A table with all kinds of gadgets, electronics, and tools stood next to them.

Elias looked up, his expression brightening when he saw me. "Ah, it's the lovely Mrs. Gerrick! Welcome, welcome. Do sit down."

I smiled and took a seat across from them. Megan offered a half wave and then returned her gaze to the electronic monocle in her hand.

"How can I help?" I asked, my stomach squirming. I felt so inadequate, especially with these two.

Elias raised a finger. "Yes! Megan told me your idea of using demons to power my tech instead of my own aura so I'm not so drained in a fight." He dropped into a seat across from me, crossing his legs and watching me as if he were my therapist waiting for me to spill my darkest secrets.

I shifted under his scrutiny. "Uh, yes. It was just an idea, though."

"Of course, but I wanted to explain to you how my

technology works and see what you think about implementing your idea." He lifted his wrist, revealing his own shiny, metal cuff. "It draws from my own source of magic. Light magic. So it's, in a sense, already bonded to me. The same goes for my gloves and goggles. They're bonded to the wearer."

I frowned and nodded. "Okay. Can you—can you let a dark caster wear it and then use it with dark magic?"

Elias shook his head. "It resets and recalibrates with each wearer."

I thought of Oliver—my demon husband—and how he was probably giving Kismet a vial of his blood this very moment. My eyes widened. "What about blood?"

Elias grew very still. Even Megan looked up from her gadget. "Blood," Elias repeated thoughtfully, stroking his chin.

"Can you, I don't know, *charge* the battery with a demon's blood and use that instead?"

Elias stared distantly behind me and then shook his head again. "No, it wouldn't be near enough power. My gloves take a portion of my *soul*. A single drop of demon blood wouldn't hold enough power to fuel it."

Recognition stirred in my mind as I remembered studying something about magical blood with Megan the other day. "But aren't blood and souls tethered together? Is there a way to attach a demon's soul to his blood and use that to fuel it?"

Elias didn't respond. His brow furrowed, and he tapped on his chin, his jaw ticking back and forth. "Perhaps. But I would have to acquire his blood ahead of time. And perform a binding spell to link his aura to his blood."

I looked from Elias to Megan. "Is it—is it possible to get Matthias's blood without him knowing?"

Megan shrugged. "If he left it behind somewhere like in a fight."

"That's not the only way." Elias slid a box toward him and started digging through papers. "Sometimes blood becomes infused with an object like an athame. Perhaps I can find traces of his aura in his blood even after it's been wiped away."

For the next few hours, the three of us researched together, going through Elias's notes and old texts, occasionally chiming in here and there with something interesting we found. Megan and Elias often corrected me—like when I suggested using Oliver and Stefan's blood since they were linked to Matthias—which reminded me that I was a novice among experts. But it was still thrilling to dive into a project. Something that stirred excitement within me.

After we paused for sandwiches, Elias moved to

another table to work on cuffs for the rebels while Megan and I continued our research. Every now and then, my gaze lifted to watch Elias as he tampered with cuffs. Electricity sizzled, singeing the air with magic. His hands glowed blue, and his eyes were fixed intently on the cuff as he worked.

My stomach swirled with apprehension. For one wild moment, I considered approaching him and asking, *Can I do the next one?*

"It's fascinating, isn't it?" Megan said quietly.

I blinked and found her watching Elias too, her eyes glowing.

"He doesn't let me help with the cuffs anymore. Not since I butchered the one I gave to you." She grimaced, her face apologetic.

The one that made me think Oliver was dead. A tiny, savage part of me agreed with Elias's decision on this, but I knew Megan had only been trying to help.

"How long has he been making them? The cuffs?" My gaze returned to Elias.

"A few years. He keeps trying to shop them around to different companies, but I think he secretly wants to keep them all to himself."

The door burst open, and I jumped to my feet, my heart racing.

Kismet hurried toward us, clutching what looked

like a small wine bottle. Her eyes were wild, and her blond hair was mussed by frizz and sweat. "It's done," she said breathlessly, holding up the bottle. "The spell is done. This potion will defeat him."

I stiffened. My breath caught in my throat, and I stood there, frozen for a full minute.

"Marvelous!" Elias clapped his hands together as if Kismet had just announced she was taking up embroidery. "And I've just finished your and Bay's cuffs, my dear. Stefan already has his, of course. And you, Desi . . ." He trailed off, digging through various items on the table before lifting a cuff toward me. "This one is yours."

"Mine?" I repeated, finally breaking out of my stupor. "Why me?"

"Well, because of your bond to Kismet, of course." He frowned at Kismet. "You didn't tell her?"

The excitement in Kismet's eyes dulled. She lowered the bottle carefully to the table and sighed, pushing her hair out of her eyes.

"Told me *what*?" I said, my eyes darting frantically from Elias to Kismet.

"Megan, be a dear and help me track down Bay to give him his cuff," Elias muttered. He and Megan left the room.

"Kismet," I said quietly. "What's going on?"

"It's nothing, Desi," she said, closing her eyes. "It's

just, Bay and I figured we might as well take advantage of our connection to you and Stefan. These cuffs will enhance that. Like how we could communicate after the twin towers were hit."

I swallowed, fighting back the trauma threatening to resurface from that awful day. "Enhance it how?"

"Similar to the way a blood oath works." Her eyes finally met mine. Her mouth pressed into a thin line.

I searched her face, and my brows furrowed. Then, I remembered how it felt fighting side by side with Oliver. When I attacked, he became weak to give me his strength. When he attacked, I did the same. We shared energy.

"Kismet," I said, my mouth dry as I fingered the cool cuff in my hands. "This will *weaken* you. If we use these cuffs, we'll both become more vulnerable in the fight."

"Yes, but we'll both be more *powerful*. Desi, we need every advantage we can get."

"At what cost?" I demanded. "What if I weaken at precisely the right moment for Matthias to kill me? Or *you*?"

Kismet's eyes tightened. "You don't have to worry about that."

"Why not?"

"Because the cuffs only work one way. They only give energy to you."

I stilled. Ice formed in my chest, freezing me in place. "What?" I whispered, horrified.

Kismet rubbed her forehead. "We already know what will happen to me. So it—"

"Yes, but you don't want to offer yourself up on a silver platter," I said angrily. "Kismet, this seals your fate!"

"It's already sealed!" Kismet yelled, throwing her hands up in the air. "My death date is tomorrow."

A heavy silence filled the air, cutting off my retort. The truth of Kismet's words swirled within me, choking me. Strangling me.

A hot bubble of agony burst in my chest.

"No," I croaked, shaking my head. Warmth tickled my eyes. "No, *Kismet*—"

She stepped toward me, her eyes full of regret. But an infuriating acceptance settled in her gaze. She was at peace with this. She was *giving in*.

I opened my mouth to yell at her—to convince her to fight for her life—but a distant boom stopped me. I blinked, looking toward the window.

"What was that?" Kismet asked, following my gaze.

"I don't—"

A closer blast shook the building, reminding me of the cannon fire from Santiago. The glass window rattled, and the furniture slid along the floor. I teetered, and Kismet's arm flew out to steady me.

The rumbling stopped, and I looked at Kismet, my eyes wide. She sniffed the air, then screamed, "Get down!"

She shoved me forward, and we tumbled out of the way as the wall exploded in a wave of debris and drywall. My head collided with something sharp, and I cried out, my vision blurring. Dust and dirt filled the air, tickling my nose and eyes. I coughed, waving a hand in front of my face.

When the air cleared, I sucked in a gasp, choking on dust particles. A gaping hole faced me, opening up to the parking lot below. Hundreds of figures stood on the ground, gazing up at the hole in the building. They surrounded a dozen demons that formed a wide circle within the crowd.

In the midst of them was a figure engulfed in flames.

CHAPTER 36

"You know what I want!" the fiery figure bellowed, his voice echoing in the parking lot. He gestured to the figures in the circle. "Deliver my sons to me, or these casters all die!"

I crawled forward, dodging debris and chunks of concrete, and squinted at the figures below me.

My heart stopped.

Those weren't demons in the circle. At least, not all of them. One of them glowed, his skin shimmering and sparkling in a way that reminded me of Persephone. He was fae. Another had giant wings fanned out behind her. Nephilim. My wide eyes moved over each individual. Though I couldn't see any distinguishable features that marked a light or dark caster—or even a Second Tier demon—I knew they were all there.

Matthias wouldn't be here if he hadn't secured every magical being he needed to cast the spell.

"Stefan, don't!" a woman screamed. She stood in the circle too. My blood ran cold. It was Isabel, Stefan's mother.

My frantic gaze flew around the parking lot, searching for Stefan. What was he doing?

Stefan's roar of fury echoed in the air, and he grunted and struggled loudly against something.

Peering over the jagged edge of the ruined staff lounge, I noticed a pair of figures grappling with each other on the sidewalk next to the parking lot. Bay gripped Stefan's arms behind him while Stefan thrashed, trying to break free.

"He'll kill her!" Stefan cried. "Let me go! He'll kill her! He wants *me*!"

"The boy is right," Matthias said, loud enough for me to hear. "Deliver my sons to me and she goes free."

"He's lying!" Isabel shrieked. "We'll die anyway! Please, Stefan—"

A demon clubbed her over the head, and she cried out, crumpling to the ground. Stefan's anguished yell pierced the air.

How? I thought in horror. *How did Matthias get everyone to agree to sacrifice themselves?* I remembered the spell said the victims had to be *willing* participants.

My eyes fell on Isabel, and my heart sank as I remembered what she'd said about doing anything to save her son.

If she thought this would save him, she would do it. I could imagine Matthias threatening the families of every caster in that circle.

I knew if he'd threatened to kill *my* family, I would've agreed too.

"Corporal Gerrick!" Matthias shouted, stretching his arms wide. "Your brother is here, ready to sacrifice himself. I suggest you join him, or the blood of these innocents will be on your hands."

Oliver.

My gut twisted. I had to find him.

I climbed to my feet, wincing from a sharp stab of pain in my side. Ragged breaths poured through me. I scanned the room for Kismet, but she was gone. So was the bottled potion to banish Matthias.

Conflict warred within me. Find Oliver, or prevent Kismet from getting herself killed?

My legs surged forward, despite my insides churning in confusion and horror. *Just move,* I ordered myself. *Don't think. Just move.* I had to trust my instincts. Though I was numb right now, still processing, I had to believe my Demonhunting skills would kick in when I needed them. So I squashed down the horror and despair that threatened to consume me, knowing we were outnumbered and doomed to die here.

Kismet knew her fate. But what about the rest of us? Would we all die here too? Would Matthias prevail against us?

I tore down the hallway, limping and gritting my teeth against the pain. My hand pressed against my side and came back covered in blood.

Great. I was already wounded, and the battle hadn't even begun.

I ran headfirst into Megan. She yelped and grabbed my shoulders to keep me from toppling over.

"Desi! Thank Lilith. Mr. Caldwell said you forgot your cuff." She handed the metal cuff to me.

I stared at it. A small part of me wanted to resist and push it away. Kismet couldn't die if I never took her powers from her.

But knowing what waited for us outside—knowing I was already injured—how could I not?

With a resigned sigh, I took the cuff and slid it onto my wrist. In a flash, energy poured into me so intensely I gasped. My spine straightened, and I no longer felt the throbbing in my side.

Then, I heard Kismet's words as she murmured them to herself: *Smash the bottle, say the spell. Smash the bottle, say the spell.*

She was going to cast the spell. Alone.

She wouldn't last five minutes out there. As soon as Matthias saw her and the potion, he would kill her.

I clasped Megan's hands in mine. "Thank you," I whispered before darting away.

My legs pumped farther and faster, strengthened by the cuff. Knowing I was connected to Kismet, I sent her an array of thoughts, begging her: *Wait, Kismet. Please! Wait for us. Don't go alone. Please!*

I sensed her falter and felt her hesitation. I pressed on. *He'll kill you, Kismet. We need more people on this. We need a distraction. We only have one shot at this.*

I scrambled down the stairs, my panicked breaths tearing through me. Kismet's resignation provided a brief flare of relief before I realized I couldn't sense Oliver at all.

Where was he?

I threw open the stairwell door and hurried into the lobby, stopping short at the sight of a crowd of rebels. A few looked up at my entrance, but most of them stared grimly out the windows at the demon army awaiting us. The looks of devastation were enough to shatter my resolve.

They all knew they were going to die. There was no doubt about it.

A quick glance around the lobby told me Oliver wasn't here. Then, my eyes found José.

He can Port! He could get us out of here.

I hurried up to him and tugged on his arm until he looked at me. His eyes were grave and haunted just like the others.

"Can you Port?" I asked, my eyes wide.

José's jaw tensed, and he shook his head. "I've already tried. He has the whole area cloaked."

My blood chilled. "Cloaked? Like—"

"Like with the twin towers."

Merciful Lilith. So we were trapped here without our powers.

But didn't that mean Matthias was powerless too? "Then how is he on fire right now?" I asked.

José offered a half-hearted shrug, his gaze returning to the window. His bleak expression said, *It doesn't matter. We're all doomed anyway.*

I swallowed and lifted a shaking hand. Focusing all my energy, I wiggled my fingers. Electricity surged through me. I flexed my fingers, pointing to a table by the doors, and Pushed.

The table fell over.

Relief mingled with confusion. What the hell? So José couldn't Port, but I still had my powers? My gaze shifted to the cuff on my wrist. But José wore one too.

"Do any of you have your powers?" I shouted, looking around at the crowd.

A few rebels shifted. Some lifted their hands like me. A scattering of fire and floating objects filled the room. But more than half lifted their hands only to drop them in disappointment.

So half of us were powerless.

Amidst the crowd, I recognized John Dickers. I hurried up to him and asked, "What's your plan?"

He blinked at me, his eyes wide and vacant. "What?"

"I mean what is the Council doing about this?" I waved a hand toward the crowd of demons. "Have you called for help?"

Dickers' mouth opened and closed. "I—no. Everyone available to help is already here. No one else is coming."

"What about the entire magical community? Witches and warlocks from around the world—can't they come to our aid? Don't you have some sort of distress signal to send out? Or an emergency alert?"

Dickers continued to watch me blankly until I grabbed his shoulders and shook him.

"Listen to me!" I roared. "He's about to summon Asmodeus! If we don't do *something*, he'll slaughter every caster on the planet!"

"I—I—I don't have my powers," he stammered.

Suddenly, he sounded like the weak, whimpering accountant he appeared to be when I first saw him.

"Then find someone who *does!*" I shouted, my eyebrows raised. How could he be so helpless right now?

But as I stared at his pale face, I finally understood. He had no powers. He was defined by them. He didn't know what to do without them—who he was or how to react. Magic was his crutch, and now it was gone.

"Tell me who to talk to," I said, my voice calmer now. "Tell me who and I'll find him." *You can just stay here and stare out the window until they kill you. Be my guest.*

"Jean Richardson. Bright, red hair." He pointed to the door. "She went out there with Bayani."

My heart dropped. Going outside would put an immediate target on my back.

No wonder Dickers stayed in here.

"Mention emergency protocols," Dickers said. Clarity broke through his hazy expression for a moment. "The Blackwood Operation. She'll know what to do if she hasn't done it already."

I nodded, muttering my thanks before I hurried out the door.

The second I went outside, a burst of demon stench filled my nose, and I resisted the urge to gag. Creatures and casters alike stood in front of me, some wearing black cloaks and others wearing street clothes like me. Matthias, still engulfed in flames, turned his head. Though I couldn't see his expression, I knew he was looking at me.

I ignored his piercing stare and frantically scanned the area for Bay. He was still wrestling with Stefan, whose face was wet with tears. Behind them stood three individuals, one of whom had short, red hair like a beacon alerting me to her presence.

I strode forward, then froze.

Something stirred within me. An inky darkness, cold and all-consuming. It clutched at my mind like long claws, dragging me down. A chill swept over me. As plain as if he were whispering in my ear, I heard Matthias's voice saying, *Come to me.*

Then, Oliver's voice: *I submit to you, Father.*

Slowly, I turned and found Oliver approaching the mass of demons, his arms outstretched toward Matthias.

"Oliver!" I screamed.

Oliver went still. He glanced over his shoulder at me. His eyes were all black.

No, no, no.

He regarded me with an icy stare that pierced me to my core. This Oliver didn't know me.

I had to bring him back—but how? Last time, I'd

kissed him, but he was too far away from me now. I doubted he could even see the tears filling my eyes.

Oliver. My mind strained from the intensity of my thoughts. *I love you. Come back to me.*

The darkness swirled, then stopped like someone pushed pause on a remote.

You're my husband. You belong to me. Not him. You're mine, Oliver. Mine forever.

Recognition stirred within him. I felt his hesitation and his disoriented thoughts.

Then Matthias said, *You're my son. We share blood. We share magic. Come to me, son. You can't fight this darkness. You've always known that.*

Conflict warred in my mind, a shadow of the chaos of Oliver's thoughts. I felt his deliberation and the confusion tearing through him. *I'm a demon,* he thought. *I'm not worthy of her. One day, I'll submit to the darkness. It's better to do it now before I hurt her. Let her live her life. Let her be happy.*

Oliver, no, I thought to him, gritting my teeth.

Matthias's hold on him was strong, but mine was stronger.

My eyes closed, and I filled my head with images: our bodies curled together on the tiny bed. His eyes, filled with hunger and desire when they drank in my naked body. The feel of his hot mouth against mine.

Our chests pressed together. Our hearts beating as one.

Oliver gasped in my head like waking from a deep sleep.

My eyes flew open. I watched him stiffen, turning to look at me with shining eyes. Green eyes. The black was gone.

Tension filled the air. Oliver was too close to the demons. If he bolted, they would stop him. Kill him.

I had to act first.

Matthias lifted his hands, but I was quicker. I thrust my arms forward and Pushed Matthias backward. His roar was more fury than pain. I barely lifted him three feet before he floated back down, light as a feather.

But it bought us time.

Oliver took my cue. He turned and ran. I waited for him to use his powers, but then realization hit me like a ton of bricks.

His powers weren't working.

I stretched my arms toward him and Pulled. Pain tore through my chest from the effort. I tugged, my muscles straining and my arms quivering.

He soared toward me, his eyes wide and his face drained of color.

"*Stop him!*" Matthias bellowed.

The demons surged forward. One of them sprouted

a mass of wrinkly, gray wings and flew forward to Oliver. Sweat poured down my face. I knew the demon would reach him before I could.

Suddenly, a rustling of black smoke appeared in front of me. Then, Bay materialized, snatching Oliver in his arms before he Ported back to his place next to Jean and the other Council members.

I rushed over to Oliver, clutching him close and sobbing into his shoulder. *I almost lost you.* I couldn't even voice the words.

His shaking hand wound through my hair. *I know,* he said in my thoughts. *But you brought me back.*

"Stefan *no!*" Bay roared.

Stefan had bolted toward the crowd of demons.

"I've got him," Jean said, closing her eyes. Her brow furrowed, and Stefan stiffened, his arms stretching by his side. Slowly, Stefan turned back to us, his face a mask of emptiness.

I blinked at Jean. She was a Thinker.

With a jolt, I remembered John Dickers' words about engaging the emergency protocol. Jean was the only one who could do it.

My heart thundered in my chest as I watched Stefan, still immobilized by Jean's magic. Then, Bay vanished in another flurry of black smoke, grabbing Stefan and bringing him back.

I stepped toward Jean, my eyes wide. "Jean, you need to alert the magical community. Use the emergency protocol."

Jean blinked, looking at me and frowning. Then her face slackened, her mouth falling open. "I—I don't know the code."

I stilled. *What? What code?*

Then, Dickers' words came to my mind again: *The Blackwood Operation.*

"Blackwood," I said loudly. "The Blackwood Operation."

Jean's eyes grew unfocused as if she stared at something beyond me. A silver tint surrounded her irises like an eclipse sparkling in her gaze. My breath caught in my throat as I watched, transfixed. Jean's small mouth opened and closed, uttering words I couldn't hear. Her eyes speared through me, glistening with an otherworldly light.

I'd never seen anything like it.

Slowly, the glow in her eyes faded. She blinked and teetered, her expression haggard. "It's done."

I swallowed and nodded, not sure what else to do. "Did it work?"

"I'm not sure. But I sent out the signal."

I exhaled. *Good. We've done what we can.*

And not a moment too soon.

The demon army reached us, and we surged into action. I shoved my hands forward, propelling three demons back several feet. Energy seeped into me, filling my veins with unstoppable power. A werewolf lunged with a dagger. I ducked, kicking him in the groin. He moaned and hunched over. I kicked him again in the face. He crumpled, and I snatched his dagger, slicing into the belly of another demon before he reached Oliver.

Oliver's eyes were wide, but his face glinted with a familiar flare. The thrill of the fight filled his face.

Warlock or no, he was still a soldier.

I flashed a grin and tossed the dagger to him. He nodded at me and slashed the throat of another demon.

A loud battle cry pierced the air, and I turned for a moment to find the remaining rebels pouring out of the building. Anger and determination blazed in their eyes, and even those without powers wielded weapons as they joined the fray.

My spirits soared. Many of the rebels, like Dickers and José, hurried forward with eyes wide with fear and uncertainty. But they were here. They were fighting. Something had snapped them into action.

I kicked another demon down. He raised his hands to try and stop me, but nothing happened. I kicked him in the head, rendering him unconscious. Realization struck me. *Half the demons must be powerless too.*

I dodged and Pushed, throwing punches and swinging my legs. Adrenaline pulsed through me. Blood soaked my shirt, but I knew it wasn't mine. Power filled me, strengthening my limbs.

A shriek filled my mind.

Stop him! Desi, stop him!

I froze. Kismet.

I lifted my arms, flinging demons backward before I raced forward, my eyes searching for that familiar pillar of flames. But the fire was gone.

Where was Matthias?

"*No!*" Stefan screamed.

The ground rumbled, cracking the concrete. The building behind me trembled. Glass shattered, raining down on us. Rebels and demons alike cried out, teetering from the earthquake.

A gaping hole formed in the middle of the parking lot, swallowing a dozen demons into its depths. More cracks spread along the ground. I stumbled backward, away from the hole that widened like the jaws of Hell.

Black magic poured from the abyss, swirling in the air like inky smoke and mingling with the fuchsia rays of the setting sun. The magic choked me, stinging my eyes. The stench was so foul I almost puked.

Flames ignited alongside the black magic. At first, I thought it was Matthias, but the fire spread, fanning out as if the sky itself were on fire. It burned against my eyes, but I couldn't look away.

Within the flames appeared a dark figure. Great, black wings sprang from his back. Claws stretched from his long, thin fingers. His eyes gleamed black, and his fangs dripped with blood. Slowly, the flames subsided, and the figure dropped to the ground, landing on his feet with a thud that shook the ground again.

When he lifted his face, my breath caught in my throat. He stood at least twenty feet tall. He had not two but *four* wings stretched out behind him. And his glittering black eyes shifted over all of us hungrily. His mouth stretched wide in a grin, revealing several rows of sharp teeth.

Asmodeus.

CHAPTER 37

My euphoria from earlier vanished like an extinguished flame, leaving numb horror in its wake. Even the demons surrounding us had stopped fighting to gape at the new arrival to the battle.

The giant demon—Asmodeus—stepped forward with rumbling thuds that made me quiver. Beside him, a small figure in flames emerged, looking pitiful next to the Demon Master.

Matthias stretched his arms wide. "See what power is on my side? Surrender my sons to me, or suffer the wrath of the Demon Master's army."

My body hardened to stone. I couldn't move or breathe. I couldn't even think.

From the corner of my eye, I caught a glimpse of Oliver's golden hair shifting with his movement.

The feeling suddenly returned to my limbs. I surged forward and snatched his arm. "What are you doing?"

He looked at me with tortured eyes, his face pale. "Desi, I *have* to go to him."

My fingers tightened on his arm. "*No!*"

"He'll *kill* everyone! I'm just one person! You already have my blood. You have the potion for the spell. I'm dispensable."

"Not to *me*, you aren't," I hissed, blinking away tears. "Besides, I have no idea where Kismet is! For all I know, she accidentally smashed the bottle somewhere and we need to gather ingredients again." The thought wormed through me, dragging my heart to the ground. *If that's the case, then we're already dead.*

Oliver stared at me, his eyes hard. Unyielding. I knew I wouldn't convince him.

I drew in a breath. "The only way I'll let you go is if you take me with you."

His eyes widened. "Desi—"

"You want to challenge me?" I snapped. "I have powers. You don't. You go without me, and I'll freeze you in your tracks."

We stared each other down. His jaw ticked back and forth, his nostrils flaring.

Desi.

I gasped, looking around. "Kismet?"

I cast a cloaking spell, but I can't get close enough on my own, she said. *And even if I could, I . . .* she paused, and I heard her utter a noise of frustration in my mind. *I can't banish him. The blood oath is stopping me.*

My mouth felt dry. I'd forgotten Kismet couldn't banish demons.

We were so royally screwed.

The potion is cloaked next to the handicap parking space directly behind Asmodeus. I circled around to avoid detection, but Matthias has already sensed me. I have to go, now. *If he sniffs me out, he'll find me and the potion. Can you get to it? Use my powers if you have to.*

I swallowed. Oliver's arm tensed in my grip, and I realized my nails were digging into him.

Desi. Can you do this? Kismet's words were slow and forceful. I knew if I showed any hesitation, she would try to do it herself despite her limitations. I was the only one she could communicate with from afar.

"Yes," I said aloud. "Yes, I can do this."

I felt Oliver's piercing gaze, but I stared vacantly at the purpling sky as the sun vanished into the horizon. The air darkened, but Matthias's figure and the flames in Asmodeus's abyss blazed like a beacon of death.

Find Bay, Kismet said. *Tell him to meet me at the rendezvous point. He'll know what it means. Get Stefan some-*

where safe. With his mother gone, he's bound to do something reckless.

Her words echoed in my mind. Stefan's mother was gone. Matthias had sacrificed her to summon Asmodeus. I wasn't sure how I hadn't processed that. My heart throbbed in my chest.

Desi, say something, Kismet pleaded. *You're the only one I can trust with this.*

Only because she had no choice. That much I knew. If half our forces weren't rendered powerless, if we weren't separated by the Demon Master and his army, if we actually stood half a chance, then literally any other rebel besides me would be more fit for the task.

But we were out of options.

"I understand," I whispered. Resolve pulsed through me, awakening my magic and the fire within me. I gritted my teeth. "You can count on me."

Kismet went silent in my head. I sensed her moving with as much stealth as she could muster. I had to let her concentrate.

My gaze shifted to Oliver, who watched me intently. "What is it?" he asked.

I tugged on his arm. "I'll tell you on the way."

We weaved through rebels and demons, who had resumed fighting. The rebels' faces were weak and devastated. I recognized one of Bay's Filipino friends, who wielded a sword, slashing through demons. Bloody gashes coated his arms, and his long, dark hair clung to his sweaty face. Beside him was John Dickers, who had fallen to his knees. A dagger protruded from his chest. His face was pale and clammy, and his broken glasses clattered to the ground. With a groan, he slumped sideways.

My heart jolted. Was he dead?

Other members of the Council fought alongside Dickers, their weapons slashing and their hands glowing black and blue with spells. But some had no magic—and they fell, just like Dickers.

They wouldn't last much longer—especially with the hell that awaited them.

Asmodeus roared, the sound so deep and piercing that my ears throbbed. The ground quivered again. His lumbering steps slammed against the concrete as he advanced toward us.

From among the crowd of demons, I heard Matthias laugh.

We were out of time.

I squinted against the darkness of dusk, trying to make out shapes amidst the battle. A blade soared toward me, and Oliver knocked it away with a gust of wind.

"What the—?" he muttered, eyes wide.

I stared at him. He summoned a ball of flame in his palm. A surprised grin stretched across his face.

Thank Lilith. His powers were back! Perhaps the rest of the rebels had their powers now too. Maybe whatever cloaking spell Matthias had used was removed when he summoned Asmodeus.

A deep roar shook the ground beneath us. Asmodeus turned toward the great abyss behind him, his lumbering steps causing the earth to quake. His huge hands came together, and a blinding red light grew from his clawed fingertips.

My heart stilled. *Magic.* Asmodeus was performing magic.

Something within the abyss rumbled and whispered as if the hole itself were coming alive.

I hurried forward, dragging Oliver with me. A werewolf lunged for me. I ducked and lifted my arms to Push him away.

Nothing happened.

A terrifying emptiness filled my chest. My heart stopped.

Fire consumed the wolf, and it howled and darted away. Oliver offered his hand, hoisting me up. The grimness in his eyes told me he knew what was wrong.

My powers were gone now. The cloaking spell had somehow been reversed.

What the actual hell? Half of us were powerless, and now it's switched to the other half?

My eyes flicked over the battling demons and rebels. Some faltered and stumbled as they no doubt sensed the same shift in magic that we had.

But I was looking for one specific figure. And he was nowhere to be found. The only flames I could see were flickering in the pit behind Asmodeus like a hungry beast waiting for its meal.

"His powers are gone," I whispered. "Matthias's powers are gone!"

Oliver looked around, his eyes sharpening. "Where is he?"

"Come on!" I grabbed Oliver's hand again and weaved through bodies, some still fighting and others motionless on the ground. Through the haze of the night sky, I could barely make out the shape of the hospital building. Last I'd seen, Bay was just outside the doors with Stefan.

"I need light," I said to Oliver.

He lifted his hand and summoned fire, lighting the area around us. Unfortunately, it also alerted several demons to our presence. A vampire pounced, fangs bared. Oliver swept him away with a gust of wind.

"Knife!" I shouted.

Oliver tossed me the blade, and I caught it by the hilt,

slashing just as a dark warlock advanced. His blood poured from the wound in his chest, and he fell over.

Panic rose in my throat at the emptiness within me. My lack of powers. The adrenaline faded, leaving me numb and cold. Weak.

In that terrifying moment, I understood José and Dickers' hesitation. The shell-shocked horror in their faces.

Without my powers, I was just a weak girl among monsters.

Desperation pulsed through me. I frantically searched the area using Oliver's light and found Bay's bulky figure, which blended in almost perfectly with the surrounding darkness.

"There! Move!" I pushed Oliver forward, dodging blows and bursts of black magic. A gunshot rang in the air, and I flinched, my ears ringing.

At long last, we reached Bay. Panting, I wiped flecks of blood from my arm and ran toward him. He grappled with a dark witch, hovering between her and Stefan to try to keep them apart. Stefan was bound with ropes on the grass, moaning and weeping.

A sheen of sweat coated Bay's face and then I realized what was wrong. He was powerless.

I flung my dagger forward, embedding it in the

witch's thigh. She shrieked and looked around, eyes blazing. She lunged for me. I lifted my hands without thinking. A swell of energy filled my chest, and fire burst from my fingertips. The flames hit her squarely in the chest. Her shrill scream filled the air. Bay tackled her, silencing her, and she slumped to the ground, her neck broken.

I stared at my shaking hands. "What—?" Then a familiar presence stirred within me.

Kismet. I'd just used her powers.

I swallowed and met Oliver's gaze. The disbelief in his face matched my own.

Bay wiped sweat from his face and looked at us, breathing heavily. "Thanks for the assist." He didn't seem at all surprised that I had the powers of an Elemental. Perhaps he knew all along what the cuff would do for me.

I swallowed, remembering the task at hand. "Kismet needs you at the rendezvous point."

Bay's eyes widened. His jaw tensed, and he stared distantly at something I couldn't see. A fierce and grim determination shone in his eyes unlike anything I'd ever seen in his face before.

I desperately wanted to know where the rendezvous point was and what it meant. Whatever crossed his mind just now couldn't have been good.

Bay's gaze shifted to Stefan. "I can't leave him. He'll go to Matthias."

"Let me!" Stefan roared. Fury ignited in his eyes. "Let me go to him!"

"You'll get yourself killed," Bay snapped.

"I can't stay with him," I said, grimacing. "Kismet told me where she hid the potion. I have to go get it."

"I'll go," Oliver said, straightening. "Tell me where it is."

Horror chilled me to the bone. "No," I said in a strangled voice. "You go, and he'll control you. He'll get inside your head!"

"Not without his powers," Oliver said. "I can do this, Desi."

"Not without *me*," I said angrily. "You're *not* allowed to get yourself killed without me. Do you understand?"

My panicked voice rang in my ears, reminding me how childish I sounded. But I wouldn't budge on this. He and I were bound, and if he planned on breaking that bond by dying tonight, then I'd die right along with him.

Silence passed between us, broken only by the grunts and screams of the surrounding battle.

A burst of black magic exploded on the ground, and Stefan suddenly stood. The frayed rope of his restraints disintegrated into dust. He stretched his arms, his nostrils flaring. "I'll go with you." His face was free of tears, and a fiery gleam shone in his eyes.

"Stefan—" Bay started, his brows lowering.

"Stop it!" Stefan roared. "I'm not a child, and you're not my Familiar anymore." He lifted his arm to show his cuff. "I have your protection."

"My powers are gone, Stefan," Bay said weakly. "I can't help you."

"No, but I *feel* your energy." Stefan pressed a hand to his chest. "I feel you here, Bay. You're with me."

We all remained silent. My gaze shifted from Stefan to Bay.

"Let me fight him," Stefan pleaded. "Otherwise, what the hell am I doing here?"

A deep roar rumbled from Asmodeus, and flames rose higher and higher from the abyss. Red jets of light poured from Asmodeus's hands into the abyss. The ground shook, and hundreds of black shapes poured from the pit. Some bore flaming weapons, and others sprouted wings and soared into the sky. A few had long fangs and rode creatures as large as horses.

My breath caught in my throat. Asmodeus's army had arrived.

"We're out of time," Oliver said sharply, grabbing Stefan's arm. "Stefan's coming with us." Oliver shot Bay a severe look, his gaze spearing through him.

Bay stared right back, unflinching. Then he nodded.

Oliver turned to Stefan. "If we die tonight, we die as brothers. For the ones we've lost."

Stefan looked at him, his face still haggard from sorrow. But a fierce gleam broke through his devastation, highlighting his features. Magic oozed from him, powerful and all-consuming. I sucked in a breath, awestruck by the energy emanating from him.

Standing there, hands clasped in a firm handshake, Oliver and Stefan looked like true warriors.

Oliver turned to me. "Desi—"

"I'm going with you," I said through clenched teeth. We stared at each other for a long moment.

Then he seized my waist and pulled my hips against his, pressing a firm, sweaty kiss to my mouth. I inhaled his musk—mingled with the stench of demon and dried blood—and then drew back.

"Then we do this together," he whispered.

And the three of us dived into the fray.

CHAPTER 38

THE SCENE SURROUNDING US WAS LIKE THOSE OF MY nightmares. Monsters roared through layers of teeth that would put a shark to shame. Some fought with several arms instead of just two. Other beasts rested on four legs, their bodies larger than elephants. Wrinkled wings, scaly skin, and clawed fingers brushed against me. Demons and monsters leapt for us. We dodged and slashed, but they were too quick to evade. The other-worldly creatures of Asmodeus's armies darted back and forth so quickly that their movements were a smoky blur. The foul stench lingered in my nose just before a skinny, six-legged creature appeared behind me, slicing a sharp knife into my shoulder. I cried out, and flames exploded from my hands, searing the creature. It shrieked and howled, collapsing to the ground.

I shot more fire into the creature's belly. Its six legs lifted like a cockroach wriggling in defeat. Its large snout opened wide, and spit flew from its mouth. Then, after I attacked it one last jet of flames, it went still.

Panting, I turned to find Oliver and Stefan both grappling with an eight-armed beast that resembled a bear with octopus tentacles. Each of its arms held a weapon, and Stefan and Oliver fought off four of the monster's arms at once.

I closed my eyes, summoning Kismet's powers, and shot a gust of wind at the creature. It fell over but easily righted itself with one of its arms. Oliver and Stefan bounded forward, taking advantage of its delay. Oliver conjured boulders with his fists and slammed them into the creature. Stefan sliced his knife into the demon's throat, and the creature collapsed, oozing green blood.

"I need a path!" I shouted, squinting at the ground amidst the chaos. I couldn't find Kismet's potion—not like this.

Oliver set his whole body on fire. I stilled, my eyes wide and my heart fluttering in momentary terror. He reminded me of Matthias. The red eyes glowing beneath the flame were so similar.

I shook my head and focused on the task at hand. Oliver swung his arms, sending demons flying in every direction. Using his flame as a light, I crouched to the ground, searching the pavement. *The handicap space behind Asmodeus.*

Asmodeus had moved. I felt his lumbering steps shake the ground, but he was farther away than before. My eyes found the fiery pit from where he came and, just beyond it, the faded blue paint of a handicap parking space.

I bounded forward, swiping my blade at demons along the way. Something sharp dug into my arm, but I gritted my teeth and pressed on, ducking and dodging blows as I went.

Soon, I reached the parking space and searched frantically for something out of place. Something magical.

A vampire lunged for me, knocking me to the ground. His claws pinned me down, digging into my shoulders.

I cried out and rammed my head against his. He jerked backward. Stars appeared in my eyes, but I jerked my body free enough to wrap my fingers around his throat. He stiffened, choking. I slammed him sideways, grabbed my blade, and slit his throat. Blood poured from his body, drenching my hands.

Panting, I scanned the area, my nostrils tingling from nearby magic. Then, I saw it. A small ripple in the air like a nighttime mirage. I stretched my hand forward and snatched the rippling object.

The cloaking spell broke with my touch, and Kismet's potion bottle suddenly appeared.

Triumph soared within my chest. I whirled around and came face-to-face with a demon twice my height. A single eye glared at me between rolls of murky gray fat. His beefy arms stretched wide beside him, and he had the hooves of a horse. Like a demonic centaur mixed with a cyclops.

I suppressed a shudder of revulsion. My brain vaguely registered his attack before he swung his meaty fist at me. It caught me in the shoulder instead of the head, and I went flying. I crumpled, landing in a painful heap several feet away. Mercifully, my grip remained on the potion bottle.

"Desi!" Oliver shouted. No longer on fire, he surged forward and sent a heavy jet of water directly into the demon's eye, momentarily blinding the creature. Stefan appeared and shoved a dagger into the beast's stomach.

The demon roared, stomping around blindly as if trying to squash his assailant.

Oliver raised his hands and cried,

"Vile demon of unholy crimes,
I banish you 'til the end of time!"

Nothing happened.

Confusion twisted in my mind, followed closely by

despair. *Merciful Lilith.* Oliver was a demon now. He couldn't banish other demons.

His wide, horrified eyes met mine with the same realization.

I sucked in a breath and lifted my own shaking hands, pointing them toward the demon. I uttered the same banishing spell Oliver had.

Still, nothing happened.

My hands glowed blue, but the demon remained. Was it because the portal to the underworld was open?

My stomach dropped. This meant the rebels fighting right now—whoever was left—couldn't banish any demons. They could fight and stab, but any demon who had the power to heal would just pop back up and resume fighting.

We had to end this. Now.

Oliver summoned heavy boulders in his hands and flung them at the monster. The demon fell, crashing to the ground. I lunged forward and rammed my dagger into the demon's eye. He screamed, the sound so loud it tore at my eardrums. I yanked the blade free and slit his throat, covering the beast in his disgusting green blood. Perhaps this was what the blood of undead demons looked like—demons from Hell.

The demon choked and gagged, his hands reaching forward aimlessly.

I swallowed down bile and stared at Oliver. His face was covered in sweat. A splash of blood coated his arm, mingling with the sickly green substance of demon guts.

"Find him," I said to Oliver over the noise of screeching demons. "Lead the way."

Oliver nodded, his eyes closing and his brows furrowing. Disgust crossed his features, and I knew I was asking him to do what he loathed most: to open his mind to Matthias.

While Oliver searched, I looked at Stefan. Hatred blazed in his eyes along with wild horror as he watched the devastation surrounding us.

"You okay?" I asked.

He blinked and looked at me. His eyes wide, he nodded. "You?"

I nodded too.

"He's close," said Oliver, his eyes still closed. "Less than a mile away. He's hiding. You're right, I think he's powerless. But it's—it's to feed Asmodeus. The cloaking spell that drained the magic from half of us—that's what he's using to fuel Asmodeus. Matthias must've altered it when it wasn't enough. His Fourth Tier powers are fueling Asmodeus right now."

My stomach twisted. I cringed at the thought of my abilities, *my* magic funneling into a lord of Hell.

"So when we kill Matthias, we kill Asmodeus," Stefan said through clenched teeth.

Oliver opened his eyes and met Stefan's stare. "Yes."

Just then, a huge bat flew at me. I raised my leg to kick it in the face. "Then let's move."

Our progress through the throng of demons was achingly slow. I tried not to focus on the lifeless rebels sprawled on the ground below me, their faces vacant and their eyes empty. I sliced through demons one at a time, dodging their blows and summoning Kismet's powers when I needed to. The demons around us only seemed to multiply. Soon, the battle around us was nothing more than a sea of wrinkled, gray flesh, oozing, green wounds, and razor-sharp claws.

There weren't any rebels to be found.

Were we the only ones left?

The thought sent a spiral of dread curling through my stomach. For a terrifying moment, I stood there, frozen.

Everyone's dead. We're the only ones left.

A cacophony of shouts echoed nearby, and my heart lurched. I flinched, expecting another onslaught of monsters, but as the yelling drew nearer, I realized it was human.

Eyes wide, I turned, my jaw dropping. A crowd of witches and warlocks surged forward, all of them wielding weapons: guns, athames, and even yard tools like rakes, shovels, and brooms.

My brows furrowed as I watched our sudden allies join the fray. Some were my age, maybe a bit older. Others had graying hair, their wrinkles taut with their determined expressions. Blue and black magic exploded in the air like fireworks.

I sucked in a gasp. The magical community had heard our distress call. They were here, fighting for us.

Hope blossomed in my chest, empowering me. A fierce burst of adrenaline swelled from within me, and I roared in anger, slashing through two monsters at once.

Stefan and Oliver, spurred on by our sudden advantage, leapt forward to take on several demons at a time. Blood spurted. Blades tore through demon flesh. Shrieks of agony pierced the air.

Only one thought fueled me: *Kill, kill, kill.* My body became a machine, my movements robotic. I didn't let myself think of anything else: not Kismet or Bay, not the other rebels who were probably dead, not Oliver and how he fared. Just me and the enemy.

Time became a blur. I felt no exhaustion, no pain, and no hesitation. Nothing held me back. The cuff at my wrist practically burned through me, powering my fury and determination.

I slammed a heavy boulder into several demons,

knocking them unconscious, and found a wide, empty pavement stretched behind them.

We'd made it.

I bounded forward, resisting the urge to glance into the fiery pit to our left. But when Asmodeus's mighty roar shook the earth, I stilled, my skin prickling.

He saw us. I was sure of it. If anyone could stop us, it was the Demon Master.

But what I saw chilled me to the bone, numbing me with horror.

Asmodeus towered over two small figures and swiped his mighty, clawed hands toward them.

My heart lurched in my throat. I recognized the brilliant, blond hair.

Bay and Kismet. They fought Asmodeus *alone*.

Bay was powerless. And I was using Kismet's magic.

My brain distantly registered that it was a miracle they were still alive. Kismet ducked and rolled, avoiding being crushed by Asmodeus's large feet. Bay drove a sword into the top of Asmodeus's foot. Asmodeus groaned in anger—but not pain. He was barely impeded by the wound.

I had to do something. I couldn't just stand there. My legs pressed forward to my friends, knowing they would die without me.

But Oliver's hand gripped my wrist, stopping me.

"They're distracting him, Desi. If you stop them, we'll be targeted. Focus on the mission at hand."

"They'll be *killed*," I croaked, not tearing my eyes away from the scene. A small, insane part of me feared that if I looked away, they would die and I wouldn't know it.

"We defeat Matthias, we defeat Asmodeus too." Oliver's voice was hard. Tense. He didn't like this any more than I did.

I swallowed. I knew he was right. Kismet and Bay knew what they'd signed up for.

So did I. This fight would kill them.

I turned to look at Stefan. Panic and terror mingled in his eyes. He saw what I saw: the Familiar who'd practically raised him would die soon. And he couldn't stop it.

"Desi, let's end this," Oliver said loudly. "Let's finish him *now*. We can still save them."

A tiny flame ignited within me—a shadow of the fire I'd felt earlier. I nodded, but I didn't believe him.

At long last, I pulled my gaze away just as Bay knocked Kismet out of the way to avoid the fire pouring from Asmodeus's mouth.

Stefan and I followed Oliver in grim silence. The fatigue of battle finally hit me. Hard. My feet trudged onward, stiff and throbbing. Pain flared in my shoulders and arms from my injuries. Sticky blood coated my skin. My brain pulsed with a splitting headache.

With the adrenaline wearing off, how could I face Matthias? How could I face *any* opponent right now knowing Kismet was about to die?

"Remember, he's powerless," Oliver muttered next to me. "But don't underestimate him. He's still a colonel, so he's a good fighter."

We stopped just in front of the mess hall. A shadow crossed Oliver's face. "He's inside," he said in a low voice.

We hesitated. The three of us exchanged uncertain glances, but as we stared at each other, a firm resolve passed between us. The feeble flame within me strengthened ever so slightly. I latched onto it, desperate to cling to that unwavering soldier within me.

Bring her back, I pleaded with myself. *I need to be strong. Brave. Unstoppable.*

But anxiety lingered in my thoughts. *Kismet will die. Bay will die. Oliver will probably die with me alongside him.*

All of us will die tonight.

"If we go down, we go down fighting," Stefan said. His voice was deep and powerful. It sounded like the voice of a man twice his age. A man seasoned by war and loss.

It spurred me forward, up the stairs and through the door. I sensed Oliver and Stefan behind me.

The door creaked shut behind us, plunging us in darkness. I stilled. Matthias was here. Hiding in the shadows.

I lifted my hand and summoned flame just as a fist collided with my face.

With a grunt, I fell over and clutched my nose as blood poured from it. Stefan screamed and lunged forward, swiping his blade with wide, inept blows that Matthias easily dodged.

I stumbled to my feet and shot a ball of fire at Matthias. He ducked, but it singed his hair. He cried out, patting down the flames.

A firm hand gripped my throat. Startled, I dropped the potion bottle and grappled with the vise on my neck. My wide eyes found Oliver's. He stared at me, his eyes an inky black.

"Oliver—" I choked, struggling to suck in a breath. But no air came. My body shuddered, convulsing.

From deep within my mind, a voice chuckled, clawing through my thoughts like a blade shredding through paper.

Matthias.

My eyes closed. Again, I focused on Oliver—on *us*.

Our arms wrapped around each other. The warmth and tears in his eyes when he saw me in my wedding dress.

Oliver gasped and released me. "Desi—"

I waved a hand, doubling over and gasping for breath. My neck throbbed. It felt like each breath drew blades up and down my throat. "Don't," I croaked. "Just . . . stop him."

A pained look crossed Oliver's face before he whirled and dived toward Matthias, who aimed his blade at Stefan's chest. I lifted my hand, trying to summon fire to search for the potion. But nothing happened.

Agony flared in my mind so intensely it numbed me, freezing me in place. Then an explosion of pain hit me like white-hot needles on every inch of my body.

I screamed, my throat ripping from the sound. The pain was so intense my vision blurred.

Gradually, it faded, and my senses returned. Then, I noticed I wasn't the only one screaming.

Stefan was too.

For one wild moment, Matthias and Oliver froze, staring at us both. Matthias recovered first and rammed Oliver with his shoulder.

Tears filled my eyes. The energy within me rose and fell, surging back and forth like the tide. A burst of light, a plunge into darkness, and then—silence. Stillness. I couldn't see or hear anything.

The frantic thrumming of my heart pierced through the emptiness in my soul. And I knew what it meant.

Kismet was dead.

CHAPTER 39

Broken sobs filled my chest. But I couldn't. Not here. Not now.

"No," Stefan breathed next to me, covering his face. "No!"

I touched his shoulder and squeezed. My eyes found Oliver, who had tackled Matthias before he could escape.

"Later, Stefan," I said hoarsely. "Our fight isn't over yet."

He looked at me, his eyes streaming with tears. His expression was broken, and his eyes were haunted, succumbing to the despair. He'd lost everything. Everyone.

I grabbed his arm. "Stefan, stay with me! Don't give in!" I sucked in a breath. "We have to finish this."

Stefan stared at me through vacant eyes. Then, he stiffened, his back arching and the veins in his neck and arms popping. He groaned, and black shadows poured from his hands.

My heart stopped. With wide eyes, I stared at Stefan. He vanished in a puff of smoke and then reappeared in front of Matthias. Matthias yelped, stumbling backward. Stefan's face drained of color, his mouth hanging open in shock. The shadows around him rippled, and he vanished and reappeared next to me, falling backward on his rear.

"What the hell?" He lifted his hands. His eyes fell to his cuff.

Flames roared in my chest, consuming me and devouring me. They burst from me, igniting my hands and my entire body.

I knew what this was. With our cuffs, we now possessed *all* of Bay and Kismet's magic.

I didn't hesitate. I barreled forward, my vision framed by the orange flames emanating from my body. I tackled Matthias to the floor. The old floorboards underneath us caught fire, spreading throughout the mess hall.

I pinned Matthias down, who screamed against the pain of my flames.

"How do you like it?" I roared at him. "How does it feel?"

His only response was more screaming. Anguish creased his face, and for the briefest moment, he looked like nothing more than an innocent mortal. Blood and sweat mingled on his face, and there was actual terror in his eyes.

"Oliver, the potion!" I shouted without looking behind me.

"Uh, Desi?" said Stefan.

I glanced over my shoulder and found the entire porch of the mess hall in flames. And amidst those flames were several dark figures.

Asmodeus's demons.

Of course. We were about to kill Matthias, and Asmodeus was linked to him. The Demon Master had to protect himself.

I pressed my hands together and shouted from exertion. Beads of sweat formed on my face. Then, I conjured a boulder the size of my head and placed it against Matthias. He groaned and struggled, but the heavy weight kept him in place.

"Don't move," I told him with a smirk. Then I bounded forward, setting myself on fire again. I twirled, igniting several demons at once. Stefan became a blur of shadows and daggers as he sliced through demon after demon.

"Oliver!" I screamed. "The potion! Say the spell! Do it now!"

Oliver said nothing. And in my heart, I knew Matthias had him again.

I couldn't fight the demons *and* save Oliver. He had to save himself. Already my mind throbbed from fatigue. I could sense Kismet's power fading. The cuff on my wrist glowed hot, searing against my hand. At first, I thought it was from my own flames but then I realized the device was overheating. The energy and magic flowing from it was too much.

We didn't have much longer now.

I slashed a demon's throat and paused to look around for Oliver. I found him bent over Matthias. Oliver's eyes were all black again.

"Oliver!" I shouted. A demon lunged for me, and I shot him back with a stream of water. "Don't you dare!" I called out to Oliver. "You are *mine*. Not his. Come back to me!"

Oliver went still. Then, a deep shudder rippled over him.

I felt him. The conflict and the darkness within him. Sharp claws grasped his mind, clinging to it. Matthias's claws. Oliver struggled and thrashed against the grip, but it was unyielding.

You're mine, I said again.

Oliver roared inside my head.

Come back, Oliver!

Suddenly, a demon's fangs sank into my shoulder. I cried out, falling backward.

Lightning flashed in the room, momentarily blinding me. Then Matthias screamed. Another bolt of lightning hit him directly in the chest.

I gasped, looking around, and found Elias at the door wearing his goggles and gloves.

My mouth fell open. *He's alive!* I'd thought all the rebels were dead.

Electricity ignited from Elias's fingers, flowing freely into Matthias's chest.

Hope soared in my heart. He'd done it. He'd tethered his gloves to Matthias's blood.

Behind Elias, a dozen witches and warlocks poured into the mess hall, engaging the demons in battle. Knives slashed. Blood spurted. Demons and casters alike roared with fury and pain.

An explosion burst in my mind, freeing Oliver. Matthias's claws broke like shattered glass as they relinquished their hold.

No, wait—

That sound *was* glass shattering.

Oliver broke the potion bottle. A murky white smoke filled the air, tickling my nostrils.

Demons roared, drawing closer to me. Like they sensed the end was near.

I set my whole body on fire and shouted a battle cry. Then, I surged forward, scorching the demons with my flames. A few of them dived out of the way, and others howled in agony as my fire burned them. I kicked and lunged as the bright orange glow of my flames stung my eyes. But I didn't feel the heat. I felt only the fearsome determination boiling inside me.

Keep them away from Oliver, I told myself. I flung my arms around, swiping my blade and cutting through demons. My fire grew higher and higher until the demons backed away in uncertainty.

Amidst the chaos, I barely made out Oliver's voice— it was thick with tears as he spoke.

"Vile demon of the fourth estate,
With this potion I seal your fate,
To suffer banishment to the depths below,
And forever leave this world we know."

Matthias bellowed, his piercing yell blaring in my ears. Even the demons we fought went still, their black eyes searching. Elias stiffened, his jaw dropping as he stared.

A white light filled the mess hall, mingling with the orange flames that continued spreading along the wooden floors.

I felt Oliver's pain and sent a gust of wind, pushing him out of the way. The magical glow encompassed Matthias's entire body until a deafening boom shook the floors. Beams from the ceiling crashed, filling my face with dust and smoke. I coughed, waving my hand to clear the air.

The glow faded. Matthias was gone.

The demons surrounding me shrieked, collapsing to the ground. They writhed in agony, green blood blossoming from unseen wounds. Then, they shuddered and disintegrated into ash.

My vision blurred. I staggered to my feet and teetered. I didn't have much strength left. I took a deep breath and sprayed gallons of water toward the fire, then swept away the ash and smoke with my wind. Then, I fell backwards and succumbed to the pain.

Kismet's blue eyes peered at me. They warmed when she realized I was awake.

I sat up and gasped. "You're alive!" I threw my arms around her. She sobbed into my shoulder.

"Not quite," she whispered.

I blinked and looked around. We were surrounded by a blinding white light. I couldn't see anything else. I didn't even know what I was sitting on.

My heart plummeted to my feet. I knew this place. This was the same weird afterlife where I'd seen my mother after Matthias stabbed me in Cuba.

Kismet *was* dead.

My broken gaze turned to her. Her mouth crumpled in a grimace. "I'm so sorry, Desi."

I stared at her numbly, not comprehending. She couldn't be dead. She was sitting in front of me as clear as day. I could feel her. Smell her.

She was here.

But in my heart, I knew the truth. A hard lump formed in my throat.

"No," I whispered.

"It's all right."

I covered my face. "How *could* you? How could you leave me like this?"

"Desi—"

I wailed into my hands, my tears soaking my palms. Agony weighed down on my heart, dragging it down to an abyss darker than Asmodeus's lair. Shadows filled me, suffocating me.

I couldn't go back there. I couldn't go back to that

place of tragedy and despair. I'd never come back if I went there.

"Desi," Kismet said again, touching my arm. "You're not alone."

"I don't care!" I shouted. I knew I sounded like a child. "I know I'm not alone, but I don't care! I want you *here*, Kiz! How could you leave me?"

"We made our peace with this long ago."

I went still, slowly dropping my hands. So it was true, then. Bay died too.

My heart twisted in knots. "Why?" I moaned, tears streaming freely down my face. "Why did this have to happen? You both suffered so much. You barely got a year of freedom together!"

Kismet smiled, her eyes watering. She pressed her cool hand against my face. "This is our recompense. We both played our part in Matthias's rise to power. Me more so than Bay, though he still struggles every day with how he betrayed you to Isko. If he hadn't done that, Matthias never would've slaughtered the Kulam coven or time traveled. And if I'd never become his slave, I wouldn't have involved you in this either. You traveled to Santiago because of me. Maybe if I hadn't performed that blood bond with him, you would've gone somewhere else. Somewhere safe."

My mouth opened and closed, my response broken by more sobs. "But I—I wouldn't have met Oliver."

Kismet's lips pressed into a thin line, and I knew what she implied. Her bargain with Matthias was necessary. And so was her death.

Would I really have been willing to give up Oliver if it meant Kismet could live?

I couldn't answer that. I didn't even want to try. Instead, I lunged forward, burying my face in Kismet's shoulder and weeping into her shirt. She stroked my hair, my back, and my shoulders and shushed me just like Mom used to do.

"I can't do this without you," I moaned.

"Yes, you can," Kismet said firmly. "You've already done so much without me, Desi. You're unstoppable."

My lower lip trembled, and my eyes burned with more tears.

Kismet drew back and beamed at me, her eyes glowing with pride. She tucked my curls behind my ear. "I'm so proud of you."

I swallowed, but a firm lump lodged itself in my throat. "You should be here to see this. You fought so hard for it."

Kismet's smile broadened. "I *am* seeing it—through your eyes. I'm still with you, Desi. I'll always be with you." She pressed a kiss to my forehead. Her eyes filled with tears again. "Take—take care of my angel baby. Please."

My heart lurched. *Her baby.* My face split, more sobs tearing through me. We clutched each other, both of us wailing and crying like children. For what seemed like hours, we held each other. Our tears rushed like a waterfall until we had none left to shed.

"I will," I whispered.

"Desi?" a deep voice asked.

My eyes flew open. I was lying in my bed in the Council's hideout—the abandoned hospital.

I jerked upright. Pain flared in my arms and shoulders. I winced, peering down at my body. Several bloodied bandages covered my shoulders.

Then, my eyes found Oliver. He had a nasty cut on his cheek, and his arm was in a sling. But his eyes brightened when he saw me.

"Desi." He leaned forward, clutching my fingers in his free hand. He closed his eyes and kissed my hand. "Thank Lilith you're awake."

"How—how long have I been out?" My voice sounded hoarse, and daggers shredded my throat. I swallowed, rubbing my neck.

"Two days."

My eyes widened, my gaze drifting around the room. We were alone. "The others . . .?"

Oliver's brows creased. Despair filled his eyes.

Part of me didn't want to know. But I had to.

"Tell me," I begged him.

"Most—most of the rebels are gone. It's just you, me, Stefan, Elias, José, and Jean left."

My mouth fell open. Horror numbed my body. So many people were gone. We'd had almost fifty rebels, including those from the Council.

Now Jean was the only member of the Council left.

Merciful Lilith. I covered my face with my hands.

"Come here," Oliver whispered, scooting into bed next to me. He wrapped his arms around me and held me close against his chest. His familiar grassy scent enveloped me, soothing me against the festering wounds of grief inside me.

"You fought him off," I said through tears. My fingers roved over his face, gingerly touching his scar.

"Not without help. If Elias hadn't been there . . ." Oliver shook his head. He pointed to his scar. "Matthias cut me with the shattered potion bottle. One last effort to stop me from casting the spell."

I winced. "But you did it anyway." I leaned my forehead against his. "Thank you, Oliver. Without you—" I stopped, shaking my head. Even *with* him, even with all of us fighting, it still hadn't felt like enough. Matthias had taken so much from us.

Agony burned in my eyes, plunging me into the darkest corners of my mind. The corners I tried so hard to stay away from since my parents' death.

Oliver noticed the despair in my expression. His own face crumpled. The grief in his eyes was so intense that I burst into tears. He drew me against his chest, and I clung to him, relying on the solid, reassuring strength of his arms around me.

We were here. We were safe.

But so many had been lost.

A few days later, Oliver and I stood hand-in-hand in a wide-open field a few miles away from the safehouse. We were surrounded by the remaining rebels and the witches and warlocks who had come to our aid. The bodies of our fallen comrades had been cremated, and their ashes were sprinkled in a wide circle. Each of us wore a cloak. It took a monumental effort for me *not* to think about blood rituals with us all hooded like this. But I remembered a similar ceremony at my parents' funeral. So instead, I focused on that.

Despite how much it hurt to relive those memories.

Kismet clutched my hand as I stared, unblinking at the pile of ashes amidst the circle of our coven. I felt so many eyes on me, but my gaze never strayed. I knew I only had an hour with Kismet. So I clutched her fingers tightly, knowing I was probably hurting her. But she never complained.

The warlock uttered the spell as a farewell to my parents, but it felt so unfeeling. So cold and empty. So rehearsed.

It felt like he was just reading from a script. And he probably was.

So I embraced the numbness in my heart, drowning myself in apathy and the void of nothingness that dulled my senses.

It was better than feeling.

I gritted my teeth against the pain that came flooding back to me. Tears streamed down my face. But with each ripple of agony came a sick sense of satisfaction.

I deserved this. If the others had to die, then I deserved to live with this anguish and torment.

A sniveling sob ripped through my chest, and Oliver wrapped his arm around my shoulders.

"Witches and warlocks," Elias's loud voice chimed next to us, his cloaked arms raised. "We gather to honor the fallen members of our coven. We assemble to share blood one last time. To pledge our lives to them and their sacrifice. To always remember what was done for us in battle. Casters, please spill your blood."

A hot lump formed in my throat. I swallowed, but it only burned. We all drew daggers from our cloaks and cut our palms. Again, I reveled in the pain as blood trickled from my hand.

This is your punishment, Desi. Embrace it.

"Summon your magic," Elias said.

Blue and black wisps of power mingled in the air as Jean, José, Elias, Stefan, Oliver, and I conjured a powerful glow in our uninjured hands. The witches and warlocks behind us did the same. The magic intensified until my fingers thrummed with energy. The warmth tickled my skin.

Then—as if the magic knew exactly what to do—the rays of light spilled from our hands onto the ground, creeping through the grass toward the pile of ashes.

I could barely see through the moisture in my eyes. The ashes radiated in a mixture of blue and black. The glow burned so brightly I felt its heat. Then, the ashes spun into a small funnel cloud, similar to the time travel spell I'd cast so long ago. The magic and ashes swirled faster and faster until I had to shut my eyes to keep from getting sick. More tears dripped down my face, and I sucked in a shaky breath.

Suddenly, the tingle of magic in the air subsided, and I felt the cut on my hand seal and vanish. I opened my eyes, and the ashes and the magic were gone, leaving nothing but emptiness and sorrow.

"*Blood of our blood, we beseech of thee,*" said Elias

thickly, his nose red and his eyes watering, *"be at rest for all eternity."*

The rest of us repeated his words amidst sniffles and sobs. The air was soft and silent. A humble acceptance of our meager offering.

It was nothing compared to what they sacrificed. Gina. Raul. Paolo. Teddy. Cameron. Bay.

And Kismet.

My eyes closed, and regret burned in my throat. I ducked my head, weeping openly. But I wasn't alone. I heard José's soft sobs, and Oliver's shoulders shook beside me. They'd all lowered their hoods, but I kept mine up, savoring the darkness.

It, too, served as my punishment.

At long last, the others retreated to the safehouse. Some muttered quietly, and others maintained the reverence of the ceremony.

Oliver's fingers laced through mine. He squeezed my hand but said nothing.

I wasn't sure how long we remained out there.

After a while, the lump in my throat subsided. An insane part of me wanted it to return. It didn't seem fair for the pain to be gone.

"They'd want you to be happy," Oliver whispered. "It's why they died; so we could live our lives."

I knew this. But it still didn't feel right.

"I love you, Desi."

I closed my eyes, my face crumpling at his words. He pulled me close and wrapped his arms around me, bear-hugging me. To be surrounded by his warmth and scent was like a soothing balm against my wounds. I felt his own pain emanating along our connection, and something stirred within me in response. Something like guilt.

I didn't want *him* to suffer for this. Just me.

Which was ridiculous.

"The remorse of losing comrades, thinking it should've been you . . ." Oliver sighed. "It's a very real pain I've had to live with. It never fully goes away. But it does become more bearable."

The knots in my stomach softened at his words. I swallowed, pressing my head against his chest and focusing on the comforting rhythm of his heartbeat. "So what do we do now?"

A heavy silence passed between us. Oliver's strong arms wrapped around me again, rubbing up and down my back. I felt his breath tickle the top of my head as he spoke. "We rebuild."

EPILOGUE

Two Weeks Later

"Jean's offer still stands, you know." Oliver wiggled his eyebrows at me.

I rolled my eyes and clutched his arm closer to mine, shivering in the chilly wind of Wisconsin's early winter. "I think I'll pass. Elias offered me a job."

Oliver's face split into a grin, stretching the jagged scar on his cheek. "That's great!"

"Yeah, it is." But I couldn't share his enthusiasm. The only reason Elias hired me was because Megan was dead.

Oliver sensed my thoughts. "Desi, don't dwell on it. You're good at aurology. You've helped him before. This is a good fit for you. And you can carry on Megan's work. You know it would make her happy."

"Right. I know."

A grim silence passed between us as we both momentarily sank into the grief that had plagued us since the demon battle.

Then, my eyes fell on a familiar house a few blocks down. Pale blue vinyl. Gray roof shingles. An American flag billowing in the yard.

A small smile tugged at my lips. "There it is."

Oliver followed my gaze and sucked in a breath. I knew what he was thinking: somewhere in that house was Kismet's daughter.

Even as I thought it, a foreign warmth filled my chest. Somehow, I knew it was Kismet bestowing her blessing on me. She trusted me to love her baby like my own. And I would. Though the notion sent quivers of fear rippling through my body, I swore in my heart that I'd keep that promise.

My hand quivered as I knocked on the door. After some shuffling, a woman with graying hair and warm, brown eyes opened the door. Her face brightened.

"Desiree! Come in, come in. And you must be Oliver."

Oliver bowed his head. "A pleasure to meet you, Mrs. Fletcher."

"Oh please, call me Jan. She's right this way. Just woke up from her nap."

The door closed behind us, and we followed Jan down the hall. My throat filled with emotion at the sight of the pictures of Cameron lining the hallway.

Another life lost to Matthias's thirst for power.

The smell of soiled diapers made me wrinkle my nose. Oliver looked at my face and laughed. "Better get used to it," he muttered.

I nudged his shoulder with mine.

"There she is!" Jan cooed, her voice soft and high-pitched—that baby voice parents use without really thinking about it.

I entered the room and stopped, my mouth falling open. My heart thrummed in my chest, pulsing along with my anxiety.

A crib sat in the middle of the room. Inside it was a baby, who rolled over and climbed to her feet, her little fingers clutching the bars of the crib wall. Wide, blue eyes stared at me curiously. Her hair was a tangle of white-blond curls. I'd expected her to share Bay's complexion, but her skin was porcelain.

She looked just like an angel. Now I knew why Kismet called her "angel baby."

"Come here, sweetie." Jan hoisted the baby up from the crib and held her out to me.

I stepped back, eyes wide.

"Oh, come now. You'll have to get over that sooner or later." Jan chuckled and slid the baby into my arms.

My mouth opened in protest, but then the baby was there, clutching my collar and burying her face in my shirt. She babbled against my chest, and I couldn't help but laugh.

"She's beautiful," Oliver murmured, stroking the hair out of her eyes. The warmth in his gaze awakened my numb senses. There was such a soft tenderness in his eyes that my insides melted just looking at him.

"What's her name?" I asked Jan.

Jan offered a shy smile. "I've just been calling her 'sweetie.' Kismet said *you* would name her."

My heart jolted, and my gaze shifted to Jan's moist eyes. Kismet had known, even then—even when she gave up her child a year ago—that I would be the one to raise the baby. That I would be this child's mother.

Mother.

The word sent a torrent of emotions spiraling through me: fear, anxiety, shock, a crippling sense of inadequacy.

But I had to do this. I had to try.

For Kismet.

I cleared my throat. The baby cooed and fiddled with a loose thread on my shirt.

I smiled. In spite of my terror, uncertainty, and worries for our future, I focused on this moment. Here and now. This sweet angel baby cuddling against me.

Warmth filled my chest. "Her name is Angel."

Want to read about Desi and Oliver's daughter? Check out *The Cursed Witch*, the start of the next series in the Timecaster universe!

Let's stay in touch! Sign up for my newsletter and get *The Raven's Promise,* a FREE short story about Kismet and Bay! Check it out at rlperez.com/theravenspromise

ACKNOWLEDGMENTS

It is an incredible and humbling feeling to know I've completed a trilogy. But I certainly haven't done it alone. Aubrey and Mary contributed the fantastic book covers and editing, and I'm so grateful for them.

A huge thank you to my beta readers, Jacque, Kari, Melanie, Janete, Ben, and Jenni. Without you, the story wouldn't be half as complete or satisfying.

I'm so monumentally grateful for my ARC readers, Barbara, Katherine, Scarolet, Debbie, Veronica, Darian, Olivia, Darcy, Peg, Janet, Mary, Chad, Kaitlin, and Stephanie. Thank you for being so enthusiastic and supportive about my stories, and thank you for your willingness to read and continue with the adventure.

And lastly, Alex, Colin, and Ellie, for your support, love, and encouragement. You all have been my rock during this incredible journey. I am nothing without you.

ABOUT THE AUTHOR

R.L. Perez is an author, wife, mother, reader, writer, and teacher. She lives in Florida with her husband and two children. On a regular basis, she can usually be found napping, reading, feverishly writing, revising, or watching an abundance of Netflix. More than anything, she loves spending time with her family. Her greatest joys are her two kids, nature, literature, and chocolate.

Subscribe to her newsletter for new releases, promotions, giveaways, and book recommendations! Get a FREE eBook when you sign up at subscribe. rlperez.com.

Made in the USA
Las Vegas, NV
20 October 2023

R00308